from international bestselling author

ARI WRIGHT

for
You

Published and formatted by Blue Eyed Books.

For Now

The Star-Crossed City, book 3

ISBN (paperback): 9781969660023

ISBN (ebook): 9781969660016

Cover Art: Sonia Garrigoux

Graphic Design: Blue Eyed Books

for my husband—
you secured this dedication the minute you offered to build me my
own personal library.
and every day for twelve years before that.
and every day since.

a note from ari

HELLO BEAUTIFUL READER!

This book and these characters are very near and dear to my heart. Their story is sweet, but a lot of the themes surrounding them are not.

Please be sure to check the content/trigger warnings before you proceed. I've included them in their own section at the back of the book to avoid spoilers for those who elect not to read them.

That being said, it is my most sincere hope that everyone who reads this story and identifies with its characters feels seen when they read these words.

Sending lots of love and gratitude.

xx,

Ari

Matilda — Harry Styles
Empress — Morningsiders
Big Guns — Ruelle
Hello Hammerheads — Caribou
When I'm Small — Phantogram
Bloodstream — Stateless
Move Slower — Mammals, Flash Forest
Got It Bad — LEISURE
Concrete Wall — Zee Avi
Sleep — The Last Bison
Tin Lover — The Paper Kites
Taro — alt-J
Don't Move — Phantogram
everything i wanted — Billie Eilish
Afterlife — Hailee Steinfeld
Stick Up — grandson
To You Alone — Tom Rosenthal
Be Be Your Love — Rachael Yamagata
Play with Fire — Sam Tinnesz, Yacht Money
Work Song — Hozier
Even If It Hurts — Sam Tinnesz
Madness — Ruelle
Way down We Go — KALEO
Waiting — Alice Boman
Quietly Yours — Birdy
In This Shirt — The Irrepressibles
her (feat. Annika Wells) — JVKE, Annika Wells
Aloha — Møme, Merryn Jeann
Wish on an Eyelash — Mallrat

"POOR THING. LOOK AT HER."

A hush falls over the group of women gathered in my mother's sitting room. I feel them all turn, craning their elegant necks while holding their bodies stiff—ankles crossed primly, manicured talons clutching teacups of gin.

Pointed stares scrape over my profile. I wince, holding back the urge to double over the book propped on my bent knees. One of the fairytale retellings I live in.

"Always sitting in that window seat, nose in a book," a different lady mutters into my mother's china.

"She'll freckle," another tuts, her Southern lilt sugared with false concern.

"And get crows' feet," someone else agrees. Her syrupy voice sharpens as she represses amusement. "All that *reading*."

There's a soft sort of snort. "Well, it isn't as if the poor dear has anything better to do. No friends. No *boyfriend*. Bless her heart."

Prickling giggles fill the entertaining space, floating over streaks of Georgia sunshine. Humiliation hunches my spine.

Everything they say is true. I *know* that—but knowing never seems to make it easier to hear.

A bolt of mortification sticks in my throat. The stinging in my eyes instinctively brings me to my feet. Mama taught me better than to cry in front of anyone. It's *unbecoming*.

Doing my best to seem casual, I shuffle from my sun-warmed window seat in the front parlor, scuttling to the foyer stairs, praying against all odds that I'll make it up to my room before—

"Alice."

Of course.

Mama marches out from the kitchen, balancing a platter of tea sandwiches no one will touch on her left hand. She reaches over to pinch my chin with the pointed fingernails of her right.

"*Alice, so help me,*" she hisses.

I keep my eyelids low, still hoping—always hoping, no matter how foolish and pointless and just plain *stupid* it makes me—that she won't see the tears.

No such luck, of course.

Her French-tipped acrylics bite into my jaw, yanking sharply until I meet her cool blue eyes. So like mine. The only piece of me she has never criticized.

She sees the wet sheen of shame glossing my gaze and scowls, her nostrils flaring in frustration. "*Upstairs.*"

Even her growl is feminine. And too low for the ladies to over-hear. Even when she adds, "And don't come down until you've composed yourself."

I grimace—it will be a while.

Ever since I turned twelve, it's gotten harder and harder to talk myself down when I get upset.

Now, I'm fourteen and it only gets more difficult every year. I suspect it has something to do with my age, but Mama steadfastly refuses to discuss puberty with me until I "blossom."

From what I can tell, that has less to do with anything biological and more to do with acting the way she wants her daughter to act. At the rate I'm going, I might never get The Talk all the girls at school chortle about.

I scurry upstairs, silently snicking my door shut behind me while I wipe my eyes on the shoulders of my T-shirt. It's a good thing she didn't escort me up to my room—the whole place is covered in magazine clippings and unspooled wrapping paper.

She would loathe the very concept of what I was up to last night. It was something I saw in a magazine—an idea I launched myself into with the sort of enthusiasm I can only muster for books, art, and daydreams.

Because, I realize, a weight sinking into my center, *that's exactly what all these clippings are.*

The silly daydreams of a stupid, optimistic little girl.

My fingers sift through the stack in the middle of my mattress, where I'd placed all the pictures and articles I deemed "a must." By the time I started wrapping the designated shoebox in pink-heart wrapping paper, the pile had gotten a little alarming. There are *a lot* of pictures here. And a few of them feature men's cologne ads I don't *quite* understand my obsession with.

I gather them all, holding tight, preparing myself to crush them in my fists. They suddenly feel so embarrassing. Proof that I'm dumb enough to dream of people who will never want me back. Pointless reminders of things I can never have.

If I've grown up knowing one thing for certain, it is the simple fact that I am going to die alone.

My mother tells me often, mourning every piece of my

appearance and each part of my personality. Constantly sighing reprimands about how I will end up on my own with a cat. Or six.

Since kindergarten, she has weighed my every attribute on the grand scale of "Attractive" versus "Unattractive."

My singing voice? Attractive.

Having my face hidden in a book every spare moment? Unattractive.

My table manners? Attractive.

My tendency toward second helpings? Unattractive.

Stuttering when nervous? Unattractive.

The way my eyebrows fold when I frown? Unattractive.

A bedroom bursting with books, paintings, magazine scraps, and sketches? Unattractive.

My pile of unappealing traits grows bigger every year, along with my waistline. And now? The situation looks dire, the scales woefully out of balance.

Mama tries to help. Keeping track of *just* how much weight I need to lose. Pointing out that my preferred floral prints only accentuate my "unseemly" figure. Pinching every roll and jiggle my clothes display.

She keeps track of which colors highlight the unnatural paleness of my skin, the dishwater tones in my hair. She's also taught me tricks to straighten and shellac the frizzy curls—always with the affection and patience a drill sergeant might show his cadets.

Self-improvement occupies every moment we spend together. I cycle through a new diet every six months. Low carb, no carb, high protein, low fat, no sugar, gluten-free, paleo, keto, vegan.

Weekends are reserved for the latest exercise craze, speech tutors, and Mama's lectures on the finer points of catching and keeping a man. Christmas and birthday gifts come as bags of new clothes—a different look this time, of course, to camouflage whatever flaw serves as her current fixation.

Our current fixation.

I've begun to feel like a piece of furniture, always undergoing renovation but never quite fitting in the corner she purchased me for. Still, she buffs, paints, plucks, and straightens. Smooths, scrapes, and putties. Changes my colors, changes my fixtures. Only to once again determine that I am just... *wrong*. All wrong.

And then, like she has so many other times, she strips me down to the studs and starts again.

Lately, though, she's sort of given up.

She's stopped fussing every time she catches me reading into the night instead of focusing on my "beauty rest." In fact, she doesn't check on me at all. Her fervor for shopping excursions and makeovers has dimmed, cooling into an exasperated hopelessness, punctuated by scoffs and dismissive flicks of her wrist whenever I debut a new outfit for her elusive approval.

She sighs about how she'll never have grandchildren. Changes the subject whenever I mention a cute boy from my class.

Somehow, it feels worse than the constant critiquing. After all, if my own mother has given up on me, I must be a real hopeless case.

Standing in my childhood bedroom, bathed in cheery morning light that makes the nauseous pain inside me seem all the more insidious, I stare down at my pile of hopes.

The image on the top page snags my focus for a moment. A picture of a tiki-hut honeymoon suite on a beach in Hawaii. My fingers curl like a reflex, preparing to crush it.

But I've always been much too soft for my own good.

So, instead, the photos wind up in my heart-papered shoebox of shame, stuffed under my bed, where I hope no one will discover my deepest darkest secret.

I may not *believe* in those hopes anymore, but I can keep them all the same. Like notes from the Tooth Fairy or letters to Santa. Only, I'll hoard pictures of engagement rings, articles about intimacy and babies, and decorating your first home as newlyweds.

No one needs to know. I can cut them out and tuck them away, just in case—maybe, miraculously—there is someone meant for me, after all.

Maybe he won't care about my flabby belly or my wild hair or the wide set of my eyes. Maybe he'll like that I read into the night and sing in the shower and stain my fingernails with my art projects.

Maybe he'll just... love me.

Even if he shouldn't.

alice

"RIDICULOUS."

The woman behind me in line, bouncing a baby on her hip as she glares, sums my life up pretty succinctly.

Because, me standing here? Holding up the entire line in this trendy café while my brain reboots?

Why, yes. It *is* ridiculous.

Thanks so much for noticing.

I swallow the snarky comment, because I'll never have the nerve to say it out loud. My best friend, Tris, claims that choking down bitterness instead of letting it out will give me an aneurysm one day. Then again, she's known for saying any and every thought that pops into her head without hesitation.

I blink at the phone wedged in my left hand, trying to recall what I was doing before the text message glowing up at me ruined my morning. I think I was about to order? Yes, that's why the people behind me are grumbling, and the shaggy-haired college guy across the counter is glowering and—

My phone vibrates. Again.

An alert from my banking app about an automated charge. The air in my chest shrivels into two lead balls. Which drop to the bottom of my lungs.

Right. I forgot about that.

My new website's renewal fee just came through. When I signed up a month ago, the thirty-day free trial seemed generous. And, I'll admit, I'm not the best with numbers—but surely the $18.99 that just disappeared into the ether won't ruin Fancy Coffee Friday.

Or was it $28.99?

I should maybe check...

"*Ahem.*" It's my biggest fan again, harrumphing from her spot at my back. My shoulders hunch as I cringe, refocusing on the menu. And the prices.

Sheesh. This place definitely deserves a capital "F" for "fancy."

These little trips to local cafés started as a tradition between me and Tris in college. We were randomly assigned roommates— and totally different in every way. But leave it to my flame-filled bestie to find any and every way to turn a stranger into a friend for life.

She decided we would get "fancy" coffee together each Friday —and it stuck.

I'm supposed to be bringing hers upstairs, to her office, right now. Because eight years later, we're still roomies. And best friends. And opposites.

As in, she is successful, gorgeous, charming, and fun.

And I am a potato.

Or maybe just the biggest idiot in Manhattan, if this woman's disapproving sneer is any indication.

My stomach grumbles as my phone buzzes more insistently. I ignore them both, because the texts are, of course, from my mother. Follow-ups to a long paragraph about how she received a late payment notice for one of my student loans—berating me for choosing a "hobby" that "doesn't pay" over a "real job."

Bold, considering she's never worked a day in her life.

I already typed an apology, letting her know I've tried to change the address for the loan statements three times. It's the best reassurance I can offer her, since I won't be able to pay this month's, either.

So maybe I shouldn't get the cranberry muffin I want.

Instead, I rattle off Tris's usual—a large cold brew with extra espresso and extra sugar—along with my usual cup of breakfast tea. Only when my belly audibly gurgles, I sheepishly ask, "How much are the pastries?"

The employee's focus automatically drops to my stomach. And not because it's growling.

"Six dollars," he replies, eyeing the love handles spilling over the waistband of my jeans.

Ironically, I only wore them because I wanted to look "nice" when I visited Tris's office. She works for one of the wealthiest men on the planet—and Stryker & Sons is practically a monument to class and success.

The February wind makes dresses and skirts completely impractical, though. And I thought dark-wash jeans looked a bit more professional than my usual leggings.

As if underscoring my point, a frigid burst of air sweeps into the café as more people huddle in from the bustling Midtown sidewalk. I huddle lower, burying my chin in my gray turtleneck. Thinking for the millionth time how much I hate the color. But it's the newest sweater I own—a Christmas gift from Mama. Intended to "downplay" my "mousy" hair color, she informed me.

Fat chance.

Remember when I said I was a potato?

Yeah, well. I should be so lucky.

The total appears on the café's iPad, and I tap my phone for contactless payment. The screen changes.

PAYMENT DECLINED.

Oh *shit.*

My heart lurches as my chest caves in. The guy across from me can't quite contain his eyeroll this time. "You can try it again."

I tap a second time, even though I know nothing will change. Because I'm sure the system is correct—and I *don't* have the funds to cover these two drinks.

PAYMENT DECLINED, it says again. Louder, somehow.

The woman behind me *groans.* I start mumbling apologies, swiping my banking app open. "I'm sure it's just—"

Hopeless.

Because when I see that my checking account has $8 in it, I know there is no savings to move money over from. And no upcoming paycheck.

The lady behind me is tall and modelesque. She openly glances over my shoulder to see my balance before muttering under her breath, "Jesus. Then move out of the way, fat ass."

I don't think she meant for me to hear, but that only makes it worse. My cheeks heat as my insides tighten. She's not wrong. I'm a mess. Wearing this ugly outfit to attempt to look decent, holding up the line, mismanaging my expenses, thinking I could ever have my dream career.

Well, what did you expect, Alice? Did you actually think you were going to "make it?"

Panic balloons in my throat, pushing small, prickling tears to my eyes. I blink and drop my hand to my side, opening my mouth to admit defeat.

"Never mind—" I start to say, "I'll just—"

A huge arm wrapped in dark fabric reached around me. The tan, brawny hand clutching a sleek new iPhone lands on top of the payment pad just as another lands on my opposite shoulder. Squeezing softly.

"Sorry I'm late, darling," a deep voice husks. "Forgive me?"

FOR THE SAKE of full transparency, it's very possible I've cracked.

Because, in all likelihood, there's no way the gorgeous man who steps around me to reach the register is *real*.

For one thing, he's enormous. Standing well over six feet, with the broadest shoulders I've seen outside of movies starring The Rock, all wrapped in a well-tailored blazer. His size alone would stop most people in their tracks. But, in addition to being huge, he's also *beautiful*.

With obvious muscles stacked under his clothing and rich bronze skin—the man also has thick hair as black as his outfit. The waves are combed into inky sweeps on top of his head, cropped slightly shorter on the sides. Close-cut, equally dark stubble covers a wide, square jaw, the area under his sharp cheekbones, and the space around his mouth. His lips are full, I note. Almost *sensual*, actually...

Until he frowns.

Then, he's terrifying.

The rugged appeal of his features transforms into something stern and intimidating as he tosses the woman behind us a pointed glare. He turns the look on the café employee next, roughing out his own order before tapping his phone again, effortlessly paying for all three drinks.

My mind boggles, unable to comprehend. Does he think I'm

somebody else? Is he about to look me in the eye and recoil in shock?

I'm so thrown, I lose sight of where I am until the strong fingers curled over my shoulder give a second, firmer squeeze. I blink, immediately surrendering to the man's unspoken directive as he guides me out of the line.

And—oh God—he's *looking at me*. But he isn't backing away. Or acting like he's made a mistake.

Does that mean he was actually just... being nice? Trying to help me save face? Why would he do that?

My mouth opens, half a dozen apologies and explanations jamming in my throat. "I—Y-you—I j-just—" I stammer, struggling to speak coherently as adrenaline drains from my body and mortification swamps my stomach.

Slashing brows form a V over the man's bottomless eyes. Shimmering threads of gold gild the brown irises, illuminating their depths. They're somehow dark and warm—a combination that matches his scowl. A muscle ticks in his square jaw, but the frown pulling at his dusky lips feels more concerned than irritated.

Which is a crazy thought. There is *no* reason for this handsome stranger to *care* about me or my coffee. Nor is there *any* reason why he would be looking into my eyes so intently, as if he's trying to read some secret inked into my soul.

Seriously. Did I fall on the icy stairs going into the subway this morning? Or get hit by a cab?

The longer he looks, the more my cheeks heat. Humiliation burns my face and stings my eyes, but there's also something hypnotizing about being caught in his gaze. The invisible fist strangling my vocal cords finally slackens, allowing me to whisper, "I'm so sorry. Th-thank you."

The man gives a steady, solid nod. I get the feeling that's how he does most things—with purpose. Deliberation. His dark eyes flit over my shoulder to the restless line. When they suddenly sail back to mine and plunge just as deeply as before, I nearly gasp.

Which might be embarrassing, if I had the capacity to feel anything other than astonishment.

"It's no trouble," he replies, even and rumbling. "You got me to the head of the line."

Oh. My insides spasm painfully, then deflate. *Right. Of course.*

Before I can spiral into a new whirl of chagrin, his mouth hitches in wry amusement. "And, unfortunately, I have a habit of saving pretty blondes."

Pretty blondes? As in me?

I almost look around, searching for some other woman he may be referring to. But he's still looking at me. Who else could he be talking about?

The man watches every flicker on my face. All traces of amusement abandon his expression. He frowns more deeply. Almost as if he's deciding something.

His mouth opens to speak, but the barista sets three drinks on the concrete countertop before pausing to skim her attention over the handsome stranger. Can't really blame her—if I weren't currently trying to look at anything *but* him, I'd be staring, too.

My eyes land on my fingers, noticing tiny flecks of green paint from my latest creation that somehow escaped my shower unscathed. A fresh swirl of shame curdles my stomach, rounding my shoulders as the man hands me my tea and Tris's cold brew.

I notice his drink looks just like mine—in a hot cup, with a tea bag string hanging down the side. His eyebrows quirk at the cup full of ice. The disapproving scowl on his face is almost funny.

"It's not for me," I blurt, mumbling too fast and too soft for anyone to hear.

My mother is always on me about that. Tris, too. Just this morning, I was muttering about how she had once again forgotten to buy paper towels, and she tossed back, *How am I supposed to hear you if you don't speak up, Alley Cat?*

Which, I'll admit, is a good point.

Horrifying nickname aside.

"I'm relieved."

For a second, I can't remember how to breathe. Did he *hear* me? Did he just... answer me?

It would appear so. The big man is locked in once again—his full focus latched on my face as I jerk upright. Waiting, I realize, for me to meet his eyes as he adds, "I'd hate for you to catch a chill out there."

Utter sincerity shines through each crease in his expression. I feel the urge to blink again, disbelief and amazement swelling in my throat. "I—"

I'm about to say I won't... but then I realize I'll likely be walking forty blocks home. Since I can't spend my last eight dollars on an Uber or a new subway pass.

I should have cancelled that website before it charged me. There will be no point to it, now. Plus, I'll have to call Mama for help and tell her she was right.

I've squandered the little I scraped together in six years at a corporate hospitality job, all before I even managed to get my first real client. Which is exactly what she told me would happen if I followed my "dream."

She always puts quotation marks around that word. Like she can't quite believe anyone would be silly or small-minded enough to make wedding planning their *actual* dream.

Though, I suppose, at this point, I can't really argue with her.

The handsome stranger is still staring at me. *Reading* me, it seems. And proficiently, too.

Without another word, he slides his hand into his pocket and pulls out a subway card. "Here," he offers, extending it to me. "So you can get home safely."

I'm... dumbfounded. Truly and completely flabbergasted beyond reason. A gorgeous man coming to my rescue? Worrying about my safety? Are there even gentlemen like this left in the world?

Apparently so, because he sets the subway card on top of Tris's cup. "W-what about you?" I stammer, noticing he doesn't even have a coat on.

But he just quirks that serious half-smile again. "I have a car. And I'm mean enough to take care of myself."

He says the last part with a somber tone I don't think I fully understand. As if maybe his words run deeper than they sound.

There's no time to figure out why. A moment later, he's in motion, picking up his cup of tea and the pastry bag beside it. Inside, I spot the cranberry muffin I wanted.

That puts something almost like a smile on my face. *If I can't have it, I'm glad it's going to the last chivalrous man in Manhattan.*

Or maybe not. Because, as I smile at my feet like the lame romantic I am, a crinkling paper bag lands on top of my drink.

The man balances the muffin on top of my cup, stepping away with a final nod. "That's for you," he says, blowing my mind one last time as he flashes the world's quickest, most earnest grin. "Darling."

I SLIDE my phone out of my pocket as a lash of winter wind hits my face.

The number is programmed as my first contact, purely for efficiency's sake. I hit it and bring today's cup of tea to my lips, wishing it were the kind I keep at home instead of whatever generic nonsense the woman in the shop ordered for herself.

Alice Moore.

I know her name—and probably a great deal more than I should about her life. But, somehow, this is the first time I've thought of her as a *woman*.

Sort of impossible not to, after actually meeting her.

The tea she chose is incredible, though. Something dark and bitter—perfect for the morning. With a pastry.

Good thing she has one.

That thought shouldn't lift the corners of my lips, but it does. I turn toward 57th as the call clicks through, connecting me to the silent presence on the other side, waiting for my word.

"She's perfect."

alice

I'VE BEEN TO STRYKER & Sons before, but it never fails to turn me inside out.

For one, the enormous building is about as cool and intimidating as they come. Endless expanses of snowy marble and onyx accents. Spiky gold fixtures, pristine tempered glass.

By the time I step off the elevator onto the open floor plan of the highest level, my hands are sweating. Although that may have more to do with the coffee shop encounter I still can't quite process.

I'd hate for you to catch a chill out there.

I have a habit of rescuing pretty blondes.
So you can get home safely.
Darling.

Like I said, it's very possible I've lost my mind.

I'd be convinced I hallucinated the whole thing, if not for the pastry bag tucked between my elbow and my side. I know I didn't order that—which means *he* must have.

Clearing my head with a shake, I turn toward Tris's department. It's on the right side of the executive floor, in the section reserved for Stryker & Sons' top real estate brokers.

My best friend may not seem like it on the surface, but she's a total shark. Some of the deals she's put together leave grown men flabbergasted. Her boss—*the* Grayson Stryker—must see her value. He's already promoted her twice in the last year. Which explains why she now has her own office behind a wall of smoked glass.

Inside, neon-purple light strips line the seams of the ceiling. I roll my eyes as I push in, noting the fuzzy pink chairs she's added since my last visit.

I suppose Mr. Stryker must not have a strict decorating policy. Either that, or he's too busy counting all the money she's made this month to notice.

Though, how one would fail to take note of the lime-green "Bad Bitch" sign above the furry sofa is beyond me.

Tris grins from her desk, looking as gorgeous as ever in today's emerald jumpsuit. She gestures at her phone with an exaggerated roll of her eyes. I shuffle closer, pretending not to eavesdrop.

"Look, Rick," she huffs. "If you're just gonna bust my balls, I gotta go. I have something tall and sexy waiting on my desk."

I smirk, leaving her (tall, sexy) coffee on the shiny white surface. Tris winks at me and tosses her shoulder-length red waves back, listening to Rick's reply. "So you get it," she quips in return, grinning again. "Call me back later."

She hangs up unceremoniously and leaps from her glittering

gold swivel chair, tackling me with a hug. "Thank you, Alley Cat!"

Don't thank me, I think darkly, giving her a weak squeeze in return. Muttering, "I can never tell if you're flirting with a date or doing business."

Tris snaps back to her full, runway-worthy height, smiling wider. "Neither can they, babe. That's why I'm the best."

There's no arguing that. Since we got to the city five years ago, Tris has gone from eating peanut butter for every meal to paying the full rent on our tiny, hideously expensive walk-up in the West Village. We're supposed to split it, but she hasn't mentioned the five-thousand-dollars-a-month once since I quit my job at the hotel conglomerate and started down the path of self-employment.

Or, you know, *bankruptcy.*

We may be opposites in every way, but Tris has a heart every bit as beautiful as her face. And she may be forgetful, raucous, and unpredictable, but she's also incredibly laid back and easy to live with.

Mostly.

"Okay, so, here's the thing," my best friend starts, skillfully keeping her hazel eyes on her phone and her posture casual. "I was thinking about your whole business situation, and I have the perfect solution."

There isn't time for me to be appropriately apprehensive. Because before I even finish furrowing my face into a frown, Tris's door glides open. Revealing Grayson Stryker, her billionaire boss... and his sweetheart fiancée, Ella.

The small blonde woman bounces forward, hugging me in a much gentler fashion than my best friend. "Oh, Alice, thank you so much!" she gushes.

The wheels in my mind grind together, then start to churn. Along with my stomach.

Oh, Lord. What has Tris *done*?!

It's difficult to look at Grayson Stryker without nearly

choking on my own tongue. He's just so damn handsome, trimmed out in a navy suit and sporting the sort of verdant eyes that only appear in paintings.

Usually, when I have to be around him, I do everything I can to shrink down to nothing. But perhaps my run-in with the mysterious coffee house man has addled my brain, because my first thought is that Grayson isn't as good-looking. At least, in my opinion.

Which may be a little biased.

The young CEO smiles when I chance a glance into his eyes and slowly return Ella's hug. "Um, y-you're... welcome?"

Ella exhales, audibly relieved. "It's just been *impossible* to find a good wedding planner! Everyone we've interviewed has been obsessed with couture dresses and tabloid articles and flying hundreds of people halfway around the world. I was *sick* at the thought of how much money and resources they wanted to waste, but I tried planning on my own, and that was a *disaster* because we're aiming for a date in May and—"

Am I sure I actually woke up this morning?

First, a series of nightmarish texts from Mama.

Then a coffee shop rescue from a modern Sir Galahad.

Now...

Well. I'm pretty sure Ella Callahan is asking me to be her wedding planner.

Or Tris has *already told her* I would be her wedding planner.

When she marries *Grayson Stryker*.

The *celebrity* CEO.

In *four months*?!

Is that even possible? With enough money, I suppose anything is. They definitely have that. But the security and the secrecy and the *media*...

My thoughts spin, reeling while sweet Ella gives me a final squeeze. When she pulls away, the sincere happiness and hope etched into her pretty features are enough to wind me.

"Anyway," she concludes, "When Tris said you had a last-minute cancellation, I was so thrilled. I know you'd never try to take advantage of Gray or burn a hole in the O-Zone just to get on Page Six. And the design ideas on your website are just *gorgeous*, Alice."

Tris knows damn well I had no clients to cancel on me—she just spun a story to make me sound desirable.

But there's a note of pleading in Ella's voice, as if she's clocked the way I've frozen solid and realizes this isn't the done deal she thought it was.

I wish I had the confidence—or delusion—to simply *take it*. I see what Tris is trying to do. She knows an event of this magnitude would launch my business straight to the stars. And the commission would be *massive*, possibly even in the six-figure range.

But I can't do this wedding! I've only done a handful of smaller ones on my own, and certainly nothing that would end up splashed across every publication in the *world*.

My designs might be pretty and unique enough for an average buffet-and-ballroom affair. But *this*?! Nuh-uh. No way.

For God's sake, I shouldn't even be *invited* to a wedding this fancy, let alone the one *coordinating* it.

My mouth falls slack, blubbing for some sort of polite refusal. The words won't come, but my middle twists as Ella's expression pinches with anxiety. Her fiancé steps smoothly into her side, his smile taking on a harder edge.

"Whatever it takes," he puts in, his tone brokering no argument. "I just want it done the way Ella's always dreamed of. As soon as possible. By someone we can *trust*."

The emphasis he places on that final phrase hits me square in the chest. Because our friendship may be new, but I care about Ella—and Grayson is right to be concerned. As I've recently learned all too well, wedding planning in Manhattan is a cutthroat business.

A lot of the boutique shops would take a sweet bride like Ella and paper over her visions with their own nonsense before she could blink. Others would be more concerned with money than ego—they might give Ella what she *thinks* she wants, but they would inflate expenses to line their own pockets with a higher commission percentage.

And the worst ones? Well, they'd take Grayson's credit card, ignore Ella's dreams, and spend the entire planning process feeding details to the media on the side.

Because the more coverage the wedding gets? The more coverage *they* get.

Which sounds more like my nightmare than my dream. But still.

An odd rush of protectiveness steels my stomach, chasing away some of my nerves. "I—I'm not sure if I can handle a wedding of this caliber," I murmur, meeting Ella's ocean eyes.

Tris interjects, slinging her slender arm around my neck, "Sure, you can! You guys should see the amazing mood boards she has in her room and on Pinterest. Oh em gee. And Alley Cat is so organized and *smart*."

My face heats, but Grayson's mouth twitches. He's clearly amused by Tris's antics, which I guess is fortunate, as far as paying our rent goes.

Then again, if I do this job... and I actually pull it off...

Despite the press interest, it *is* my dream. The only one I've allowed myself to keep.

There's a voice in my head, though, shrieking that I can't do this and never could. She's loud and shrill enough for me to flinch down, away. Metaphorically stuffing my tattered wishes back into the shoebox under my bed.

I glance up to stammer some lame excuse, but Ella's eyes stop me.

She's so *hopeful*—and clearly every bit as nervous as I am.

A softer voice hums under the blare of my impostor syndrome, reminding me, *She didn't ask for any of this. She never wanted to be famous or rich. She's just a sweet girl who fell in love. And she needs help to make her wedding dreams come true.*

I'm somehow shaking and petrified. But, damn it, some things are more important than fear.

I swallow hard, doing my best to steady myself. "If you want me to try," I whisper. "I will do my absolute best."

Ella *glows*. Grayson pulls her into his side, brushing a kiss on her temple before turning back to me with a businesslike nod. "That's all we could ever ask for." A flinch darts across his face. "Oh, and I'm afraid I'll have to ask for your forgiveness as well."

All three of us pause, even his fiancée. His cringe deepens into a grimace as he addresses her instead of me. "I had to, Ellie, as a matter of security. To protect you."

Ella's expression morphs to a gape. "Grayson, you *didn't*."

"Just this once," he replies, low and even. "Only for a few hours."

Tris opens her big mouth, but Grayson beats her to it, turning back to me with a contrite wince. "Alice, I apologize, but I had to have my head of security look into your background, and he took it upon himself to familiarize himself with your routines and temperament, as well. To ensure you wouldn't pose a risk to Ellie."

The haunted look in his eyes, his lowered brow and heavy frown... My stupid, romantic heart can't even hold his shocking revelation against him.

Of course this man wanted me vetted before he hired me. He *adores* his wife-to-be; I'm sure he would move heaven and earth to keep her safe, if he had to.

It's like something out of a fairytale.

And, unfortunately, I've always had a soft spot for those.

And, unfortunately, I have a habit of saving pretty blondes.

My thoughts trigger the memory of the chivalrous stranger yet again. His voice replays on a loop, drowning out Grayson's next statement as he gestures to the open doorway behind him.

Where a tall, broad man suddenly appears.

Wearing all black.

Holding a cup of tea identical to mine.

alice

THE IMPOSING man doesn't flinch or squirm as I gather the courage to meet his eyes.

I have a feeling, even if I hadn't studied them twenty minutes ago, I would vividly remember the clear, dark brown irises. Their rich color—and the unflappable air of control layered beneath it.

My heart spasms, twisting in two directions. The stupid, silly flutter of excitement at seeing him again so soon. And the jagged, slicing sting of realization that he wasn't actually flirting with me.

He was only nice because he *had* to be. As part of his *job*.

I can practically hear my mother scoffing. Of course *he had a* reason *for flirting. And of course it had nothing to do with actually liking you.*

The phrase sounds dumb, even in my own head. Because, really—who *thinks* like that? I'm *thirty,* for crying out loud.

My cheeks flame as mortification liquefies the butterflies in my stomach. I immediately turn my gaze to my walking shoes, struggling to swallow past the lump that appears in my throat.

"Oh," I say to my feet. "H-hello again."

The big man exhales quietly. In my periphery, I see him offer another of his solid nods. "Miss Moore."

My last name rolls off his tongue in a low baritone. And somehow, despite all my embarrassment, I find myself raising my chin. Seeking out his gorgeous, solemn, impassive face.

See? He's real, after all, my brain chimes. *And now the whole encounter makes perfect sense.*

In the most depressing way possible.

His etched mouth presses into a straight line when our gazes touch. He extends his huge hand, hovering it in the space between us. "Marco Amir," he offers. "It's a pleasure to meet you."

Marco Amir.

And he's acting like we didn't meet downstairs.

I mean, I suppose we *didn't,* technically... but I still sense a snap of urgency flashing in his deep, espresso eyes. Perhaps asking me to play along? Or forgive him for deceiving me?

No, that can't be it. Because why would he care?

I'm too frozen and stubborn and nauseous to pretend. Seconds pass, and I don't reach for his hand. Ella jumps in, giggling nervously as she rests her palm on my forearm. "Marco is always super formal," she stage-whispers, clearly teasing Grayson's head of security. "But I think we'll be able to break him eventually."

Grayson laughs under his breath. "Good luck with that, ladies. Many have tried, and many have failed. Either way, I have a meeting downstairs, so I'll leave you to it."

Ella squeezes my wrist, whispering a promise to come right

back before she follows him into the hallway. Tris stands between Marco and me, glances at each of us, and blurts a chipper, "I have to pee!"

Her heels clack out of the room, but I can't turn to watch any of them leave. I'm too busy keeping my chin up, ignoring the large, brawny hand extended toward me.

Marco finally drops it. His lips part, but I shock myself by cutting him off.

"It's fine," I murmur. "You were working."

His next nod looks more like half a shrug. As if he can't decide whether or not I'm right. "In any case," he starts, "I should still—"

A sharp stab hits my chest. I'm not sure why, but if this handsome stranger *apologizes* for flirting with me, I have a feeling I'll simply crumble into dust. Instead, I step back and shake my head. "J-just forget it. I-I—"

Have to get out of here.

And possibly flee the country.

My words flail into sputtering silence, as they do all too often. I brace, waiting for the imposing man to interrupt with his dreaded apology. Or try to guess what I was struggling to say.

He does neither, though. He just... waits. With his eyes steady on my face and his stern mouth shut. Watching me. Listening.

The pressure should probably make me more nervous, but the weight of his full attention feels settling. I blink twice, awed at his patience, before peeping, "I need to t-talk to Ella. T-to schedule our first meeting."

Marco absorbs that, but *still* doesn't interrupt. He takes one step closer. My nerves flutter back to life. "If you'd excuse me," I nearly gasp. "I-I'll just..."

I try to slip around him. But I'm too big.

Or, rather, *he's* too big. Taking up the entire doorway like a cologne-model-meets-Navy SEAL-shaped barricade.

I'm already impressed by his manners, even before he automatically steps aside, bowing his head in deference. I start to scurry past, but a warm, firm touch lands on my upper arm, carefully curling just above my elbow.

His hand. On me.

"Miss Moore."

My eyes automatically snap up to his. Again. His reaction is so immediate, I barely catch the millisecond smirk that flits over his mouth before he flattens it. His other hand reaches for the inside pocket of his black blazer, extracting a charcoal business card. Engraved with a phone number.

"Call me when you have a date set for your meeting. I'll pick you up."

five

MARCO

I KNEW I wouldn't sleep well.

I never do, after the tough jobs.

Yesterday's assignment should have been an easy one, though. The fact that I grappled with it until my head hit the pillow had me questioning if I'd lost my edge. And launched me into one of my recurring nightmares.

Long shadows, stakes of wooden crates. A haze of smoke and the smell of gunpowder. Blood that runs between my feet.

This is all my fault.

I jerk awake, my body launching into a familiar, defensive

position. The readout on my bedside alarm glows white in the spartan, darkened bedroom.

4:56.

Fucking hell.

I slept for maybe two hours—and none of it was restful. With a groan, I roll to my feet. I'll have to do something about my sleeplessness soon, if I want to keep functioning the way I need to.

Doctors and Web MD articles like to blame my insomnia on my time in Special Ops. Or maybe my days working for the NYPD. Or, most recently, running security for a billion-dollar company.

Stress. I have *stress*.

But, actually, the constant need to stay alert has more to do with *me* than my circumstances.

Even before I had so much to worry about, I was never good at quieting my mind. Ironic, since "quiet" tends to be my most consistent personality trait. Right alongside "observant" and "intimidating."

All positive attributes for someone in my line of work.

Serene silence greets me as I stretch the stiffness from my limbs. *Stupid. Waste of perfectly good adrenaline*, I grunt internally, my bleary eyes taking in the world outside my windows.

It's as dark and peaceful as Manhattan gets. In fact, this view is the reason I chose my new apartment. The quiet calm of being so high above the rest of the city is still my favorite thing about it.

The building is also new and well-built. Solid. Soundproofed. It helps that it's on the West Side, only a few blocks from the Hudson.

Each time I look around, I shake my head in disbelief. Just three and a half years ago, I was nobody. A former soldier. A disgraced police officer. Too quiet, really, to mix well with others in general.

A week after the incident that cost me my spot on the force, I sat down with a notepad, intending to write out all the qualifications I could put on a résumé. I wound up with one.

A driver's license.

The next morning, I went to the nearest chauffeur service and took the first job they gave me. Turned out, some trust-fund kid in Manhattan needed a driver to cart him from Columbia University to his father's development firm Downtown. A kid named Grayson Stryker.

It didn't take long for me to realize he wasn't a kid at all. He was twenty-two with a sick father, a new girlfriend, and an empire to run. He needed help. When he hired me from the car company, we became a team of sorts. Three years later, he promoted me from his personal bodyguard to the director of security for his entire firm.

He also offered me more money than I ever thought I'd see. Enough to pay off all my mother's debt, buy her a new home in Queens, and get myself a three-bedroom apartment in town.

The open-concept space has a modern, masculine feel to it. I like the aesthetic, but not as much as I like the clean sight lines. From my bed, with my bedroom doors wide open, I can just about see every inch of my new apartment. Which is the way I prefer it.

Even now that I've "made it," part of me will always be looking over my shoulder.

Because I learned my lessons the hard way.

Not wanting to think of it, I reach for my dresser. It's black, like all the clothing inside of it and the four guns laid out on top.

I throw on workout gear and strap my Glock to my chest, sliding a magazine of bullets into the pocket of my joggers. Thinking better of it, I add a second magazine to my other pocket.

"Cautious" bordering on "unreasonable"—more words from the mandatory psych report the NYPD conducted before I left my job. I didn't like them, at the time. As the years go on, though, I get the sneaking suspicion their shrink may have had a point.

Hence, the knife built into the sole of my left trainer. And the Taser I keep in my gym bag.

It all comes with the job, of course. I am the security director for one of the largest and wealthiest companies in the city. Stryker & Sons has enemies. Which means I do, too.

Sometimes, even my workouts aren't really breaks. I spend many mornings sparring with Grayson. He likes to feel prepared, should anyone ever come at him. Or, more importantly, should anyone ever come at his girl.

Ella Callahan—soon-to-be Stryker—deserves every bit of effort. She's a sweet person, and she's suffered enough to last her a lifetime. After witnessing just how determined her demons were, I take my duty as her protector very seriously.

Most mornings, I do my own workout before I go over to Ella and Grayson's and kick the crap out of him. They had a date last night to celebrate their new wedding plans, though. He told me he would be "too tired" from "going out."

More like exhausted from a sex marathon.

I thought I would get used to the pangs of envy by now. Instead, their romance serves as a constant—daily, *hourly*— reminder of what I want but might never have.

True love. Soulmates.

Maybe most single guys would be thoroughly nauseated by that. But I watched my parents orbit around each other for twenty-seven years before my dad was taken from my mom.

My eyes squeeze shut as I inhale through my nose, doing everything I can to not return to that night. Instead, I grab my keys off the kitchen counter and bolt out the door, jogging to hail the elevator down the hall. Within seconds, I stride into the building's gym, finding it blessedly empty.

Normally, as soon as I hit the treadmill, my mind starts to clear.

Not today.

I didn't have a choice, I argue with myself. *I had to follow her.*

Right now, Alice Moore poses the single greatest security threat to the Strykers. Being their wedding planner means she'll have access to Grayson's credit cards, Ella's schedule, their townhome, and our office. Plus, she's planning the *actual* event—if she were an untrustworthy person, she could easily sell them out on the day of the wedding. God knows, there are plenty of people who would pay good money to harm them. And even more people willing to go to any length to sensationalize their nuptials in the press.

Goddamn it, that's *true*. So why does it feel like bullshit?

I've been repeating the facts to myself from the moment our eyes met in the coffee shop, but it hasn't helped one bit.

I suspect the guilt gnawing at my guts might be more rooted in the way the light hit her clear blue eyes. Or how tightly her sweater pulled across her chest.

And the fact that I noticed both things. Dozens of times over.

Maybe I shouldn't have approached her the way I did. It wasn't strictly necessary—I'd already done a background check and tailed her for hours. I knew she wasn't a risk. From what I could tell, the woman didn't have the nerve to order the muffin she wanted, let alone scheme up sabotage.

But watching her squirm when her card declined made my insides itch—and I figured paying for her breakfast was the least I could do.

Making her smile was just a happy accident.

Liking her smile was unavoidable.

It won't happen again, though.

I'm just not that lucky.

THE SMELL of coffee on a Monday morning is decidedly *not* a good sign.

Tris only brews her own coffee on the not-so-rare occasions when she has overnight *guests*. And she only brings *me* coffee when she needs a favor.

An unholy combination, I assure you.

My door bursts open without warning. Then there's some bustling. The sound of my stuff hitting the floor. The sheer of my curtain ripped to the side. My shoulders are already hiked up to my ears, even before an all-too-chipper, *"Good morning!"* rings out.

Her voice only gets louder as she plops onto my mattress. "Up and at 'em, Alley Cat."

I crack one eye open, squinting against the meager light from my brick-wall-facing window.

When we moved into the tiny Greenwich Village walk-up on Bleeker Street, we decided Tris would take the room with an actual view. It's bigger, after all, and she pays our rent.

Not for long, I hope.

"Tris," I whine, closing my eyes again. "I need to *sleep*."

While she was out, I spent the evening on my laptop and three new concept boards. It took half the night, but I managed to come up with a handful of themes for Ella to use as a jumping-off point. We have our first planning session this afternoon—and I'm so nervous, I barely got any sleep at all.

Ignoring my protests, Tris flashes her wide, white, winning smile. "I made you coffee."

Wary, I lurch upright. "Tris... what did you do now?"

Still grinning like the Cheshire Cat, she shrugs her slender shoulders and swipes the auburn fringe of her side bangs off her forehead. "What are you talking about? I just made coffee." She stands abruptly, showing off her lithe figure in an electric-blue jumpsuit and matching heels. "I have to run, though," she goes on, casual as ever. "Big meeting with my boss. Your boss, too, now, technically."

That is too true. When I originally left my old job, I naively believed I'd be my own boss. Turns out, we all work for someone.

The man from the coffee shop rolls over my other thoughts. An irrational burst of hurt follows, then a lash of hatred. None of it makes any sense. It's been three days, and the guy was simply doing his job, trying to keep my friend safe for her adoring fiancé.

How can I possibly hate him for that? And why am I still so embarrassed?

I'm not sure. If I figure it out, I'll let you know. Though I suspect it has something to do with the way I basically slunk off in shame after Ella and I made our plans for this week.

I gently nudged her into doing our first set of sessions at her townhome. That way, I figure, she won't need security to tail her anywhere. If I have the smallest pinch of luck, it's possible I won't even run into *him*.

Marco Amir.

His name rings in my head without permission. I do my best to mentally crumple it, reminding myself I have much bigger fish to fry.

Namely, a *celebrity wedding*. In less than four months.

Unfortunately for the rabid press, if her Pinterest boards are any indication, Ella's taste trends toward the understated. Except when it comes to her crazy color palettes... and the dessert table. I've made a custom-painted vision board to bring with me today, although I'm decidedly unexcited about hauling it in and out of the subway.

Because I'll be damned if I use that business card Marco gave me.

Instead of leaving my coffee on my nightstand, Tris carries the mug to the door of my thimble-sized room, waving it slightly to tempt me out of bed. "Up, up, *uhhhhp!*" she sings.

With a grumble, I roll to my feet and reach for the robe wadded up at the foot of my tiny full-sized mattress. The mirror shoved into the opposite corner doesn't do me any favors, reflecting my pale, haggard face back at me, along with my limp blonde hair.

At least the robe covers most of my body. The fluff layered around my middle, the rolls under my ribs, the cellulite padding my thighs.

Ugh. I pull the sash tighter.

Edging carefully past the half-finished painting on my easel and one of the corkboards laden with the Strykers' wedding details, I barely make it out of the room without toppling everything. I almost breathe a sigh of relief. Then I step into our living room.

"*Tris*," I hiss. "*What* in the..."

At my side, my best friend shrugs one shoulder again. "Sunday Scaries."

As if that explains the two—not one, *two*—naked men face-down on our sofa and rug.

"You had a *threesome* in our *living room*?" I whisper-shout.

"Well, it's not like all of us would have fit in my bedroom, silly," Tris replies, rolling her eyes. "And, technically, it was a four-some. The other girl went home. She was nice. *Great* boobs."

Lord, have mercy. "You had an *orgy* in our living room?"

Dark red brows knit over bright hazel eyes. "Is four people an orgy? I feel like that implies a minimum of five."

I clench my teeth together. "Beatrice Eleanor Dunn. You let *three strangers* in here?"

"Mellow, Mom," she scoffs. "Everyone was safe. Nothing is stolen or broken. And they aren't *strangers*. I know them from the karaoke bar."

I open my mouth to argue, but my roommate is already in motion. She rarely pauses, in general. "Anyway, Alley Cat, I'm outie. I have that showing so... Have a great day!"

I grab her elbow. "No way are you leaving me here with them!" I hiss. "What am I supposed to say when they wake up?"

"Tell them..." Tris slips out of my grasp and makes for the door, outpacing me with her long legs. "...the coffee's fresh! Okay-gottago, loveyoumeanit, byeeee!"

"Tris!" Desperate, I lunge to grab the door handle just in time for the slab to slam in my face.

Frantic, I dash into the kitchen before either man rouses. There really isn't any place to hide, though. The whole "room" barely covers six square feet from the doorway to the fridge. And I only have enough space to turn between the brick wall and the four-foot wooden countertop along the only stretch of cabinets.

I glare at the full coffee pot, hating everything it stands for. *Ridiculous Tris with her stupid coffee bribes and her orgies....*

Someone shifts in the living room, and I press further back, my butt bumping the black fridge and the collection of Christmas cards still taped up there. I've asked my roommate to throw them out at least once a week since New Year's, but Tris is notoriously horrible at cleaning.

Rolling my eyes, I rip them down, ignoring my stab of guilt. They are all hers, of course. Postcards and pictures from high school and college friends, exes, clients, her extended family.

Only one has my name on it—typed onto a label, clearly mass-printed from some sort of master list. I flip the thick piece of cardstock over in my hand, giving the picture on the front one last glare.

My mother looks gorgeous, as always. Coiffed to perfection in a cheerful red wrap dress, perched with her manicured hand casually resting on her husband's shoulder.

Richard looks as fit and wealthy as ever. While my mother grins, he keeps his expression stoic and stares the camera down, daring it to disapprove of how much he doesn't care about some silly Christmas card.

But he still sat for the picture. Because *not* sending out a Christmas card *doesn't look good*. And Richard cares about appearances almost as much as my mother does.

By the time I finish shoving all the cards into the trash can stashed under our tiny sink, I hear the front door open and close. When I bend out of the small strip of space, I see that one of Tris's hookups—Floor Guy—has fled, leaving The Man On The Futon behind. He stirs, moaning quietly and twitching against the morning sunlight.

Still totally naked.

I sigh at the pot of fresh coffee on the counter. Knowing I'm about to end up offering this bare-butted stranger a cup. And wondering if my roommate will ever remember that I prefer tea.

seven

MARCO

OF ALL THE streets Ted Stryker could have chosen, it had to be this one.

For weeks, I have spent hours double-parked in rented black SUVs, surveilling the still, silent walk-up. And every damn time, the smell of dumplings frying two doors down threatens to distract me.

That is one downside to my size—no matter how much I eat, I am *always* hungry.

Shifting in the driver's seat, I squint out the windshield, forcing myself to focus.

Come on, you bastard, I grumble internally, willing the disgraced Stryker to show his face. *I know you're in there.*

One of our newest hires confirmed that fact. He isn't good for much, yet, but the guy can trace a cell phone faster than any other man on my team.

Otherwise, Pierce Williams is just a baby-faced kid fresh out of the police academy. He had perfect marks and passed his law enforcement exams with flying colors... In the end, though, he decided to go corporate for more security. He has a newly minted wife at home, expecting their first baby.

I'm not sure if that contributes to his overall nervousness, but the kid practically twitches every time I call his name. It probably has something to do with his age—at twenty-two, he is, by far, the youngest person I've ever employed.

And, God help me, he *acts* like it.

Behind him, our other recent recruit, Brad Forrester, cracks his knuckles. A habit that might not annoy me, if he didn't do it every four minutes. After three hours, I don't know if I'm closer to breaking out a timer or making sure they're *permanently* cracked.

While Pierce doubts everyone—including himself—Brad is cocky. He scoffs, rolls his eyes, and generally has the attitude one would expect of a little shit who couldn't hack it in the Marines.

But he also wrestles like an MMA prize fighter. And he can shoot nearly as well as I do.

Both of them make me feel as old as hell itself.

We sit in our unmarked Escalade. Brad pops his joints, and Pierce taps his fingers against his thighs the way a drummer might hit a solo. "Are you sure you want me to do this by myself?" he asks, his voice breaking over the last word.

"Yes," I answer, projecting the calm I wish he'd summon. "You can do this."

I believe that. More or less.

He is an awkward kid, but he obviously looks up to me. I don't have the heart to tell him his admiration is entirely misplaced. After all, I have failed myself and the people I care about in a few *very* crucial ways over the years.

I sigh, counting the minutes until I can call this off. The week has worn me down and sharpened my determination in equal measures. I'm not sure why, but with every passing moment, I feel something coming for me—for *us*.

It seems to beat in the air, in my ears, in my chest. I feel, in each moment, seconds away from a reckoning. And, somehow, ages away from a resolution.

What if I'm looking in all the wrong places? Maybe the danger isn't Ted Stryker and his piece-of-shit, rapist son. Maybe this is something bigger than protecting Ella from the men who tried to harm her in the past and keeping the rest of Grayson's family safe from his evil uncle. If that's the case, there may not even be a threat lurking in this Chinatown walk-up.

Except, I feel it. Here, on the dim, still street. In my apartment at two a.m. Every time I drive away from the Stryker's townhouse.

Something sinister is loitering, filing its nails. Playing the long game.

I hate that I don't know how long it will wait.

Or who it truly wants to hurt.

alice

"MAMA—"

I'm not sure why I even bother trying to cut her off. I only know I am twenty minutes late for my first meeting with Ella and my mother *will not stop talking* about her doubles partner's step-daughter's back acne.

"Alice, it is *unbecoming* to interrupt," she chides. "I spent two hours at the mall last weekend choosing clothes for you, and you wouldn't even FaceTime me to try them on. The least you could do is listen while I'm speaking!"

She's right, of course. She went out of her way to buy me a

new batch of sweaters and work pants. I don't have the heart to tell her that the pants are two sizes too small and the sweaters mold to every roll of fat on my frame. No matter how many times I work up the courage to mention my current size, she always "forgets" and buys clothes that are too small.

I can't tell if it is malicious encouragement or wishful thinking.

Tris suggested we burn the "fugly" pants either way and send my mother a picture of the ashes.

"Mama," I say again, huffing and puffing as I hitch up the giant vision board tucked under my arm. The sidewalks on the Upper West Side are usually wide and empty, which will leave plenty of room for my glorified poster and the frigid wind. Unfortunately, I have to get out of the train station first.

Unfortunately, I have a habit of saving pretty blondes.

I swear, if my brain doesn't stop replaying random snippets of that humiliating encounter, I will pull the New York equivalent of an *Anna Karenina* and jump in front of the next subway.

And to think that man had the nerve to tell me to call him for a ride, I think. *Like I'm some charity case who can't make it Uptown on my own.*

We won't talk about how he's sort of right—Tris had to give me a loan to get me through this first meeting, where Ella will hopefully pay my deposit.

And—okay, yes—the card I used to get on the train is the one Marco gave me when we met...

But *still*.

I don't care how hot he is or how good his intentions were. He didn't have to *flirt* with me. Or buy me that damned muffin.

"Alice!"

I jump at my mother's screech, nearly dropping my phone and the board. Two men approaching from the steps stop short, staring at my collection of fabric samples and color cards.

Shit. Why would they do that? They wouldn't want to steal it, right?

When one of them takes a camera out of his backpack and aims it at me, I realize why.

Oh God. The names.

Last night, I painted a ribbon along the top of the board, emblazoning it with *Ella & Grayson*. Now, as the stranger elbows his buddy, fear sticks in my gullet.

Did Marco want me to call him for a ride because he knew there would be paparazzi at the subway station near Ella's house? Or am I just being paranoid?

"I-I really have to g-go, Mama," I interrupt again, ignoring my pinch of despair when I think of all the scolding I'll receive later. "S-sorry!"

"Alice," she snips, sharp.

I don't bother telling her I'm not stammering from nerves, but because my teeth are chattering and there are now two groups of people with their phones out. "*Sorry,*" I say, emphasizing each crisp syllable. "I'll call you tomorrow."

My numb fingers fumble my phone as I shove it into my satchel. As I do, one of the guys grabs the edge of my board, his light eyes gleaming hungrily. "This for *the* Strykers?"

The moment feels surreal on a horrifying, out-of-body level. The man tugs harder, nearly ripping one of the fabric samples off, and some fight-or-flight instinct kicks in. I whirl and dash for the station's stairs.

It all happens so fast.

The element of surprise gets me to the top of the steps, but the second my foot lands on the sidewalk, someone rips the poster board from my hands. The sharp tug throws me off balance just as a blinding flash bursts in my face. I blink to try and clear my vision, but a hard shove rams into my side. I go sailing to the left, thrown into the railing separating traffic from the mouth of the underground train station.

My body bounces off the cold metal, and I stagger, nearly regaining my footing just in time for the other man to tear my purse off my shoulder. I flail and fall, crashing onto the cement as hard as one would expect for a woman my size. I recoil from the cold ground and the sudden pain that jolts through me.

As I expected, the street in this residential, posh part of Manhattan is mostly quiet. Which means my surprised shriek echoes off the twenty-million-dollar townhomes and barrels back into me.

I try to lurch up, but my head spins. The air stings my throat as I drag in shallow, panicked breaths. The quickly dizziness wins out, and I have to grasp onto the dirty metal fence behind me to keep from tumbling down the stairs.

"Fuck," one of the guys mutters. "Hurry up."

The other man is taking pictures, I realize, holding my board up and snapping shots of it while his accomplice rifles through my wallet. For a moment, I'm oddly grateful there isn't anything valuable for him to take. Unless he wants the loyalty card from my favorite book shop.

He only takes one thing, though. "Come on," his buddy grunts, throwing my tattered vision board on the sidewalk beside me. "We should run."

The first one tosses my purse down, too, clutching my single card to his chest like it's a priceless treasure. They disappear in an instant, but my breathing doesn't slow. My thoughts thin and dim.

And I barely hear the sound of tires screeching before I slip into the dark.

alice

"MISS MOORE?"

Oh God.

"Miss Moore?"

Oh *no.*

I can't decide if I'm dead... or if I *want* to be.

Because I know that voice. And it means I've either lapsed into some dream-like state between this world and the next—

Or Marco Amir actually found me, crumpled on the street like a discarded Starbucks cup.

And if he did, he clearly brought me... somewhere? I'm not sure, but it's warm here. The surface behind me feels soft, too.

My head pounds dully as I peel my eyes open, revealing Marco and Ella. My friend's pretty face is soft with concern, while her head of security looks utterly *pissed*.

Can I blame him, though? I just lost all their wedding details to a couple of paparazzi punks. On *my first day* as their planner.

Ella doesn't seem angry, at least. The second I flutter my lashes, she cries, "Oh, thank goodness you're awake!"

She turns sharply, long golden hair falling over her navy sweater. "It's okay!" she calls out. "She's awake!"

My bleary brain whirls, trying to work out who she's speaking to. Across the lavish parlor—*wow, is this her* house—I barely catch a group of EMTs being halted on the threshold. Another security guard, in a suit similar to Marco's, keeps his arm stretched in front of them, awaiting his boss's orders. Almost as if—

Oh. *Marco* called the ambulance?

I suppose that makes sense, given the state I was in when he found me. *If* he was the one who found me.

Marco's swirling eyes snap over my profile. He makes a frustrated sighing sound and nods at the wide archway. The other guard and the medics begin to file out. Ella follows them, humming something about handing out scones for their trouble.

The air in the room somehow gets tighter. My bleary brain can't comprehend the sensation, until my gaze snags on Marco's glare.

Oh GOD. He's *furious*.

His thick brows crouch lower. "Are you alright? They said you passed out from panic and you don't have any head contusions. But I can make them come back if you're feeling—"

Fresh mortification clenches my middle. "N-no," I rasp. "P-please."

To try and prove myself, I push upright. The room blurs for half a second before refocusing. Marco's frown somehow—impossibly—deepens. "You're really fine?" he husks out.

I'm not, but I nod anyway. His expression only grows tenser, though.

"Good," he bites out, stepping closer. "Then I suppose we can move on to *why the hell* you were on the subway, alone, when I clearly told you to *call me for a ride.*"

My face pulls into a cringe. What can tell him?

You're too handsome? I was trying to avoid further humiliation?

Ironic.

Marco isn't done. He closes the gap between us, looming less than a foot away while he scowls down at me. "What were you *thinking*, Miss Moore? Those bastards got all of the details on your wedding board *and* they took your driver's license."

Ah, so that's *the one card they took.*

Bizarre. Why would they want my ID?

And how does he *know* all of this?

Marco sees the befuddlement quirking my features and continues glowering. "We're hooked into every CCTV camera for several blocks surrounding this property. When you didn't call for a ride, I assumed you'd taken a cab—which still would have been risky—so I monitored the street views to ensure no one harassed you when you pulled up. Imagine my surprise when, instead, I saw you racing up the subway steps *a block away*. Being *chased* and *assaulted*."

Wow. He is *mad.*

I suppose that makes sense. His entire job hinges on his ability to protect Ella and Grayson. Now I've gone and compromised their event details mere days after being hired.

It's only sheer luck that I didn't have the wedding date or location anywhere on the poster. Today's meeting was set with the purpose of locking that information in, so I could add it later. It never even occurred to me that painting their names on the custom inspo board would cause them any trouble.

So stupid, Alice.

The thought is mine, but the shrill tone is one I've heard in my head for my entire life. I clasp my hands in my lap to hide my shaking. "I-I'm sorry. R-really. I-I didn't r-realize there would be paparazzi w-waiting around."

Just like the morning we met, Marco doesn't use my stutters as an excuse to interject. He waits, as patient as he is pissed off. Though, the more I stammer, the softer his scowl seems.

"I—I shouldn't have this job," I go on, knowing it's the right thing to do. "It's c-clear I'm really not equipped for it. I—I'll just tell Ella she can hire someone else. Someone *better*."

Marco finally exhales, his shoulders relaxing a fraction. "You would give up this big event?" he asks flatly. "And the commission?"

I wince at the thought of my empty bank account. But my issues aren't Ella's problem—and she obviously needs a more experienced coordinator. The thought fills me with equal parts sadness and relief.

"Honestly?" I answer, "I d-didn't want this job in the first place."

Marco's thick brows arch. "Then why did you take it?"

I look around the opulent sitting room, noting traces of Ella's simple, no-frills nature, strewn about in stark contrast to the Strykers' wealth. The half-finished knitting creation on the arm of a priceless antique armchair; the small pot of daisies sitting on the bar cart beside crystal stemware.

My bruised shoulder aches as I shrug, admitting, "I f-felt bad. Ella was having a hard time finding someone to work with who won't take advantage of her. I figured the only way to help was to—"

This time, he does finish my thought for me. Only he does it with an incredulous murmur. "Do it yourself."

I nod. "Yeah."

Marco truly has the deepest, most beautiful eyes. He holds my gaze for a long moment, searching it. Whatever he finds there has him sighing, dropping down to sit on the edge of the coffee table next to me.

"I'm not sure why," he replies, "but you're the only person I trust for this job, too."

The depth of his sincerity matches his bottomless brown irises. It helps quell the rising panic pinching my lungs.

Because I'm starting to see; there's no way out of this. For either of us.

No, Marco is stuck with me and I'm stuck with him until the wedding is over.

Or until it implodes.

I am going to kill *Tris for getting me into this.*

Marco watches his words sink in. He glowers once more as he adds, "Despite the fact that you've now compromised your identity as their planner, gotten your personal information stolen, and you seem to have a self-sacrificing stubborn streak."

My face pulls into another wince.

He isn't *wrong*.

I can't let this man continue to be nice to me out of a misplaced sense of duty, though. I have more pride than that, at least.

But the most pressing reason isn't my dignity. It's the way my heart squeezes when his dark, intense eyes bore into mine again.

"Stubborn doesn't scare me, Miss Moore," he husks. "But the things I'm trying to protect you from should definitely scare *you*. So if you think you can continue trying to avoid me, you ought to think again. Because keeping you safe is now *my* job. And I'm very good at what I do."

ten

MARCO

"FUCKING *FINALLY.*"

Well, I *am* late.

My smirk feels bleak as I drop into the barstool beside my friend, thumping his slumped shoulder. "Hello, Xander. Good to see you, too. Thanks for waiting."

"Don't start with me," he grouses. "And, by the way, you're buying. I've been sitting here for two hours, so I've been *drinking* for two hours. Which I can't afford because I'm broke as shit. And I don't want to hear any complaints. Your shoes cost more than my car."

I flip the menu over, wondering which whiskey he's volunteered my wallet for this time. Knowing Xander, it will be the best one they sell.

"You don't have a car," I remind him.

"And you have twelve. Hence, you'll be picking up the tab, and I'll"—he waves his hand to snag the bartender and lifts his empty glass—"have another."

If I had to describe Xander in a single word, I'd probably go with *direct*.

I could also say he is a motherfucking asshole with questionable morals, minimal emotional intelligence, and the sort of self-serving social skills indicative of a psychopath. He can charm a room full of superiors within an hour... then turn around and stab every last one of them in the back while he scrabbles up their shoulders to reach his ultimate goal.

He also happens to be one of the smartest people I've ever met. He grew up in trailer parks and homeless shelters, with an education cobbled together from dismal public schools and whatever resources he found at bombed-out local libraries across the Midwest. Still, he graduated from high school two years early and joined the Army, hellbent on finishing college during his five-year stint.

In the end, he did one better. While I completed my criminology degree, Xander got his undergrad and started medical school. Now, he is a second-year surgical resident at Columbia Presbyterian.

A broke, pissed-off one, apparently.

He hates dealing with other people's feelings and only allows himself one sort of sentiment: anger. I can't decide if his reptilian range of emotion will make him a good, level-headed surgeon or a sociopath with a literal license to kill.

But Alexander Carmichael is also, for better or worse, the only friend I've managed to keep over the years.

"The cars aren't *mine*," I point out. Though, I did recently purchase an Aston Martin for myself. I don't mention it to

Xander, since he can barely afford to feed himself on his resident's salary. "But, yes, these are nice shoes. Armani. And I'll buy. You can owe me."

He knows I'm full of shit. I've never called in a single debt against him, and there have been plenty. "I owe you fuck-all," he returns calmly, sipping his new glass of whiskey.

"You did save my life," I allow.

"Twice."

My teeth grind at the memory of him digging shrapnel out of my shoulder... and, on another occasion, my lower back. "Twice."

Neither of us likes to talk about our time overseas. It wasn't exactly Call of Duty, but our unit got caught in the crosshairs a few times.

I clear my throat, banishing the memories. "Anyway. You know all you have to do is ask, and I'll gladly add you to the payroll. I doubled our team, and we're still short."

Obviously. Based on the fact that some assholes assaulted Alice today. And now they have her personal information.

My teeth grind, residual frustration rearing up in my chest. Honestly, I don't know what the hell I'm supposed to do with that woman. If she won't let me protect her, I can't properly protect Grayson and Ella, either.

Not to mention how I would feel if anything happened to the stubborn, quick-witted little wedding planner...

Xander snorts. "As if I would abandon the promise of a surgeon's salary to be one of your bitches. In four years, I'll be running the whole neurosurgery unit. The dinosaurs they have running the place right now are jokes. I'll kick their asses the second someone gives me a shot."

He has a point. My job pays well, but I'm the only one on my team making millions. Grayson insisted I have an "executive" salary when he promoted me. Barnes, my second, makes nearly what I do, though.

The cranky old man started as an MI6 agent. After retiring from the British intelligence agency, he worked as private security for the Stryker family for decades. I have no idea how much money the man has or where he hides it, but he lives in a studio apartment on the river and hardly ever strings more than ten words together at a time.

Despite the fact that I am easily half a foot taller and twice as broad, I get the distinct feeling the distinguished Englishman could kill me with a bendy straw if he wanted to. Every single piece of personal information about him in any database is redacted.

Nearly four years after meeting, I still don't know the man's first name. Or maybe his *last* name. It's unclear which one "Barnes" is.

My own glass of whiskey arrives. I ordered whatever Xander has, and it turns out to be a glass of Blanton's single-barrel bourbon. Expensive as hell, as I suspected.

I knock back a smooth, smoky mouthful, peering around the room, surprised that a dingy college bar up in Morningside Heights would even offer such an expansive selection.

Xander sighs. "I'm supposed to ask you how it's going, right? That's the social norm here?"

I smirk into my drink. "Yes."

"Fuck. Alright. How's it going?"

After the second time Xander dug bullets out of me, we made a pact not to bullshit each other. So, because it's him, I blow out a breath and admit, "It's fucked."

He swallows, unconcerned. "Let me guess," he drawls. "You had sex with a woman who isn't your *'soulmate'*"—he throws up agitated air-quotes—"and now you feel guilty about it."

That has happened many times in the past, but not recently. My last few hookups were women I met through Stryker & Sons' business. One happened sometime around Thanksgiving, when Ella's best friend Maggie came on to me after I gave her a ride home from one of their girls' nights.

We had fun, but Maggie made her boundaries clear from the outset. She didn't like monogamy. I *only* like monogamy. We hooked up a few times before she wanted to move on. I agreed, eager to get back to waiting for the right woman.

Of course, that didn't stop me from taking Grayson's new PR consultant home a few weeks back. I didn't have an excuse; she was a gorgeous woman who caught me in a moment of weakness. One hour in bed definitively proved that we were incompatible. I still want to cringe every time I think of that night and the regrets it left with me.

Xander reads the look on my face and scowls. "You know, they've done studies on this. Celibacy can increase your chances of prostate cancer."

"Yeah, and banging every nurse in the tri-state area will increase your chances of getting an STI," I shoot back. "You know I don't like the casual bullshit. I like to be able to *trust* the women I take to bed."

"You're the most pitiful motherfucker on Earth," Xander laments, shaking his head. "And way too noble for your own good. I say you put your conscience in a corner and stick your dick in something. Tonight. That's my official, medical opinion."

This is an old argument between us. I roll my eyes. "Jesus. I've got bigger problems here."

I decide that the need for an impartial opinion outweighs the very slight risk associated with Xander knowing the details. He is a total recluse who didn't give two shits about celebrity gossip or the Strykers' world. And he's a brilliant guy with a calculating mind.

By the bottom of my glass, I've explained the security situation. Xander nods along, his gears turning, hazel eyes squinting as he peers across the bar at nothing.

"More bourbon," he declares, thinking.

I signal for another drink and wait for him to receive it before prompting, "Any day now, asshole."

He knocks back a sip. "When did they hire the wedding person?"

"Planner," I correct automatically. "Last week."

Xander's expression remains impassive. "And this subway thing was your first major security incident in months?"

I count back in my head. *Carajo.* "Yeah..."

Prior to Alice Moore's stubbornness, our last threat was Grayson's uncle, Ted, moving back to town—and the threat of his cousin, Daniel, being released from prison. Both men will stop at nothing to harm Grayson, his father, and Ella. But for the most part, while Daniel has rotted in prison, Ted has remained oddly quiet.

Xander's smile is chilling. "So you're telling me this wedding girl caused the first breach your team has had since autumn, but you're not doing anything about her."

I sigh through my nose, not liking the bent of his thoughts. "Wedding *planner*. But, seriously, this woman is..."

Lovely.

I bite down on the word, refusing to admit it. Especially to an ass like Xander.

It's true, though.

The mousy, awkward woman who stammers and bites her nails and hides her blushes... She's also kind. Dreamy in an artistic sort of way, with her head in the clouds.

The world isn't kind to people like Alice. I'm not sure why that's never bothered me before.

Xander raises one of his light brown brows. "She's someone with access to their private relationship details, their addresses, their schedules. Plus, she profits from the publicity if her wedding shit goes viral."

He's right. It was the reason I had to investigate her in the first place; the more famous Ella and Grayson become, the more coverage their wedding—and Alice's business—will get.

My gut tells me to trust her, though. And, more than that... "I think she's in trouble, here."

God knows what that paparazzi guy will do with her address. It's possible that more people like him will start hanging around her building, trying to get in to see what they can find. Or attempting to corner her and extract information.

Xander shrugs. "So she's been compromised. Whatever. Get a new planner and make sure it's announced publicly that the Alice girl was fired."

A thud whacks my stomach, the memory of her ashen face when her bank card declined playing across the forefront of my mind.

"No," I deny, too quickly, then clear my throat. "She's Ella's friend. They're not going to want to fire her without cause."

"So you're stuck with her as a risk, but can't get her to agree to let you help protect whatever assets she has," Xander puts in, ponderous. "Stubborn girl. Just my type. Does she have a husband? A boyfriend? A really smart dog?"

I swallow the urge to grit my teeth again, mentally running through the background check I conducted. "None of the above."

"Great," Xander chips in. "You can fuck her."

My lungs stutter. "What are you talking about?"

He shrugs again. "Date her, woo her. Whatever. You're the romantic son of a bitch around here. My point is, she's single, and you're single. You both work for the same people. Would it be *so* crazy if you asked her out? Pretended to take an interest in her and used that as a way to keep an eye on things?"

Who knows if it's the liquor or Xander's bullshit? Either way, I find myself muttering into my glass, "I wouldn't have to *pretend*." I think about the mysterious paint staining her finger-tips. The books that fell out of her bag when those men knocked her down. Her infinitely blue eyes. "She's—"

Different.

Fascinating.

Beautiful.

All of those things are true, but none of them are reasons to invade her privacy. And after seeing the look on her face at Stryker

& Sons the morning I crossed the line in the coffee shop... I never want her to feel misled by me again.

Especially since I'm starting to think my interest—this interminable itch in my veins—might be something more than professional concern.

The fact remains, though; she's in this, now. Part of the Strykers' world—part of *my* world. Which means she's mine to protect.

Even if she makes me work for it.

eleven

IS THERE some scientific law mandating that salon chairs and mirrors *have to* turn you into an ogre?

Cringing, I cast my attention away from the floor-to-ceiling reflection in front of me, distracting myself from the way my stomach pooches and my limp, gray-blonde hair. Tris catches my eye with a wink, holding up her complementary champagne with a wide grin. "Is this not *to die for*?"

The salon really is beautiful. The sort of place I'd never be able to afford in a hundred lifetimes. Every mouthful of bubbly I swallow has me wondering how much this congratulatory gift cost her.

So far, I've been waxed from my eyebrows to my ankles, scrubbed, wrapped in seaweed, manicured, pedicured, moisturized, and now, apparently, someone will do my hair. All because Tris found a special for both of us and decided to book it to celebrate my first real paycheck.

I started to argue with her, but she pointed out that I needed headshots for my website. Now that I can afford them, I figured a little trim couldn't hurt.

But leave it to Tris to dream big.

She holds a palette of pastel hair extensions beside my face, pursing her lips as if a cotton-candy mane is a true possibility. I bat her away, giggling. "Don't even *think* about it."

My best friend pouts for half a second before resuming her musings, isolating one of the lighter yellow shades and holding it beside my face. "I keep *telling* you how good light colors look on you, Alley Cat."

My eyes start to roll, but they snag on the image across from me. I still look like I crawled out of a swamp... but I have to admit, she has a point.

"Tris," I start, "You know what my mom says about dyeing it and my natural skin color..."

My mother is nothing if not an expert on my many inadequacies. Over the years, she's tried just about everything to help me look "presentable." She paid to have my natural hair straightened and covered in keratin. She took me to every makeup counter imaginable, lamenting that none of the cosmetics could quite disguise my paleness, my plump cheeks, or—worst of all—the "caveman" ledge of my eyebrows.

I can just picture her horrified face staring at me through FaceTime, berating whatever Tris's hairdresser attempts to do to the flat, ashy-blonde-brindle tresses hanging around my face.

"Your mom can kiss my entire ass," Tris announces, flouncing into the seat beside mine. "If having it done the way *you want* for once will piss her off, all the better."

My mother and best friend have long-standing mutual hatred for one another. Mom thinks Tris is loose, spoiled, and about fifteen other words that are all Southern Belle Code for "slutty and stupid." Tris, on the other hand, thinks my mother is bitter, callous, and, in her words, "the world's most insufferable bitch."

I think they both give me a headache.

"But, Tris—"

She cuts me off with a whine. "Oh, *come on*, Ali. Damien is amazing. Just let him do your hair this once, and if you hate it, I swear, I'll help you dye it back to Dull As Dishwater Blonde, m'kay?"

I swallow a lump of hurt and look at my lap. I can't exactly argue with her. I've spent most of the week hating how self-conscious I feel every time I'm around Ella, in their fancy town-house. Or—worse—if Marco happened to be lurking in the background.

Blinking at my own image, I tug on the oatmeal-colored sweater I hate and comb out the wet ends of my frizzy hair. Tris has a point—these are all my mother's choices. Do *I* like any of them? Would changing anything make me feel more confident?

Before I can decide, a long, lean man with gorgeous dark skin, a head full of shiny braids, and a gold septum piercing saunters into the salon space. "Okay, gorgeous, what are you—"

He spots me in his chair and stops short, his eyes leaping to Tris. "And... who is this in *my* chair?"

Tris goes for nonchalant, turning to me first. "Damien is the most sought-after stylist in the city. He only sees pre-vetted clients by appointment, *but...*" She tosses Damien a playful shrug and nods at me as she informs him, "She's going to take my appoint-ment today."

The beautiful man rakes a critical glare over my hair, crosses his arms, and shakes his head. "Nuh-uh," he says, evil-eyeing her. "No ma'am."

Tris flashes her dazzling smile. "Damien," she purrs. "You beautiful genius. Meet my best friend in the whole wide world, Alice Moore. She's fabulous. You'll love her."

Damien's glower doesn't so much as flicker. He stares her down, tapping his black boot against the lacquered floor. "Mmhmm."

At his sarcastic dismissal, I shrink. Tris doesn't seem bothered at all. "She's planning the Wedding of the Century, D," my best friend pushes. "She needs to look the part. And everyone knows you're the best in town. And the best stylist in New York is *basically* the best in the world, no?"

He blows air out of his nose, his slim shoulders falling forward. "Pain in my ass," he snaps at her, closing the distance. He comes up behind me and offers a wry smile in the mirror. "Hello. Your friend is the worst."

It's hard to stay offended when he is so funny. "I know. She really is."

He sifts long fingers through my locks, scowling once more. "Now, tell me, what sort of heinous criminal did this to you?"

Without waiting for an answer, he lifts my tresses, examining the hair around my neck. "Lord Jesus," he mutters, shaking his head again. "Beatrice Dunn, you owe me."

He cuts her a look before once again regarding me in the mirror. His eyes soften when he sees the mortification staining my cheeks. "You ready?"

I hesitate. "W-what are you going to do to it?"

Damien grins. "Oh, baby. *Everything*."

Tris keeps us all entertained while Damien works. She asks about Ella's latest color selections—our bride is still on a pink kick, though I don't tell either of them—and whether Grayson ever walks around shirtless in front of me. That leads to an in-depth retelling of Tris's antics last Sunday.

Damien moves with leonine grace, brushing various serums and creams over my hair without bothering to explain his process. I recognize foil for highlights and the burn of bleach wafting in the air. After a wash, he gets to work with scissors, knocking a few inches off before adding layers, plus a few shorter pieces around my face that he calls "The Moneymakers."

I expect him to pull out the hairdryer and a round brush like every other stylist I've ever met. Instead, he brandishes a diffuser and a bottle of gel.

"Here's the deal," he announces. "If I ever hear of you straightening this beautiful hair again, I will come to your house and slap the bejesus out of you."

I blink at my reflection, noting the lighter blonde woven into the kinky, wet clumps. "Umm... then, what am I supposed to do? It's a mess if I don't straighten it."

He glares at me. "It's a mess *because* you straighten it. Baby, I don't know what kind of disastrous white-bread bitch told you to use a flat iron, but they're assholes. You have curly hair. Gorgeous curls. I'm going to show you how to do them." He rolls his head toward Tris. "And Miss Thing over there is going to buy all the products. Right?"

Tris grins. "Right."

When I pout, Tris giggles. "Come on, Alley Cat. You look *hot*. And you never know when a gorgeous man will show up on your doorstep, right?"

I almost snort. *Yeah. Right.*

twelve

I FREEZE my ass off on Bleecker Street for ten minutes before finally trudging up the steps.

It's Saturday night, and all I really want is a cup of tea and some fucking silence. I spent the better part of my "day off" planning for the Strykers' last-minute engagement party and wrestling with the best way to deal with my latest security risk.

Which is right behind this door.

I shift on my feet, staring at the red slab labeled "2B." *Okay,* I think. *I'm just going to update the security software on Alice's work laptop to protect the event details from hackers. And check to make sure her locks are in order. Possibly suggest a couple of cameras for this hallway...*

Her indignant face when I suggested this on Monday flashes through my thoughts. I don't know whether to smile to myself or wince. *If she's mad and I need a distraction, I'll ask her advice about a gift for the engagement party next weekend.*

The best covers always contain a bit of truth, and this is no exception. Because I wasted the afternoon trying to get my team in hand, I now only have six days to find an appropriate present for the people I work for.

Shopping at Williams Sonoma sounds almost as bad as taking a bullet. Possibly worse, depending on where the shot hit.

Carajo. I'm stalling.

I didn't expect to be so daunted by this little woman. True, I've avoided casual dating as much as humanly possible, but I *have* done it. Rarely, and usually not for long, but still. I'm a grown man with a job to do here. I shouldn't be *nervous.*

Although, I can't recall an occasion when I've shown up on a woman's doorstep without any notice. This would be uncharted territory, even without the whole security angle.

This direct approach may not be the best way to get to a girl like Alice. She seems shy. Overt interest could spook her. Would it be better to start slower?

Jesus. Start *what*?

I'm here to make sure she's safe, I remind myself. *Nothing more.*

Because it doesn't matter how much time I've spent wondering what she hides under her thick, shapeless sweaters. Or how clear her eyes might look without a frown furrowing her brows.

This is just me doing my *job*. Doing the *right thing*, protecting an innocent, single woman.

I smooth my hands over the front of my black T-shirt, wondering if I should have gone with something more suave. In truth, I didn't think about my clothes *at all* until this very moment. The dark jeans seem normal, but, in retrospect, steel-toed boots may have been a little overkill.

Too late now. I force my apprehension back and knock.

Tris's voice rings out as her long-legged stride approaches the door. She throws it open and blinks at me before grinning. "Hi, handsome. Can't say I was expecting this, but you can knock on my door *any*time." She tilts her head coyly. "Did you realize you simply could not live without me and rush right over?"

Tris has been toeing the line between flirtatious and professional since the day we met. Even if I found her lithe figure and boisterous personality attractive, casual shit just doesn't do it for me anymore. I want something deeper—and I want the *right* woman. Now, just one that's right for now.

This is Alice's best friend, I tell myself. *Be charming.*

"Miss Dunn," I return, smiling. "I'm flattered, of course, but I'm actually here to see Alice. Is she home?"

Tris's hazel eyes bug out, but she recovers quickly, grinning once more. "My little Alley Cat? Yep, she's... here! Come in, Tall, Dark, & Handsome. I was just on my way out." Her smile takes on a wicked gleam. "But you are *welcome* to wait."

I step over the threshold as she gathers her purse and coat from the rack crammed beside the door. "Alley Cat!" she shouts, not the least bit bothered by yelling beside my ear. "I'm leaving! Love you!"

Some muffled reply comes from the back of the apartment. Before I can ask Tris to let Alice know I'm here, she spins out the front door, dropping the deadbolt behind her.

Well, then.

I turn to face the room. One room. The whole apartment seems to exist within it, but the cramped space is nice.

Really nice. Homey.

The place itself needs some cosmetic updates. Chunks of missing plaster leave patches of bald brick scattered throughout the white walls. Their kitchen looks to be a small galley straight across from the front door, the standing space no larger than an average coffee table.

The main room holds one area for seating. Its yellow futon showcases an array of indigo, pink, and orange throw pillows, along with a chunky knit blanket. A blue-patterned chair sits at an artful angle, facing both the couch and a white trunk topped with a small television setup. Under my feet, their worn rug weaves yellows and pinks and blues together in an oriental pattern.

Everything in the space ties in with a large watercolor canvas hanging behind the futon, a few feet from the door. Though the scene is unfamiliar, I somehow recognize it.

A lake, tranquil and still, holds its breath beside a lone tree silhouetted by sunrise. It's a place I've never visited—perhaps one that does not exist. But I feel like I've been there. That I could close my eyes and go there this very minute.

I know little about art, but I can tell it's an exceptional piece. Full of light, shadow, and feeling. Perfectly coordinated and yet completely out of place in their tiny, simple apartment. The painting seems more fit for the Met than the corner of Bleecker and MacDougal.

While I admire it, a small voice drifts out of the short hallway behind the TV. I assume Alice must be in her bedroom as she calls something I miss, followed by, "... and don't forget about the laundry!"

Laundry?

A basket lies on the floor next to the steamer trunk. It looks clean and fluffed, obviously unfolded. I gather that was Tris's job, but she's left without completing it.

With a shrug, I sit on the edge of the futon and pull the laundry basket over. It's all I can do while I wait, since she doesn't have any of her personal stuff in the main area. Maybe I'll get lucky and fish something useful out of a pocket. Like a hint as to what the hell I say to this woman.

Unlikely. The apartment seems meticulously tidy. There aren't any papers, pictures, or electronic clutter hanging around.

Even the one and only surface in the place—their coffee table—is bare aside from a dark blue candle, flickering as it fills the room with a pleasant citrus and amber scent.

I push the candle to the side and start to fold the clothes. Most are obviously Tris's. Lots of long, thin strips of neon and spandex. But the other items... confuse me.

They aren't the shapeless gray sweaters or thick wool skirts Alice usually wears. At first, I think they can't possibly belong to her at all. But they are clearly too big for Tris's flat frame.

I hold one of the lacy tops up, turning the silk in my hands. Covered in flowers, with thin, wispy straps. A moment later, I unearth a matching pair of satin shorts.

Huh. It's pretty. *Sexy*, actually. *Maybe I was wrong. Maybe Alice actually does have a boyfriend.*

That shouldn't annoy me, damn it. Knowing she has someone to look out for her would be a *good thing*. I still have to pry my fists open slowly, shaking out the slight wrinkles I made in the floral fabric.

For some reason, I set the pajamas aside and lay them on the very top of her stack when I transfer the folded clothes back into the basket. I finish placing it all where I found it just as one of the doors in the hall swings open. Mumbling reaches my ears. The scent of lavender wafts into the room.

"... swear if she forgot to fold the clothes again, I'm going to—to—well, do nothing. I'll do nothing. Which is why she *keeps* 'forgetting' to fold them in the first place. Which is why I'm basically walking around in a napkin—"

Alice breaks off on a shriek as she steps into view.

Wearing a tiny towel.

And *nothing* else.

It's hard to tell which of us is more shocked.

I lurch to my feet, and she freezes, allowing my wide eyes time to travel over every bare bit of her. From her polished toes, over short, shapely legs, to the feminine flare of her hips, where the small towel stretches taut to keep her decadent curves covered. It hangs a little bit looser around her torso, though I can't help but notice the top edge is every bit as tight as the bottom, pulled across her breasts in a vise.

Her hair is different—and even prettier than before. Instead of straight and cool, the pale blonde is mixed with warm sand. A head full of curls frames her rounded cheeks and the delicate bow of her chin, bouncing around the soft lines of her face.

Her *petrified* face.

My hands automatically fly up to hang beside my shoulders, palms out. A classic I-come-in-peace gesture. I fall back a step, dropping my eyes to my shoes.

"I'm sorry," I exhale. "Tris told me to come in. She didn't mention that you were..."

Naked.

So naked.

Naked and soft and blonde.

And I can't keep my eyes off her. I keep forcing my gaze away only to find it right back on Alice before I can develop a second thought.

Have I ever noticed the specific texture of a woman's bare shoulders and throat before? No. Yet her skin, in particular, fascinates me. Like spring roses steeped in frost—a bright, light blush blended into smooth ivory. Her lips are the same pretty pink—full, and puckered in panic.

"Marco?!" she squeaks, pulling the scrap of terrycloth tighter around her body. "Is Ella okay?"

I can't even remember who Ella is. My stare leaps from the creamy curves of Alice's shoulders to the edge of the towel, where her breasts prove rounder and higher—not to mention, *bigger*—than I imagined.

I bet her nipples are the same color as her lips. That would be striking.

My dick twitches to life, the sensation hurtling me back to reality. *What the hell am I doing?* I snap my eyes to the floor and grit my teeth through a surge of lust.

"She's fine," I force out, mentally tracing the pattern in the rug. "I only came to upgrade the security on your work laptop. The Strykers' firewall system has been inundated with cyberattacks. They've insisted I ensure your security software is up to the challenge, should anyone try to gather wedding details off your device."

More like *I've* insisted.

That's an irrelevant detail, though.

I pull the silver thumb drive out of my pocket, presenting it without raising my eyes from the carpet. "This has an upgraded system on it in case yours needs to be swapped out."

Alice seems to tremble slightly as she backs toward the hallway. "O-of course. I'll go get my stuff. H-hold on."

The moment she leaves my sight, my brain recalibrates. *What just happened? I need to focus.*

Holy hell, now is *not* the time for a hard-on.

I rearrange my jeans, lowering myself onto the futon and dropping my head back. I start to count by threes, but that doesn't work nearly as well as the sight of the watercolor hanging overhead. I fall into the tranquil colors and blurred edges of the scene, relieved when my blood starts to cool.

Through the wall behind the television, I hear shuffling and a few thumps. Within five minutes, Alice reemerges wearing a pair of navy leggings and one of the frilly tank tops I noticed while folding her clothes. I wish she had forgone the fluffy pink cardigan layered over it so I could see the thin straps and the lace skimming her bare chest.

Damn it. My erection resurges as she bends in front of me, setting her laptop up and accidentally flashing me a quick glimpse down her top. *Get a grip, Amir.*

When I force myself to concentrate, I note that she doesn't offer her password. Instead, she unlocks the computer and then retreats to the only other chair in the room, watching me.

Good girl.

I'll never sleep again if she doesn't start showing some initiative where her own safety is concerned.

Breathing deeply, ignoring the damp whirl of lavender perfuming the air, I sit forward and get to work. The system on her device is as outdated as I would expect for someone working with her budget. I'll have it upgraded in no time.

She moves in my periphery, and I tell myself it's human nature to look up. Is it my fault that my eyes latch on to the gentle sway of her hips or the bounce of her ass?

Yes, my more gallant side answers.

Jesus. I'm here practically against her will and now I'm ogling her. No wonder she shoots me wary glances every few moments.

I work hard to keep my eyes on my task, breathing a sigh of relief when I hear her humming in her closet-kitchen, knowing the small room's galley style will hide her from my view.

Frowning at the desktop, it occurs to me that I might have been too quick to give her credit for protecting herself. From what I can see, everything is laid out on her home screen, each clearly marked and color coordinated. Ripe for plucking.

She has tons of folders, full of event images. Vendor contacts and contracts. Only one email account. The same commonplace Facebook and Instagram accounts I've already perused. And something girly called Pinterest, which is also overflowing with wedding photos, arranged into various inspiration boards.

Though, there are some "secret" boards. But those mostly seem to consist of lingerie pictures and... honeymoon destinations? Why?

For fuck's sake, I curse myself internally. *What am I doing* looking *at these?*

My father would have knocked me in the back of the head.

A new spiced, floral aroma joins the others swirling around the tiny room, warming my nose. It smells so incredible that curiosity gets the better of me. I lift my head just in time to watch her cross the living room, moving with unhurried poise, carrying two teacups balanced on saucers.

With her eyes cast down, she places one beside my left hand and backs into the blue-patterned armchair. "It's hibiscus tea, with just a tiny bit of spiced honey. Y-you ordered tea at the café that morning, so I thought you might... like it."

I do. I *love* it, in fact. Not just for the hundreds of varieties and dozens of different preparations, but because tea has always held a special place in my relationship with my dad. He wasn't able to bring a lot of his cultural traditions with him when he immigrated, but proper tea remained one of his sacred rituals until the day he died.

When we all lived under one roof, I often found him sitting alone at our kitchen table well after my mother had gone to sleep. Usually, he had a mug of *yerba mate* in one hand and some philosophy book in the other. But if I caught him staring at nothing, lost in space, I went to join him, pouring for myself before sinking into his silence.

Those were the nights we tended to have our deepest conversations. The nights we talked about the meaning of life, the dreams he had for me and my mother.

Over tea, he taught me every lesson I needed. How to listen well. The importance of respect for myself and others. How to treat a woman. All the male-female dynamics that mortified me in my youth.

I never realized how lucky I was to have a dad who spoke to me about everything. Other guys I met in the military and the police academy considered themselves fortunate to have fathers who deigned to watch the game with them on Sundays... But I had a real teacher. A role model.

Until I failed him.

I stare down into the fresh cup of tea, unnerved by the morose bend of my thoughts. What is happening? I've gone from determined to turned on and now, depressed. All in ten minutes. And I never even answered the woman.

"I do like tea," I force out. "Thank you."

thirteen

THE SOUND MARCO makes sends an electric charge through my body. A low, growly moan rumbles around his lips as he swallows a mouthful of tea and pulls the cup back, blinking at it like it's a mystical mug of ambrosia.

"That is incredible," he tells me, his voice matching his dark velvet eyes as they flicker to my face. "Really. Alice."

He has never said my name before. Ordinarily, I'm "Miss Moore." The memory of the last time I saw him—after the incident outside the subway—makes my face flame. I basically ignored all of his offers to help me, yet here he is. *Complimenting* me.

A spark ignites in my lungs, burning up my breath. "Thank you," I murmur, looking down into my own cup. "This has been my favorite, lately. I-I found it in a tiny Indonesian tea shop."

Marco stares into the liquid, a look of true awe on his face. "It's *great*."

He seems sincere. And very surprised. It puts a giggle in my voice as I reply, "Is that a shock?"

Marco's features turn from wildly handsome to absolutely *devastating* when he grins. The white flash of his teeth against his dark tan skin and black stubble sends another jolt straight through my heart.

"I'm particular about it. I usually only enjoy my own. And Ella's, although she really can't make it right. She means well so I just drink it anyway. I was worried yours would be like hers," he admits, his smile taking on an irresistible, rueful quality. "But you make better tea than I do. This blend is the best I've had. Ever."

I find myself smiling back at him. *Well, in that case...* I stand and dip into the kitchen to take the kettle off the two-burner stove, along with a sachet of dried herbs. When I return and place the tea on the low table between us, he stares at it.

A wave of shyness comes over me as I sink into my seat and pull my sweater closed over my center, hoping he won't notice the belly pooch under all my layers. "T-take it," I stammer. "I can get more."

Marco's ponderous frown is almost as beautiful as his smile. "No one appreciates a good blend of tea more than me. I'd never want you to part with yours."

But he's tempted. I can tell from the gleam in his warm brown eyes.

"Seriously," I insist. "Take it as a thank you for..." I wave my hand at my computer, though I can't begin to describe what he was up to. "... whatever you're doing."

His brows snap together. "The new software is just

installing," he murmurs, shifting slightly. He clears his throat. "It will only be another moment or two."

I try to ignore my stab of disappointment. *Of course he isn't going to stay long. It's Saturday night. He probably has plans. A girlfriend at home.*

Thinking as much, I glance at the small canvas bag I offered him. "Hope there's enough in there for two," I fret, mumbling to myself. "I never thought I'd need extra..."

Just like that morning in the coffee shop, he hears me when someone else wouldn't. His head snaps up, that dark gaze snaring mine. "Two?"

My cheeks and chest heat under his direct regard. When he doesn't drop his eyes, I know I have to clarify, "You and your girlfriend."

Another broad, wry grin. "Ah. No worries on that front, unfortunately." He looks back at the tea and then smiles wider. "Or, fortunately, in this case. More for me."

It's been a long time since anyone was so complimentary about something I made. Another pleased giggle skips up my throat. As I laugh, his focus flies over my lips. A second later, he blinks back at the computer.

"I think this is done," he announces, removing his thumb drive and snapping the screen shut. "It should work normally. Call me if it doesn't."

I open my mouth to attempt to force out a reply—or perhaps an apology, for not calling him the last time when I clearly should have. But he reaches his large, brawny hand out to me. "Give me your cell. I'll add myself to your contacts. Since you clearly won't."

His stern side-eye makes my stomach squirm. When I place my cell on his palm, he gives one of his enigmatic half-smiles and patented solid nods. "Good girl."

My insides erupt in jitters, butterflies pouring into my abdomen. As he finishes typing, Marco clears his throat and shifts a bit more. "I don't sleep much. So if you're ever out late and get stuck, I want you to *call me*." His dark eyes snap to mine, blazing with shocking intensity. "Got it?"

"Uh-m," I wobble, my breath pinching. "O-okay."

Lord, why does his scolding *melt* me? I blink, trying to come up with something else to say. "I—I have a tea for insomnia, too, if you want it," I offer. "It's lavender and honey."

His eyes darken. "Lavender?"

"Mmhmm." I nod, standing to go back to the kitchen. "It's from the same shop. You'll probably like it."

Even with a gorgeous single man the size of an ox as a distraction, our kitchen practically gives me hives. Drying dishes, the toaster, and Tris's blender clutter our small strip of counter, making every move precarious. I try to keep the space as tidy as possible, but it always feels like the whole thing could tumble down at any moment.

Our 'pantry' is just a cabinet above the narrow refrigerator. Tris can reach everything easily... but I usually wind up using kitchen tongs and jumping on my tiptoes to get things from the highest shelf.

I huff as I brandish my utensil and stretch as far as I can, only barely missing the purple tin I aimed for. I startle at Marco's low chuckle rumbling at my back.

He followed me.

Between his height and the impressive width of his shoulders, he practically fills the room. I scoot over, trying to make space for him without tripping on my own feet and falling against the wall of his chest.

"Here," he says quietly. I get a full hit of his leather-and-manly-man scent as he stretches right over me and collects the lavender tea tin, bringing it to the place between his torso and mine. I expect him to back up, but his massive frame hovers close while he gazes into my face.

A quiver trickles down my back. His features relax, the tension evaporating from his thick brows. "Alice." Marco blinks. "Your eyes are so blue."

Something about his stunned expression strikes me as funny. I laugh lightly, unsure what to say. "Yeah... they, um, always have been?"

My mother tells me that my eyes are my best feature. Or, in her words, *"my one saving grace."* Tris often chuckles about them, too. She likes to say that she thought she had the most unique eyes in the world until we met. Then she'll usually flash a grin and add, *"You bitch."*

Of course, Marco says neither. He bends a little closer, laser focused. "They're beautiful."

Liquid warmth fills my lungs to the brim, cascading into my middle. A sense of complete calm washes over me, chasing away my nerves. I stop shaking and simply stare back at him, our gazes locked.

For one breathless moment, I have the insane idea that he might kiss me. He looms so close, his focus flitting from my eyes to my mouth and back again before he clears his throat, remembering himself as he straightens.

"Sorry," he mutters.

Another apology for flirting with me.

Because this is his job. And he's chosen to accomplish it by leading me on.

Will that ever stop feeling like a stab to the chest?

Marco sways slightly, but his eyes linger on mine. Full of intensity—regret, probably. Pity, maybe.

So I straighten and hand him the tea he retrieved, doing my best not to sound breathless. "I think you'd better go."

fourteen

BEAUTIFUL.

Two days later, and I still can't get Alice's face out of my mind. The way her brows curved up. The way her pink lips parted. The shine in her gaze.

My praise—the single word I told myself I said because it was the thing I *had* to say—changed her.

That's the simplest way to describe it. When I complimented her, she relaxed. Every feature softened. The defensive panic in her eyes melted away. And she let me in.

It *was* beautiful.

Almost as beautiful as her eyes themselves. The soft, almost-violet blue, rimmed with a band of dark indigo and filled with splinters of ice. They remind me of the way light shines through frost on sunny winter mornings.

Worry gnaws at my gut, recalling the single deadbolt on her door and the dearth of cameras in the building. When she saw me to the exit Saturday night, I offered to install some, but she claimed their landlord wouldn't have it.

I *might* have sent the man a rather brusque email this morning. Until I hear back, though, there's nothing I can do but wait for my phone to ring.

Because I used up so much of my "weekend off" working, I carved out this Monday afternoon to help my mother move her stuff out of my childhood home. Grayson is on an international conference call, and Ella plans to stay home writing. So, in theory, my bases are covered...

My mom's sniffles interrupt my unease. She shuffles into the living room, swiping at her eyes.

This was the last place my father ever lived and the last place Mami saw him alive. As I watch her shoulders slump over a box of old photo albums, I release some of my frustration. It's good that I'm here—I don't want to leave her to face this alone.

I thought I'd be more attached, myself. After all, apart from a few temporary rentals during my years on the force and my new place, this brownstone is the only home I've ever known.

I'm not sure when I started to hate it so much.

When my dad first died, and I moved home to care for Mami, it was comforting to be in our family home again. I spent many nights sitting in my father's customary place at our round wooden table, praying I could somehow absorb the last of his wisdom through some physics of position.

He always seemed peaceful here, in his chair, with his tea. I wondered: if I sat there, if I stayed still, would I inherit his peace? Would I be able to forget what had happened?

The answer, by the way, is no.

That's the hardest part about the way he died. Sure, it was violent and unfair and so sickeningly *wrong*. But, worse than any of that, is the knowledge that I let him down. I didn't analyze the situation quickly enough to save his life. And, once he was gone, I didn't honor his memory with my reaction.

The relief from gunning down the man who shot him receded almost immediately, leaving me with nothing aside from the difficult truth:

My dead father would have been disappointed in me.

Ever since that sank in, I've made it my life's mission not to let him down again. For the most part, it's simple. He raised me with the same values he upheld, so my conscience tends to guide me the same way he would have.

When things get complex, though, I'm never sure I do him justice. Would he be proud that I finally put my foot down and told Mami she needed to move out? Or would he be upset that I was trying to help the woman he loved move on from his shadow?

I had to do it for a lot of reasons. For one, she needs space for my grandmother now, and Abuelita can't manage the stairs here. As the years passed, taking us further from the worst day of our lives and into the future... this small house becomes less of a reminder of what my family had and more of a relic to everything we've lost.

"*Mijo?*"

My mother's voice interrupts my reverie. I realize I'm standing where the kitchen table used to be. With a sigh, I pivot, finding her silhouette in the doorway to the empty living room.

I grew up hearing that my mom was the most beautiful woman in any room. My father told me so, often. He told everyone who would listen.

And people *believed* him. So much so that Mami had a reputation in our neighborhood for being a great beauty. It took years for me to see that, truly, her looks fell just north of ordinary. What really set her apart was her attitude. She had so much joy and humor and kindness.

Some of that has returned, lately. As she drifts closer, I note the old laugh lines creasing her face, though they're pulled into a frown now. Her dark eyes flash with disapproval.

"You are too tired," she tuts. "Why aren't you sleeping?"

Because there's a beautiful woman in an unprotected apartment way too fucking far away from mine.

Because my phone is always ringing and it's never her.

Because something is fucking wrong, *and I cannot figure out what it is.*

An image of her parted lips and shimmering blue eyes flashes through my mind. She shut her reaction down so quickly. I don't know why, but it's clear that my praise truly touched her, for a moment. And if that's the case, why did she slam a wall between us?

A fresh pang of doubt turns my stomach, followed by a wave of frustration.

Who are you, Alice Moore?

alice

"ALLEY CAT!"

Tris's nickname fills my mind with images of mangy, begging felines living in dumpsters. I roll my eyes as I fluff out my curls, checking the reflection in our bathroom mirror. Damien was so right; my hair seems to prefer the curls.

I haven't gone through the whole process of re-styling it yet, but I feel inspired to at least try. The loose spirals create volume that makes my features seem more delicate and actually complements my round eyes and nose.

It's still exhilarating, looking in the mirror and realizing that *I like* what I see. Yesterday, a random man did a double-take when I walked down the block for a bottle of dish soap—and I actually felt *good*. Though, Tris claims that probably had less to do with my hair and more to do with my "sweet ass" being "an absolute dump truck."

As if I'd conjured her, my best friend appears in the doorway to our tiny bathroom, leaning leisurely against the jamb as she drinks her coffee.

"I have the hot goss for you, baby cakes. Guess who got engaged last week?"

Tris loves celebrity gossip. I feel my eyes skirt skyward again. "Uh... Khloe Kardashian? Ariana... Gigante?"

"It's Grande," she smirks. "And no. This is a couple you actually have a shot at styling for. Someone we know."

I rack my brain before shrugging. "Who?"

Her smile takes on a wicked gleam. "Graham Everett proposed to Juliet Rivera."

I gape in disbelief. Tris tried to tell me that she thought there was something going on between Mr. Stryker's lawyer and his broker, but I didn't believe her. I should have known better; Tris can pick up on sexual tension from three blocks away.

"What a bad bitch, right? She met *Graham Everett*—the biggest man whore in Manhattan—*six weeks ago* and already wore that motherfucker down. Five-carat diamond from Tiffany's and everything." She shakes her head in awe. "A legend. I've gotta ask her for blow job tips."

I snort as I brush powder over my nose. "I'm sure that won't be weird at all. Next time you guys have a boardroom meeting, fire away."

Tris chortles. "I don't know why you don't make more jokes. You are hilarious, Alley Cat."

"Probably too busy trying to adult," I muse, mulling over her new-client suggestion... and recalling the voicemail I found on my phone this morning. *I need to call Mama back... I've been avoiding her all week.*

"Uh-oh," Tris chirps, reading me easily. "You have your Mommy Dearest face on."

I groan into my perfectly prepared cup of coffee. "She wants to *visit*. She says that the wait from Christmas to Easter is too long."

Tris scoffs. "Tell her to enjoy the Marriott."

Ah, yes. Last time Mama visited, I believe Tris's exact words were, *"If she thinks she's staying under my roof while she calls me a ho, that Southern Belle Bitch can bite me."*

I don't realize I've started nervous-humming until Tris begins singing along. Apparently, I was halfway through the second verse from a Madonna song. She hits a high note, and I glare from across the living room.

"Okay, okay," she giggles. "Where are you off to today?"

I think about my favorite little bookstore and its tiny coffee corner and smile. "I have some calls to make for Ella and reading to catch up on. I'll be at Book Club."

Tris shoots me a look as close to scolding as she's capable of. "Remember, you're out of shelves. And money. And for fuck's sake—*do not* get on the subway."

BY THE TIME I get to Book Club, my cheeks are wind-burned, and I don't even want to know what my curls look like. I avoid looking in the mirrored wall along the front of the shop as I step off the pavement, entering through the wide glass door.

Inside, the long, narrow space is blessedly quiet, apart from an espresso machine whirring on the bar along the right-hand wall. Beyond that, shelves cover every inch of the space, laden with books of every color and size. A single stained-glass window with mismatched panes shines with morning sun at the back of the shop, illuminating a small circle of vacant leather club chairs.

"Alice," Amber, the barista, grunts. She isn't friendly, but she does remember me. Usually. "What do you want?"

I bite the corner of my lip, debating. I only have ten dollars budgeted for today. But is it rude to sit and work without ordering something? Ordinarily, I'd get a pot of their oolong tea... and I *am* thirsty after walking twenty blocks.

While I try to decide, the door opens again, sending a burst of fresh air into the space behind me. "Whatever she's having," a familiar voice says, followed by heavy footsteps. "Double it."

alice

AMBER ROLLS her eyes so hard, I hear it. "Your order, Alice? Sometime *today*, preferably."

I force out my words, squeaking as I blink up at Marco Amir. "Oolong, please."

Amber waves us off, muttering, and I pivot to face the man who has to be a figment of my imagination. Maybe my brain is so desperate to find an excuse to order my favorite tea that it created a mirage.

But no. Because when he reaches into his pocket for his wallet, his arm brushes mine. And it is very solid and very real.

I blink at it, thrown, and then turn my gaze back up to his square, chiseled face. A flicker of humor touches the curves of his lips. "You seem more agreeable in this coffee shop than in the last one."

"I—I like books," I blurt. My skin seems to know I've embarrassed myself before my brain does—by the time I realize that I sound like an idiot, my cheeks are already burning.

"Ah," he replies, his smirk slightly more obvious as he drops a twenty onto the bar. "So, it's all about proximity to books and nothing to do with me surprising you?"

Just like the first time, it feels like he's flirting with me. But why? Last time he was trying to vet me. Is he still?

Oh God. Is that why he came over last weekend? To keep an eye on me?

I've been so stupid, I realize, my eyes burning as he smiles at me. *Of course this is all part of his job.*

My chest and neck flame along with my face. I pray he can't see either under my marled blue cardigan and the matching navy camisole layered underneath.

But Marco's too observant for that. He leans back slightly, widening his stance and slipping a hand into the pocket of his black slacks. I realize he doesn't have his whole suit on this time. Just the onyx pants and an equally dark shirt, rolled up at the sleeves to reveal two bulging forearms roped with veins. One wrist has a watch, the other a simple braided band of black leather.

His dark eyes flick right down to my chest and back up again. His lips don't move, but somehow, his smile turns cocky.

My pinch of mortification smolders into offense. Before I can overthink it, a scoff bubbles out of my mouth, followed by a taunt I ordinarily would have swallowed. "You surprised me last time, and it definitely *did not* help my mood. So it's probably just the books."

That earns me a broad, mind-melting grin. It moves over his face slowly, as if every bit of it is a deliberate choice he makes to reveal his amusement to me. Even after he returns to his usual stony expression, the stunning sight lingers behind my eyelids like a camera flash.

Awkwardness starts to press down around us, and my stammer returns. "I-isn't it a work day for y-you?"

The tense line of his brow relaxes slightly, softening the sharper edges of his features. "Yes. It is."

Basically admitting this *is his work. Watching me while* I *work.*

I don't realize I've started scowling until he frowns, staring at my face like he finds the whole scenario every bit as infuriating as I do.

But his velvet voice stays deep and quiet as he gestures to two couches. "Shall we?"

seventeen

MARCO

ALICE CARRIES OUR SMALL, individual pots of oolong tea to a circle of brown suede seats at the back of the bookshop.

She sets each on the table with care, hesitating while she tries to decide whether to put mine in the place next to her seat or across from it. In the end, I tamp down a smile and try to look casual about lowering myself in the seat perpendicular to hers.

The more time I spend around her, the less her little awkward moments of uncertainty bother me. Now, I realize, they are almost sort of... cute? *Endearing*. She clearly cares very much about pleasing the people around her, but often seems to have no notion of how to go about it.

Sweet. She's sweet.

I pause, trying to decide on an approach. The truth is, I have no idea why I'm here. Sure, I guess I "needed" to check in with her this week as part of my work duties... but that's just an excuse. Because, in all honesty, when the security software in her laptop pinged, alerting me that it had been removed from her home, I leaped into action so fast, anyone observing would have thought there was a bomb threat.

I hated myself the whole ride over, wondering why I couldn't just leave the damn woman alone. Knowing she's been clear in her disdain for me... and having good reason for it.

Now that I'm here, though...

I'm not leaving.

Remembering the way she warmed under my praise back at her apartment, I find myself waiting until she settles herself and turns to me. When our eyes meet, I stare right into hers and speak with complete conviction. "This is lovely. You chose the perfect spot."

Her posture changes; her back straightens, along with her neck. A pretty arc of milky white that leads up to her dimpled little chin.

Most of her features are rounded and soft, as if God drew her in circles and curves before carefully blurring the edges to add shading where her cheeks nip in. Blonde hair bounces around her shoulders—windswept, this time, which only leaves it wild and even more appealing. I wonder if the curls feel as smooth as they look. My fingers twitch against my legs.

As I push the idle thought aside, I blow out a breath and busy myself with pouring her tea, then my own. Trying my damnedest to come up with some pretense for sitting here with her.

Like she's read my mind, Alice reaches into her bag and takes out a small paperback with worn edges. The front displays a detailed drawing of a man in a pirate's costume. He's half-naked, with long, flowing hair.

Alice's cheeks blaze when she sees me looking at it, but the determined pout I've gotten so fond of appears on her lips. "I've decided to work later tonight. I'm just going to read now. So..."

You can leave.

She clearly expects me to be indignant, but my only reaction is a disconcerting burst of fondness. And... longing. Hell, when was the last time I sat and read with purpose instead of carving out time for it while chauffeuring Grayson?

I check my watch, noting that I have three more hours until he needs me at the office. Alice watches me shift and pull a small, thin paperback out of my back pocket. "Sounds great."

Her wariness briefly morphs into disbelief. I swallow another smile, pretending to be engrossed in this week's philosophy text. It was my father's—a book by Kant I found when I was helping my mother pack.

After a long beat, Alice sighs and places her own book in her lap. She tosses me one sideways look, her pale brows lifting. As if asking, *Seriously?*

She doesn't say the word, but I hear it in my mind, clear as one of her little squeaks. The question swirls in her eyes, filling the blue with something hesitant and fragile and... *gorgeous.*

My throat thickens. Worry coils tight around my insides, squeezing in a painful spasm.

Does she think I don't want to be here?

I watch her, trying to read her emotions. Her gaze flickers, scanning something in mine. The corner of her rosy mouth wobbles slightly... and then she flings her focus away. To her paperback.

Jesus, this woman. I *worry* about her. For no fucking reason.

Gradually, her tension ebbs and mine follows suit. She turns a few pages. Contentment floats off her, filling the air between us. It seeps into my chest, easing some of my suffering as I settle back, stealing glances at her every few moments.

The fifth time I look up, my gaze sticks while she shifts to lie against the arm of her loveseat, blowing a few curls off her cheek. I stare, waiting. As if to prove a point, she turns another page and keeps on reading, engrossed in her story.

My focus still doesn't return to my own book.

The sun shifts, filling the stained-glass window behind her with gold, silhouetting her with its glow. My brain crashes to a halt. My breathing stops.

Because she is *breathtaking*.

Like a Renaissance painting. All buttered light and flowing, untamed blonde and pale skin and *curves—God—*draped over the arm of her chair.

The more she relaxes, the more exquisite she appears.

And I know I should. But I can't look away.

TWO HOURS LATER, Alice huffs, setting her teacup in its saucer with a delicate clatter. "That's ridiculous."

I shrug, doing my best not to smile at her. "Kant didn't think so."

I never thought I'd see timid, mumbling Alice roll those gorgeous blue eyes at me. But the ice-and-violet orbs skirt toward the ceiling while she snorts. "Of course he didn't disagree with his own theory," she argues, neither squeaking nor stammering. "He came up with it!"

We've been at it for the better part of an hour, arguing circles around each other. The conversation started when I set my book aside to pour each of us a fresh cup from the teapot. Alice looked down at the page left open on the tabletop and stunned me when she recited one of Kant's three fundamental questions. My favorite one, naturally. Giving the impression, once again, that she sees far more than most others.

When I tried to offer a retort, we lapsed into a discussion of ethics and metaphysics. I was surprised when she tended to agree with me on most points. And oddly delighted when she put up a fight about transcendental idealism.

I mean, really. How many people even know what that *is*?

Not only does Alice know the theory, she knows her opinion and has a thoughtful argument for it.

Turns out we're well-matched. Alice is as quiet and calm while we fight as she is when she reads. Aside from the occasional smirk or eyeroll, she keeps her tone diplomatic and listens carefully. She also has no problem offering concessions when warranted.

It makes me better. I listen harder. I think more carefully before I speak. By the time we work our way to the end of Kant's published philosophies, I'm leaning forward in my seat with my forearms braced on my knees, totally invested in Alice's every word.

She shifts from leaning on the right arm of her overstuffed chair to the left, leaving our faces only a few feet apart. One of her curls keeps falling over her brow. She blows it away a few times, but it floats back down eventually. The fourth time it starts to fall, a smile I can't quite hide curves my lips. I nod while she continues, reaching over to carefully weave the single strand behind her ear.

There, I think, satisfied.

The hair is smooth. As soft as her earlobe and the patch of skin beneath it. When my fingertips trail over her pulse, it leaps.

Carajo.

I *like* her.

She's *smart*. Kind and gentle and centered in a way I never expected. Now that I've seen her in her element, I feel a pang of concern when I remember how scared and scattered she seemed the last time I surprised her in a coffee shop. *Her nerves must be as bad as her self-esteem.*

I hate that thought. Viscerally.

And I want her to feel as interesting as she truly is.

"Well, you obviously know what I'm reading." I shrug. "What are *you* reading?"

The pretty pink flush on Alice's cheeks darkens along with her eyes. "It's, um... it's a romance novel?"

The squeak is back, I note. That fills me with equal parts shame and amusement. I hate that I made her self-conscious, but her cringe is cute. Does she think I'll disapprove of her book?

A wicked thought tweaks my brows up. "Is it a romance novel or a *romance* novel?"

She sucks the corner of her lower lip between her teeth and peeps over it. "Both?"

Oh fuck. She sat next to me, reading smut, for an *hour*, and I had no idea? Why is that so *hot*?

I reach for my tea, needing an excuse to shift around and conceal the bulge now pressing into my fly. I keep my voice offhand while I lock my gaze back on hers. "Anything good?"

The creamy skin of her throat tightens on a swallow. "I—y-yes, actually."

Adorable. The urge to tease her bleeds into the thick pulse of arousal simmering at my center. I curve a brow and hold out my hand. "Give it."

My favorite shade of roses-in-frost warms her chest as she inhales a sharp gasp. I don't relent. My fingers curl, silently underscoring my order.

Alice extends the paperback to me. I turn it over, scanning the synopsis. *Damn.* It doesn't look half bad.

I smile despite myself. "I'm intrigued."

She wrinkles her nose and giggles, the sound sweet and tinkling. "You are?"

I nod, handing the book back. "Don't tell anyone," I warn, setting my face into a stern mask. "Or I'll have to kill you."

Her eyes drop to the Glock strapped to my hip. Her gaze goes wide. "Yes, sir," she whispers.

Which does not help the state of my cock.

Thankfully, Alice's focus doesn't linger on my weapon. She meets my gaze. Expectant. Waiting for me to continue our conversation.

"Where would one find such a book?" I ask, sipping my tea. "You know, out of curiosity."

That earns me another giggle. "Oh, you could just borrow one. I have *tons*."

Her embarrassment catches up to her quickly. She slaps her palms over her cheeks while a fresh blush stains her skin. "I—I mean—"

My lips curl into a slow smile. *Can I get her to tell me her favorite one? What is it about?*

"Alright." After making sure my erection won't press right out of my pants, I push to my feet, knowing my alarm is about to go off. I have to go, but I refuse to leave without setting another date. "Would Friday night work?"

Alice blinks up at me, her lush pink lips forming a small "O" that teases my raging cock. Especially since standing beside her puts her mouth at just the right level for—

"For what?" she asks.

I realize she isn't answering my thoughts this time—she wants to know what I want with her on Friday night. I clear my throat, slipping my Kant book into my back pocket. "To borrow one of your books." *And install the security cameras, limp-dicked landlord be damned.* "Would that be good for you?"

She flounders for another moment. "G-good for me?"

My smile is entirely involuntary as I lean down and place my fingertips under her chin, closing her mouth before I do something impulsive like pressing mine over it.

"Yes," I murmur. "Eight o'clock?"

She agrees, her reply no more than a slight quivering breath. "Okay."

I don't realize until I've left the shop and walked around the corner that I never asked about her work once.

MARCO

"FUCK."

My nightmare hurtles me into consciousness just before my lungs collapse. They heave as I throw myself out of bed, automatically reaching for the loaded gun on my nightstand and drawing it.

It takes me several breaths to realize I'm pointing the damn thing at an empty room. *My* bedroom.

Blood, panic, and pain whirl through my head in a kaleidoscope of misery. Shots ring in my ears, deafening me to any sound apart from the rough breaths scraping out of my chest.

I know I'm alone, but I click off the Glock's safety and clear the apartment anyway. When I am certain it was all part of my bad dream, I drop into my father's seat—at the kitchen table I took from my parents' house—and stare at the dark window across the living room.

After setting the gun aside, I curl forward to drop my head to my hands. Eventually, the noise inside of me quiets, replaced by the dull roar pressing down around me.

Silence.

Because I'm alone.

The thought hits differently in this moment. It isn't just a fact. Or a placation. This time, it's the worst kind of realization. *The truth.*

I am alone.

Still. Always.

I stay there for a long time, staring at the dark void outside my window, waiting for the first strains of dawn to touch it. For the first time in a long time, I don't want to go to the gym and pound myself into submission. I just want to sit with the truth. With my choices.

I don't know how long I stay there before the sky lightens from pitch black to silvery slate. Long enough to work my way through all of my thoughts and back again.

Gradually, reality steals me out of my introspection. It's Friday. And that means—

A spark settles into my center. *Alice.*

"*FUCK.*"

Grayson spits the curse along with a mouthful of saliva, lunging up from the ropes surrounding his boxing ring.

I swallow a smirk. I've knocked him back four times, even though I'm going easy on him. I don't want to give him a black eye to match his tux for his engagement party, but he's making it easy.

In my professional opinion, his legs are too loose. Every boxer knows what causes *that*.

"Watch your left," I remind, raising my gloves to demonstrate. Again. "Keep your shoulders lax and step with your right foot."

"Yeah, yeah, yeah," he grumbles, putting his fists up. "We both know I'm horseshit this morning."

I jab left to throw him off and swing a right hook. He barely dodges it, pivoting to face me again.

"Long night?" I drawl, hoping to provoke him. I only get a chance to goad my boss when we're in the ring. Sometimes, if I rile him up enough, he really comes at me. I need the challenge since I skipped my usual gym session this morning.

"Longer than yours," he shoots back, striking quick enough to get a piece of my torso.

While his arm is extended, I uppercut and hit him in the diaphragm. He grunts, losing a step. I take another swing and land a blow to the side of his head. "How would you know?"

Shaking me off, he raises a sardonic eyebrow. "You obviously have a bit of frustration to work out."

He has a point. I haven't had a decent night's sleep or satisfying sex in months. Maybe years. And the recent image of Alice in her damned towel doesn't exactly help. Nor does my brain's new habit of projecting the picture into the forefront of my mind the second I lie down.

Grayson's fist slams into the side of my jaw. "Watch your left," he taunts.

I have to laugh. "Yeah, yeah."

We both round, snarling as we go for each other again. After another four rounds, he finally falls back, panting. "Okay, I give."

The thrill of victory pours through me. I do my best not to grin. "Ella should take the night off every once in a while. Give you a fair shake in the ring."

Grayson glowers, tugging his gloves off. "I'll be sure to pass that along."

I toss my own gloves aside and reach for my water bottle, chugging half in one go. "Is she ready for tomorrow night? I know she likes big parties about as much as I do."

His scowl morphs into a grimace. "Which is still more than *I* like them." He sighs. "She's been a good sport about this one. I think she feels bad for choosing so many wedding details that my mom disapproves of. She's trying to be upbeat about the engagement party because she thinks it's Mom's one chance to have things her way."

That sounds like Ella. I nod, my mind spinning through the dozens of details I have to review before the following night, not to mention their actual wedding day.

That will be its own logistical nightmare.

"To be honest, I'll be happy when this is all over," I grouse, mopping sweat off my forehead with the hem of my tank top.

Grayson agrees, nodding. "Hopefully, people will stop being so insane once we're married." He sighs again. "It can't come soon enough. I'm supposed to pay the rest of Alice's planning fee by tomorrow, and then there are only three months to go."

Strange relief bleeds into my chest. *Good*, I think. *Alice needs that money. Maybe she'll be able to pay her bills soon. And get some more tea for herself. It was generous of her to give me any in the first place. I never should have taken them. I suppose I could go to the shop and get her some more—*

"Marco?"

Carajo. I keep *doing that.*

"Sorry," I apologize, tuning back into the conversation. "What?"

Grayson squints slightly. "I asked if you thought Miss Moore was a little… off? I've been thinking about it ever since those paps got hold of her. She barely said a word about it afterward."

I don't like the flash of fear that seizes my lungs at the memory of that man. And the knowledge he still has her address. I also don't like Grayson's implication that her silence was anything but pure terror. I've seen the way she clams up when she feels stressed or scared.

A pang hits my heart. I know I was with her when she woke up, but I should have been there when it happened. She must have been terrified.

Poor sweet girl.

"She's just so quiet," Grayson continues.

I think of all her mumbling and humming. Our long, lively debate. For a moment, I almost contradict him.

But those small pieces of her feel like secrets. My secrets.

"She seems… soft."

When I reflect on why I find it so impossible to maintain a proper level of suspicion around her, that's the word I keep coming back to. Soft and sweet—and seemingly neglected by most people she knows.

Grayson's expression turns sympathetic. "Poor girl."

Too late, I realize how my reply sounded to him. He doesn't know I've spent any extra time with Alice. As far as he knows, she's just Miss Moore to me. The awkward wedding planner I suffer for Ella's sake.

He thinks I was making some sort of veiled insult. Using the word "soft" as a placeholder for "pitiful."

Why does that make me want to roundhouse kick him?

I don't have time to think it over too much. The elevator on the far side of the basement gym dings. As the doors part, Ella's petite form appears.

Grayson grins, immediately distracted. "You missed Marco kicking my ass," he tells her, dropping his drenched shirt in the hamper beneath the laundry chute. "It was pathetic."

Ella glows as she smiles up at him. "You could never be pathetic," she soothes.

I laugh. "Oh, I wouldn't be too sure about that. His head was in the clouds."

Grayson tucks a piece of his fiancée's hair behind her ear. "Your fault," he mouths at her. A brooding pout pulls at his features. "At this rate, I may as well not bother getting back in the ring after our honeymoon."

Ella giggles, turning her deep blue eyes on me. "Want a victory scone? I baked some to go with your tea."

I think of Alice again, wondering if she'll make me tea when I see her later. "Actually," I find myself saying. "Could I take two to go?"

alice

"WALK ME THROUGH THIS AGAIN..."

I've put this conversation off as long as I could, knowing it would make me feel like crap.

It isn't Tris's fault, really. If anyone else heard that Marco Amir had asked to come over to see *me*... well, I suppose they would have equally incredulous reactions.

It's understandable. The man is a sexy, single millionaire with a muscle-stacked body and a secret, sensual sort of smile.

And I am a potato.

If my thirty years of ignominy haven't driven that point home sufficiently, one look in my mirror after ten hours on my feet sure does.

I spent Friday pulling off three separate events that my last employer contracted out to me. Small jobs that paid a pittance—nothing they wanted for themselves, in other words. My day started at six a.m. with a corporate breakfast. Then came a bridal luncheon at a Japanese tea garden. And, last, a baby shower at three p.m.

The one highlight in my otherwise dismal work came courtesy of Ella Callahan. She called me after her Friday yoga class and asked if I would be willing to meet with a friend of hers. Apparently, the girl is set to marry one of the city's richest bachelors—a former classmate of Grayson's—but she doesn't have a planner yet. We set a breakfast meeting for Sunday morning.

Now, as twilight darkens my viewless window, Tris sprawls on my bed, kicking her heels up behind her while she watches me grimace at my reflection.

"You're saying that Marco—*the* Marco? Big guy? Glossy black hair? Soulful brown eyes? Former-military, muscle-bound, could-pick-you-up-and-literally-fuck-you-sideways, *Marco?*—is coming to our apartment in forty-five minutes to 'borrow' a *romance novel?* From you?"

I rip my hair tie out of my hair. And instantly regret it. Hours pulled back and kinked up only made the whole mess limp and tangled.

While I groan in hopeless despair, Tris carries on. "*Marco?*" she sputters again. "Sexy bodyguard? Black clothes?"

"Yes, Tris," I snap. "That Marco. He asked to come over and borrow a book after work. That's it."

I squirt some goop into my hands and follow the bottle's instructions, smoothing it over my hair before scrunching it into the ends. Miraculously, it starts to tame some of the frizz.

"On Friday night?" Tris asks, then rephrases, "*He* chose tonight?"

I huff out a frustrated snort. "Yes! Lord, is it that impossible to believe a guy would want to come borrow a book from me?"

"Noooo," she drawls. "But it *is* a little surprising that a man like Marco Amir invited himself over for a hookup. I've been throwing him invites left and right for *years*, and he's never even sent me a dick pic."

"Beatrice Dunn," I shriek. "Ew!"

She grins, cocking her head to the side. "Just sayin'. I didn't have him pegged as the forward type. But I must have been mistaken, since he invited himself over here to get it on with you."

Get it on? I scoff. "Oh yeah, *sure*. Of course not! I mean, that's what you're saying, right? That there's no way Marco is *actually* forgoing a night out with this week's supermodel to get a piece of *this*?"

I gesture at my recycled gray skirt and the matching charcoal turtleneck. Tris eyes the outfit with outright disdain. "That's not fair, Alley Cat. You know how much I hate that skirt."

I throw my scarf at her. "Just... listen, I know this is impossible, and he doesn't like me as a woman or probably even know that I am one, but could you *help me*, please? I'm pretty sure he's only doing all of this to keep an eye on me while I work for your boss, but I'd like to give the impression I at least own a hairbrush!"

Tris isn't known as the most empathetic person, but I can tell from the look on her face that she understands my desperation. Sympathy fills her hazel eyes before they dash to the phone lying beside her. "Forty-one minutes," she announces, leaping up. "Let's do this."

Thirty-some minutes of primping later, I almost feel human again. Tris convinces me to wash off the day's dirt and makeup, leaving my skin clear aside from a light layer of "glowy" moisturizer, as she calls it. She also talked me out of my work clothes and into a camisole, leggings, and a light, open sweater.

As her last trick, she teases the knots and kinks out of my hair before spritzing it with a spray bottle and re-winding the curls around my face that make the most impact. The rest, she leaves looser, though whatever nonsense I raked into them seems to help a bit.

While she works on me, she also adjusts her own hair and makeup. Apparently, she has a date she's going to be "uber late" for, but it doesn't seem to bother her.

As a "finishing touch," Tris spreads mascara over my lashes and dabs shiny gloss over my lips. "Okay, baby cakes," she crows, hurrying out of my room and into hers. She throws her cosmetics onto her bed and whips on a shimmery sequin jacket. "I'm out of here. Smooches."

With one last pucker of her painted lips, she twirls out of the apartment. Nerves seethe in my stomach, reminding me that I've only eaten scraps at events all day. I wander into the kitchen and put the kettle on, deciding that's a nice, normal thing to do when someone is dropping by. In a moment of weakness, I also put out a plate of the chocolate chip cookies Ella sent home the other day.

I pick an English blend for the tea. It's bold and dark, intended for those who like to put milk in their brews, so I fill a little ceramic pitcher with milk, too.

The white porcelain got cracked in one of our ill-fated Tris-does-the-dishes incidents. Because the tiny carafe was one of my favorite little trinkets, I pieced it back together. Now, the long, thin scar running diagonally through the side feels like a metaphor for my general inadequacy.

It sits in the middle of my coffee table along with my favorite candle, two teacups, and the cookies—mocking me as I wait for the man who, in all likelihood, won't stay long enough to notice I'm making tea at all.

This is so stupid. He's going to knock, take the book, and go about his Friday night. He did nothing to indicate that he would stay. Why would he? To talk to me? Of course not. See? Stupid.

My hands fidget in my lap, the chewed-up fingers knotting. Looking at them reminds me of his large, solid hand, stretched out to demand my book. His thick, smooth skin. The rich color, the square nails.

Everything about Marco is like that, come to think of it. Straight, sharp. Chiseled. Masculine.

Much too handsome for the likes of me.

Telling myself that over and over actually helps calm me down. *He has no interest in me outside of making sure I don't ruin his boss's life,* I reassure internally, recalling the moment I realized the handsome stranger from the coffee shop was really a bodyguard investigating me. *All the flirting is just his way of being sneaky about it. If I act like a normal, competent person, maybe he'll finally leave me alone.*

My heart pinches at that thought, but I shove the hurt aside. I should be *offended,* damn it. Not sad. Or, worse, sympathetic toward the man.

Sure, he's shockingly chivalrous. And earnest... most of the time.

But still.

The Smart TV's clock says eight on the dot when three hard raps hit my door. Ever punctual—I wonder if it's because he used to be a soldier. Then I mentally slap myself. Because *I shouldn't care.*

Blowing out a long breath, I shake my arms and legs to dispel some jitters before shuffling over to let him in... just before my mouth falls open so far that my jaw practically unhinges.

Oh. My. God.

In a black cashmere sweater, black slacks, and an open, tan coat, Marco looks like he stepped out of a men's cologne ad and onto my landing. My gaze absorbs how his pants cling to his thick thighs, then roam up to the slight V of his bare chest revealed by his thin sweater, all the way to the crisp lines of his facial hair. A heavenly scent creeps into the space between us—warm, manly spice with a touch of leather.

I feel like one of the heroines in my Victorian romances, about to swoon over the very *sight* of a man. And then he *smiles.*

"Sorry, I'm overdressed. I came straight from work. Can I come in? It's freezing."

I squash the burst of excitement at how hopeful he looks. *Of course he wants to come in,* I chide myself. *He's trying to make sure I'm not a loose end.*

"Uh—sure," I bumble, pulling the door wide open.

Marco steps into the apartment, instantly filling the room with his broad strength and sheer size. Power rolls off him in a fluid ripple as he shrugs his coat from his shoulders and hangs it on our coat rack. His dark eyes glance over my face as his smile turns rueful.

"The tea smells amazing. I'm embarrassed to admit how much I'd hoped you'd make some. In fact..."

He reaches into one of two large pockets concealed in the satin lining of his coat. Two bags appear in his grasp—one a white paper sack and the other a familiar sachet from my favorite tea shop. "I brought some to replace what you gave me last time. And a couple of Ella's scones."

A nervous giggle trips out of me. "I just put out Ella's cookies. And I brewed the perfect tea for scones. It's English Breakfast. Darker, to go with milk."

Realizing I'm rambling, I swallow the rest of my words. Marco hovers close, lingering with both our hands wrapped around the scones. His eyes flicker from my revived hair, down to my exposed chest, before looping back up to my face and zeroing in on my mouth.

"Perfect," he praises.

Perfect? Me?

But he means the tea, of course. He proves as much when he suddenly steps away, edging into our living room and dropping onto the edge of the light yellow futon. He looks almost comical there—his wide frame, dressed all in black, dwarfing the tiny pastel couch.

Unable to come up with anything clever to say, I silently fetch the kettle. It's just shy of boiling, which is my secret for brewing tea properly. I pour it into the pot with the bags and carry it in on an oven mitt, laying it beside the plate of cookies and adding Ella's scones on top.

I don't realize I've started humming until Marco raises his brows at me. "Are you alright?"

"Alright?" I choke out, lowering myself onto the blue-patterned armchair. I don't want to lie to him, so I can't say *yes*... "Why do you ask?"

Like a gentleman, Marco pours a cup of tea for me and then one for himself. He places a cookie on each of our saucers before thinking better of it and cramming scones on the plates as well.

"You were humming," he points out. "You do that when you're nervous."

I swallow a knot of chagrin. "No," I deny. "I—I like to sing."

Marco surprises me by nodding in agreement. "I know. You sing when you're happy. You hum when you're stressed."

With a start, I realize he's *right*.

"How do *you* know that?" I murmur, biting the side of my thumb again. "Do I do it that often?"

His smile melts from teasing to kind. "Not really. I just noticed that you normally hum in stressful situations—like last week when you were getting the tea out of the cabinet and couldn't reach it. Then, on Wednesday, while you were reading, you were relaxed. And you sang under your breath every now and then." His gaze burns into mine. "I like the singing."

A shiver skirts up my sternum, lodging in my throat. "Y-you do?"

With a confident calm, Marco picks up his tea and sits back with it, nodding easily. "I do."

I can't figure out why he would go out of his way to compliment me. I know he has some agenda, but I'm already here. With myself and my place both totally accessible to him.

It's almost cruel for him to be so gallant when he doesn't need to be. Still, one of my mother's rules comes to mind. *A lady never refuses flattery.*

"Thank you," I reply, wooden.

Marco starts to frown, then takes an absent-minded sip from his teacup. His attention snaps down to it, earlier concern forgotten. "Damn," he mutters, drinking more. "Thank *you*. This is perfect. Again."

He shakes his head at himself. "I tried to recreate your hibiscus blend at home. It wasn't nearly as good as yours. I thought it was a fluke, but..." He holds up his cup. "It seems I'm outmatched."

I feel a blush bloom over my chest and neck. "Thank you," I say once more, the words quivering this time.

Marco gazes at me over the rim of his teacup, deep brown eyes warm but sharp. They linger on my cleavage for a beat too long before sliding up to meet mine. We stare at each other, neither of us speaking, until my nerves get the best of me.

"I, um, I should get you that book. I'm sure you have places to be."

He takes another sip of tea before setting the cup back on his saucer and rolling his massive shoulders. "Not at all. Do you?"

I almost laugh. "Uh, no."

His beautiful smile melds with the warmth of his gaze. "Great. Then we'll both stay in."

I WATCH, enraptured, as Alice pours some milk into her black tea. Light from the flickering candle burnishes her blonde curls and bathes her flawless skin, catching on all of the dips and hollows of her throat.

She moves with the same care she seems to show everything else. Slow, deliberate, always careful to treat everything gingerly.

Which makes the large crack in the side of her cream carafe curious. I eye the thin fracture, noting the way candlelight reflects off the lustrous adhesive. "Is that gold glue?"

Alice's thick lashes flutter with surprise each time I take any interest in her. She blinks down at the pitcher before her face breaks into a slight grimace. "Yes. Tris tends to stack things... precariously. She broke it one night, and I pieced it back together."

She hands me the jug for closer examination. Up close, I see that the painted crack is the sole point of interest on the smooth white ceramic surface. It would be unremarkable without it.

"I read about it in a Japanese philosophy book, of all places," she blurts. "Fixing broken pottery lends itself to their practice of embracing imperfections as part of one's individual beauty."

There are her depths—shimmering intelligence and a mysterious soul. I wonder if she knows anything else about Zen philosophy, since it happens to be one of my favorite attitudes.

I don't need to give her a lesson. Instead, I simply say, "It makes a lot of sense to me."

Her timid little smile appears, softening her features just so. "Me, too." She looks at her lap, lightly brushing her hands over her middle while her expression takes on some ruefulness. "I imagine there's a sort of... tranquility in accepting one's flaws outright."

Well-versed, as I suspected. But I don't know which flaws she's referring to. I don't see any from here, apart from the way she's torn into the skin on the side of her thumbnail.

We both drink our tea, soaking in the silence. I know from experience that sitting beside her without speaking won't be awkward. We're both friends with the quiet.

When our eyes meet again, a beat of understanding passes between us. She opens her mouth, then closes it again before finally working up her nerve. "Marco..."

My brows tweak. "Hmm?"

As I wait for her to finish her offer, a swell of want rises in my center. There are a lot of things I want to do with this woman—and I suspect I will think of dozens more by the end of the night.

My favorite pink creeps into her cheeks as she whispers, "Why are you here?"

Fear froths in her cool blue irises, but she holds my gaze and keeps her chin high. Waiting for my answer with a determined wariness I don't understand. Does she think I don't want to be here with her? It was my idea.

"To borrow a book," I say slowly, reminding her of the alleged reason for this visit. Guilt pokes my stomach, and I decide on the spot I can't lie to her. Not even a lie of omission. "I'm also going to measure for some cameras in the hallway before I leave. Your landlord finally relented."

"Oh." Her shoulders deflate. "Okay."

Fuck. I hate the way her shoulders hunch. "Like I said," I try, "I'm in no hurry. What do you want to do?"

There's wariness in her eyes, but something else too. *Hope*. It pierces some tender place I didn't know I had as she whispers, "We could read together again?"

Her invitation is, quite simply, lovely. As lovely as her tea and her voice and her gorgeous skin.

She wants to sit with me. Just to have me here. Is there a bigger compliment than that?

The size of the knot in my throat surprises me. I'm... touched? Flattered. Warmth expands in my chest and trickles down to my stomach. I press my palm there, holding onto the feeling while I give a nod. "I would like that."

"Alright," she says, bouncing up. "I'll be right back."

Her hips sway as she delicately makes her way to her room. I'm beyond caring about whether I should be checking her out, memorizing her curves. The fact is, I am. And I can do my job while also being insanely attracted to her.

Case and point—I have a measuring tape hidden in my coat to fit the hallway for cameras. And I paid her landlord a little visit earlier on my way upstairs. After a fistful of cash, he came around.

I hear some shuffling in an adjacent room. Seconds later, Alice reappears with four books folded between her arms and her chest. She looks sheepish as she glances at them and then back over to me. "I—I didn't know what you would like the best. I tried to choose a few... They're probably stupid. I'm sorry."

She doubts herself at every turn. Does she really spend her whole life apologizing for who she is and what she likes? Has anyone ever even *asked her* what *she* likes? Or why?

"Which is your favorite?"

She blinks, taken aback. "Oh. Um. Well..."

With a shaky hand, she extends one of the paperbacks. I can see that she treats her books with care. The pages are pristine, though I note slight creases along the binding from repeated reading.

I take it from her, absorbing the cover. A woman in a voluminous purple gown stands with a man at her back. The title hangs over them in scrolly cursive. *The Wallflower.*

I smile before I can help myself. Of course this is her favorite. But it still feels important to ask. "Why?"

The look on her face as she gazes at it sends a crack of pain through my chest. *God.* She seems *staggered.*

Has no one ever asked *why* she likes these books? Why doesn't anyone care?

I double down, invested in her reply. "Why do you like this one, Alice?"

"I—well, it's about a girl who's kind of a shy, bookworm type. Sort of p-plain." She clears her throat, flushing. "And sh-she meets a man who sees another side of her. And h-he falls in love with her. The *real* her. The one—"

"Underneath." I finish her thought automatically this time, unable to help myself.

Alice stands completely still as she swings her big blue eyes up to meet mine. "Yes."

The sharp stab in my center takes on the sweetest edge of agony, thinking about Alice seeing herself in that character. Her heart connecting to that story.

It fucking *hurts.*

I don't want her to feel more insecure. If I can somehow validate one of her interests, I will. I carefully keep my gaze and my voice steady as I repeat my earlier praise. "Perfect."

Instead of joining me on the couch, she walks over to her tote bag and pulls out a different sort of book altogether. One I recognize.

"Interesting." I can't quite get a grip on my grin. "I think I've seen that somewhere before."

Alice giggles softly at the Kant philosophy book in her hands. "Our debate and the notes you showed me in the margins of your copy inspired me to try reading it again. This one is from the library. No notes from brilliant fathers, though."

A fresh bolt of disgrace hits me. My dad would have been ashamed by the way all of this started, with me approaching her in the coffee shop the way I did. He always taught me that my honor as a man was my most sacred possession. In the end, he *died* for his.

While I stare at her copy of the Kant book, I think of what my father would want from me. He always followed his instincts and let his conscience guide his choices. If he were in my position, he would've gone out of his way to treat Alice with the utmost respect, especially given how I feel about her now.

"Here," I say, my throat tight. "Hold on."

Dad's book is in my coat, tucked into the second interior pocket with my Glock. When I slide the slim white book out and stretch it over to her, Alice's bright blue eyes widen.

"No," she whispers. "I can't take that. It has all your father's private thoughts in it. What if Tris uses it as a paper towel next time she overfills the coffee maker?"

Examining her crystalline irises, I suddenly realize: there isn't one other person on Earth I would give Baba's book to. But... I trust Alice. Despite all logic, I've trusted her from the moment I laid eyes on her.

"Seriously, take it. Keep it for as long as you need. Then we can talk about it some more."

She likes that idea. Excitement electrifies her gaze. Her joy is irresistible. My lips pull wider, and I reach for her hand, placing the worn book in it. "You'll take good care of it, right? Keep it safe from Hurricane Tris?"

Alice swallows, the creamy lines of her throat working. "Of course," she vows softly, peering down at the faded cover. "You don't think your dad would mind? I mean, these are his private musings, and I'm a stranger."

Her mind works in the oddest, loveliest way. Who else would consider the wishes of a dead man they've never met?

My hand curls around hers, holding the book between our palms. Our gazes click together. "I don't think he would mind," I decide, staring into her. "I actually think he would have really liked you."

Her brows twitch together in a quick frown. "Me?"

"You," I confirm.

We've drifted closer again; I've taken three steps toward her, bringing our bodies inches apart. My head spins from the lavender warmth rising off her skin.

Fucking hell. Did I ever think this woman was *just a job*?

No, some steady, quiet voice inside me says. *Never.*

That's why I swept in to save her at the coffee shop when I was supposed to be keeping my distance. It's why I called her darling, pretended to be her boyfriend. Touched her. Bought her a treat. Made sure she had a way to get home.

I liked her before I even spoke to her.

And now that I *know* her...

Alice seems to sense my turmoil. Her blonde brow creases, betraying some inner conflict I still don't comprehend. She leans forward, though, moving slowly at first, and then all at once.

Her lips flit over mine, quick and delicate as the beat of a hummingbird's wings. I keep my eyes open, watching her as she slides our mouths together for the briefest, softest kiss.

The voltage in my veins amps higher, a current radiating into every corner of my body. My fingers clasp her chin, stilling her as she tries to pull away. She only manages a few inches before I stop her, our faces hovering close.

The trepidation in her eyes undoes the last threads tying me to my manners. I swallow a growl, pulling her body into mine and pressing my open mouth to hers. Her lips part on a gasp, allowing me to sweep inside.

She tastes like her perfect tea and smells like lavender-honey. The combination makes my cock throb as it presses into her belly.

Fuck.

I can't control the way my fingers curl, dimpling the soft flesh of her hip and holding her face in an iron grip. The blazing aggression seems to turn her on. She makes another breathy sound of pleasure, stretching up on her tiptoes so she can meet my tongue with hers.

The moment she succeeds, a jolt vibrates through her shorter, rounder frame. She tears herself out of my grasp—or tries to, at least. Again, I hold fast, keeping her close as wide, ice-blue eyes regard me nervously.

A fresh pang strikes my heart. *Sweet girl.*

I keep calling her that in my mind. There's no helping it. She *is* sweet. The sweetest thing I've ever seen, especially in this moment.

"Sorry," she whispers. "I knew if I didn't do that now, I never would."

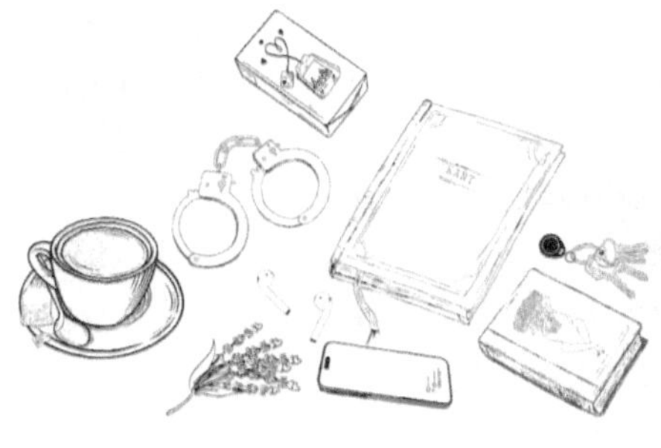

twenty-one

STUPID, *silly, sad sack. Why did you* do *that?!*

There's no excuse, really. I was standing there, in the candlelight, looking up at the most beautiful man I've ever been alone with... and something in me snapped.

For a moment, I didn't want to be boring, invisible, or a means to an end. I wanted to *believe*. And let myself fall into the feeling of being wanted by someone like Marco. Even though it isn't real.

He looked so conflicted, too. Brooding, the way he did the day we met and the afternoon he had to rescue me.

No matter how much I want to hate him for flirting and leading me on to make his job easier, his turbulent gaze did strange things to my heart. Pinching and pulling. Prodding until it swelled large enough to find compassion for him.

The same way it does for Tris. And my mother. And everyone else who makes me feel bad without meaning to cause any real harm.

Because, really, this guy doesn't know about my past. To him, this game he's playing is probably just a fun diversion. One I just encouraged by throwing caution to the wind for a delirious moment.

But, God, he kissed me like he was trying to save me. Or himself. How could he fake something like that?

That realization sinks into my stomach like a stone, and I hate myself for how much it *hurts*.

Why can't I just be like Tris? Why do I have to want romance and love and the whole stupid thing? Can't I just settle for this very hot man being willing to make out with me? Who cares if it's under false pretenses??

I do. Unfortunately.

The brawny fingers holding my chin flex gently. His espresso irises swirl. So serious, even when his lips kick up into his mysterious half-smile. "I've never had a beautiful woman apologize for kissing me."

Of course not. Because he's some cross between a Greek god, a warrior king, and a GQ ad.

Deep down, I suppose I don't actually regret it. Even if he leaves now and I never see him again—well, at least I got to pretend he actually wanted me for a few heartbeats.

I turn my face, twisting out of his grasp. Looking at the wall and not his horribly handsome face. "Sorry," I say again, reflexively. Then force a steadying breath before I ask, "Do you need anything to measure for the cameras? I only have Tris's tool kit—it's pink and only has two screwdrivers and some double-sided tape, but you're welcome to borrow it."

I can't see his expression, but there's a beat of silence before he clears his throat. "No, that's alright. I brought a tape measure. I'll be out of your hair in a few minutes."

There's another pause before he adds, "I'll see you tomorrow, right? At the engagement party?"

He won't. Since the entire soiree is Grayson's mother's way of placating her *team* of event planners over not being selected to coordinate the actual wedding, I felt it was in poor taste for me to show up.

But I'm sick of this man having unfettered access to me. I signed up to be his boss's wedding planner, not a prisoner. He can't keep tabs on me, twist my feelings at will to manipulate me into making his job easier. Or, at the very least, I don't have to help him.

"Sure," I lie, mumbling to my feet. "I'll see you tomorrow."

Marco doesn't make me look at his face again. Instead, he looms close enough for the warm, masculine scent of his throat to envelop me and presses a fleeting kiss to my crown. "Tomorrow," he repeats, stern and somehow soft. "Sweet girl."

twenty-two

BARNES and I stand over Mason and Jacqueline Stryker's townhouse blueprints, scanning for possible security holes.

He stabs his finger at one of the service elevators, not even bothering to grunt.

"Brad," I reply. "It's in his zone."

"Aye, but he can only cover one floor at a time."

"He'll be on the first, I'll be on the second. You're watching all the camera feeds, anyway. Pierce has the front area of the house, where all the guests will be. We have four men on the roof. Two on each fire escape. Three in the basement. One for the kitchen, one for the garage. Not to mention everything but the damn front door will be locked up tighter than Fort Knox."

I say it more to reassure myself than him, trying to shut down the instinct screaming that this whole party *isn't safe.*

No, more than that; it feels like a fucking *trap.*

Every time I run through the plans and protocols, I see Ted Stryker's smarmy smile. The bruises his son left on Ella. That too-still, too-silent apartment.

God, how do I know he didn't hire those paparazzi assholes to attack Alice? Maybe he wanted the information so he could sabotage the wedding. Or find a way into tonight's event.

I can't shake the instinct that something wicked is coming. And, if I'm right, it makes sense that Ted would be the one pulling the strings.

I've had him under heavy surveillance all week, but nothing has changed. It's starting to make me feel insane.

Barnes tilts his neck, cracking it as he steps away from the table and settles his eerie steel eyes on me. "You've dealt with the lass?"

Alice. Because as far as all my men are concerned, the time I've spent with her is purely professional.

It strikes me suddenly how fucked up that is. I shake my head. "Alice Moore doesn't need to be *dealt with.* She's smarter than any of our men, and she's learned her lesson about breaking protocol."

Behind me, Brad and Pierce enter the room, both laughing about a YouTube video on Brad's phone. Barnes says nothing, but his metallic glare darkens.

I sigh. "She's important to me. Our objective is to *protect* her, not treat her like a loose end."

Brad drops his elbows to the blueprint and shoots me a shit-eating grin. "Did you *gain access* to her place yet, boss? I bet you did."

My jaw locks while Pierce elbows Brad, shaking his head.

"What?" Brad snickers. "I'm just *saying*—"

"Nothing," I interrupt sharply. "You are saying *nothing* because there *is* nothing to be said. Miss Moore is a *lady*. I went to her house last night for a social call. That is *all*. Anyone who would like to insinuate otherwise can take it up with me."

Brad tries to bite his lip. "*Social call*," he snorts quietly.

Pierce covers his face with his palm. "If he kills you, I don't think I'll miss you."

I know *I* won't. "Enough. Do either of you jackasses have your quadrants memorized, or should I just fire you right now?"

The guys grumble, each turning their attention to the white-board covered in notes at the back of the room. Barnes eyes them with distaste before turning the full force of his disapproval on me. "You should put someone else on the wedding planner."

"No." The word rips from my throat without polish. "She's *mine*. This subject is closed."

Barnes sees too much. Hears too much. Of all of us, he's the most highly trained. The only person who has experience with interrogating the sort of people you question under a bone saw. His eyes flicker while he listens to me.

And I don't like it.

I swallow a growl and murmur too quietly for the others to hear, "You leave her alone, or we're going to have a problem."

Again, he doesn't speak. But his face does. *This doesn't feel right.*

But neither does letting anyone else near Alice.

Still, I scrub a hand over my face before turning back to my notes. "I know," I tell him. "I know."

twenty-three

"EXCUSE ME—*WHAT*?!"

After lying in my bed for half the morning, trying to sort surreal memories from my night with Marco, I finally call for reinforcements. I had to bribe Tris with a fresh pot of coffee and her favorite hangover mélange of sausage gravy and a buttered bagel, but she finally drops down onto the couch and listens to me recount the entire evening.

By the time I get to the endearment he used and the way he kissed the top of my head, her mouth hangs open.

"You *kissed* him?" she shrieks.

I wince. "Yes."

She lurches up onto her knees, her face alight with awe. "He called you '*sweet girl*?'"

"Um..." I'm still unsure. Did it really happen the way I remember? What other explanation is there? "I really think so."

"He gave you his book?" she squeals, bouncing. "He kissed you back with tongue?" Before I can answer any of her questions, she hits her grand conclusion. "And you *made him leave*?!"

I expected her to be shocked, but I didn't expect *this* to be the reason for her disbelief.

In all honesty, I *had* to ask him to go. It just isn't healthy to let my foolish hope run away from me. It isn't as if he will ever want *me*—he wouldn't even look at me twice if he wasn't being paid to watch me.

And I'm pretty sure if he so much as stripped his shirt off in front of me, I'd faint.

How would that even work? I wonder. He is so *big*. Large and —if the feel of him when he swept my body into his was any indication—completely *covered* in muscle.

The whole idea makes me slightly manic. "Well, he couldn't *stay*! Tris, that would be like giving a Maserati to someone who just got their learner's permit and asking them to win—to win—I don't know, whatever competition a Maserati races in!"

Instead of laughing, she takes on a grim air. "You don't think you can take him? Why not? Is he hung?"

I throw a pillow at her head. "Tris! This is serious! I'm not going to talk about h—his—"

"Cock?" she supplies, overeager. "Oh my God, have you *seen* it? Does it curve to the left? I don't know why, but I have him pegged for a Southpaw penis."

I groan, dropping my head to my knees. "Can you *please* stop asking me about his *penis* and *help me*?"

"I *am*," she huffs. "Listen, Alley Cat, I know you haven't been on the dating scene in... well, *ever*, but shit's wild out there. A man like Marco Amir probably gets laid five nights a week. He's *definitely* not used to sitting around *reading*, waiting for the girl to get a clue and take his pants off."

Stinging mortification prickles my cheeks. *Great. I can't even get used properly.*

I slump back, letting my eyes fall to my hands. I didn't even *kiss* him well. On the off chance he may have had some real interest in me... I'm sure he doesn't anymore.

I can't say anything in my defense, apart from the truth. "I— It never occurred to me that he w-would want that."

Tris's shoulders fall forward in an exasperated slump. Sympathy fills her fine features, pinching her auburn eyebrows under her bangs. "Alice," she says, her voice quiet, "that makes me so sad."

"Sorry," I peep lamely.

She sighs, reaching over to pat my hand. "Babe, as a rule, when a man invites himself over for some dubious purpose and then finds excuses to stay and make out with you—he wants you to take his pants off."

Tris obviously knows more about men and the removal of their clothing than I ever will. But I'm too embarrassed to tell her the real reason I'm hesitating. If she knew he'd been manipulating me with his charm, she would rip his (possibly-left-leaning) dick off.

I bite my lower lip so hard, I feel it blanch. "He asked if I'm going to the Strykers' party tonight."

Panic wells in my middle anytime I picture myself actually attending. I only have one dress that's formal enough—a pale blue recycled prom dress that's over a decade old. And, of course, I'd turn into a stammering, sweaty mess whenever one of Mrs. Stryker's wealthy society friends asked about the wedding.

If Marco witnesses that, after last night, he will probably cringe at the thought of me. He will *definitely* regret trusting me with his prized philosophy book. Hell, he'd probably be mortified to admit he even *pretended* to be interested in me.

"I can't go," I cry. "No way."

My best friend jumps to the edge of her seat. "Are you crazy?! Of course you *have* to go! You have to keep him wanting more—so you show up and look gorgeous and then let him make the next move."

I blink, thrown. Unable to even envision what she's describing. "Tris, this is *me*. *My* life. Not yours."

Tris shakes her head. "No, Alley Cat. This is *romance*. A tall, dark, and handsome man inviting you to what is basically a ball? Literally sweeping you off your feet last night? Jesus, babe, what more do you want?"

I want it to be real.

But I can't tell her that.

So I guess I'm going to have to shave my legs.

twenty-four

I TRY—REALLY and truly try—to focus. But no matter how hard I force concentration, I can't turn my attention away from the one question running through my mind on a loop.

Where the hell is Alice?

The second-floor landing is my favorite spot for observation at Mason and Jacqueline Stryker's opulent manse. I've spent many philanthropic events and social gatherings perched here, watching Grayson move through the enormous entertaining space at the foot of their grand, curved staircase.

Tonight proves no exception. Though now, I keep my eyes

trained on my boss *and* his future wife. Keeping tabs on Ella is easy enough—in her white gown, it's impossible to miss her. It helps that Grayson tends to stick close to her side.

Which is good. Because I need all the help I can get.

My head isn't even in the room. When my mind isn't racing with all the things that can go wrong at any moment, it's back in Alice's little pastel apartment, basking in her enticing warmth.

Finishing *The Wallflower* this afternoon didn't discourage my new fixation. As I read it, I couldn't help but imagine Alice's eyes running over the same words, her mind conjuring the same sensual images. My body had a *distinct* reaction to that thought. One so potent, I had to relieve myself before I could turn my meager focus to tonight.

It didn't make much of a difference, in the end. I remained distracted while I donned my requisite black tuxedo. All during the drive to retrieve the guests of honor. And throughout the final briefing I gave my team before the party commenced.

Now, I have to actively yank my mind back to the task at hand every few minutes. Exhaling in frustration, I shift from one foot to the other and scan the Italian marble foyer. A fresh stab of aggravation assaults me when I realize: I'm not even looking for potential security threats.

I'm looking for *her.*

Where the hell could she be? She told me she'd be here. She's never flaked on anything else for the Strykers.

Fuck. Focus, Amir.

During the first hour, I was on edge and overeager. During the second, I got angry. Almost indignant. By the third, worry has crowded in.

What if she is hurt? Or sick? She could have been in a traffic accident or gotten mugged on the subway again.

My stomach turns leaden with dread. Repeatedly, my hand twitches for my phone. I narrowly catch myself every time, internally chanting stern reminders that I am *working*. Doing the job that garners me millions of dollars and changed the lives of my entire family. Keeping people I care about safe from the threats circling their heads like vultures. Screwing around with my phone during a high-risk event is unthinkable.

Yet here I am, thinking about it.

I blink down at the scene below, noting that Grayson stands off to the left, but Ella does not. When he meets my gaze, he subtly rolls his head up and to the right, indicating the level behind me. His lips mouth, *"Bathroom."*

Instantly, I raise my watch to my lips, speaking into the speaker hidden there. "Who has a twenty on the bride?"

Pierce responds first, his voice filling my ear via the earpiece I wear. "I had her about three minutes ago. She was in my quadrant, en route to the elevator in the west wing. I thought you'd catch her when she exited. She was going up to your floor and planned to cross over the landing to the bathroom in the east wing."

Damn it. I *would* have caught her if I weren't so damn distracted.

"Barnes?" I growl. "Do you have a visual?"

The old Brit hates being in a storage closet full of monitors. Every time the situation necessitates it, the task turns him more stoic and surlier than usual. But he is the one who knows this house the best.

"Second floor," he snaps back. "West wing, heading east."

Toward me. Good.

"I'll intercept her at the top of the stairs," I determine, blowing out a gust of anxiety. "Next time, someone better fucking call me."

Pissed, Barnes clicks off without a word. But Pierce's voice takes on a conciliatory note. "Understood, sir. I'm in the dining room; I'll keep a twenty on the groom."

Great. The sarcastic tone of my thoughts is uncharitable, and I know it. Pierce has diligently given up time with his new wife all week. He can handle watching our boss drink a martini.

I still don't like handing the reins of Grayson's security to another person. For years, I took sole responsibility for his safety. It feels unnatural to forfeit the job, but my boss made one thing exceedingly clear—Ella's well-being now supersedes his own.

It is a noble notion. One I agree with and understand. Honestly, I know I would make the same choice if I were in his shoes.

If Alice and I were in danger, of course I would want her to be safe before me.

The errant thought surprises me. What the fuck am I doing? I am *at work*.

A strange tendril of indefinable certainty creeps up my insides. It isn't new—and it seems to reach farther and deeper each time I think of her. Problem is, I don't understand the sensation. It's warm and solid and real... but *what is it*?

Carajo.

I've gotten distracted again. For two minutes, my smart watch informs me.

Two minutes. That seems like a long time for someone to walk from one side of the house to the other.

An instinctive prickle skitters down my spine. It doesn't matter how long I do this kind of work—I always forget this feeling until it returns. The solid certainty mixed with soaring adrenaline. How it sharpens my mind and sends an anchor dragging through my gut.

Something isn't right.

My eyes snap to the crush of people below, scanning. Not knowing what I'm looking for until I find it.

But I find it.

I always do.

Tension grips my lungs. I've trained myself to ignore the urge to panic, though. And years of practice have given me the ability to think around the fear.

It's the trick no one teaches you; being a good soldier doesn't require the absence of fear. Just the humility to treat it with respect. So you can move *through* it, instead of tripping over it.

I hit the speaker on my smart watch. "I need backup on level two, east wing. Whoever has eyes on Ella, move in."

Brad bleats back, "Heard," just as Pierce adds his agreement. Barnes's "aye," is belated, but I don't have time to think about that.

Striding as quickly as I can without making my concern obvious, I stalk down the grand staircase, keeping my gaze trained on a head of ashy brown hair.

The color is all wrong. It should be blond. And the face hidden under it may be gaunt and half-insane, but I recognize it. *Him*.

Ted Styker's son, Daniel. Ella's tormentor from her past life. Grayson's sick, son-of-a-bitch cousin.

He's supposed to be behind bars. I put him there myself—slammed the door on his cell and everything. How the fuck is he here?

It's another mystery I don't have time for. Not now.

Because the fucker has his target in his sights, weaving his way through the throng to get to—

Ella.

She's there, floating toward Grayson with Pierce right behind her. He's focused—*good kid*—and doesn't see me. I raise my watch back to my mouth.

"Hold her there," I bark. "*Now*."

It all happens too quickly.

The worst things tend to.

Daniel watches as Pierce yanks Ella to a halt. She whirls, surprised, and Daniel flashes his teeth. I take the opportunity to reach for him, but he sees the way the crowd has to part to let me through—and he launches himself at his mark.

Grayson senses the commotion and turns. He shouts something—and the split second it takes for me to tune into his voice is all Daniel needs to draw a gun.

My scalp tingles, lungs stuttering as he raises it at Ella. My *friend*. My love of Grayson's life.

I lunge, intending to tackle him or block his shot. But I'm not fast enough.

By the time I land on the marble floor with Daniel Stryker under me, smoke and the reverberation of a gunshot hang in the air. The room is silent as blood creeps up Ella's white gown and pools underneath me.

twenty-five

"HOW THE FUCK DID THIS HAPPEN?"

The moment we are alone, Grayson spirals. He's already been banished from Ella's hospital room. After he snapped at every single person who tried to touch her, she finally lost her patience with him and sent him out to the hall. Now he's pacing and trying to figure out how the hell his cousin got out of prison. And into our event.

He's wasting his time. I've already considered every angle multiple times. And the only explanation isn't one either of us is going to like.

"How the fuck did this happen?"

He keeps asking. Again and again. I'm unsure who he wants an answer from. Me? Himself? God, maybe.

He shoves his hands into his hair, pulling at the roots. The quiet clack of heels approaches, and Jacqueline Stryker appears, looking both ethereally elegant and devastated beyond all words. Her pale lips move while the rest of her face remains wreathed in pain. "I'll stay with him, Marco. You ought to go get checked out and make sure you don't have a concussion. Mason wants to speak with you, as well."

Hopefully to fire me.

That is what I deserve. All of this is entirely my fault.

With a somber nod, I leave my head bent in apology. "I'm fine, ma'am. I'm only sorry I was too late to stop any bloodshed."

I'm not sorry Pierce shot the fucker, though. No matter how stained the carpet ended up. Or how frenzied this will make the media.

Alice.

I've thought of her a hundred times in the last three hours, praying she got my texts and stayed home. It isn't safe for her to be out alone. Especially not now.

Whoever took her personal information could have sold it. Everyone knows she's Grayson and Ella's planner—and with this bombshell of an evening? It's never been less safe for her to be by herself. Even at home.

Goddamn it. I should have finished installing those cameras last night.

There isn't enough time to properly flay myself for any of this. Not now. Grayson's father, Mason Stryker, is hovering a few yards away, looking jaundiced in his white tuxedo shirt. Throughout his three years of failing health, I'm not sure I've ever seen him look so broken.

My dress shoes squeak against the linoleum while I close the space between us and stand across from him. Folding my hands in front of my torso, I hang my head, waiting for his dismissal. "Sir."

Instead of reaming me out, his gruff voice lowers to a whisper. "Is he really dead?"

Images flash through my head; pictures of the limp body under mine. A bullet through the head. Blood rapidly pooling around us. Pierce, horrorstruck, standing in front of Ella, his shaking hands wrapped around a smoking handgun. The body of Daniel Stryker, lifeless and pale on the coroner's stretcher.

My stomach tumbles as I bite back bile and grit, "Yes, sir."

Mason looks haunted. "Someone has to call Ted."

His brother. I wonder if he feels any grief at the notion of losing the monster that was his nephew. Or if he feels any sympathy for the man he grew up with.

I don't.

"The police did it. They have to notify next-of-kin, even if the person killed is a scum-sucking piece of shit." I clear my throat, embarrassed by my outburst. "Apologies, sir. I know he was your nephew."

Mr. Stryker simply stares back at me. "Not anymore, it would seem. I ought to thank that new agent. He did us all a service, ridding the world of Daniel. Though, I wish it hadn't happened in my house. With two hundred guests inches away."

Carajo. Barnes and Pierce have been handling that nightmare. One thing is certain; the kid proved his mettle beyond all doubt. Any lingering apprehension I once harbored evaporated as he gave his statement to the police, reliving his heroic act without a hint of pleasure. I understand that feeling—he hates that he's taken someone's life, but he would do it again. If that doesn't solidify his loyalty, I don't know what will.

Brad, on the other hand...

Someone had to let Daniel into the engagement party—or at least look the other way while he snuck in. Barnes, Pierce, Brad, and I each swept a different wing of the house an hour before the party started. None of us found anything to indicate any other way in. Someone had to take his invitation and look him in the eye as he entered.

Unless he scaled the building and broke in through a window.

But how would Barnes not *see* that? He sat over the monitors all night; he should have caught anyone coming in or out. The old house may not have as many cameras as Grayson's, but it still has eyes on every door and window. Barnes is a former MI6 agent—how could he miss a strange man busting in?

I'll have to review the footage myself. Assuming I still have a job.

Mason's yellowed eyes meet mine. "How did that monster get into my house, Marco?"

Even hunched and sickly, he is a formidable man. A titan, really. I resist the urge to fall back and square my shoulders, prepared to take full responsibility. "It's my fault, sir. The security for tonight was under my authority. However he penetrated the system... I am responsible."

"I don't disagree." Mr. Stryker regards me stonily before raising one brow—a gesture his son often mimics when staring someone down. "But how did Daniel do it? Who let him out? Did he have some key? A disguise of some sort?"

The short answer is, I have no answer. But as I start to rattle off the various security concerns I brought to Grayson's attention ahead of the party, Mason shakes his head, sighing.

"Too many holes," he mutters. "I told Jacqueline this party was a bad idea. The paparazzi will be fucking ravenous, now. We'll have to lock Ella up in the townhouse."

I've had the same grim thought.

"You'll need an updated security plan for her," he goes on. Before my face registers my shock at not being terminated on the spot, Mason's frown deepens. His voice drops low. "Tomorrow, of course. We'll need you here tonight. Grayson can take Ella to one of our rental properties and hide out there in the meantime."

I nod again, speaking around my surprise. "Of course. I'll call Barnes and have him bring you and Mrs. Stryker some other clothes from the house. Then I'll contact Grayson's housekeeper to do the same for Mr. Stryker and Miss Callahan."

"Good." He casts his eyes down the hall, fixing them on the room I commandeered for Ella's cautionary exam. "I should go join my wife and my son. I trust you'll run interference in my stead if the police have more questions?"

With a final jerk of his head, he clips his way down the corridor. I stand at the other end, frozen under the fluorescents.

The weight of everything that's happened crashes down onto my head. A tsunami of guilt. My knees buckle while black spots bubble around my peripheral vision.

Shit.

I have to keep it together, but it feels like I'm about to pass out. Did I knock myself in the head tackling Daniel? Or is it just the simple fact that I watched him point a gun at someone I care about?

Neither explanation makes sense. I've been in combat. I watched my own father die. And I remained upright every time.

I push both hands through my hair, doing my best to breathe deeply as I close my eyes. *Food*, my mind rasps weakly. *You didn't eat anything all day.*

Too late for that, though. I have a job to do. Before I lose the ability to stand, I spin on my heel, intent on finding a quiet corner to make a few calls.

And there's Alice.

twenty-six

AT FIRST, I honestly think I'm imagining her.

She looks... like an angel. Floaty ice-blue tulle swishes around her legs and hugs the beautiful canvas of her cleavage.

A gown.

She was on her way to the party, after all.

It's sickening to think I was mad about her absence. All I have thought since they hauled Daniel's body away is *thank God Alice wasn't there*. I never would have wanted her to see that shit.

She must have left her house in a hurry. Her shoulders and arms are buried in a gray cardigan she clearly threw over her outfit before rushing out. It hides some of the curves I want to see, but that doesn't matter. Especially when she gets close enough for me to see her face.

Wide azure eyes beam up at me. They touch each part of my face, as comforting and tangible as any caress. For a moment, I let her look at me, just to feel it, even though I swear she's a mirage.

Her small, cool hand smooths over the sleeve of my formal shirt. "Marco? Are you alright?"

My chaotic emotions rise like a tide. Chagrin and concern mixed with relief. Both seep into my expression. "What are you doing here?"

Shyness colors her cheeks as she shrinks back. "I-I—" She blows out a little huff, frustrated with herself. "Tris t-told me the party was evacuated because s-someone had a *gun*. I just... I was scared for you."

I blink down at her, shocked. "Me?"

She clearly doesn't understand my disbelief. Confusion pinches her eyebrows, then quickly morphs into embarrassment. Her cheeks glow pink. "Y-yes? Tris said you were okay, but I wanted to try to do something to help, so..." She raises the arm twisted behind her back, offering a thermos and a takeout bag to me. "I thought you might be hungry."

When I continue to stare, she looks at her own hands, forehead furrowing as if she's made some sort of mistake. "I just figured you might be here late, and I thought you probably didn't get to eat anything, so I just—I thought—"

Of me.

When she heard there was an emergency, she thought of *me*.

No one ever does that.

People don't worry about me. I'm a good man in a storm. Others know, no matter what, I will soldier through.

But Alice is concerned. About *me*.

Lightning snaps through my center, an electric current that crackles in my blood. The surge short-circuits my brain and jolts my limbs into motion.

I haul her up, sweeping her body into mine and pinning her to the nearest wall. My lips find hers, crushing them under the weight of my desire and my desperation to get closer.

Alice gasps, letting me slip my tongue into her sweet mouth, sliding it against hers, tasting tea and mint. Her lush pink lips are even plumper than I realized during our one brief kiss. As they gently rasp over mine, an answering bolt of arousal hits below my belt.

I skim my hands down her sides, and a moan catches in her throat. I love that there's so much of her for me to touch, even if it's hidden under her sweater. My fingertips tingle, stroking soft, rippling curves that intensify the ache in my balls with every passing second.

Her free hand curls into the back of my tuxedo jacket, clinging to me while I ravage her with deep, licking kisses, beyond all rational thought. It doesn't help that every little shift presses her sweetly curved belly right into my rock-hard cock.

Some sort of alarm clangs in a nearby exam room, our surroundings intruding just long enough to burn off the fog of arousal blanketing my mind. I pull back slightly, panting and gazing down at her bewildered face.

The crinkle of the bag still clutched in her hand reminds me why I lost control so completely. A deep, hidden spot, buried in my chest, starts throbbing. My voice turns hoarse. "Thank you," I murmur, humbled.

As I take the takeout from her, her beautiful blush deepens. "It's a steak sub. I didn't know what to get you... But there's a salad in there, too. And chips. I hope it's okay."

A steak sub sounds incredible. As I stare at the bag and the thermos, it hits me; she bought the meal but brought my drink from her house. In a hot thermos. "Did you make me tea, too?"

She nods, blonde curls bobbing around her head. "It's the hibiscus one with spiced honey."

Shame and gratitude simmer in my middle. She shouldn't have paid for my dinner. I've seen the meager way she lives.

Despite the much-needed cash influx from Grayson, Alice has debts and business expenses.

She can barely afford to feed *herself*, but she sacrificed some of her limited budget for me. It makes her gesture even more touching. And impressive. Few people possess that sort of generosity.

Feeling protective of them, I curl my hands around her offerings. The hitch in my throat turns into a quiet rasp. "I don't deserve you, Alice," I confess, meaning every word. "But I'm starting to doubt that anyone could."

Her entire face changes. Softening into awe... before immediately turning stricken. "Marco..." She drifts back, putting space between us. Shaking her head sadly as her eyes drop to the floor. "I wish you would stop saying things like that."

"True things?" I reply, narrowing my eyes. "Or compliments. Because with you, they're one and the same, sweet girl."

Something almost like anger flashes through her gaze. "Like *that*! 'Sweet girl?' W-why would you ever need to call me that? Haven't I gone along with all of your requests and let you do your job since that day on the subway? I—I don't understand why you're still trying t-to—"

The only thing I've tried to do since that day is keep a professional distance.

And when that failed miserably... I was honest with Alice about my attraction to her. My opinion of her. My regard for everything about her.

My insides go numb as I realize. "This whole time... you thought I was manipulating you?"

Alice blinks those gorgeous crystalline eyes. "Yes," she whispers. "Obviously. Just like the day we met, at the coffee shop. It's —*I'm* your job." Her gaze trails over my hardened jaw. Her lashes flutter when I burn my focus into hers. "Ar-aren't I?"

OF ALL THE stupid mistakes I've made, underestimating Marco Amir might be the dumbest.

Or the most dangerous.

It's too easy to forget how deadly the man must be. He's always been a gentleman with me. Treating me like I'm delicate.

But now?

His dark eyes *blaze*. So full of fury and feeling. I suck in a silent gasp, trying to step back. The wall blocks me, and he follows, his big body crowding into mine.

His jaw flexes as he stares into me, lighting me on fire from the inside out. "*No.*"

I have to blink, forcing my mind to rewind. I asked him if this is really what I've always known it to be—part of his work. An elegant solution to keeping a close eye on me. Maybe, if Tris is right, a bit of flirting and fun on the job.

And he's saying—

"*No,*" he repeats, more vehemently. "Jesus, Alice. Is that really what you've been thinking this whole time? That I'm using my dick to lure you into letting me do my job?"

A fresh blush heats my face, the shame smoldering all the way to my core. Nausea flips my stomach—both from the mortification of being called out and the fact that, really... I let him use his good looks and gallant manners to lure me into letting him do his job. Exactly like he said.

There's something else, too. An insidious voice that tells me he's still conning me. Leading me on. Trying to gaslight me.

Because there's no way in hell this big, beautiful man would have any other reason to call me sweet girl. Or buy me muffins. Or tell me I'm perfect.

Right??

But then, why is he looking at me like this? As if I've wounded him to his very core—insulted his pride and his honor and maybe—

Maybe even hurt his feelings.

"Marco..." I start again, "I'm sorry. I just—"

None of this makes any sense to me.

I don't say the words, but Marco has an uncanny knack for knowing what I mean even when I can't form words. His brawny hand snaps up to my chin, clutching it as he stares down at me. "You want me to explain?" he roughs out. "Tell you how I hated myself for not being able to keep my distance from you that day at the coffee shop? Or how nervous I was showing up at your apartment last weekend?

"I tracked your laptop to the coffee shop because I couldn't damn well help myself. I went to your place last night just to spend ten fucking minutes with you—because it was the end of the week and there was only one person I wanted to see. Have I ever been anything but clear? I like you, Alice. More than I ever meant to. Because you *were* my job. And I should have stayed objective. But I fucking *couldn't*."

His fingers trail up my cheek, his thumb skirting across my lips as they part in shock. He presses his core to my belly, branding me with the thick heat pressing into his fly.

"My cock has been hard since you kissed me yesterday," he growls, his deep brown gaze sparking. "A man *died* tonight because I was so distracted by you."

He rubs his erection against me slowly, letting me feel it. "Do you think I could fake *this*?"

I try to speak, but I can't even swallow. A lifetime of longing and shame has my heart and my mind taking off in different directions.

Of course he's faking his attraction to me.

Unless he's actually everything I've ever wanted.

"I'm not a man who plays games with women he's interested in," Marco concludes, stepping back and dropping his hand.

I finally inhale, but I have no clue what I should say. Another apology? Or more interrogating questions?

The sad fact is, this *can't* be real. Because *I'm me*.

For the first time since we met, Marco doesn't wait to hear what I have to say. Instead, he straightens, casting a dark, hardened glance down my body.

"We'll have plenty of time to talk tonight," he determines, "because you're coming with me."

Going with him? As in, to his place?

Tonight?!

I finally manage a thick swallow. "W-why?"

Marco's lips kick up in his enigmatic half-smile. "Because,

according to you, your safety is my job. And, according to me, you're the woman I want in my bed. Either way, your apartment isn't safe tonight, so we'll have to go to mine. You can decide which of us is right on the way home."

twenty-eight

IT'S possible I've lost my mind.

So far, I don't miss it.

If I were my usual self—overthinking, strategizing, weighing the morality of every minor shift—there's no way I would have this trembling, beautiful woman next to me. Quivering in silence as I drive us to my apartment.

I tell myself it's the only way, knowing that's a lie. A flimsy one that would fall apart if I only pulled on a thread or two.

We could have stayed at the hospital. I could take her to a hotel. Or, hell, put her on one of our private planes.

But no. She's here because I *want* her here.

Because I need her to know *just how much* I want her here.

And, goddamn it, I do. Despite the knife she sank into my gut when she told me to stop calling her sweet girl, complimenting her, or kissing her...

I *want* to see her, listen to her, hold her.

I *want* to take her out and spoil her.

I *want* to stay in and curl up with her.

Hearing her quiet laughs and feeling her soft lips on mine. Stripping her out of her mismatched clothing and dragging my mouth over every creamy curve and rosy blush.

While I lead her into the elevator to the thirty-ninth floor and turn for the junior penthouse, urgency roars in my veins. Nudging me harder on every heartbeat.

Now. Now. Now.

As my front door swings open, I even start to tell her that her time is up—she has to choose which path we're going down.

But then I see her face.

Alice stands just outside the entrance, gaping with pure *awe*. Like she can't *believe* she's at my apartment. Or, maybe, like she can't believe *I'm* here with her.

She stares right up at me, her features open and vulnerable. Full of heartbreaking confusion and a tinge of shimmering *hope* that tears the breath from my lungs.

It's like I said before: I'm not worthy of a look like that. No one is.

Except maybe her. Despite everything she said at the hospital, Alice is still the purest, sweetest, wisest woman I've ever met. And so fucking *beautiful*, standing there with her heart on her sleeve and wariness in her eyes.

How can I stay mad at her?

Do I want to?

If anything, the fact that she thought I was duping her for the last three weeks only makes her more incredible. All that time, she must have felt sick to her stomach with shame and hurt… but she was kind. She welcomed me into her house and made me tea. She shared her books and her brain. She worried about me so much that she showed up tonight with dinner.

One I sorely needed, considering I wolfed it down in the time it took her to call Tris and use the ladies' room before we left.

Alice watches my throat work and catches the corner of her lower lip with her front teeth, worrying it. As if remembering where we are, she blinks quickly and then slides her gaze over the sparse furnishings half-filling the big, open space.

Her light laughter knocks the wind out of me. Dizzy relief rolls over us, breaking the tension stretched taut in the air.

"Oh boy," she giggles, the sound musical. "Need a new decorator?"

It's as bad as I thought, then. She smirks at my black leather sofa and the matching coffee table. Both of which could have come from a store exclusively for bachelors with no taste. Which, I suppose, is fitting.

I wonder if she notices my family's dining table and the way it doesn't coordinate with anything else. Or her—*extremely* erotic—book lying on my kitchen island with a bookmark situated toward the end.

"I'm hopeless." I mean the words as a joke. A dark one, for me, given how true I know they often feel.

Alice shrugs delicately, moving with her captivating blend of poise and deliberation as she picks her way around the living space. Curiosity gets the better of her, and she turns to the bedroom's double doors.

It's still just a bed, a dresser, and some milk-crate nightstands, but at least it looks clean. My years in the Army ingrained the habit of making my bed every morning.

I wave her on, holding back a smirk. Normally, getting a woman into one's bedroom is a game of sorts. I love that shit like that doesn't even occur to Alice.

Still thinking about décor, she happily floats down the hallway before jerking to a stop once she's inside. Her eyes widen at the array of weaponry laid out on my dresser. I hear the words she doesn't say.

That's a lot of guns.

When she looks back at me, I cock my head to the side and try for another wry smile.

Occupational hazard, baby.

Her answering grin flashes bright and burns out just as quickly. I hear a sticky, thick swallow. She looks down at her shoes and shifts, uneasy.

"A-about what I said before," she starts. "I really didn't mean to insult you. I'm so sorry I did."

"Alice." I move toward her, not stopping until I come close enough to mold my hand around her waist. The movement feels instinctive. It comes from some unfamiliar part of me that knows what she needs and aches to provide it.

I dare to drop my forehead to hers, relieved when she doesn't flinch. Her eyes fall closed on a tense sigh, and my chest aches. *She really doesn't believe this is real.*

"Do you want to tell me why you feel this way?" I ask, "Is there a reason you still don't trust me?"

She casts one quick glance at my face before lowering her head again. "I—It's not important."

"The hell it isn't," I murmur, turning her to bring us front-to-front. "You don't have to tell me if you don't want to, but I think all your thoughts are important."

I mean it. She isn't the kind of person to fill her brain with idle, meaningless chatter. She's brilliant and compassionate. Everything she's shared with me so far hints at fathomless depths.

I have no doubt they're as beautiful as they are unique. But I've barely scratched the surface. If I dare to dive, how deep does she go? Will she let me find out?

What the hell is holding her back?

Alice blows out a breath so quiet, most people probably wouldn't have heard the way it quivers. "I, uh... I'm embarrassed. I don't r-really know how things like this go. I haven't..."

I wait intently as she takes a moment to gather herself. Sometimes, Alice needs that. Just one fucking minute to process and piece her words together. People often don't give it her, and then they have the audacity to judge her for stammering or going silent. I will give her all the time she needs.

Finally, she exhales deeply and lifts her head, squeezing her eyes closed and pushing out words like ripping off a bandage. "I haven't been alone with a man in his bedroom in a few years. And the last time..." Her voice dips and shrinks. "I-I thought he liked me, but it turned out he... didn't."

I'll kill him.

I don't care that I don't even know the vague outline of the story yet. Anyone who puts that look on her face is getting strangled. Or shot.

"What—?"

She shakes her head, cutting off my growl. "It's not important," she says again. "Besides, I'm sure I'm completely misreading this whole—It's weird for me to think you even want to—I mean, you're probably tired, and I'm sure you don't even want to—"

The thread binding me to my honor snaps.

It was already frayed from days of aching for her and hours spent reading her dirty books. But the heavy realization that she will never believe I actually want her until I *show* her finally does me in. Untethered, I pull her body flush with mine and bend to hover my lips over hers.

"I *want* to fuck you."

The words are a breath, and Alice sucks them into her lungs on a gasp before I seal my mouth over hers.

Holy fuck.

She *blooms* for me.

The way a water lily opens—only under the dark cover of

night, and with a slow, luxurious sort of grace. The petals of her lips brush over mine so softly that tingles spark in my chest, racing down to rouse every nerve below my belt.

That easily, she has me.

My hand moves up the back of her arm, over her shoulder, and into the warm hair at her nape. As my fingers tangle in her curls, I press her face closer, slowly sliding my tongue over her full lower lip.

She surprises me again, gliding out to meet me instead of retreating. The tip of her tongue tastes mine with short, delicate touches. Teasing me.

A growl builds in my chest as I snatch her off the ground, hauling her lush warmth into my arms and turning to toss her onto my bed. A soft moan of surprise vibrates against my lips, but she doesn't break away. Her legs part for me while she slips her tongue around mine and locks her hands together at the back of my head.

I sink into her, groaning when my throbbing erection meets the softness between her thighs. I love the way she feels underneath me, her lush, feminine figure molding to all the planes of my body. Padding my hips, my abdomen, my chest. Her big, gorgeous breasts pressing into my shirt.

My hands roam up her sides, tracing the curves of her hips to the slight nip at her waist. Heat seeps from her body into mine, teasing my cock even more. When I shift and grind it into her hip, she gasps into my mouth.

"Your gun," she says. "You forgot to take it out of your pants."

Damn it, she's so cute. Grinning, I brush my nose along hers. "That's not a gun, sweet girl."

Her wide gaze flutters. "Oh."

"You're so warm and soft and curved. My body loves the feel of yours." It occurs to me that I'm not exactly displaying gallantry. I frame her face with my hands. "Do you want me to stop?"

Alice graces me with one of her hummingbird kisses. "No,"

she whispers into my lips, slowly tilting her lower half against mine. "I—I like it."

I watch in wonder as she tilts her hips against mine, gliding upward slowly, molding her core against my erection. Her hands trail over my torso with untold reverence, moving to unhook my buttons.

I still don't know why she's hesitating, but it's clear she doesn't trust me. Yet. She will, though. With every passing second, I am more determined. I will earn her.

I should be thinking about how.

But I can't see anything apart from the admiration gilding her blue irises as she pushes the shirt off my shoulders. She gasps again, a little louder than before. "Marco..."

She starts at my shoulder, trailing over the healed pock marks. Shrapnel scars. They're nearly invisible, but she feels them. Slowly and gingerly, her fingertips trace each one before gliding down to my chest.

Something about her touch tears right through me. My heart speeds while I absorb the guileless awe and concentration etched into her features. She looks mesmerized, memorizing pieces of me.

When she makes her way over each of my abs and skims the waistband of my pants, her pretty eyes flit up to my face, running over my expression on an anxious loop.

Which is when I notice the rusted smear along my hip.

Blood.

I didn't think I had any on me—my tuxedo pants must have hidden the worst of it. Part of me braces, expecting Alice to recoil. But she just exhales quietly, shaking her head.

"I'm so sorry you had to go through that."

There it is again; her selfless concern. For *me.*

An unfamiliar intensity burns through my body, spurring me onto my feet. With one hand, I flick the fly of my pants open, nodding over my shoulder.

Her breath shudders out of her as she tilts her head to take me in, her expression a compliment unto itself. No one has ever looked at me with so much raw desire, mixed with heartrending reverence. Wonder, almost.

It puts half a smile on my face as I walk backward. "I'm going to shower. If you make up your mind about what you want this to be, come find me."

twenty-nine

MARCO LEAVES the door wide open as he disappears into the ensuite. Clear as day, I hear his tuxedo pants falling to the floor. As I hold my breath, the shower sputters to life, filling the room with the echo of rushing water.

Paralyzed by disbelief, I sit on the edge of his bed, my fingers still burning from his heated skin. My mind reels, trying to come up with excuses for his actions, all the reasons I must be misinterpreting what pretty clearly seems like an invitation to join him in the shower.

Past experience tells me there is no way he actually *wants me.*

But isn't that the point of his challenge? Deciding if I can truly believe him?

I can still feel the pound of his heart against my palm, the way it leaped out to touch me through his flexing pectorals. And the hard throb of his erection, the heat of it radiating through his clothes and branding my thigh.

All of Tris's warnings about men and their expectations run through my brain.

Oh my God, I think stupidly. *He actually wants me.*

My body rejoices, humming with renewed desire as I scramble to my feet. I make it halfway to the bathroom door before I realize...

Oh my God. He's going to see me naked.

A spike of panic impales my lungs. No man has ever seen me totally naked... or even partially so, in the light. It was always dark, or I kept most of my clothes on.

Neither will work here.

I peek at the open door, assessing how bright the room will be. From my vantage point, I see a long built-in counter, the same gauzy gray as his kitchen's quartz. A wide rectangular mirror fills the wall above sinks, reflecting the open door, a towel rack, and the corner of the shower's fogged glass.

Glancing down at myself doesn't help. In that moment of self-doubt, my form-fitting gown highlights all my insecurities. My belly, my thighs, the rolls at the back of my waist. What if he sees all of them and doesn't want to see me naked ever again?

But, if I don't get in the shower with him now... will I ever get another chance? Is this my one and only opportunity to experience some of the things I thought I'd never have? How will I ever forgive myself if I let it pass me by without even trying?

I won't.

I can't tell if my hands or my breathing shake harder. Either way, I force shallow gasps in and out while I squeeze my eyes shut and peel off my dress. I leave it in a pile beside the door, along with my panties.

Focus on Marco, I tell myself. *He's in there, naked, too. Naked and wet and covered in all those muscles...*

Steam starts to billow over the glass enclosure, thickening the air. The scent of his body wash tightens my nipples, puckering them into buds. The pulse between my thighs sends tingles down my legs.

On an insane burst of lust-fueled bravery, I dart into the bathroom and open the shower door, revealing the large onyx tiles inside, along with the most gorgeous man to ever exist.

He is a statue come to life. Only better, because instead of dull stone, he's all warm bronze skin. With his back to me, my gaze works over the ripples and ridges of his massive shoulders, the slabs of muscle encasing his sides, his impossibly thick quads, and long, bulging calves. Not to mention his bare butt—which is every bit as chiseled and tight as the rest of him.

Marco stands with his palms pressed flat to the dark tile in front of him, his face turned up, the hot water streaming down his body. With his eyes squeezed closed and his chest expanding on deep breaths, he appears to be fighting off some unpleasant emotion.

I want to comfort him. My hands reach out, landing on either side of his spine. He stills for a beat as I slide them around his ribcage and step against his back. Before I can consider retreating, he drops his head—whether to look at my hands on his abdomen or because he's lost whatever internal battle he was waging, I don't know.

"Alice..." His voice is low and gruff as he shifts away from the wall, clasping each of his enormous hands over mine and leaning into my embrace. "You feel incredible."

I press my face against the center of his back, nuzzling all his strength. "So do you."

My reply is so quiet, I barely hear it. But I know he will. He always does.

To calm my nerves, I concentrate on the feel of his large, hard torso, reading its cues. Under our entwined hands, his chest moves too quickly, his breathing deep and fast. Soap slicks the skin under my palms. When I rub my hands over his abs, washing the ridges, he rumbles, the sound reverberating against my cheek.

I press closer, fitting my ungainly curves around the hard planes of his lower back... and the even firmer bow of his ass. As soon as I do, I feel the tension gripping him, the strain in his thighs.

It all clicks in my mind at once. He's so hard, his entire core has seized up. It sends me over the edge. The last of my fear disappears, evaporated by the heat burning low in my belly.

Leaving his hands behind, I ghost mine down the sides of his torso, to the deep grooves carved into the firm flesh of his hips. Without my sight, I follow the lines until a dusting of coarse hair tickles my fingertips.

Marco grunts, the sound pained. "Alice, you don't have to—"

I don't let him finish. I can't. I know if I don't act now, I will never get the nerve up again. Before he gets his gallant words out, I cup his cock, fisting my right hand at the base and stroking up.

A tremor runs through him as a foreign word sloughs up his throat, rough with unbridled emotion. Encouraged, I replace my right hand with my left, moving them in tandem, drawing one all the way up to the wide, throbbing head while the other clings to the base of his shaft, waiting for its turn.

Against the side of my face, his back muscles swell on a pant. "Fucking hell," he growls. "*Alice.*"

I feel feverish. Restless. My hips grind tight to his backside while his muscles flex on every tug, ticking against me. He spreads a brawny hand on the tile, bracing himself, and reaches the other around both of our bodies to fondle my ass. The second he touches me, a desperate, broken groan rips from his chest.

The serrated sound is tortured. So full of feeling, it tears at my heart. A familiar swell of tenderness floods me, the same one I felt when I saw his expression after I brought him dinner and made him tea.

I get the sense he's rarely on the receiving end of selflessness. He takes care of others, but who takes care of him?

Me, I decide. *I want it to be me.*

I kiss the spot between his shoulder blades and rub my cheek against his spine, gentling him. "I won't stop. I've got you."

He swells in my hands, pulsing so hard I feel every separate throb, even with the warm water sluicing over our skin. I notice the way his hips jerk every time I close my thumb and the side of my forefinger over his wide tip and double down, adding the motion to each pull.

A powerful gasp explodes from his lungs. His head falls back. "*Fuck*, Alice, how did you—" He loses his words on a particularly powerful stroke, moaning over the rest of his question.

No one understands losing their words better than me. I press more kisses onto his bare skin, not wanting him to feel self-conscious. Besides, the fact that he can't form a coherent thought feels like the sincerest form of flattery.

When his balls start tightening with every pass of my fingers, curiosity gets the best of me. I lean to the side, peeking around his broad back.

A fresh burst of molten heat trickles down my thighs as I take in the glorious length of his cock. It is slightly darker than the rest of him, with a thick purple head and veins beating up the sides.

An embarrassing mewl flies from my lips. I watch, fascinated, as my fists move in succession, rubbing him harder, only slowing to roll over the place where his shaft meets the tip with extra care.

Unable to bear the heavy tingles in my breasts, I rub my nipples against the side of him, moaning quietly at the sensation of our wet skin slipping together.

Marco likes it, too. The hand spread over one whole cheek of my ass clenches, his blunt nails biting into me while he groans my name again. Bucking forward, he sets a slightly quicker pace, and I follow, slipping down his length faster than before, squeezing the head on every pull.

Jagged breaths shudder out of him. I brush my lips over his

shoulder, his spine, his side. When I wrap both fists around his cock and lightly suck just below his nape, his muscled frame locks down.

"I'm going to come," he growls, pumping his hips harder. "Alice—God, baby—I'm going to come so hard."

With one final nip of my teeth, I bend to watch while he finally unravels, sliding into my clutched hands one final time before spilling. His release gushes over my fingers, propelling thick bursts of white onto the black tile in front of us.

When he's finished, I carefully let go, holding my hands out to let the water wash them before I hold him from behind.

Marco completely freezes, barely even breathing.

thirty

I AM WRECKED.

Undone. Obliterated.

I've been with more women than I care to admit, and I've done things far more intense than a hand job in the shower.

But no one has ever made me *feel* so much.

I can't fucking *breathe*.

It wasn't just the way she touched me—as if she somehow read every twinge in my body and spoke its silent language. It was the way she nuzzled her cheek against my back. Her sweet, quiet reassurances.

She *gave.* So much more than just her hands on my skin.

I move all at once, spinning and snapping her into my arms. Hitching her legs around my ribs, banding my arms under her ass, and burying my face into her throat.

Shaking, I press tender kisses along the curve. Alice wraps her forearms around my nape, combing through my wet hair.

Hot water rains over us while I pant into her neck. Turning, I feel the tile to make sure it isn't too cold and then press her into it, balancing with her legs twined around my waist and my face buried against her.

Ordinarily, I could do squats for half an hour with her strapped to me. But my knees are weak from the force of the climax she coaxed from me. And I want to make her come.

As soon as I've regained control of my faculties.

I can't believe how *good* I feel. Most sexual encounters leave me uncomfortably sober, mired in some dark, disjointed disappointment that hits almost the instant my orgasm ends. I remember it so clearly—the sudden, fierce urge to be alone.

Being with Alice could not be more *different.*

My body hums, heavy and sated. Intense euphoria clouds my mind, obliterating everything aside from relief and gratitude and Alice.

I want to sink into her and never resurface.

And she lets me.

Instead of turning to her own needs or rebuilding the walls that lie in rubble around us, Alice holds me. She weaves her delicate fingers into my hair, gently soothing me while I recover from the tumult flipping my thoughts inside out. After a few moments, she moves on to the tight muscles in my shoulders, massaging them, even though her wicked hand job has already stripped every bit of tension out of my body.

I want to praise her and thank her and give her everything she's given me. But every time I try to form words, my throat feels too thick. And the longer she hugs me, the more I need her not to let go.

I'm decimated. And completely at the mercy of little blonde Alice, with her magic fingers and her hummingbird kisses. Her deliciously slippery skin. The molten heat of her core searing the spot above my navel.

Am I... getting hard? *Again?*

I can't recall a single occasion in my life when I've finished and recovered so quickly. But thinking about Alice's naked pussy pressed into my abs does it. One day, I will get her off by rubbing her over them until she can't take it anymore. That will make every abdominal workout I've ever done more than worth it.

I go from nuzzling her neck to kissing it, lightly sucking beads of water off her creamy skin. Her hands pause mid-massage while her breath hitches, thrusting her chest into my pecs.

I leverage myself upright, finally taking in the glory of her naked breasts, drenched and on display. They are bigger than I imagined. Large enough to fill my hands and spill out of my grasp, which is saying something.

I almost smile when I see the pink of her nipples. Just as I suspected the day I found her in her towel, they *do* match her lips. And the combination is truly striking.

All cream and roses and soft, luscious woman. She's so fucking pretty. Stunning, especially with the dark tile behind her, playing up the pale glow of her skin and her curls.

While I stare, Alice's mouth hangs ajar, dragging in loud breaths. Her blue eyes widen and blink, projecting innocence and hunger.

My shy, sweet girl. Something about her gets to me in a way nothing and no one else ever has. She slips right between my ribs, sails through my heart, and sinks into my soul.

Before, it bewildered me. I didn't understand it, so I couldn't enjoy it. But here, in this moment of vulnerability, I don't *want* to understand how or why she got in there. I just want her *to stay*.

The scalding water has cooled to a comfortable warmth. I lap it off her skin, bending to follow the curve of her breast. She arches her back, gasping when I suck one furled nipple between my lips and tug.

I hold her steady with one arm banded around her soft, thick waist. The other hand reaches for the full curve of her ass, kneading the supple skin while I make my way to my ultimate goal.

The place between her thighs is silky and hot. I run my bent finger over her, parting her lips to graze my knuckle against the bud pulsing at the top of her folds.

"You're such a good girl, aren't you, Alice? Getting so wet for me."

Another breathless sound slips out of her. "Marco," she cries. "Please!"

A roar builds in my chest when I touch her clit, feeling it pulse. It's wide enough for me to press two fingertips over it, working it with both pads at the same time.

With my thumb, I trace along her lower lips, skimming back to dip into the liquid desire pooled at her opening. She's so tight, I have to gently twist my way in. The second I do, a slick rush gushes over my hand. The sensation rips the air from my lungs just as a cry tears from hers.

"Is that good, sweet girl?" I nip at her throat and brush my lips up to her jaw. "God, you sound beautiful when you moan for me."

The hands gripping my hair tug harder. Another moan echoes through my bathroom, louder. I hide a smile against her shoulder. For all of her stammering and mumbles, my sweet girl can get *loud*.

I fucking love it.

"Look at you," I groan into her ear. "I've never seen anything so perfect."

This time, she *keens*. And gasps my name again, tightening her legs, squeezing closer. Her reactions finally click in my mind, reinforcing something I've suspected since the first night I went to her apartment.

Praise.

She doesn't just *like* it. It *gets her off.*

Alice wants to be told just how amazing she is while I make her come.

I am so turned on by the thought, I move to kiss her, wanting to swallow her sounds after I say, "Just like that. Good girl, Alice."

Our open mouths settle in a graceless graze, our tongues meeting in shallow flicks and deeper plunges while she mewls. Her slick essence runs down my hand. Her clit throbs under my touch, and she comes all over my fingers.

For all her moaning and screaming before, she only lets out the smallest whimper while her pussy spasms around my touch. I hear it, though. And the sound sends a vicious throb of joy through my chest.

Her body melts in my arms. Our eyes meet through the fog steaming up the shower stall.

The ecstasy hazing her blue irises fills me with pride. She blinks, fluttering her lashes the way she tends to when she gets nervous. She opens her mouth to speak, but stops as her gaze roams over my features, collecting clues as to my thoughts. Instead of speaking, her lips start to tremble.

I understand. I don't know *what* I understand, but an overwhelming rush of feeling presses against the wall of my chest, too, rising up to block my throat.

I drop my forehead to hers, cupping her jaw in my hands, trailing my fingers up to her hair. Something inexplicable passes between us while we stare through the fog.

Keeping her pressed between my body and the wall, I eventually reach for her hands and gently soap them, tracing a tiny smudge of blue paint along her thumbnail. I smile involuntarily—even her stray streaks of paint are sexy. More evidence of all the secret depths I get to see up close.

And I don't know what Alice's final decision about me will be.

But I know mine.

I'm going to keep her.

thirty-one

REMEMBER when I said Marco Amir was dangerous?

Well.

I stand on the threshold of his living room, with my mouth hanging open as he takes a phone call. The morning sun shines through the apartment's picture windows, burnishing the golden skin of his back while he—

Makes tea.

"—understand that. But until I have full confidence that the danger has passed, I'm afraid I must insist."

I bite down on a goofy grin. Whoever he's talking to is getting the gruff, no-bullshit Marco who pinned me to the hospital hallway last night. I'm sure they would never know he's practically naked, in only a snug pair of black boxer-briefs...

Sporting scratch marks on his shoulders.

Oops.

I try my best to quell my embarrassment, but it's only one item on a pile. After all, I have no makeup or hair products to fix the effects of our late-night shower. Not wanting to put my dress back on left me with no choice but to don the clean white T-shirt he left out. It fits, but the way it hugs my hips, belly, and chest makes me feel a bit more jiggly than I bargained for.

Even though I look like something that got caught in a drain, Marco still grins as he turns toward me, holding out a mug.

"Not as good as yours," he mouths, then frowns sideways at his phone. "I'm sure it's not my place to tell you," he snaps, then rolls his eyes. "Goodbye, Tris."

Tris?

I nearly drop my cup of tea when I balk. Marco tosses his phone onto his island, rolling his shoulders as if my roommate has thoroughly stressed him out.

"What was that about?" I whisper.

"You," he replies, quiet but easy. He bends to kiss my forehead, nuzzling there. "More specifically, keeping you safe."

His dark eyes swirl, beaming with intensity. "It isn't safe for you to go back to your apartment for now. We can have the police clear the paparazzi gathered there this afternoon, to allow you some time to grab whatever you need... but you have to find somewhere else to stay until the media frenzy dies down."

There's more he wants to say—I see it germinating in my mind as he assesses me, weighing my expression. I do my best to breathe through my anxiety, nodding minutely. "A-alright. I suppose I could rent a room with Tris or—maybe stay at Ella's for a few nights?"

They have space, but I wince at the thought of intruding on my clients in that way. Renting a room for the week would be expensive, though. Not to mention living in one shared space with Tris...

Marco's brows snap lower. "I thought you might consider staying here. With me."

IT TURNS out Marco can be *very* persuasive.

The blend of panty-melting authority and genuine concern bowled me over before I had even finished my tea.

It's a little after noon by the time he gets the call he's been waiting for—his men have helped the police clear the hordes of paparazzi camped out in front of my apartment, hoping to get a statement from me about the party I didn't even attend. They're keeping the sidewalk cordoned off at either end of the block until we get there and do what we need to do.

Marco drives one of the Stryker & Sons' company cars, a white Mercedes like the one we used last night. When he takes me down to his garage—dressed in a pair of rolled-waist joggers and a borrowed hoodie—I see a whole row of vehicles just like it, all in various sizes. Parked alongside one truly terrifying black sports car.

Thankfully, the ride to my place doesn't take long. Marco insists on parking and walking me up, intent on securing the whole place himself and finally installing his remote cameras while I pack.

We're in the midst of another philosophical debate while we climb the stairs, Marco nodding along as I make a point. He suddenly freezes. His eyes snap forward, locking on something I'm not tall enough to see yet.

"Down."

He hisses the command at the same second he strikes out his arm and pushes me into the wall of the stairwell. Before I can breathe, his body flattens mine, back-to-front. I fight to fill my lungs, choked by shock and the unexpected impact of his broad back.

His protective stance feels severe enough to keep me from asking any questions. My fingers automatically twist in the fabric of his black T-shirt—the same one I slept in.

He moves with practiced efficiency, reaching his right hand to his left hip and drawing a gun I hadn't realized he had hidden. His other hand dips into his back pocket and extracts a magazine of bullets. In a single smooth motion, he locks it into the handgun and clicks the safety off.

For just one moment, he hesitates. His dark eyes leap from whatever he saw on my landing to the empty stairway behind us and the empty street beyond.

"Damn it," he mutters quietly. "Alice? You're going to have to stay behind me. Can you do that?"

I feel like I've swallowed my tongue. But I nod.

"Good girl," he murmurs. "Hold on to my shirt just like that. If I say 'down' again, you hit the floor. Got it?"

With one more bob of my head, he starts to slink up the last flight of stairs. When we reach the landing, I see what all the fuss was about: there is no sign of Tris... but our apartment door hangs open ominously.

Marco moves with capable grace, slipping into the living room without making a sound. I try to step where he does and keep my breathing shallow while he clears the room, thoroughly checking every corner, behind all the doors, in each closet—even on the other side of our shower curtain. He finally lowers his gun and flicks the safety back on.

Footsteps angry, he storms to the front door and slams it shut. I finally manage to force some air down my narrow throat, glancing around.

Everything looks normal. Untouched.

Damn it, Tris.

"Maybe the wind blew the door open?" I squeak, embarrassed. "Tris sometimes forgets to lock up."

Marco stays rooted to his place in the middle of the room, facing away from me. His shoulders rise and fall while he breathes hard, staring straight ahead.

"Marco?"

My voice snaps him out of it. He exhales before he turns and opens his arms, waiting for me. I hug him, letting him wrap his strength around my body. "I reacted on instinct," he whispers. "I'm sorry if I scared you. I—"

It's rare for him to lose his words. I lean back, reading his face. He stares down at me, his features full of confusion and worry. "I need you to be *safe*," he finishes, fervent. "I always did, but it feels different, now."

My heart trembles. Will I ever get used to him being so forthright? Saying such beautiful things? I'm still convinced I'll wake up any minute and find myself on the sidewalk beside Ella's subway stop with a lump on my skull.

"Okay," I assure softly. "I'll be safe."

He scowls while he looks around my place, as if not totally trusting it. "I'm putting up those cameras. Now. Pack your things, sweet girl. Bring anything you wouldn't want to lose or have strangers rifle through. Just in case."

I hide a smile. He's a bit overprotective. And a touch on the pessimistic side. Though I suppose that's how he keeps everyone safe.

He really does carry the weight of the world on his shoulders. Only he does it so gracefully, I doubt anyone else ever notices. I'm grateful I have.

Stretching up on my toes, I press a kiss to his jaw. "Yes, sir."

thirty-two

YES, *sir.*

Alice's breathy, teasing voice loops through my mind again, leaving another dumb smile on my face as I sort through the shit-storm on my desk.

The weekend's events left me with a hell of a lot of paper-work. I'm grateful I forced myself to keep to my routine, waking early and working out before heading to the office to greet the dawn.

It was harder than most mornings. Harder than *ever*, perhaps.

Leaving Alice on her own went against every protective

instinct rumbling in my middle. I knew I had to, though. Despite the way she gave in to me on Saturday night, the woman clearly doesn't trust our situation at all. I can't blame her, given how quickly everything's changed.

Still, I'd be lying if I said I hadn't wrestled with the stab of disappointment all night. She chose to stay in the one guest room that has any furniture, snuggling on the spare sofa in there and falling asleep with a book in her hand.

I might have chalked it up to a coincidence—we didn't sleep much the night before, after all—but I noticed the tidy way she kept all her things stacked beside the door. As if ready to be asked to leave at any moment.

It would frustrate me if it didn't make my chest ache.

The tablet propped up beside my computer flickers. I lean closer, narrowing my eyes as the feed of Alice's apartment hallway refocuses.

Damn it. Nothing.

I know she wants me to let the whole open-door incident go, but I can't. Which I know is insane, given the amount of real work I have to take care of. I just can't shake the feeling that there's a missing piece at play here.

Why would someone go into her apartment if they didn't intend to ransack it or steal anything? And why leave the door open if their hands weren't full?

Leaning back in my leather chair, I scowl at my subpar cup of tea from the downstairs café and swipe open the contact I need. Pierce answers on the fourth ring, clearly fresh out of sleep. "What do you need, boss?"

I need him to tap into the street cameras on Alice's block and pull any footage showing someone entering or exiting her stairwell from the last week. I also ask him to look for an angle that will give us a view of the building's fire escape.

Then I tell him I want the names of every guy who has been added and subsequently deleted from Alice's social media accounts in the previous four years. I have a hunch.

If Pierce hears the venom in my voice, he doesn't let on. He just takes down all the information I want and promises to get back to me within the hour.

I hang up and stare at my phone. Hating myself for what I have to do next. Making the call anyway.

"Everett," Graham answers, most decidedly awake. I hear him muffle the speaker. "Shh, *Bijou*, behave yourself. I'm on the phone."

Hell. Aren't they supposed to be getting ready for work? I don't need to hear this. "Everett? It's Amir."

"Yes," he snorts, "Marco, I know. You don't have to say your name every time you call."

I hear a slap and a squeal. *God, give me strength.*

"So... hit me," Graham goes on. "I'm moving into my new office space today, and my assistant—while very sexy—keeps distracting me."

As ever, I have to admire his audacity. The guy has absolutely no shame and balls as big as his ego. Which makes my next request especially hard to scrape out.

"Flowers," I grit. "I need to know where you get my cousin her flowers every week."

I should have known he'd be a dick. He could have just given me the name of the florist graciously, like a gentleman. But then he wouldn't be Graham Everett.

"Hmmm," he drawls. "Flowers? Whoever for?"

"Everett," I growl. "Mind your own business and give me the name of the shop."

Graham chuckles darkly. "Marco, where are your manners? I didn't hear the magic word. And you didn't answer my question. Who are you buying flowers for?"

Next time I see the bastard, I'm going to dead-leg him.

"A woman, okay?" I snap. "I need flowers for a woman I'm seeing. Please don't tell Juliet."

He makes a tsking sound. "Can't help you there, *primo*. I would never lie to our formidable Miss Rivera. If she asks me why you called, I'll tell her the truth. But I'll convince her to be discreet, of course."

Honestly, how can I be mad? Do I *want* him to lie to my baby cousin?

"Don't call me *primo*," I mutter. "Ever. So? The florist?"

"Eh." I can picture his signature shrug. "What sort of cousin would I be if I didn't make time for your personal problems? Tell me about this mysterious lady of yours. Where have you been hiding her?"

"You gossip like an old woman," I grunt. "No wonder Abuelita likes you so much."

Graham laughs again. "Fine, fine. I actually do have to go, so I'll text you that name. Though, depending on her location, you might be better off asking someone closer... and, depending on the girl, you might be better off with chocolates or jewelry. Lingerie, even."

Cristo. The bastard is digging. "Just text me the name," I demand, unwilling to divulge any more information. "And Everett?"

"Yeah?"

I hesitate, knowing I may be crossing a line, but feeling an instinctual pull, I blow out a deep breath. "I think you should stop by Stryker's at some point today. Grayson might want someone to talk to after this weekend."

Surprised silence swells over the line. "Understood," he finally says, appropriately solemn. "I'll send my recommendations your way. Get ready to pay out the ass. I have *very* expensive taste."

He hangs up. I try to ignore the awkward tug in my chest. Gratitude and... amusement? *Carajo.* Am I actually starting to like *el pinchao*?

By the time the sun peeks over the next building, Everett comes through. Links to three different florists—Downtown, Midtown, and Uptown—as well as web pages for Dean & DeLuca and something called Agent Provocateur.

Perhaps the pretty boy has a point. Alice arranges flowers as part of her job. She probably has opportunities to bring bouquets home all the time. If I forgo flowers, that leaves some sort of dessert or...

Lingerie.

I remember the collections of frilly photos on Alice's computer, saved on a secret Pinterest board. *She would like something beautiful. It would make my romantic interest in her clear. Maybe not anything* leather... *Not yet.*

My mind keeps doing that. Thinking of Alice in the future tense.

And I like it.

thirty-three

I'VE NEVER SLEPT at a man's place before, so I can't be certain...

But I'm pretty sure it isn't normal to wake up to a *gift*.

By the time I stagger into Marco's kitchen, his condo is still and silent. Given that I can't even catch a whiff of his cologne, I'm guessing he left well before the sun came up.

Part of me is relieved, at first. This situation feels so awkward —I barely had half a day to wrap my head around this man wanting me in any capacity... and now he won't let me leave?

Should that make me giddy or nauseous?

Split the difference?

My mouth dries when I find the things he left on the counter beside his stove. A teapot, a mug... and this gorgeous silver gift box.

The note on top is undeniably from him. Bold, slashing, and masculine.

GOOD MORNING, SWEET GIRL—

TO MAKE UP FOR FLATTENING YOU IN THE HALLWAY YESTERDAY, I LEFT YOU A PRESENT THIS MORNING

The wrapping looks... *sensuous*. And expensive. I turn the metallic box in my hands, admiring the black satin ribbon around it.

The second I touch it, I know it cost him a pretty penny. The fabric is thick and luxurious. A subtle damask pattern textures the iridescent cardboard. When I see the label emblazoned on the box underneath the paper, my heart stutters.

Agent Provocateur.

Most decidedly *not* a casual gift between friends.

With a thick throat and a pulse in my core, I sift through the tissue, unearthing a delicate silk robe. The fabric slides right through my fingers, as thin and fine as a cool breeze. Handmade lace adorns each sleeve, its meticulous loops forming frothy floral patterns.

I've never been given anything so exquisite or luxurious. Not to mention *sexy*.

I don't know what it means. But I know I *love* it.

My cheeks hurt from grinning when the phone in my hoodie buzzes. I jump, fishing it out with my heart thumping all the way to my fingertips.

Marco Amir, the screen reads.

My lungs feel fluttery as I stammer, "H-hello?"

I hear a smile in his voice. "Hi," he says. "Good morning."

"It certainly is," I giggle, gazing down at my present. "I've never woken up to a *gift* before. It's... too beautiful for words, Marco. Truly. Thank you so much."

Satisfaction warms his reply. "It was my privilege. I'm glad you like it."

"I *love* it," I emphasize, still unsure how to adequately express my gratitude. "I—I don't think I've ever owned anything so lovely. I want to put it in Plexiglas and hang it on my wall."

The moment the words escape, I hang my head, mortified. *Oh dear Lord.*

Then I remember the cameras—*he can* see *me*—and blush all over again.

But Marco's heated chuckle sends a shiver down my spine. "Don't do that," he murmurs, a low rasp tickling my ear. "Then I won't be able to see you in it."

I nearly gulp. "O-okay."

"Maybe tonight," he says casually, as if the idea doesn't make me ache. "In the meantime, how about dinner later? I can pick something up and bring it home after work. Anything you want."

As Tris would say: my flabbers are gasted.

Is this man real? Did I actually wake up this morning?

"W-whatever you like is fine," I peep.

"Hmm." He sounds stern. "That won't work, sweet girl. Because I want whatever *you* want."

I have to bite my lip to keep from grinning like a loon. "Maybe Chinese?"

I hear him smiling, too. "Exactly what I wanted."

With a giggle, I swipe out of the call and into my planning app. "Just let me check my calendar."

The iCal app looks clear, but a message leaps from the bottom of my screen, displaying the one name that sinks my stomach. Hovering over a single text.

We'll speak tonight at 6.

"What's wrong?" Marco asks, sensing my anxiety. Or possibly seeing it. "You okay?"

"I-I'm fine," I lie. "No big deal."

"FOR THE LOVE OF FUCK," Tris moans, "you have *got* to calm down. You look like a cartoon character. Is your head about to spin off in an animated cloud of smoke, Alley Cat?"

"Don't call me that," I snap, adjusting the angle of my phone. "How about now? Can you still tell I'm not at home?"

Tris blinks, wide-eyed, then winces. "Babe, that place is like the Fortress of Solitude. There's no way she'll think that's our apartment."

I know she's right. My mother has eyes like a hawk. If I dared to move an end table in my living room, she would have something to say about it.

Tris has confirmed that our apartment is still surrounded by media leeches, though. She tried to go home after work and wound up heading back to whichever guy she's staying with. Which leaves me no choice but to FaceTime Mama from Marco's condo.

Dejected, I hunch my shoulders with a groan. "She's going to have a million questions."

"Bitch, I have a million questions!" Tris chimes. "Like how the hell did you end up in a hostage situation with the city's sexiest bodyguard? And also, can I come watch?"

I glower, and she laughs at her own joke, adding, "But seriously. Don't think I haven't noticed your new robe."

The humiliating truth is that I've worn it all day while working from the enormous, mostly empty apartment. I know I should get dressed like a normal person, but every time I go to change out of it, I hear Marco's rumbled words.

Maybe tonight.

Still, I can't wear it for my call with Mama. She will lose her—

"*Shit!*" I hiss as my screen flickers. "She's early."

You know it's bad when Tris doesn't have anything funny to say. Her hazel gaze widens. "May God have mercy on your soul, Alice Moore." Then, before clicking off, "And tell Thundercunt I said hi!"

Shit, shit, *shit*.

Tris's call disappears, leaving my mother's. Ringing.

I make a mental list of things to brace myself for. Aside from being in a strange man's apartment, she also hasn't seen that I changed my hair. I need to somehow rush her off the call in less than twenty minutes if I want to keep Marco from crossing paths with her. And I still haven't decided how to answer if she makes any snide comments about my—nonexistent, as far as she is concerned—dating life.

Little does she know.

Maybe tonight.

Have I mentioned—*SHIT?!*

Frantic, I run my eyes over the area around me, searching for any scrap that might set Mama off. She will take advantage of anything she sees to lecture me—the title of a romance novel, a new article of clothing in the "wrong" shade, carbs.

I re-angle my phone screen, ensuring she will only see my face and the boring gray wall behind me. *Maybe I could say I'm at work? In someone's office?*

... in a robe?

If she only knew that a full-blown single man had it waiting for me this morning.

Doo-dooo-doo-doop-doop-dah-doo. The ringtone skips, then starts up all over again. I jump to answer, knowing that every missed chime will only make Mama more difficult.

Sure enough, as the screen flickers and fills with a view from my mother's prized black granite kitchen, a perfectly made face scowls back at me.

Once upon a time, my mother was a striking woman. She even won pageants, if the photos on her mantle were to be believed. Nowadays, she wears a lot of makeup and keeps her signature bob shellacked into a helmet of blonde.

At least Richard is out golfing or something.

"*Alice Lillian Moore.*" Mama's voice rings through the room, softly Southern and breathy with indignation. "*What* is going on?"

thirty-four

I SHOULDN'T BE HOME YET.

After a hellish day fighting through crowds ten men deep, I planned to sneak in another workout before I came upstairs.

It seemed polite, too. I know Alice has a call with her mother —and I suspect she isn't ready to explain any of this to her yet. Especially since Alice can't seem to accept any of it herself.

That's a mystery I need to unravel. After her breathless gratitude over this morning's gift, I'm more convinced than ever that wanting what I'm offering isn't the issue. Which means there must be something else.

Despite my burning curiosity, I had decided to give her as much time and space as I could stand. I practically kidnapped the woman and dragged her back to my place like a pillaging Viking. Letting her go about her business without my eyes glued to her every move seemed the least I could do.

Well. The best laid plans.

Perhaps I should have taken the whole "give my skittish, sweet girl space" concept into account before I picked out that goddamn robe. Because once she put it on...

I definitely checked the cameras more than I should have.

It's almost become a reflex, at this point. Sliding my home security app open, checking on her. Making sure she's still quietly singing to herself while she works and hasn't escalated into an anxious humming frenzy.

I do it as I walk onto the elevator, pausing halfway to pressing the button for the building's gym level.

Alice is there, sitting at my kitchen table—but she's biting her nail to the quick, wincing as she listens to whoever is FaceTiming her. Since she's still wearing her new gift, I'd guess it's her mother or Tris on the other end of the call. When she flinches, her shoulders hunching with shame, instinctive fury pours through me. I smash the button for the thirty-ninth floor without thinking at all.

I know how to keep my entry silent, carefully maneuvering the door and my footsteps so I don't disturb Alice. The second I enter my apartment, a shrill voice edged with a Southern accent sails down the hall. I only catch bits and pieces at first.

"*... start explaining yourself!*" the voice insists. "*Why on Earth would you be in a man's apartment?*

I grit my teeth, pushing back the urge to walk right in and explain *exactly* why.

Because I brought her here.

And I'm damn well keeping her as long as she lets me.

My deep-seated possessiveness knocks me back a step. *Jesus.* This woman isn't even mine. Not yet. Not even *close.*

There's a distinct chance she won't ever get over the way we met. How she believed I was just a stranger, flirting with her, and how humiliated she felt when she found out I had an ulterior motive.

The depressing thought seems all too likely when I turn my head, peering into the guest room she slept in.

It's virtually untouched. And I notice she hasn't brought any of her art supplies or extra books.

Meaning she doesn't plan to stay very long.

"Can you sit up straight for one measly minute? Your posture is distracting me, Alice. And I deserve an explanation! My God, what have you done to your hair?"

If I'm trying to impress this woman, telling her mother to go fuck herself probably isn't the best place to start.

I only walk into my guest room to keep myself from charging into the kitchen and snatching up her phone. Fresh guilt swamps me as I examine what little she brought with her. Just one vanity case, her work bag, and—oh. What I thought was a duffel bag is actually a fabric hamper of clothing.

There's a dryer sheet stuck to one of her socks. She must have grabbed the basket of clean laundry because it was faster than packing a proper bag.

"And get your thumb out of your mouth. It's horribly unbecoming."

So is your voice, pero loca, I think as I start to fold Alice's clothes. Intent to at least stack them for her.

"I'm not surprised no one will hire you when you can barely scrape out a basic explanation."

My fists wrap around one of Alice's dresses, flexing against the impulse to stomp out to the living room.

Someone did *hire her*, I mentally growl at the faceless woman berating my sweet girl. I heard Ella tell Grayson that Alice has more work on the way, too. One of their wealthy acquaintances is planning their own high-profile wedding. I can't wait for Ella to let Alice know so I can tell her how proud I am.

The clothes in the hamper quickly dwindle, revealing a few items she must have tucked underneath to hide them. A smile spreads across my face when I see that she did bring some of her wicked paperbacks. *Her Errant Earl*, this time. My smile widens into a grin. *Along with a pirate one that has the word* Swashbuckler *in the title.*

Fuck, that's cute.

So is the last item in the basket—a shoebox, wrapped in separate layers of ancient pink-heart-speckled wrapping paper.

It's cute. Innocent. The kind of thing a teenager might do. Very Alice, too, to randomly decorate a box. She has little craft projects like that spread around her place.

It feels light enough to be empty. I don't think twice about opening it; I figure I can use it to store the socks and panties I rolled up.

" Mama," Alice says, "I-I can't really t-talk right now—"

"So dramatic with the stammering, Alice," the woman mutters back. *"Am I really so horrible to talk to? It's simple—tell me where you are and why you're there. In a robe, of all things. With your hair in absolute disarray."*

Does her mom seriously care what she does with her *hair*? What *for*? Is Alice just expected to cower to the woman's insistence on picking her apart?

I pick up a wad of socks, then freeze.

I wasn't prepared. I didn't expect to find anything in the shoebox.

Let alone the assortment of papers that stare up at me, looking faded and long-forgotten.

What is all of this?

My investigative instincts take over. With care, I lift each piece of paper up, examining closely.

Clippings from wedding magazines and travel articles. Honeymoon packing tips. Lingerie ads. Reception setups. Flowers, candles, cakes. Hawaii, Bermuda, the Bahamas. Baby names.

She has lists, written in a young girl's handwriting. They are all hopeful and achingly innocent. One anthologizes all the things she wishes would happen on her honeymoon. Most are simple, easy things like ordering room service or watching the sun set. My heart clenches at the dates in the margins, which place them some-time in her high school years.

A vise tightens around my throat. The most recent ones are from her early college years. I can see a marked difference. They're more dubious than the childhood lists. Instead of presuming she would eventually get a wedding and honeymoon, they focus on dating in general.

"Romantic Dates," one reads. Then, a few pages later, *"Ideas for Surprises."* But none of them are meant for her. They are all thoughts of things she might do for someone else, should she ever have a partner.

The last few take a darker turn. Dated around the end of her university tenure, they no longer mention love or romance at all. Instead, there are ways she might improve herself or make herself more attractive. One even lists foreplay skills she wants to master.

The final sheet physically pains me. It isn't dated at all, but it has water stains sprinkled over the lines. *Tears.*

I don't see a title, so I start to skim the bullet points. Most are short, just a few words apiece. *Holding my own baby*, one says. *Picking out a wedding dress. Making love.*

The floor falls out from under me.

It's a list of all the things she thinks she'll never have, things she's tried to let go of.

All her hopes. She hid them away. From the world. From herself. Because someone convinced her that they were embarrass-ing. And impossible.

Who the fuck did this to her?

Alice Moore has never hurt anyone in her life. But she must have been hurt badly.

Have I made that pain worse? Should I have left her in peace?

Would I even have been able to?

Deep, true shame cuts me to my marrow, throbbing like an

open wound carved into my diaphragm. Tension grips my neck and shoulders while I clutch the papers, unsure how to proceed.

Should I read the lists? Maybe they will give me ideas for how to make her happy. *But it would be an invasion of privacy.*

Alice's voice sails down the hall on a cry that lifts the hairs on the back of my neck. "Mama," she says, her voice underwater, "Can you just listen, p-please? My hair isn't even d-done right now."

"Isn't done?!" the older woman screeches. *"It's* hideous. *Isn't your face chubby enough without adding a perpetual cloud of frizz around it?"*

She lets her cruel question hang in the air for a moment before layering false woe into her voice. *"Oh, Alice, you have to think about these things! I know your genes didn't help. You got your father's horrible nose, his eyebrows... and that* figure, *ugh. There's no help for any of* that, *but your hair is another matter entirely! I try so hard to help you, and you defy me at every turn! Now, hang up and go brush out those ridiculous curls. They make you look cheaper than dollar-store hooch."*

...

I think the fuck not.

This bitch is lucky I can't shoot her through Alice's phone.

My rage roars. I quickly fix the lid on the shoebox and slide it into the hamper. Then I muss up all the clothing I folded, putting it back the way I found it. Alice never needs to be embarrassed about me seeing this.

An instant before I rush out into the hall, their call ends with a telltale thud. I stop short on the threshold, surprised to find her seat at the table empty.

A sniffle pricks my ears. I follow it into my bedroom, where my feet fail. Cementing me into place as my lungs heave.

Alice doesn't see me. She stands in the bathroom where we nearly made love two nights ago, staring into the mirror. She touches her curls, her lip trembling while fresh tears blaze down the dried tracks on her cheeks. No trace of her pretty pink glow remains. Instead, she's pale and crushed, like a rosebud trampled in the snow.

The dejected slump of her shoulders sends a white-hot burst through my chest. I open my mouth to speak, but her small, sad voice reaches my ears as she picks up my comb and starts to drag it through her loose hair.

"—stupid for me to think this looked better," she tells herself. "Why do I keep trying to fix it? Nothing ever works. I *know* that."

As she speaks, she yanks harder and harder, ripping through her once-glorious curls, leaving a cloud of puffed blonde in her wake.

She speaks through clenched teeth, berating herself. "Marco probably thinks I'm ridiculous. Wearing my hair like this for him... wearing this robe for him. Like he would actually *want* me?!"

God. It hurts to listen to her. It also pisses me off. And insults me, on some strange level. After all, I *do* want her. Lust after her. Want to keep her.

The comb starts to look more like an instrument to inflict self-harm. Furious, I stalk across the room and pluck it out of her hand.

Stricken, Alice whirls her blotchy face toward me, blinking in shock. "M-Marco," she stutters, shrinking down. "H-how long have you b-been here?"

Overwrought, I glare at her, holding the weaponized hair tool out of reach. "Long enough."

She hiccups. "D-did you h-hear... any of that?"

With her hair half-mangled and her ice-blue eyes bright with tears, she still looks lovely. She still looks like Alice. And even though I'm angry, overcome by a foreign slurry of feelings I have no name for, I suddenly want to kiss her.

Need to kiss her.

So I drop the comb and reach for her wet face. "I always hear you."

MARCO IS STILL SCOWLING when he pulls his face away from mine, having shut me up with a press of his stern, chiseled mouth to my tear-damp lips.

The second our eyes meet, his anger dissipates on the spot, leaving softness in his dark gaze. His big, brawny hand floats up to my scalp.

"You'll hurt yourself," he murmurs, drawing soothing circles over the tender skin. "And you're wrecking your pretty hair."

With exquisite gentleness, he touches his knuckles to my cheek, wiping at the tear tracks. His dark eyes bore into mine.

"Your mother is wrong," he says, his voice ringing with quiet conviction. "*I* want to look at you. I *love* your curls. You look *lovely* with your hair loose and your skin scrubbed clean. And you are *not* cheap. At all. Ever. I'm furious she said that to you; if you hadn't hung up, I would be having words with her right now."

He seems to pick up steam as he goes. His free hand curves around my other cheek.

"*I want you,*" he repeats, vehemently. "Do you think I have bad taste?"

I can barely shake my head. His eyes flash, and he jerks his chin toward his bathroom counter. "That's my good girl. Now, sit."

Chastened, with eyes wide as saucers, I manage to balance myself on the granite. I blink as he turns to the sink, filling a cup with warm water before flinging open a medicine cabinet.

He looks sexy as sin in all black, particularly the thin V-neck sweater under his suit jacket. As I watch, he takes his top layer off and pushes his sleeves up, revealing muscled, bronze forearms.

Without a word, Marco stretches over me, scrunching water into my hair. He moves with practiced efficiency that I can't help but admire.

"How do you know how to do this?" I wonder, sheepishly absorbing the concentration carved into his handsome face.

He sighs. "When my father died, there were a few months when my mom struggled to take care of herself. She struggled with basic tasks like doing her hair and choosing clothes. I wound up doing both for her for a time."

Thinking of strong, silent Marco bottling up his own grief to help his mother through hers sends a fissure through my heart. My hands reach for him of their own volition, brushing over his chest. "I'm sorry."

He dries off with a basic white washcloth and shrugs tightly. "It's coming in handy, now. Have to take care of this pretty blonde hair. I'm a bit of a sucker for it, if you haven't noticed."

The notion that such a big, sexy man could ever be a "sucker" for any part of me seems absurd. An incredulous giggle bubbles out. "Really? You like my hair?"

He gives an emphatic nod, stern once again. "I do," he replies, bending to loom right in front of me. "But, Alice, it's more than that. I like *you*, okay? It wouldn't matter what you did to your hair. My feelings aren't about your hair. They're about *you*."

I feel dizzy. Feverish. Embarrassed and awed and maybe sort of... *happy*. Breath quivers out of my lungs as he pulls me into his arms, holding me against the length of his hard body. The warm scents of cologne and leather envelop me along with his muscle-bound frame.

"Alice..."

The rough timbre of Marco's voice is the only warning I get before he presses closer, his hips tight to my torso. One hand skims down my chest, tracing the gaping edges of my new robe, while the other cups my cheek, lifting my chin.

For a long moment, he just stares.

At me? Why?

I imagine how red my eyes must be—and how low my breasts hang without a bra to prop them up.

Unbecoming.

My mother's favorite word flashes through my brain, trimmed in neon. Wincing, I open my mouth to apologize. Before I get the words out, Marco says my name again. This time with... *meaning*.

"*Alice.*"

He sounds agitated and growly and...

Well.

Sexy. He sounds panty-meltingly sexy.

I blink at him and try my best to read the dark intensity filling his face. Is he... mad? No. His eyebrows aren't plunged together. Annoyed? I don't see a tick in his jaw... or any brackets around his lips...

Maybe... hungry?

He looks sort of hungry. *Wild*, actually. Heat glows in his dark irises, like smoldering coals.

Heat. Hunger. Oh.

OH.

He *wants* me. The side of his mouth twitches up when mine falls open on a soft, surprised gasp. One he, of course, hears. And, as always, Marco hears all the things I *don't* say, too.

Yes, his small, sensual smirk says, answering my unspoken question. *Good girl.*

Maybe I should have been more prepared for the look on Marco's face after everything that happened in the shower on Saturday night. He told me how beautiful he finds me. He spent time making me feel good, holding me, drying me off, and cuddling me in bed. And I'm still here, ensconced in his apartment.

But, no.

I have to remember *why* I'm here. And tell myself every day that this is part of his *job.*

Not real. Not forever. Just for now.

But that isn't what I see, burning silently in his eyes. Only that bottomless entreaty. And lust hot enough to melt all the muscles in my core.

I don't know what to do with it. In all my years of etiquette training and personality tweaking and makeovers, no one ever bothered to tell me what to do if I *actually* managed to attract a real, live man.

Marco watches my lashes flutter, reading my insecurity so easily. Electricity snaps through his depths.

Without a sound, he straightens and drop back a pace. Despite the scalding heat radiating from his features, his movements are measured. Unhurried, but not casual in any way. Slow and intent. A man who knows what he wants and knows it will wait for him.

He starts to remove his belt. My throat goes dry when he continues undressing, never pausing for a single beat. His fingers dip into his waistband to retrieve his gun before floating up flick his fly open.

His watch comes next. The clink of the metallic links against the bathroom counter feels jarring in the tense silence that swells between us.

Marco doesn't seem to notice. He has already slid out of his socks and his shoes. His eyes burn into mine, staring while he finally shrugs his sweater off.

Even when my focus drops to where his erection bobs—the straining length curving toward his navel—I still find his gaze waiting for mine when I finally look back up at him.

My Lord, he is glorious. Just an absolutely perfect specimen of a man. The kind of male form I would pay to paint, if I had any talent for painting people.

I don't, but I could imagine trying to recreate him on canvas. All square angles, only softened by the round bulges of muscle rippling over his abdomen, filling out his pecs and his shoulders. The shadows pooled beneath every hard ridge. The unique bronze shade of his skin. Even the smattering of scars peppered over his left shoulder seem like part of a masterpiece.

My fingertips tingle, aching to touch. Marco doesn't make me wait long. He takes a handful of quick, deep breaths before he finally closes the space between us.

And drops to his knees.

The position puts us face-to-face, pressing his impressively hard length into the edge of the cushion underneath me. Our gazes hold for a long moment.

I blink. *Hi*.

Every bit of irritation abandons him, leaving his gaze molten and soft. *Hi*.

His hands band over my hips, rubbing the fine silk covering them. For a moment, his stare blazes a hot path behind his hands, following them to the frothy lace adorning the sleeves, over the simple sash tied at my waist, and, finally, up the fabric parted at my breasts. He pauses there, running the tip of his finger along the exposed skin below my collarbone.

His eyes snap shut while he leans closer, pressing his forehead into my thigh. "Alice," he murmurs, as if he has any right to be as breathless as I am. "You look so fucking sexy in this robe. It makes me want to do so many things to you, I can't decide where to start."

My lashes flutter in shock. "L-like what?"

When I stammer, a tiny smile touches the stern curves of his lips. "Like put my head between your thighs so I can finally taste you."

"I—I—" I don't even know where to begin. *Finally* taste me? As in, he has been thinking about it for a long time? And by 'taste' me, does he mean...?

What else *could* he mean? We've already kissed. And I doubt he wants to know what the inside of my knee tastes like...

"N-no—" My voice shakes so hard I have to bite my tongue and cut off the rest of my confession.

His brows arch, surprised. I brace myself for judgment or disappointment, but he only nuzzles his nose against mine. "No? You don't like that?"

Lord. Eventually, I will run out of ways to humiliate myself in front of this beautiful man, right? Hopefully?

I swallow a sticky wad of chagrin and look down at my hands while I reply, "I don't know if I like it. I was trying to say, no other guy has ever offered to—or, um, *wanted* t—"

Marco stretches up, his lips brushing over mine. "I'm offering," he says, with a bite that dares me to doubt him. "*I* want to."

His next kiss is quick, but desperate. He leans back just enough to bore his gaze into mine, underscoring his utter sincerity. "If you'll have me."

The ache between my legs throbs until my thighs clench around it. I don't know why I'm hesitating. Habit, probably. While he waits for my reply, my mind automatically tallies up all of my inadequacies.

Surely, if he goes down there, he will see... *everything.* Up close.

And, yeah, I shaved pretty thoroughly this morning... but I

honestly have no idea what the situation *down there* will seem like, up close and personal. Not to mention the cellulite on my thighs. And what if the waxer missed a spot? I didn't bother to check. I never dreamed someone would be *staring directly between my legs*.

Marco senses my panic and brings both of his hands up to my face, cupping my cheeks until I look back into his warm, dark eyes.

"I want you to know two things," he rasps, his gaze turbulent. "The first one is that I will never do anything—*anything*—you don't want me to do."

He means it with every fiber of his big, muscled being. I see the steady resolve in his eyes. The steel of an oath.

I touch his cheek and whisper my own truth back to him. "I knew that even before you said it."

A flare flashes in his eyes, leaving them even more intense as he grabs the hand touching his face and presses it into his skin, as if he can imprint me on his cheek.

"The second thing," he roughs out, "is that I have never been on my knees for another woman."

I balk slightly. "Ever? You've never..." I don't know if I should feel relieved or apprehensive.

But Marco shakes his head. "I have. But never on my knees. I've never..." He blows out a breath. "I've never wanted to kneel for anyone but you."

The depth of that simple statement strikes me like a blow. Marco isn't loud or domineering, but he conducts himself with dignity. The unmistakable air of a proud man. The fact that he wants to lower himself for me—even figuratively—stuns me speechless.

I can barely agree, moving my head in a couple of stiff nods before slowly shifting my legs out from under me. Marco keeps his gaze trained on mine but drops his hands to smooth over the silk covering my hips.

I remember that I don't have any panties underneath the same second his fingers skirt the hem of the robe. "This looks exquisite on you," he rumbles, turning his attention back to my body. "I'm buying you at least two more to keep here." He tugs on the sash and stares as the fabric parts, heat simmering in his eyes. "Make that three."

His large hands feel deliciously calloused as they skim over my naked sides. So good that I forget to suck in my stomach and sit as straight as possible. When I scramble to correct my stance, Marco suddenly stops touching me.

Without missing a beat, he pushes to his feet and scoops me up. I squeal, but he just presses a kiss to my forehead, carting me toward the bed.

"I want you to relax," he says, gently setting me down before resuming his position on the floor. "Lie back if you want to."

I think about his view, wincing. "But my—" I swallow my words, not exactly keen to point out any flaws he hasn't noticed yet.

Something glimmers in his gaze. He drops a hand to his cock and pulls back to stroke it from his place between my knees. "Do I need to give you another demonstration of how much I want you? Because I will."

My mouth falls open while I watch him fist the thick length in a series of hard, fast strokes. Color floods my cheeks, but I can't look away.

"When I think about putting my mouth on your pussy," he growls, tugging at his dick faster. "It makes me so hard, it hurts."

Sure enough, his erection jumps against his palm, the head so dark and swollen it almost looks purple. As if he isn't torturing himself with his right hand, the left skates a leisurely path from the base of my throat to my belly button, gently pushing the robe open further. He hisses. "Fuck, you look so hot."

I don't know if I believe him, but I'm officially too turned on to care. Watching him touch himself has me desperate. I rub my own palms over my thighs before I even realize what I'm doing.

A spark lights his gaze while he tracks the movement. His fist slows and then stops. He leans forward, planting his hands on either side of my hips and dropping a kiss to my mound, lingering just long enough to murmur, "Good girl," before trailing his lips lower.

I gasp and jump, my body already straining to get his mouth closer to my core. His lips curve into a smile while they skim my slick, parted lips.

There, he stops, breathing hard against me for a long moment. Only, it doesn't feel like hesitation. More like he's run some sort of horrible marathon and finally crossed the finish line.

And *I'm* his prize.

"Here, sweet girl." His brawny hands slide under the robe as he grips my hips. Without any more words, he arranges me just the way he wants me, pulling my lower half to the edge of the bed and moving back to give himself the proper angle.

I watch, fascinated. Not knowing what to expect, since I've never really let myself imagine experiencing such a thing before. As if reading my thoughts one last time, Marco pauses before he bends over my lap and shoots me the world's most handsome grin. Victory shines in his smile, like this really is some priceless honor.

Then he grabs my hand, kisses the knuckles, and drops it on the back of his head.

Why would I need my hand on his—

"Oh!"

There isn't a word to describe the sound that flies out of me as Marco opens his lips over my center. His tongue follows, licking a straight line to my core before slipping up to nudge my clit.

Oh. My. God.

The part of my brain that hasn't melted figures out that he's moving slowly on purpose, mapping me out as he goes. When he traces the bottom of my clit a second time, and my hips buck, he hums and wraps his tongue around the same spot, sucking lightly.

I cry out, and he groans, the sound appreciative. "You taste so good. So sweet. I knew you would," he mutters, working his way back down to my entrance. "My sweet girl."

I whimper while he works his tongue into me, thrusting in shallow flicks and deeper licks until I keen, my fingers tangling in his thick black hair. There's a throbbing place inside of me that he almost reaches with his tongue, but *not quite*. Just when I think I'll go mad, he licks up to my clit and slides one of his fingers into me.

"*Marco!*"

He rubs the perfect patch along my inner wall, stroking over it again and again while I moan. "Is that it?" he rumbles against me. "Is that our spot, baby?"

Our spot. The words alone nearly make me come. Then he seals his lips around my clit and sucks, lashing at me with his tongue while his finger pumps over the secret place inside.

My body twists off the bed. I come, whimpering his name and soaking his face. Marco groans so loud, I think he's coming, too.

"You're going to ruin me," he pants, lapping up all the ecstasy pouring out of me. "I'll be on my knees for you every goddamn night. I don't want to fucking *stop*."

So he doesn't. He stays there, gently working me over with soft sucks and fluttering licks until a second orgasm rolls through me. This time, the pleasure feels deeper, cascading out from my core. Smooth, slow, and golden, like honey in my veins.

He finally straightens, swiping his palm over his face. I start to reach for him, my hands shaking visibly when I lift them to his cheeks. Marco catches my fingers instead, holding them against the nape of his neck while he leans forward and nestles his cheek against mine.

I close my eyes, grateful he can't see me as I gather my courage and push out my request. "Fill me up."

He kisses me slowly, pressing his lips to my temple, my cheekbone, the place under my ear.

"Yes."

thirty-six

ALICE LETS me pick her up so I can tear the damp comforter down.

She still shifts around and hangs her head, but I tighten the arm under her torso, cinching her closer. It really isn't hard. I deadlifted close to four hundred pounds this morning. Compared to that, holding Alice feels like carrying a pile of pillows.

One day soon, I plan to take her against a wall and hold her weight the entire time, just to prove a point. If I break a sweat, it will be from doing my best to stave off a climax, not because of her size.

I'm not sure how well I'll fare once I actually get inside her. If she feels anywhere near as good as she tastes, it will be the end of me.

God. She has the most beautiful pussy I've ever seen. The same pretty pink as her mouth, with equally full lips. She smells so sweet and has an earthy, musky taste. The combination of the two is the perfect cocktail. Delicious and intoxicating. I wasn't kidding when I told her I want to lick her every night.

Just the thought makes me so hard it hurts. My cock thumps while I lay Alice back on my bed, arranging her on the edge of the mattress.

My lungs burn at the way she looks up at me. Gratitude and awe shimmer in the violet blue, so open and earnest that I can't *breathe.* Can't speak or think past the crushing thought that *I'm* not worthy.

I remember her lists. The hopes she hid away. Making love is one of them. Because she never thought that anyone would want her and care for her at the same time.

I need to fix that. But I also need somewhere to put all the intensity thundering through my blood. And I want to know what her preferences are before she has a chance to learn mine.

I hold her face with one hand, rubbing my thumb over her lower lip. Too many feelings teem in my body, turning my voice into a rough whisper. "What's your favorite?"

Alice beams up at me through her lashes. The lust she reads in my eyes reflects in hers. Desire darkens the irises, her pupils blurring into the dark rings of indigo along their edges.

"You don't want to—"

I shake my head, shucking my shirt and pants. "No. I want *your* favorite. Show me."

Her breath quivers as she moves, gliding to the middle of the mattress... and rolling onto her hands and knees.

Holy fuck.

My sweet girl likes to get fucked from behind? A dizzy surge of lust roars through my veins. All my muscles tense like strings on an instrument, tuned too tight.

"Is this okay?"

Is it *okay*? I've never seen anything hotter. Still draped in her open robe, Alice balances on all fours and looks over her shoulder at me, raising her brows in question.

I lunge.

"No, it's not fucking okay," I growl. "It's *perfect*. Every time I think I can't want you more, you do something that wrecks me. Dirty, perfect girl. Come here."

I fit my body around hers, grasping her fine-boned wrists and balancing her forearms on mine. I leverage the strength in my core to pull us both upright, nudging her toward the headboard and guiding her hands to grip the top of it. Nipping her neck, I slide the robe down until it pools at her waist.

"Take it off," I implore her, rubbing my lips over her spine. "I want to *see* you."

Her nervous swallow tempers my impatience. I settle, breathing hard against the curve of her back while I wait for her to work up her nerve. Finally, she takes the robe off and lovingly sets it on the pillow beside her.

My throat dries, and my mouth waters. *Good God.*

Her *skin*. It *glows*. Alabaster and frosted rose. Creamy curves and wide, plush hips in perfect proportion to her round ass. I smooth my palms over her sides, following every luscious swell and dip to her backside.

When I reach between her thick thighs, I find her slick and scorching hot. My cock swells to a painful point, pulsing while it grazes the side of her ass.

She whimpers as I touch her. "Marco, please."

I reach over to my nightstand and pull a condom out, bending to murmur into her shoulder while I slide it on. "Do you know how gorgeous you look like this? Stretched out so perfectly? On your knees just for me?"

She shivers. I move closer, pressing my chest into her back, nuzzling her blonde halo of curls. Sweet lavender warms my nose. The scent tugs at my lungs, grounding me in the moment.

Alice.

She's here. She's mine. And I want to give her everything.

I position her just so, spreading her legs wider and angling her hips back. "You like it deep?" I guess, gliding the head of my pulsing erection against her soaked center. "Fast or slow?"

Her voice is barely a whisper. "Yes. Deep. Slow."

"Whatever my sweet girl wants," I promise.

Resting my forehead on her shoulder, I grunt as I work my hips in a circle, pushing past the narrow ring of her entrance. She's so impossibly *tight*. Her pussy clings to me, squeezing hard on all sides.

I want to feel her snug heat tugging at my entire length, but I have to take my time. Learn my sweet girl.

Halfway in, I feel the rough patch that drives her wild. It grazes the underside of my cockhead, and Alice goes rigid, a loud moan tearing from her lips.

"There's our spot," I murmur, bearing down slightly as I rub my shaft over it. Her body gives a glorious clench on every plunge. "Feels so fucking perfect."

Alice mewls at the praise, grinding her ass back for more. I shove in deeper, almost to the hilt. "You take it so well," I tell her. "And you look so gorgeous with me inside of you."

She feels like *heaven*. Soft and wet and squeezing me harder than a fist. A serrated groan rips out of me when I finally hit the end of her, barely screwing my entire length in before I run out of room.

"Fuck, Alice," I pant, working my hips in small circles and slow, deep drives. "You were made for this cock."

Her loud moan, desperate and unrestrained, sends lightning up my spine. My hips snap harder, pushing and pulling faster. Alice thrusts her own back, meeting me, making sounds I wish I could record and replay forever.

Every gasp and cry reverberates through my body. The

muscles in my base tauten as my balls draw up, aching for release. I cinch an arm around her waist and pull her closer, burying my face into her neck while I alter the angle of my thrusts, carefully rubbing the ridge of my head over her secret spot. The hand sprawled over her belly slips down to press against her folds. Two fingertips work over her clit.

"*Marco!*"

She screams just before she comes, grinding herself back and forth between my hand and my cock. All her inner muscles flutter and seize, squeezing me so hard my vision goes white.

"*Alice.* God, *yes.*"

My release feels life-altering. World-ending. Like I'll open my eyes and find myself surrounded by rubble.

Aftershocks rock both of our bodies. I clutch her closer, banding both arms around her torso and leaning back on my knees. When she sniffles, I cup her warm cheek and turn her face toward mine, catching her lips for a kiss.

A tear melts into my fingers. Alarm flares in my chest. I nestle my nose against her, nudging. *Did I hurt you?* I ask without words.

No. She shakes her head so slightly, I have to feel it instead of seeing it. Her watery eyes meet mine.

There's an apology there. And dazed confusion over why she can't keep her tears at bay. She gives her head another small shake, exasperated with herself as more emotion wells in the luminous blue.

She doesn't speak, but I understand the look all too well. It contains everything I can't put into words, either. I smooth her hair away from her flushed face, nuzzling our noses and lowering us onto the bed.

Me, too.

thirty-seven

I AM NOT in the fucking mood for a dead body.

Not when all I can think about is Alice, sated and sleepy-eyed in my bed.

And the erection I assumed wouldn't abate until I made it back to her side.

But a dead body does the trick.

Grayson taps his fingers on the center console. It's odd to have him in the front seat with me, but this is no ordinary car ride.

I knew the second Brad's name appeared on my phone—some new horror had come to light. And as much as it killed me to leave

Alice after everything that happened tonight, I have people to protect.

Of course, it helps that I know my sweet girl is as safe as she could possibly be.

The Chinatown side street is awash with chaos. We unbuckle in unison, both jumping out of the Mercedes sedan without a word.

Up ahead, a surreal scene unfolds. Two cop cruisers sit at diagonals in the center of the street. Cold blue light swirls up into the chilly damp, casting sinister shadows on the vacant apartment building. Between the police cars, a black van sits idle, one word emblazoned on its side.

Coroner.

Grayson and I push into the throng of officers gathered around the side of the van. I extend my hand to their captain. "I'm Marco Amir, head of security for Stryker & Sons. This is Grayson Stryker."

The captain gives a sympathetic nod. "Ah, yes. Good of you to come so quickly. We'll need one of you to identify the remains. Though I have to warn you... they aren't pretty."

My boss and I look at one another. His jaw hardens while determination steels his green gaze. "I have to do it," he decides, stepping forward. "Show me."

They lead us to the open doors at the back of the vehicle. There, on a flat stretcher, is a black plastic bag, six feet long. The coroner unzips the top part, revealing a sallow, bloated face.

Grayson and I both stare down at the somewhat-familiar man. I hear him swallow hard, voice thickening. "Yes," he confirms. "That is Theodore Stryker."

At least... it *was.*

The man was never as good-looking as his brother or nephew, but his corpse is positively grotesque. Fit for the state of his soul.

The slight stench tells me he's been dead for more than a day, at least. I level my gaze at the coroner.

"How long?"

The tall, thin man frowns thoughtfully as he re-seals the bag. "I'll have to run some tests back at the morgue to confirm," he hedges. "But based on the ambient temperature in the apartment... I would say he died Saturday night or very early Sunday morning."

"Cause of death?" Grayson intones, his voice strangely hollow.

"Gunshots," the coroner replies. "Two in the heart, one in the head."

Old school, I think. Modern-day soldiers are no longer taught to execute enemies on sight, but decades ago, in the fifties and sixties, most intelligence agencies considered the three-shot style of dispatching an unarmed enemy compulsory.

"The shell casings are missing," the police captain informs us, preempting my next question. "Most likely taken by the perpetrator. We'll run ballistics on the wounds, in case they match a gun in our system. I understand there was an ongoing search for this man?"

I nod. "He's wanted for interrogation regarding another investigation. We believe he had information about a violent assault perpetrated by his son. Who was supposed to be behind bars—but we just found out he made bail on Friday."

That was the latest piece of information from Barnes, who dug into the prison-break side of things all weekend. We thought the ten-million-dollar bail would be enough to stop Ted from getting his son out—but apparently it didn't.

Not that it did either of them any good.

My gaze snaps to the stairwell across the sidewalk, my mind working through the situation systematically. "May I inspect the scene?"

"As long as you don't disturb anything," he agrees, gruff. "Your associates are up there, too. They called us when they discovered a key broken off in the door. Whoever shot him must have done it on their way out, to keep the landlord from coming in."

Damn it. Pierce and Brad have been here four times since Saturday night, and they only just noticed the lock? Sloppy work.

Rookie work.

And, ultimately, my fault. I'm supposed to be teaching them, not holding wedding planners captive in my apartment and watching them on my cameras at all hours of the day.

I take the steps two at a time, charging upstairs to find a sad, unlit landing with three doors. The one on the right hangs open, revealing a single, sparsely furnished room.

The moment I see it, Daniel's bail makes sense. Ted must have mortgaged everything he'd ever owned and sunk every penny he'd ever embezzled into freeing his son. A shit investment, if you ask me. Considering I have mountains of evidence that would have ended up convicting the evil fucker either way.

Not anymore.

Now they'll both rot where they belong.

A dark pool of dried blood occupies the center of the concrete floor, soaked into the cement for all eternity. Off to one side, Pierce and Brad stand talking with a forensic officer. As soon as Pierce sees me, he breaks away.

"Hell of a night," I mutter, surveying the stark, sour room.

Brad shakes his head, his eyes fixed on the indelible stain on the floor between us. "No shit," he mumbles. "We were doing our usual surveillance, checking to see if the door was unlocked or if anything in the hallway had been disturbed to indicate movement. But then I noticed the key snapped off in the lock. I knew that would give the police probable cause to search the place, so I called them and you."

I clap a hand on his shoulder. "You followed protocol. Good man."

Pierce scuffs his boot on the floor. "I should have seen that damn key in the lock," he admits. "I was here so many times. I came up here last night... I can't believe I didn't notice that the whole handle was jammed."

Really, it's my own fault for trusting a rookie to think like a seasoned detective. Most people would presume a door is simply locked when the handle doesn't budge. It takes experience to think outside the box.

"You did what you could," I tell him honestly. "Now the real work starts."

"R-real work?"

His nervous stuttering and wide eyes send a pang rebounding through my chest. *Alice.*

My hand twitches toward my phone, but I quell the impulse, inhaling deeply. "Yes. Ted is a murder victim, which makes it a hell of a lot easier to get access to his financial statements and phone records. It should be simple enough to find our suspect based on those."

Brad comes closer, frowning. "What do you mean?"

I sigh. "Someone wanted this man dead—but only *after* Daniel was shot. There has to be a reason. I'm assuming there was a third person working with Daniel and Ted to bring Grayson and Mason down. Or perhaps pretending to work with them. They probably smuggled Daniel into the party somehow, came here to collect their payment before word of Daniel's death could reach Ted, and then shot Ted to tie up loose ends. Now, they think they've gotten away without leaving any accomplices behind."

We saw double-crossing all the time when I worked in the NYPD's Organized Crime division. My father used to quote Benjamin Franklin on such occasions. The famous words return to me as I stand in the former apartment of two of our three targets.

"Three men can keep a secret if two of them are dead."

Anger tightens Pierce's expression, along with a touch of denial. It's natural, I suppose. We keep stepping on cockroaches only to find more. It's like Whack-A-Mole.

"How do we know Ted was the one paying off the accomplice?" he asks.

I shrug, numb. "We don't. But it feels logical. Ted poured all his money into this—he posted Daniel's bail, paid for all the lawyers. We've always suspected that he kept some of the money he tried to embezzle from Stryker & Sons. It seemed like, no matter how many times we stripped his resources, he always came back with more."

Pierce chokes on his outrage. "That's—"

"I know," I say, staring down at the dried black blood. *Fucking karma.*

My focus flickers over to Brad, who—I now see—keeps dribbling his weight from one foot to the other. *Huh.*

"You guys were both here all night?" I confirm, raising my voice to make sure they both hear me.

When Brad turns from speaking with the forensic specialist, his eyes are wider than usual. He looks at Pierce before he answers me. "Yeah... all night. Since, like, what? Four? I think Barnes left around four."

My eyes narrow. "*Like* around four?" I repeat. "This is a fucking murder investigation, Forrester. We can't deal in approximations here."

Pierce shoots Brad a dirty look. "We got here at four," he confirms, solid. He glances back at me. "Barnes left right after we arrived."

But there is something neither of them is telling me. "... and?"

A silent argument ensues. They both send severe glares at each other until Brad finally shifts on his feet again. "I, uh... I had to step away. For about an hour. Around six."

Pierce stares right at his partner. "Tell him *why*, Brad."

A dark flush seeps into Brad's ruddy face. *Oh, for fuck's sake. Am I running a fraternity?*

I throw up my hands, halting him. "If you left your post to get your dick wet, I don't need details."

The forensic officer snickers in the corner, smirking over her clipboard. *Carajo.*

When Brad doesn't protest, I know I'm right. I shake my head. "I'll dock your pay for the hour. But consider this your one and only warning, Forrester. Leave your post again? You might as well not come back."

He swallows audibly and shuffles his feet again. "Yes. Sir. Understood."

I still don't like his posture. I make a mental note to try to look into whoever he met up with. If it's someone the Strykers know.

Because I have a feeling that whoever this third person is?

They aren't done.

And the wedding—the one Alice is *killing* herself to create—is the perfect target for someone with Ted's cash and a grudge against the Strykers.

I just don't know who it is yet.

Pierce's cough interrupts my train of thought. He stares down at the blood stain like it disgusts him. "This is sick."

He isn't wrong. The scene in front of me speaks of someone methodical and cold. A seasoned murderer.

They walked in, lifted a gun, and shot the man three times. He probably died before they even bothered to tell them that they'd gotten his son murdered, too.

I wonder if the two Strykers were surprised when they saw each other in hell.

alice

I CAN FEEL how late it is before I open my eyes.

Even though I tried to follow Marco's instructions to wait up for him in his room, I eventually gave in sometime around midnight and went to sleep. He texted me right as I settled onto the sofa in his guest room, telling me he would call me when he was done working, but he understood it might be too late for me.

I warred with myself over whether I should stay in his room or return to where I slept before. In the end, I figured that, while it was life-changing for me, a man like Marco probably has sex like that—or better—all the time. I'm sure he wouldn't want me assuming I belong in his personal space just because we hooked up... again.

When I blink awake sometime in the small hours of the morning, though, I find I'm no longer snuggled under his spare comforter. Instead, my body sways as a set of bulging arms gathers me into an equally hard chest.

"Shh," Marco hums. "Don't wake up, sweet girl."

It's impossible not to, though. He smells freshly showered, and his skin is softer than usual, as if he had to wash off his night before he came to get me.

... and bring me back to his bed.

He doesn't speak as he lays me on his big mattress and rolls into place behind me. Or as he locks his arm around my middle, snuggling me into his body heat.

But just as I start to think I might be dreaming, his low voice rumbles in my ear.

"From now on, you sleep with me."

"ALICE?"

Ella's melodic voice, tinged with a trace of amusement, invades my daydreaming.

I blink, remembering where I am. A blush sweeps over my cheeks.

"So sorry," I mumble, shuffling a stack of the catering menus strewn around us. "I was just thinking about—"

Marco's dark eyes sinking into mine right before he put his mouth on me. His hands dimpling my thighs while he tugged me closer. The way he stroked his hands over my body this morning and ground his hard cock against my ass. How we've now done it on the bed, the bathroom counter, the couch, the—

"—chicken or fish."

Ella smiles kindly, letting me have my fib. "Huh. Alright. Well, according to Grayson, if we don't serve some fancy fish, his mother will 'die of shame.'"

I nod seriously, even though I know she's kidding. "We can do both, if you want."

My bride bites her lip. "*And* the ribeye?"

That was Grayson's one and only menu request. I wince. "I suppose so."

We share a worried look. This has been the theme of our planning sessions—both of us cringing over every penny of Stryker wealth we spend.

The budget Grayson has provided is, quite frankly, ludicrous. I wouldn't be able to use that much money on ten weddings, let alone one featuring the least materialistic bride of all time.

Seriously. It was a *struggle* to convince the woman she needed new shoes to go with her gown. I finally talked her into letting me and Juliet go with her to try some options sometime in the next couple of weeks.

Assuming Marco lets us out of his sight.

He's been more intense than ever this week. Insisting I stay at his place until further notice, checking every camera feed for his place, the Stryker's, *and* my apartment. Bundling me into his own bed every night.

Which I'm sure has more to do with keeping me safe than anything else. Because it's his job.

That argument becomes harder to believe every day. Especially today, when I woke to a note on his kitchen island, asking me to dinner this weekend.

Which is probably a terrible idea, right? I mean, aren't I making enough of a fool of myself as it is? Walking around with butterflies in my stomach, all because he calls me sweet girl and likes to put his hands on me?

There's no possible way this could ever last past a fleeting diversion for him. It's only for as long as his business interests align with my safety. I'm sure.

But, still. Where he managed to find a single pink rose to place beside his note at six a.m. is still a mystery to me.

If I'm honest, I wish he would stop being so damn romantic. Won't this be hard enough for me to move on from, once it ends? Does he really have to look like a cross between an ancient warrior king and a male model? And does he need to spend evenings reading next to me on the couch before utterly *destroying* my body? Or get *more* overprotective with every passing day??

He only deemed this outing safe because he has the Strykers' house locked down tighter than his own. Even now, there's a scary British dude looming in the far corner of Ella's second-floor living space, watching us with flinty, unwavering focus.

"I suppose that's okay," Ella hums. "I know it's more expensive to offer three options, but—"

"It will be *perfect*," I promise, squeezing her hand gently. "Grayson will love it."

That phrase has become my secret weapon. Once I figured out that the billionaire truly lights up at the prospect of anything that gives Ella joy—and vice versa—all I have to say is that their significant other would be thrilled. And suddenly they're both on board.

It's almost too adorable, even for me.

Grinning, I go down my mental checklist. "You've got the location, flowers, officiant, dresses, tuxedos, and place-settings. Once I give the caterers their final marching orders, we're just down to choosing a band, photographer, and videographer."

Ella exhales, looking as relieved as I feel. "Thank God."

No one is more shocked than I am. I never dreamed I'd be able to pull this off. We've managed to get a lot done very quickly —mostly because every vendor in the city wants a piece of the Wedding of the Century. And thanks to Marco's subtle intimidation and several well-placed NDAs provided by his cousin, Juliet, there haven't been any leaks yet.

Marco is still upset about the ominous way my apartment door hung open last weekend. I'm sure it was just Tris—especially since none of the wedding binders or my technology were taken. I miss my roomie, but she is truly the definition of a Hot Mess. Just this morning, I was cleaning out my purse, and I found one of her earrings, her least favorite sunglasses, her stray Metro card, the key to her locker at the gym, and a dead AirTag—probably one meant to help her keep track of her locker key.

The girl is a walking junk drawer, I swear.

I need her help, though, if I'm actually going to go on a date with the sexiest man in the city. She'll know what I should wear. Hopefully.

Ella notices that I'm drifting into outer space again. Her teasing smile returns as she tilts her head at me. "You know," she remarks, "Marco told me you've been staying at his place."

Panic sticks in my gullet, but her grin only widens. "Now, I know Marco is dedicated to his job, but I've never heard of him bringing work home with him."

Oh Lord. *What do I say? Do I spill my guts and tell her everything, like a friend would? Or should I try to act professionally?*

There is *nothing* professional about the way Marco and I have been this week.

"I—I—I'm—we—"

Ella interrupts my stammer by placing her hand on my arm. Warmth swells in her eyes. "Whatever it is, I think it's great," she murmurs. Her gaze slides to the side before she lowers her voice, ensuring our current guard can't hear her as she adds, "He's a little bit broken, though, Alice. Just be careful."

There's something about the earnest concern creasing her face that socks me in the gut. I try to swallow. "W-with him? Or because of him?"

Ella sinks her pearly teeth into her lower lip again. "Both."

thirty-nine

I WILL PROBABLY NEVER GET USED to seeing Marco naked.

I have a sneaking suspicion he's trying to slowly inure me to his physical perfection, though, since he's used every opportunity this week to strip his clothes off in my presence.

The first couple of days, he mostly stuck to rolling his sleeves up and kicking off his shoes at every opportunity. Next, the shirts started to disappear. Now, just five days into this temporary kidnapping, he doesn't seem to own any clothing apart from sweatpants and boxers.

By the time he emerges from his post-workout shower, in nothing but a pair of black joggers, I have settled on his couch with my latest book. Marco's dark eyes skim over the robe I wear as often as I can, then stray to the teapot and cups I set out on his coffee table.

His expression is as devastating as it is rare. I've never seen him smile like this for anyone else—wide and dazzling. Always too quick to be anything but genuine and always with a wry glimmer, like he is as surprised to be smiling at all.

No. So far? This look seems to be reserved for... me.

This time, his grin flashes over his features while he drops his eyes and shakes his head. Almost as if he can't believe his luck.

Absurd.

Why would having me on his couch, in a robe he paid for, make him feel *lucky*?

I'm the one who clearly did something good in a past life to end up here. Every time he smiles like that. Or takes my stress-bitten, paint-stained fingers in his and brings them up for a kiss. Or skims his lips over the pulse point in my neck. Or carries me to his bed to make sure I sleep there... I have to do a double-take.

Is this real? Does this strong, handsome, perfect man actually want *me*?

When he catches me staring—probably with my mouth hanging open in outright disbelief—Marco's grin grows. His brown eyes warm and soften, the depths as clear and dark as the strongest black tea. They twinkle at me. *Hi, sweet girl.*

I feel my lips curve into a moony smile. *Hi.*

He takes the seat beside me, settling as close as he can get without dragging me into his lap. My copy of *Her Errant Earl* takes up residence in his lap as he props one leg up on the coffee table. A brawny hand curls around my thigh while the other flips to the page marked with his bookmark.

While he starts to read, I start to stare. He's just so impossibly *handsome*. His square jaw, black stubble, thick hair, and bronze skin. The tiny twitch of his lips that tells me he feels my eyes tracing his face, but doesn't plan to call me on it.

After a moment of marveling at him, I notice the deep purple smudges under his eyes. The slightly deeper frown lines bracketing the stern curves of his mouth. He hasn't slept well during the week—I know because he occasionally jerks awake and typically rolls out of bed long before his six a.m. alarm.

My mind races. *What's bothering him so much that he isn't sleeping? Is it something to do with Ella and Grayson? Or because I'm here?*

Maybe he hates it. I bet I'm every bit as burdensome as I feel, and he's counting the seconds until—

"Hey."

Warm, brawny fingers wrap around my palm, pulling my thumb from my teeth. He brings my abused hand to his mouth, nuzzling it with his lips. Dark eyes snap with soft intensity as they bore into me.

"Don't hurt my sweet girl," he warns, the dangerous rumble vibrating into my side. He cocks an eyebrow, lightening his tone. "She still hasn't agreed to go out with me yet."

A giddy thrill bursts under my lungs. I laugh, but the sound is breathless. "I thought you were kidding," I half-fib. "I mean, why would you want to go out? I've been here all week."

Marco's thick brows knit together. "Because I'd like to take you on the kind of evening you deserve. And show you off."

I open my mouth to reply, but there are no words to describe the sheer, illogical panic seizing my insides. Because I'm starting to suspect the one thing I might be more afraid of than this being some sort of ruse... it *is* real.

"I—" The explanation tangles in my throat. I try to swallow around it, forcing myself past the fear I don't quite understand. "O-okay."

Marco reads my expression. His eyes seem troubled, but his mouth eventually flits into a half-smile. "Tomorrow night. Be ready at six."

forty

MARCO

THE USUAL DREAM wakes me in the usual way—with panic and flaring pain, all tinged with dark red.

But this isn't my usual place or situation.

I flail, my body jolting itself into consciousness. My hands slam into something covering me, shoving it off. My arm sweeps out solidly, removing the chains keeping me—

Oh.

Fuck.

A small scream scrapes my ears, followed by a sickening thud and the rattle of plates clattering to the floor. Fear takes root inside me as I snap my head to the side, bleary eyes burning against the overhead lights.

Because I'm not in my bed.

This is my *living room*. And the weight on top of me wasn't trying to smother me into a puddle of my father's blood.

It was *Alice*.

I curse viciously, flying upright. Alice stays perfectly still, sprawled against the table and the gray rug underneath. She looks afraid, like she went to sleep with a beloved pet and woke to a rabid beast.

I scramble forward, chest heaving, back covered in a sheen of sweat. Shame cramps my lungs, my hands reaching for her immediately.

"*Alice.*"

I drop to my knees, not giving a damn if the broken stoneware —including my father's last tea mug—cuts me. She trembles as I gather her into my damp chest, squeezing tenderly.

"I'm so sorry," I rasp. "Jesus. I'm *sorry*. Are you okay?"

I pull back to run my eyes and palms over her shoulders, her wrists, her sides. Suddenly, she catches my hands.

"I-it's okay," she warbles, still wheezing. "I'm okay."

Pain ripples through my marrow. She's *not* fucking okay. *Because* of me. I *shoved* her into a table.

A lump thickens in my throat as I drop my hands from her body. Realizing I have no right to touch her ever again. My shoulders shake as I jerk backward, falling against the couch. "God. I could have—Fuck, I'm so sorry."

Alice hesitates for half a second before launching herself at me. I catch her at the last second, instinct barely overriding my shock.

Why would she want to hug me right now? Why isn't she *afraid* of me?

"Marco," she murmurs, turning her face into my neck. "That dream sounded awful. Are you alright?"

Am I...?

Her compassion doesn't even compute. I still can't fucking believe I had a nightmare in front of her. Lashed out in my sleep. *Hurt* her.

And now she's worried about *me*?

While I freeze, my lungs aching along with the swollen mass in my gullet, my sweet girl slips her arms around my neck. Her fingers find the sweaty hair at my nape, combing it gently. "You were talking," she whispers, "Y-you said, 'not him.' D-do you want to tell me...?"

God. She's so faultlessly *good*. Pure of heart, with the sharpest mind and endless empathy. I shudder in her embrace, my own flexing around her. Wishing I could pull her inside my body for safekeeping. Nothing so precious should be walking around unprotected.

Her soft touch skates down my spine. My teeth grind as I recall my dream and all the horrible realities that preceded it. "It's a pretty hideous story."

She cuddles closer. "You can tell me, if you want. Is it... something that happened overseas?"

Another shudder wracks me. "No," I reply, the word bitter on my tongue as I mutter, "I have a whole other set of nightmares about that shit."

None of this is her problem. I cup her delicate jaw in my hands, tilting her head back to look me in the eye. "It never even occurred to me that I might hurt you during a nightmare," I vow. "I've had them for years, and I usually just... wake up. Eventually. If I'd known you could have gotten hurt, I would have warned you or avoided sleeping near you at all. I'm supposed to *protect* you, Alice. That's all I've ever wanted to do."

Her soft features shatter into an expression of pure pain. "Stop that. I'm *fine*. What about *you*? Have you ever talked to anyone about these nightmares? M-maybe that would help."

Jesus. Her pure, blue eyes. They cut right into my soul. Extracting words I really shouldn't say.

"I haven't talked about them," I admit. "Because I've never told anyone else this story. Not the real one."

forty-one

I FEEL my eyes go wide while I will the rest of my body to remain motionless, hoping my stillness might help him continue.

He turns his head, flinging his gaze out of the windows around us. His body relaxes a bit as he stares. I've noticed that he seems to find the same comfort in horizons that I do—even when they're dark ones.

"I was a rookie cop," he husks, speaking quietly while he continues to focus on the starless sky. "After I finished my Army stint, I came home and decided I'd be an NYPD officer like my father. It seemed honorable, and I like a challenge. I figured nothing would ever shock me, after what I witnessed overseas."

Marco swallows, the sound thick. "I did my training and did well enough to have my pick of departments. I wanted homicide." A distinct note of derision enters his voice. Aimed at himself, as always. "Of course. Thought I was tough shit."

He shakes his head. "Stupid. My mom wanted me to do something somewhat safer, like Organized Crime or Internal Affairs, because my father was in Internal Affairs. Organized Crime was overwhelmed. Both departments needed more men.

"But my father *argued* with her." I hear his remembered surprise—clearly, his dad did not argue with his mom very often. "He got *angry*. He told her I would be better off dealing with serial killers in homicide. I was insulted, and I signed on for Internal Affairs against his wishes, to spite whatever notion made him think I couldn't handle it."

Marco suddenly pauses, his eyes falling to the mess of broken dishware around us. With a solemn scowl, he whisks me off the floor, moving us a safe distance from the shattered mugs. "It didn't take long for me to realize why my father didn't want me in that division," he grunts, arranging me in his lap.

He bows his head, as if the next part of his story somehow shames him. "Once I was on the force, I found out that my dad had been hiding things from my mom. He was deep into an investigation—closer than anyone else in the division to determining which of the men on our force were really working for a big organized crime family. So close that he was getting death threats. Daily."

I try to imagine the scope of the evil he describes, but it boggles my mind. Marco sighs. "My father hadn't told me or my mom anything because the information was classified, and he didn't want to scare us. When I saw what he was up against, I couldn't believe it. They were threatening to come after us from every angle. They had his address, sent him pictures of his car parked around town, and had copies of his schedule. I couldn't believe he hadn't even told my mother when he could have been abducted or killed at any moment.

"It was the only real fight we ever had. I thought he should tell her, and he said he wouldn't. Couldn't. That he'd made a vow to keep classified information a secret. That it wouldn't matter anyway; if someone killed him, he would rather my mom feel safe and happy until the day he died, instead of living in fear."

I see the weight of grief sink into his gaze. "That's what happened, isn't it?" I whisper, my nose stinging. "They killed him, and your mom didn't know why."

"Yes," he agrees softly, his focus shifting between my watering eyes. Shame darkens his visage. "She's the only person who knows what happened that night."

"Because... it's classified?"

A self-loathing mockery of a smile touches his lips. "It was, here I am, telling you."

His head bows as he looks into the space between our chests and roughs out a breath. "The truth is, even she doesn't know everything. And I almost didn't tell her at all, because I was—*am* —ashamed."

He lifts his face back to mine. "Because I was there that night. With him."

My heart leaps and starts to race. Turbulence roils in Marco's bottomless depths, but he doesn't drop his gaze again. Noble and honest as ever, even when admitting to something he clearly hates.

"I was worried. One of his prime suspects for the double agent was a man he frequently partnered with. They were both on duty that night and got a tip about a small human trafficking deal going down across the river. I was just coming off shift when the call came in. And it just felt *wrong*. I had an instinct about it. So I clocked out... and then I followed them."

His teeth grind while a sheen glosses his eyes. I can barely move my chest to keep breathing.

"It was a trap," he bites out. "The other cop, his *partner*, was the one working with the organized criminal network. He knew my father suspected him and had to dispose of him before anyone else found out. That piece of shit drew his gun, and so did my dad. Dad fired first, but the gun didn't go off. Someone had tampered with it. The other guy fired back less than a second later. One shot, straight to the head. My dad died instantly."

No, please, not him.

So fervent. So *angry*. His tone makes sense, now. I flinch toward him, my hands automatically flying up to his tense jaw. My whispered reply sounds as wet as my cheeks feel.

"Marco, I'm *so* sorry."

He winces while I stroke over the planes of his face. "Alice—" He swallows hard, his throat working while his eyes widen. "There's more to this, but—"

The words die as his molars clench. A flare of anger burns through his expression before fresh shame crowds in. "If I tell you," he finally grinds out. "You might hate me. Or be afraid of me. Which would be worse, somehow."

I try to hide the frisson of fear that goes through me at his words. Smoothing my palms over his skin, leaning closer.

"There isn't..." I pause to make sure I say exactly what I mean. "You can tell me. I don't think much could change how I think of you."

"That isn't true," he says, the words a pained, quiet hush. "I wish more than anything that it was, Alice. But it isn't. I've done things. I—"

The intense guilt that sometimes settles over his eyes completely covers his features now. He's drowning in it, choking on it while he tries to keep speaking.

I'm scared. Terrified he's about to tell me this has all been some big scheme. But I have to know what's under that look, or I'll never be able to move past it. "You can tell me," I assure him. "I'll listen."

Marco's entire body slumps toward me as he exhales harshly. Our foreheads brush while his eyelids drift shut.

"I... I killed him," he murmurs. "After the man shot my father.

I shot him, and I killed him. On purpose. That's the part I never told my mother—or anyone. I didn't do it in self-defense. Not really."

I feel myself gasp, but no air hits my lungs. He stares into me, patiently waiting for condemnation. Or disapproval.

Maybe I should feel both. But I only experience overwhelming, heartrending grief. Grief and... *shock*. It's hard to imagine the calm, principled man before me being driven to such lengths.

Then again, I know how much he adored his father. And who wouldn't react violently after watching their parent being murdered in cold blood? A shiver moves through me when I imagine what might have happened to Marco if he hadn't disposed of the double agent on the spot.

Would he have been the next victim? That horrible organized crime family could have caught wind of everything and come after him and his loved ones, just for good measure. By acting so decisively—for better or for worse—Marco probably saved numerous lives.

By taking one.

His confession clearly costs him. Every hard slab of muscle on his body tweaks tight, but his face almost looks vulnerable. Open. Defenseless. Still waiting, I realize, for me to judge him.

He was so *brave*. To follow his father that night. To take on that crooked cop. To shoulder the blame. To carry it all these years. Even to tell me, now.

It doesn't make any sense.

"W-why?" I finally manage. "If you haven't even told your mother... why did you tell *me*?"

It takes him a second to absorb what I just said. A shaky breath hisses out of him. "I don't know, sweet girl," he admits. "Maybe because I want you to trust me. And you deserve to know the facts, if you're willing to keep sleeping next to me. You should understand why I am the way I am, so you can decide how to keep yourself safe."

Because he's a good man.

And, for him, I'm starting to believe this is as real as anything ever could be.

I run my hands over his shoulders and his arms, wanting to comfort him. "You did the right thing, Marco. I know it probably doesn't feel like it, but you did what you would have done for any officer who was shot in cold blood, right in front of you. That man was a violent criminal. And he threatened you and your family. It *was* self-defense."

"I wanted him to die," he whispers back, shaking his head. "I wanted his *blood*. And then, back at the precinct, I found out he had kids. *Kids*, Alice. They came in—without a mother or any other guardian— and I... I couldn't even *look* at them."

I press my fingertips to his lips again, silencing his spiral. "It's awful. So awful for everyone. I'm so sorry you had to go through that, but what that man did isn't your fault. He was dangerous, Marco. I won't tell you not to blame yourself, but *I* don't blame you."

He flexes his arms, tucking me into him and holding fast. For a long time, neither of us speaks. I feel the way his breathing stutters and know he can't say any more without breaking. I'm content to let him hold me and stroke my hands over his shoulders while he slowly winds down.

When his posture loosens, I stand and draw him to his feet. Silently, I lead him to his room and push him onto his bed. He goes willingly, watching me with wary eyes. Like he's sure I won't stay. Or maybe like he's worried I never existed to start with.

I look down at him, weighing everything he told me. All the horrors he's endured. And the burning, fanatical need he has to protect me.

Neither of us says a word as I slide into his bed. And despite the mess we left in the living room, I've never felt safer.

alice

"OKAY, so, are we going more for, like, sexy-classy... or are we going more for make-him-come-in-his-pants-as-soon-as-he-sees-you?"

I probably should have known better than to ask Tris for fashion advice.

But I am wildly out of my depth when it comes to picking an outfit for a *date*.

Because that's what I have. A date. A real, live, pick-me-up-at-the-door, "the reservation's at eight" date.

In fact, I'm fairly certain the only reason Marco cleared me to come to my apartment for the afternoon is so that he can pick me up like a proper suitor.

That and the video cameras all over the hallway.

I blink at my roommate. Tris assesses my expression and nods, all business. "Got it. He'll have to change his pants before dinner."

After a lot of bickering and at least three more references to Marco's manhood, we eventually settle on one of the cocktail dresses I've never had the courage to actually wear—creamy satin covered in vibrant watercolor roses and dark green leaves.

"This will look ah-mazing with those titties of yours, Alley Cat." Tris flings a lacy white bra at me and tilts her head. "If you skip panties, do you think your puss will freeze? It's only, like, forty degrees outside, but you don't want panty-lines in a satin dress."

"I'm not going commando to a five-star restaurant," I hiss, arranging my boobs in the bra before tugging my dress over it. The fabric skims my waist and floats away, flattering my hips and legs.

Up top, a loose, draped scoop-neck and thin straps reveal *a lot* more cleavage than I bargained for. Tris insists it's fine, but I still feel partially naked... even after I add panties and a blood-red pashmina from Tris's closet. She also shoves a pair of nude, strappy heels at me.

"Don't bother with lip gloss until you're in the car," she advises, shrugging. "He's just going to kiss it off the second he sees you."

Marco's heavy knock sounds at the front door. I do one last check in the mirror, debating the gloss. My reflection surprises me. With my hair carefully fluffed out, and just enough makeup to draw attention to my eyes, I almost look... good?

My date seems to agree. When I open the door, Marco's impassive expression instantly falls off his face. His eyes flash as they flow over my hair, my chest, my dress.

Tris probably expected him to slam me into the wall and maul me the way one of her dates would. But Marco silently brings his gaze to mine, showing the intensity burning there. I can practically hear the sensual bent to his thoughts as his mouth tips up in his small smirk. *Hi.*

I feel myself grin. *Hi.*

He steps over the threshold, angling his big body around mine in a stance more intimate than any kiss. "These are for you," he murmurs.

Marco lifts his left hand and brings a bouquet between our chests. For a second, I can't focus on the flowers. I only see his onyx dress shirt and the casual way he's left the top couple of buttons undone. Not to mention how the column of his throat meets his thick, muscled chest...

I blink, forcing my eyes down to the over-the-top arrangement in his equally large hand. It's *gorgeous.* White orchids, spring lilies, and snowy snapdragons, each so pristine their petals sparkle.

They look so similar to one of the pictures I keep shamefully stashed under my bed, my cheeks heat. I finger the powder-blue ribbon tying the whole thing together, still not believing my luck. "You picked these out?"

"For you," he says again, dropping his arm and my flowers to his side. "I'll put them in water in a minute."

Marco stares down at me like he can't *not.* His gaze skims my lips before burning a path back to mine. "You're exquisite."

His knuckles brush over the blush flooding my face. Another small smile touches his features. *Cute,* he seems to say, amused by my rosy embarrassment.

I run a fingertip along the upturned corner of his lips. *Unfairly handsome,* I toss back mentally.

His eyes soften, reading my thoughts and pulling me closer with the arm twined around my middle. We stare at each other for an endless moment, somehow communicating things that can never be put into words.

He... *likes* me. Really likes me, if the glowing reverence in his dark gaze is to be believed.

Before long, a wolf whistle echoes from the hallway. Marco sighs, leaning his forehead into mine while he calls out, "Find somewhere else to be, Tris."

"And miss the show?" she scoffs. "You clearly don't know me very well, big boy."

Wry amusement flashes across Marco's features, but he never so much as glances her way. "What are the odds she leaves us alone?"

I bite down on a smirk. "Pretty much zero?"

"Alright then." He presses one sweet kiss to my mouth. "Let's get out of here."

AM I proud of the fact that I went back to review the contents of Alice's hidden shoebox?

No.

Am I willing to do anything necessary to get over whatever wall she's keeping around her heart? Hell fucking yes.

There were dozens of images to use as inspiration. Most of them aren't current, though. The resorts and vacation destinations will probably be easy to track down... but the restaurant and clothing pictures were ripped out of magazines over a decade ago.

Still, I got the concept. A very romantic atmosphere, a tucked-away table. Ambience and privacy. I could do that. In fact, I had a great idea.

Alice is *everything* I've been waiting for.

No one will keep me from giving her the first date she deserves.

Especially not the woman herself, who does just about everything she can to convince me I don't need to take her anywhere "fancy" as we walk into our first destination of the evening.

God, she looks lovely. The oncoming twilight just makes her eyes even bluer, her skin creamier. I'm internally counting the minutes until I can run my hands all over the silky floral dress covering her curves.

"You're forgetting something important," I murmur, trying to sound urgent as I wrap myself over her, and my lips graze the tip of her burning ear.

Her azure eyes go wide with worry. "W-what?"

I flash the smile that usually makes her squeeze her thighs together. "I *want* to take you somewhere fancy. I want the whole city to see who I'm out with."

She doesn't believe me. That's okay. She will. I have no plans to retreat. I hold her gaze so she can soak in how earnest I am as I add, "You make me very proud."

Her eyes gloss while she bites down on her lip. "Maybe... let's just go back to your place."

She isn't entirely kidding, and that has me laughing out loud, even when my cock jerks at the jest. "Oh, we will," I promise. "After I show you off properly."

Le Coucou boasts the best French food in town and an undeniably romantic atmosphere. The white brick walls and rounded passageways make the interior intimate, despite the high ceilings, enormous windows, and all the finery.

I check-in with the maître d' and steer Alice away from the main dining room, toward the picture-perfect bar area. A vintage chandelier glows over the antique black bar's marble top. Delicate, shimmery aqua blues and forest greens make up the mural surrounding the room's arched doors and the large mirror behind rows of gold shelves filled with expensive liquors.

Her mouth briefly drops open. "Marco... it's *gorgeous* in here."

"Then you fit right in," I inform her, my tone not to be argued with. "We're just staying here for a couple of drinks. Here's our table."

Alice blinks when I pull her chair out for her. She tries to hide her surprise, dropping into her seat and smoothing her skirt nervously. I fold myself into the seat beside her instead of one across the table, handing her the wine list. "What's your favorite?"

The same question I asked the first time I had her. The flare of desire that lights in her eyes makes my cock twitch.

It darkens as quickly as it appears, though, replaced with a sort of sadness I don't understand. I reach for her hand, but she leaves it limp in mine, looking at me with pure dismay.

"You really shouldn't have done this," she murmurs, gesturing around at the buzzing bar.

I'm not sure how to answer her; she hasn't even seen my real plan yet. I squeeze her fingers. "What do you mean?"

Alice has never looked more beautiful than she does when she lets her rigid posture fall lax and tilts me a hefty dose of side-eye. Her gaze rolls as her perfect, lush lips tilt into a sardonic smile.

"I mean... a date is one thing," she jokes, "but this is just mean. You're going to make it impossible for me to go out with anyone else ever again."

I should probably be alarmed by how deeply satisfying I find that thought. Instead, I frown at her. "Why would that be a bad thing?"

She half-shrugs. "Because this is temporary. I know we've been having fun this week, but I know that doesn't mean anything. We can't be forever. Just for now."

Fucking hell.

It isn't the first time she's said that. Before, I thought she had low self-confidence. Then, when I heard how her mother spoke to her, I assumed it had something to do with a chronic lack of approval.

I spent the whole week worshipping her body and praising her every chance I got, though. And after last night, if she still doesn't think I see a future for us...

I'm absolutely out of ideas as to why she would ever believe that.

"Alice..." I start, unsure how to phrase my suspicions. "If there's a reason why you think we could never be in a real relationship, I think you need to let me in on it. Because I can't think of a single goddamn thing. You're the kindest, smartest, loveliest woman I've ever been on a date with. Any man would be lucky to have you as his girlfriend."

It's quick, but I catch the naked pain that bolts across her face. And why does she suddenly look so *ashamed*?

Alice bites her lip, worrying it. "You—No. That isn't true."

I don't know how, and I don't know when, but whoever is responsible for this look on her face is going to pay. Using my free hand, I lift her chin and cup her cheek, asking her to go on without saying a single word.

Her answering sigh trembles. Watery mortification fills her vivid blue depths. "I... It—" Her head shakes from side to side. "It's not a nice story."

I've taken blows to the head that hurt less than seeing tears in her eyes. I hate that it's happened two nights in a row—last night because of my past and now because of something in hers.

I brush my lips across her cheek, wanting to chase the bad memories off her face. "Shhh, sweet girl. You don't have to tell me."

I'm not sure I *want* to know. Or if I can take it.

We sit in heavy silence for a long moment before Alice sighs quietly again. Our eyes meet once more, hers conveying that whatever she needs to tell me won't get easier with time. She ducks her head slightly, but slowly starts.

"When I met Tris, I couldn't believe she wanted to be friends with *me*," Alice whispers. "Everyone loved her. Guys. Other girls. She was *it*, you know? She's always had that thing that people can't resist. Everyone loves her."

My jaw hardens, both at her dismissal of herself and her assertion about Miss Dunn—a woman I've never been drawn to for even a minute.

Oblivious, she goes on, "When we moved to the city together after college, we went out every Tuesday night to this one bar. Tris loves karaoke, and this place had everything. Good drink specials, cute boys, great DJ."

I wonder which place she is referring to and whether I've ever taken Ella there. She's joined Tris for her weekly karaoke nights a few times, but I don't recall ever seeing Alice with them. I know I would have remembered her.

A waiter brings us a bottle of water, asking what we'd like to drink. I point at the first bottle I see and wave him off. Alice shifts beside me, clearly growing uncomfortable as she continues her story.

She darts her eyes around to make sure no one else is listening and exhales hard. "Th-there w-was... There was this one group we saw every week. Five or six good-looking men our age who liked the open mic night, too. They all worked in Midtown, like Tris, and, of course, it only took a few weeks before they were eating out of the palm of her hand."

My fingers curl around Alice's thigh, not liking her ominous tone one bit. "What happened?"

"One of them picked *me*." She says the words with remembered shock. "Tony. He started sitting with *me* every week, buying *my* drinks, asking about my work and my hobbies. One night, he... he held my hand. Out in the open, on top of the table, where his friends could see."

God, it hurts how much that one simple act surprised her. I

swallow a knot and bring our joined hands to my mouth, kissing her knuckles. "Lucky bastard."

Instead of gifting me a giggle, Alice winces. Her shoulders hunch.

"I'd been with other men before," she admits quietly. "In college, after parties, and stuff. Fumbling around in the dark, tipsy, and all that. But I'd never had a... a date. And he asked me out on one. S-so I went, and then he wanted me to come home with him, s-so I did."

Her words break. Instinctual fury pours through me. "What did he do?"

So help me God, if he hurt her.

She finally whispers, "He kept asking me out. Sleeping with me, calling me his girlfriend. And I was so, so happy. I'd always wanted to be in a real relationship."

I ignore the burn of envy in my gut. Which is wise, because a second later she blurts, "I didn't notice at first how often he asked me to do things for him. It started small, with dry cleaning or groceries. Then he wanted meals and foot massages. He asked for money toward our dates, but almost never planned any."

Fucking *jackass. Tony what,* I wonder. *I could probably find him. Pay him a little visit and—*

"It t-turned out that it was all a j-joke. A b-bet, actually."

—and kill him.

A *bet?*

She lets that sink in for a moment. My skin prickles, heating as rage simmers under the surface.

Our waiter returns, uncorking the red wine I selected and pouring enough for a taste. I don't take one, pointing to Alice's glass with an expression that must be close to murderous. No wonder he scurries off as soon as possible.

"What do you mean?" I bite out.

Alice's cheeks flame. "Th-there was... It was joke from a TV show, I guess," she stammers quietly. "When two girls were out, and one was beautiful, and the other one was ugly, the joke was that a guy's wingman would have to 'jump on the grenade' so his buddy could score the hot one."

She sniffs once. "I found texts on his phone one night. A group chat. They were all coming up with things for Tony to get me to do. Errands, chores. Some, um, sex stuff. They had money on how far they could push me until I finally realized they were messing with my head."

forty-four

WELL, *this has been fun.*

Thanks for joining me, but I really ought to get going.

Remember when I said we could be a long-term thing? Well, actually...

My mind plays through all the polite ways for this man to extricate himself from my pathetic presence. Meanwhile, Marco gapes at me like I've just told him I have three weeks to live. Horror. Shock. And—worst of all—pity.

I fix my posture, too restless to sit still. But he is frozen, with his sharp, dark eyes boring into my face as I nervously take a sip of wine.

Moments tick by. Gradually, his hands fist in his lap. The molten emotion in his gaze hardens into iron. "I need a last name."

Realizing what he means, I almost choke on my next swallow. My head shakes furiously.

"Tell me," he rasps, balling his fingers tighter.

"Marco, n-no." Just thinking about the two men meeting mortifies me. Scalding tears sting my vision. "P-please."

A rough breath vaults out of him as he reaches down and tugs my chair closer with one swift yank. His solid arm winds around my waist, pulling me into his solid strength. He holds me fiercely, not giving an inch, but his hands are gentle; one against my hip and the other cupping my chin.

"I want to find every person who's ever made you cry and make them regret it," he rumbles, gruff. "If you won't tell me his name, at least tell me you kicked him in the balls before you dumped him."

He's kind to phrase it that way, knowing full well the guy was neither my boyfriend nor the one who got "dumped." I shake my head again, a hopeless, watery laugh bubbling as I recall, "Tris did it. I don't know what she said or what she did, but I never saw any of those guys at that bar again."

Marco's embrace constricts. He doesn't speak, but he drops his forehead to rest against my shoulder, and, somehow, his ragged breathing says more than words ever could.

He regrets upsetting me on our first real date. He's *furious* on my behalf.

And he isn't planning on going anywhere.

WITH MY FLOODGATES FIRMLY OPEN, Marco makes it his mission to find out every possible detail about me.

He asks if I like the dry Italian red wine he's chosen and then insists on hearing *why* I like it. While I tell him all about my misadventures in Tuscany with Tris, he listens as though I'm explaining the secrets of the universe.

Then, he wants to know *more*.

He asks about high school—torture, for a nerdy fat girl. If I was in any clubs—I begrudgingly admit to my membership in the Future Librarians Club during sophomore year.

Which class was my favorite? And how did I pick my small, liberal arts college? Did I like it there? What about my major? Did I ever regret leaving Georgia to come to the city after graduation?

The questions themselves aren't unusual for a first date, but his intensity is. He absorbs every word like it's vitally important for him to understand everything about me. Every follow-up question delves a bit deeper, peeling back layers no one has disturbed for years. If ever.

He asks about my childhood, frowning thoughtfully when I describe growing up in my country-club-centric hometown and all the Cotillion nonsense I endured.

"What about your mom?" he asks, pouring me another glass from the obscenely expensive bottle. "What is she like?"

My chest heats while I try to come up with an honest, diplomatic answer. "She's... very put-together."

His brows twitch. "As in 'organized' or...?"

I roll my lips, considering. "She values beauty. Her own and others'. She likes to carefully curate the way everything looks." *Herself, her house. Me.* "It can get a little tiring."

"Hmm." He doesn't like that, I can tell. "And your father?"

My throat tightens. "I don't know him. My mom never—I guess they were a casual thing, because she gave me her maiden name and has never mentioned him at all. By the time I was old enough to ask, she had married my stepfather, and she usually just shut me up by telling me that *he* was my father, now."

Marco's scowl deepens. "And is he? Like a father to you?"

A very unladylike snort tears from my lips. I promptly hide behind my wine glass, mumbling, "He's more like an annoyed, distant great-uncle."

Marco hears me loud and clear. His mouth quirks at my sad little joke, but his warm hand envelops mine, squeezing gently. "So he never intervened? In raising you?"

I shake my head. Marco clearly has a hard time picturing the whole arrangement. He keeps frowning while he asks, "What does he do?"

"Some sort of insurance?" I've honestly never bothered to nail down the exact details. I only know one other thing about him for certain. "He plays golf a lot. My mom usually *deals with me* on her own."

Lord. I know the bitterness in my bearing isn't attractive, but I can't help it. Every kind word Marco gives me only underscores how few I get from my own family. Or *anyone*. After a week of his attention, I have a whole new kind of clarity on my relationship with my mom. Especially after Monday's FaceTime episode.

The intent focus in Marco's eyes takes on a harder edge while he remembers the same incident. "I didn't like the way she spoke to you this week. If she were ever to talk to you like that in front of me, I'm not sure I would be able to stop myself from having words with her. Would that bother you?"

A wave of anxiety rolls over me. "T-Tris has tried," I stammer. "My mom doesn't listen, and it just ends up being a big, dramatic scene. I-it's not worth it."

Marco lifts the hand entwined with his and presses his lips to my knuckles. "It is absolutely worth it," he says, staring right into me.

I open my mouth to argue, but his stern lips pull tight.

One sharp shake of his head. Another reverent kiss to my hand. And words I might replay forever. "The more I get to know you, the more convinced I am. *You* are worth everything."

alice

IN CASE I didn't believe him, Marco makes sure to prove his point an hour later when he informs me that we are not actually eating at Le Coucou.

Instead, he leads me to our true dinner destination.

At first, when he parks his insanely sexy sports car under an unfamiliar condo building, I think maybe we are going to a party of some sort. He notices my nerves, of course, and gives me a warm smile while we ride up in a clean, quiet elevator. "Just the two of us," he assures me.

Suddenly, I can't wait one more second to touch him. The

three glasses of wine have my libido purring... and a big, sexy man who knows me so well and seems to find my social anxiety endearing is just too much for me to take.

I throw myself at him, and he catches me as if he's secretly been waiting to haul me into his arms all night. Our lips brush together, settling into a lush kiss. He angles his mouth over mine to lick deep, cupping the back of my skull in one enormous hand like it holds a delicate treasure.

The elevator dings, and he surges forward, striding out of the vestibule as if I weigh nothing. Like he walks around with a fully plus-sized woman clinging to his neck all day, every day. His mouth doesn't even leave mine until a bracing gust of wind sweeps around us, distracting me.

Are we... outside?

I break away, frowning in bemusement while I turn my head. Still plastered to his front, I can only see the elevator and a wall behind him. We are definitely outdoors, though, standing on a rooftop? In the cold nighttime air.

With a wry little smile, Marco sets me down and slowly turns me, pressing his chest into my back. "I thought we'd have a special meal tonight."

Every bit of breath quivers out of my body. My muscles lock up, frozen in absolute awe.

Because it's... *perfect*. A dream.

My dream.

We are on a private rooftop with a modern glass fence gating the platform, offering completely unobstructed views of Manhattan in all her glory. Across the open space, a sumptuous table for two glitters—a champagne tablecloth with flickering candles and rose-gold place-settings. Strings of warm fairy lights sway in the open air above us, luminous and romantic.

Two restaurant-style space heaters flank the arrangement. They'll make the table perfectly comfortable, I realize—and they're probably keeping the exotic floral arrangement laid in its center from shrinking in the chilly air.

"Marco…"

I can't move. Can't speak. I am sure the second I do, it will all disappear. And I'll wake up, alone in my bed, listening to Tris have a four-way down the hall. Underscoring just how lonely I truly am.

How lonely I *used to be*.

The heat of Marco's body slides against my side, pressing into my hip as if to reassure me. Like he *knows* I can't believe this is happening. His lips skim my temple while he gestures to our table. "After you, darling."

forty-six

I FLOATED through our dinner and all the way back to Marco's.

At this point, it's possible my feet won't ever touch the ground.

All of Tris's theatrics about taking a risk, giving this a chance. Enjoying what I can while I can....

She was right. Because even if this ends, I'll always have the memory of this man converting a Manhattan rooftop into our own private restaurant. How he blushed when he offered to dance with me, admitting he's terrible at it. And the way he leaned over the table when our three catered courses were through, brought my hand to his lips, and murmured, "Ready to go home?"

Home.

The word echoes in my dizzy, delirious thoughts as I watch Marco's profile. He frowns in concentration, swiping his electronic key card through the front door's lock mechanism.

It beeps, and he cracks the slab open, pausing to slant me a look that's half-teasing, half-consternation. "Fair warning," he begins. "I have one more surprise for you."

Astute man that he is, Marco doesn't give me time to overthink it. He promptly shoves the door out of the way, deftly spinning me over the threshold so I can see the final piece of his plan.

Hundreds of white rose petals line the wood floor of the hallway, forming a trail to the ice bucket and champagne laid out on the kitchen table. The only light in the whole apartment comes from dozens of candles. They flicker from clusters on the floor, the countertops, and the coffee table.

The door shuts behind us, but I barely hear it. My eyes sting as I blink, trying to clear the dream-like vision in front of me. Hoping I'm wrong.

This can't be happening. I'll never recover from losing *this.*

Tears drip down my cheeks, blurring the scene. No matter how many times I flutter my lashes, it's all still there.

Two thick fingers press under my chin. Marco turns my face toward his, a new question blooming in his eyes. Wondering what he's done wrong.

You've ruined me, I think, praying to God that he won't be able to read my mind. His warm depths ignite, swelling with all the things that are so uniquely, sincerely him.

Pain and determination. Possession and lust. Solid and steady, but somehow threaded with that open, obvious tenderness.

It's already all the things I never thought I would have. Then he opens his mouth, his voice gravelly as he issues his final request.

"Let me make love to you."

IF I REALLY AM DREAMING, I've decided not to wake up.

Nope. No way. I'll just die here in Dreamland, thank you very much.

Marco waits, looming over me, all dark sensuality and reverence. I'm sure I practically climb his body in reply, because two seconds later, he has me in his arms once again.

I expect him to set a brisk pace and stride right for the bedroom. Instead, he cuddles me close and nuzzles into my neck. "Sweet, beautiful girl. So good to me."

His praise touches my heart... then slides down to pool in my core, contracting the muscles until they throb. I whimper, and he hums, kissing a slow path to my mouth. He sinks his tongue against mine, moving with languorous, thorough thrusts.

Marco takes a few steps and balances me against the cased opening to his great room, slipping his jacket off before trailing his fingertips up my forearms. They tingle while he pulls Tris's crimson pashmina from my elbows, letting it fall to the floor beneath me.

"You look incredible tonight," he whispers, lifting my arm to brush his lips against the pulse in my wrist. My legs tighten around his hips. "You made me so proud. I loved showing you off. I'm going to take you to every five-star restaurant in the whole damn city, just to make sure everyone who's anyone knows you're *mine.*"

My heart pounds, heavy with the depth of my emotion. "Thank you," I breathe, on the verge of tears again. "Thank you so much, Marco. For all of this."

His kisses return to my face, more purposeful than before.

"We'll do it again," he promises. "*All* of this. We're aren't just for one night, Alice. I'm going to take you out and bring you home and make love to you every chance I get."

My eyes spill while I nod, gasping around a sob. "O-okay."

He *tsks*, holding me closer. "Come here, baby."

Marco bends and easily sweeps my body to the side, holding me bridal style as he starts toward his bedroom. There are roses and candles everywhere—the kitchen table, the floors, the counters—but I can't appreciate them.

I only see Marco. His chiseled jaw, dark with stubble, taut with all the emotion he keeps inside. The way his eyes shine, hot but also full of feeling. The concentration tightening his square features, the determined set of his massive shoulders.

He carefully places me on the edge of his bed and shucks his shirt before going to his knees. The air rushes out of my body while he reaches for my ankles. His fingers make quick work of the straps, sliding my heels off before taking my feet. He sets one on his shoulder and begins massaging the other, running his open mouth along my inner thigh.

"God," he exhales, lightly biting the plump skin. "Fucking heaven."

His tongue smooths away the sting just as his thumb works my instep. My hips jerk forward, and I moan. The sound echoes off his walls, drowning out the quiet beat of whatever song pumps from the speakers in the ceiling. I bite my tongue.

Good Lord. I really am noisy.

Just as my tide of shame rises, Marco nips me again. I look down to find his dark eyes glowing with heat. "Louder," he demands.

For a second, I flounder. But then his free hand smooths up the back of the leg draped over his hard, hot shoulder, and his fingertips brush the wet lace covering my core.

My audible gasp makes his lips twitch. He goes back to licking a path up my thigh while he strokes over the soaked panties, lightly teasing my clit through the rough fabric until I mewl.

He gives a low sound of approval while he lifts my other ankle to hook my knee over his vacant shoulder. He pushes the skirt of my dress to my waist, baring the ivory thong underneath. "Look at you," he murmurs, staring. "I can't wait to taste you."

He doesn't waste any time. With a few more reverent brushes of his mouth to my upper thighs, he pulls the panties away from my pussy and settles his mouth over me.

Unlike the starved, possessive licks he gave me the first time, his mood tonight seems more loving. He takes his time lingering over every inch of me, working me into a frenzy with slow, deep plunges inside and sweet suction over my clit.

The hand that isn't busy holding my underwear to the side reaches up. At first, I think he'll grab my breasts, but his palm settles against my cheek instead, holding my face while he pleasures me.

The tender way his thumb brushes over my mouth sends me over the edge. The next time he slants suction over my throbbing core, I come, crying his name while Marco groans.

We both pant. He straightens, sliding his hand back to my nape as he gets to his feet. "You're incredible," he praises, stepping between my legs and bending over me.

I ache to have him naked. My fingers fly to his belt. The fine fabric of his suit falls to his feet, and I push at his boxers, too. Marco steps out of it all and slowly lifts the hem of my dress, pulling it off. I remove my bra and my sopping panties just in time for him to wrap both of his muscle-bound arms around my middle.

He hugs me close, rubbing our bare skin together, and easily maneuvers us into the middle of his giant mattress. Lying on such a big bed, with such a big man on top of me, I actually feel like I'm the right size, for once. Especially when his body settles between my legs, and he trails kisses up my stomach before capturing one of my nipples.

I dig my nails into his solid shoulders, moaning and arching under him, pressing his pulsing erection between our bodies. His breathing picks up, but his pace doesn't. He clearly wants to take everything as slowly as he can stand to.

For *me*.

To make it romantic and sweet for me. Because he already knows me well enough to know exactly what I want.

Fresh emotion fills my eyes while I run my hands down his back, feeling the hard flesh. He rears up just in time to distract me with the masculine perfection of his body. Flickering candlelight moves over his muscles, bathing his glowing bronze. I trace down over his abs and take his rigid length in my hand.

"Alice," he groans, tipping his head back while I stroke him. "I love the way you touch me."

I remember what set him off last time and use both hands, clasping around the head of his erection on each draw until pre-cum wets both of my palms. When he starts to pulse on every tug, I look up to find him staring at me, chest heaving. He pulls out of my hands and crawls over me.

"You're everything I've ever wanted," he whispers, pausing to press a kiss to my heart. "Better. *More.*"

But he has it all wrong. *He's* the answer to *my* prayers, not the other way around. The dream I thought I'd never have... and he is truly so much more than I ever imagined.

Marco tenses, dark eyes skirting to the nightstand. I instantly shake my head, my hand floating up to touch his cheek. *No. We don't need a condom. I just want you.*

He stares at me, eyes smoldering with every kind of intensity I can fathom. Including guilt. With a regretful expression, he reaches over and takes one out anyway.

"You're all that matters to me," he whispers into my hair, leaning as he rolls it onto his length. "I'll make sure it's safe for you, and then we can stop using them, okay?"

In answer, I put both hands on the back of his head, tangling them in his thick black hair, and pull his mouth to mine. Marco settles between my thighs. The blunt head of his cock brushes against my pussy, slicking through the wetness seeping from my center.

He sets his forehead against mine, eyes falling shut as he groans. "*Alice.*"

The way he feels... the way he *looks*... I'm suddenly *terrified* to be so happy. Part of me panics, sure that he'll change his mind at the last minute—fling himself off me or reveal a hidden camera or something.

I move to grip his sides, pressing him down while I spread my legs wider, rushing to get him inside me before it all goes wrong. Marco senses the frantic edge to my movements and opens his eyes, reading all the fears pricking at my middle.

His features crease, pained. He frames my face with his hands, balancing on his forearms as he stretches over me. His dark depths glow fervently.

"You don't have to be afraid, sweet girl," he says, staring right into my eyes. "I'm not going anywhere." Another flash of feeling echoes in his gaze. "I promise."

Tears stream down my temples while I blink up at him in amazement. "You're sure?"

"Yes," he says, the word almost harsh with his insistence. "More than ever before."

He doesn't give me a chance to doubt it. The second he finishes his confession, he surges forward, filling my body with one deep thrust.

I moan too loudly, but he doesn't care. Marco strokes over my hair and my cheek while he brushes our lips together.

His chest vibrates on a ragged grunt as he starts to move. He sets an achingly slow pace, sliding almost all the way out of me every time, angling his hips to hit the throbbing place inside me on each plunge. While he rolls his body against mine, grinding and rotating, his mouth swallows every moan and gasp.

He's tireless, working himself into me until I've melted into the mattress twice. When he finally comes, he keeps his face right over mine, letting me see the moment he loses control and spills into me with a mournful cry.

THE PILLOW under my face smells like lavender.

I burrow closer, groaning but smiling to myself.

Shit. Alice *wrecked* me.

For someone so small and quiet, she is voracious. We spent *hours* making love. Again and again.

My sweet girl truly possesses an endless wealth of sensuality. I love that she keeps it under wraps, one of the many layers hidden from the rest of the world. We're alike in that way—choosing not to show most of ourselves to most people. Which only makes my current exhaustion more rewarding.

She picked *me*.

And *used* me. Thoroughly.

My entire body feels loose, especially at the joints. I stretch my arms over my head and open my eyes before I notice that I haven't done my usual anxious survey of my surroundings yet.

Slanting sunlight tells me it is likely mid-morning. Extremely late, for me. It makes sense, though, given how late we kept each other up.

The scent of breakfast food curls into my room. With another smile, I realize I've never eaten anything Alice cooked, aside from tea. I haul myself upright and shove my hand through my hair before finding a clean pair of black boxer-briefs on my way to investigate whatever smells so good.

I find Alice in my kitchen. A few pans of food sit on the stove behind her, each covered and off the heat. Along with my kettle. Of course.

She's facing away from me, enjoying my view of the Hudson while she tinkers with something on the island in front of her. I stop on the threshold to watch her because I can't help myself.

Golden morning light shimmers off her silk robe and catches in her wild curls. She presses her hips into the gray granite counter, resting on her elbows and holding...

A paintbrush.

She shifts from one foot to the other, the bounty of her curves jiggling under her robe. I start to smile again, but the object in her other hand stops me cold. She holds it up to the light streaming in from the windows, squinting at my father's favorite mug.

How did she possibly piece it back together? I broke it during my nightmare and picked up the broken shards the next morning. Throwing them in the trash left a lump in my throat for far longer than I cared to admit.

But now—it's whole again.

Glued together with shining *gold*.

My breath shatters in my lungs. And for a moment, some distant part of my brain wonders: Is this how the guy who discovered diamonds felt? The wonder of realizing that under the right conditions, certain unassuming rocks became priceless, one-of-a-kind treasures?

Did he know what he was doing? Or was he just so fucking *lucky*, like me?

Alice hasn't heard me yet. Her head stays high while she gazes at her handiwork, turning the mug to make sure she's filled every crack. The smallest, sweetest smile curves her lips when she determines she's finished. With care, she sets the piece—more beautiful than ever—on the other side of the island and tilts her neck, her eyes intent on the horizon. Her features smooth, and I wonder what she's thinking about.

Always something deep, I muse, painful warmth bleeding inside of me. Respect and admiration. Fondness. Gratitude. *Alice doesn't have shallows. Only depths.*

A wave of certainty builds behind my heart, swelling high and cresting over the top. Warm contentment trickles down. A swooping burst of joy crowds my cramped lungs, stealing what's left of my breath.

But I don't feel panicked. Only peaceful. My whole being relaxes while my very soul snaps to attention.

Her, it says. *Her*.

Just like that, I *know*.

She's the one. And I love her.

I SPEND a lot of time thinking I look horrible... but this time, I think it might actually be okay.

Tris and I spent the better part of Thursday night arguing over text about what I should wear. She kept pushing low-cut dresses and short skirts at me, insisting I play up my *"ass-ets."*

A month ago, I would have told her that I didn't *have* any assets. Now, that doesn't feel true.

Marco truly seems to love running his hands over my hips and my backside... following the line of my spine with his fingertips while he takes me from behind... propping me up in his lap to focus entirely on the way my breasts loom in front of his face.

And then there are the sweeter things. He still likes to gently pull my fingers away from my mouth when I start to bite them. He never grimaces at the paint-stained cuticles or makes a single sound of reproach. He only brushes his lips across the abused skin and tucks my hand into his iron grip for safekeeping.

Whenever I laugh or sing or smile at a scene in one of my smut books, his stern lips soften into a smile of his own. When we spend our evenings snuggled on his sofa, sharing a throw blanket he barely fits under, he listens to every word out of my mouth. Even the stammers and mumbles.

Marco Amir is not a man who softens. But he does for me.

Case in point—he's planned *another* date.

Insisted on one, actually.

The thought banishes the anxiety crowding my lungs. I stare at the navy-blue dress Tris and I finally settled on and give myself an encouraging nod. Marco will like it. He seems to like everything I wear.

He somehow finds redeeming qualities for even the ugliest, least flattering pieces. My terrycloth robe that always highlights my round mid-section? Also offers a tantalizing flash of my boobs. The yoga pants that bunch around my thighs? Make my ass look great, apparently. The stretched-out panties that I forgot to change out of before he came home one night? He liked that *I* didn't like them, because it meant he could tear them in half in his single-minded quest to get his mouth between my thighs.

I'm starting to suspect that maybe he just... likes my body.

I'm starting to think that maybe I do, too.

The navy dress is pretty. I put it on and stand in front of Marco's full-length mirror. It's tucked into his huge closet—which is entirely too big for the man who only wears black suits, exercise clothing, and barely there boxers.

Last weekend, he claimed it "just made sense" to move my

things in here while I stay with him. You know, since he has all this extra space...

The memory of his gruff, muttered explanation and embarrassed flush puts an almost-smug smile on my face. I've been at Marco's place for three whole weeks and—despite the paparazzi losing interest in my apartment—he has vehemently argued every time I suggested going back to my own place.

I'd maybe start to suspect he simply wants me to stay, but Marco has also proven truly fanatical about my protection.

My phone buzzes with a FaceTime call, and I swipe at the screen without looking away from my reflection, assuming it's Tris. She was supposed to call me an hour ago.

"Alice!"

My mother's shriek freezes the blood in my veins. I instantly have to fight the urge to duck and hide.

"M-mama?"

Sure enough, when I peer at the screen wedged in my hand, there's my mother. Wearing a pink wrap dress, holding a martini in her manicured hand. Glaring at me.

Gulping, I glance around, trying to figure out which wall looks the most like my own apartment. But it's a lost cause. This is *clearly* a man's place. And I'm obviously in his closet.

A nauseating thrill darts through me when I realize there's nothing to be done. She's going to disapprove... and *I don't care.*

She huffs around the rim of her glass as she takes a fortifying sip. "Well, now I see why you've been avoiding me. Are you still in that man's apartment? It's been *weeks*, Alice. And you haven't fixed your hair yet, either?!"

She's right when she assumes I'm avoiding her. More than anything, I didn't want to explain Marco.

She knew about Tony... and then I had to tell her how and why it ended. Given how much better Marco is than Tony in every category, I'm terrified of what she'll say about Marco's interest in me. Especially once she sees a picture of him and finds out just how out of my league I truly am.

I angle the screen away from his belongings, digging deep to find the insane burst of courage I had seconds before. Drawing from it. "I-I like the curls, Mama. I'm g-going to keep them."

Her painted pink lips pucker while she rakes her eyes down what little of me she can see. "Is that a cocktail dress?" she demands. "Where are you going in a dress on a Friday night, anyway? Do you have an event?"

I repress a wince. "I have a dinner," I hedge, trying to avoid the word *date*. "And I have to leave in a few minutes, so..."

She starts to offer some unsolicited opinion just as the bedroom doors open. *Oh dear sweet heavens. It can't be—*

"Alice?" Marco's deep timbre reverberates as he approaches the closet. He sounds irritated.

Wide-eyed, I snap my head to the side. My grip on my phone turns clammy. "Is that him?" my mother asks, putting her glass down with a *clank*. "The man who has you over at his place so often?"

My mouth gapes while I try to scrape out words. An explanation for Mama. A warning to Marco. An excuse to slam the closet door or end the call. Something. *Anything.*

But, of course, it's me. So nothing comes out.

Marco appears on the threshold, looking ridiculously handsome in a thin black sweater, black slacks, and an open camel-colored coat. Even set in a ferocious frown, his face could steal my breath. If I were breathing.

"Alice," he starts, not realizing I'm on a call. "Sorry I'm late, sweet girl. Traffic was a nightmare and—"

"Alice Lillian Moore!" I cringe as my mother's tinny voice bursts from the phone speaker. "*Who* is this man? And don't even *think* about lying to me! I can *see* you."

Marco's eyes fly to mine. *Your mom?* he mouths.

Again, I have no words. I barely manage a weak nod. Mama sees me silently respond to someone off the screen and starts up again. Addressing Marco directly, to my horror.

"Young man!" she calls, shrill. "I can *hear* you! It is unconscionably rude to interrupt a conversation without even bothering to introduce yourself."

The easy resignation that falls over Marco's face surprises me. He doesn't seem angry to have to deal with my mother. Instead of rolling his eyes or fleeing, he places a steady hand on my shoulder and steps into the space behind my body.

"Mrs. Moore," he says, looking into the screen and ignoring the sour look on Mama's face. "It's a pleasure to meet you. I'm Marco Amir."

Mama visibly startles. Shock fills her face while she examines his. Seeing, of course, how horribly outmatched I am.

"It's Mrs. *Campbell*," she snaps. "Mrs. *Richard* Campbell." As if that means anything to anyone outside their silly country club. "Are you the man my daughter has been seeing, *Marco Amir?*"

She *sneers* his name as if it's an insult. Her creamy features pinch as much as her Botox will allow.

Marco subtly squares his shoulders, arching his brow. "I am," he replies, brusque but calm. Brokering no argument. "And I'm the only man she will be seeing for as long as she'll have me."

My insides flutter and liquefy. I can't help but turn my face up to his, seeking the solid sincerity I know I'll find in his dark eyes. When it glints at me, surrounded by steely resolve, I almost smile.

My mom chooses that moment to scoff.

I expect her reaction. Really, I do. I've dreaded it for weeks, knowing that she'd balk the second she heard a gorgeous, successful, intelligent man had set his sights on me.

So I'm not sure why watching her gasp and then smirk—because, clearly, this *has* to be a *joke*—hurts me so deeply.

But it does. Her scornful face hits my heart like a bullet, ripping straight through to the other side. Marco watches my features crumple on the screen and immediately forgets about my mom. He pivots to me, reaching one hand up to cup my cheek.

My mother says something else, but I don't hear it. I've fallen into Marco's clear, bottomless eyes. They tighten when he reads my expression. *She's upsetting you. Let me tell her to go to hell.*

I subtly shake my head. *That will just make it worse for me later.*

I don't miss the way his jaw hardens as he turns to the screen wedged in my frozen fist. His body stays angled toward mine in a distinctly intimate way. My mother notes his stance with another scathing scowl.

"Exactly how long have you two known each other?" she asks, the very picture of indignation. "A proper gentleman would have introduced himself to me before pursuing my daughter."

She looks offended, but her tone still holds the same mocking edge. Like, at any moment, I will admit this is all an elaborate prank and she needs to be able to say she knew it all along.

Marco stares back at her, undeterred. "I believe it's been about six weeks. We met through work. Alice is coordinating an event for my employer."

Mama's tweezed blonde brows arch. "Your employer," she repeats, acidic. "And *who* might that be? Alice doesn't have any clients."

The hand on my shoulder squeezes; a gesture of pride. "Actually, I think she's up to four now, right, sweetheart?" The look he shoots me would be conspiratorial and amused, if not for the hard edge of his tense jaw. "But I work for her largest client. Grayson Stryker."

Of course my mother knows I have the Stryker wedding. She only said I don't have any clients because she "doesn't count" Ella as a "real" client due to our friendship. I would have told her about the other commissions that have started rolling in, but anytime I bring up another bride, she cuts me off. It's part of her constant crusade to convince me to get "an actual job."

Mama leans back and regards Marco with a supercilious air, narrowing her made-up eyes. "And what is it *you* do for him?"

The outright insult instantly knocks me out of my stupor.

"*Mother!*" I cry, aghast. "Don't speak to Marco that way! He—he's—"

Marco's expression turns utterly flat, aside from the anger burning in his gaze. He runs his hand down my back in a comforting caress. "It's okay, sweet girl," he murmurs.

A sardonic smile touches his stern lips. "Actually, Mrs. *Campbell*, I'm an executive at Stryker & Sons. I oversee all their security —both in-house and for all their external holdings."

Mama's lips purse while she flicks her gaze over his face, looking for a lie she won't find. I'm so mortified I think I might cry. Just before I open my mouth to cut her off, she issues another insulting inquiry.

"And how much money do you make?" she demands. "As a *security executive?*"

I blink, utterly dismayed. But Marco's dark humor blossoms with a sharp smile. "Well, if you don't count the housing allowance, company vehicles, travel reimbursements, and bonuses, I believe I'm up to two million dollars a year."

Mama's mouth smacks shut. Her face pales while she reaches up to fiddle with the necklaces layered over her sternum. A nervous gesture I recognize from observing her around Richard's wealthy parents and women who don't like her at the club.

Marco's grin warms into something genuine when he turns to look at me. "Are you ready, darling? We don't want to be late."

"Darling" isn't new; he only uses it when he's teasing me or being unbearably romantic. I can't tell which it is, at the moment. But I love it.

"Of course," I smile back, only sparing my mom one final glance. "We have to go, Mama. Call you later."

She starts to reply, but I hit the end button, dropping the phone to the floor like it burns my palm. Marco stares at it for a long second before he scoops me into his arms and turns to his bed. "Come here."

forty-nine

TRIS

Ohmygodohmygodohmygoddddd

Aliceeeeee

ALICE LILLIAN MOORE

ALICE

WHAT?!

TRIS

Ok. So I just got a text from a friend of a friend and GUESS WHO GOT ARRESTED

Hint: starts with a T

Ends with —ony the Insufferable Piece of Shit

ALICE

Wait... are you serious??

TRIS

Yep! I guess they did a random search of his work computer and found a ton of evidence of insider trading?

They perp-walked him out of his office in front
of all of Wall Street.

ALICE

...a *random* search?

Is that normal?

TRIS

I guess?

I mean, who would have had the right
connections and wanted him to get caught?

ALICE

...

I can only think of one person.

TRIS

Probably the same guy watching you walk
around his apartment all day every day.

ALICE

He does not.

TRIS

Wanna bet, Alley Cat?

"HAVE WE CHECKED THE—"

Brad and I both interrupt Pierce, "Yes."

"But what about the—"

"Yes," we say again.

"And the—"

"*Yes*," I grit a third time. Sometimes, it feels like we have combed footage from every camera in the damn city. I have hundreds of files from dozens of street cams, all ripped from the night of the ill-fated engagement party.

None of them has been helpful. Every time I think about how many man hours we've wasted going through it all, only to come up empty, I want to put my fist through my office wall.

Every other pod on Stryker & Sons' executive floor boasts floor-to-ceiling windows at the front and back. I insisted on taking the one office that was built into the cylindrical floor's only solid segment, beside the elevators.

Without a front wall and door made of glass, no one can peer in, and I don't have to worry about employees seeing things above their pay grade. Or watching me punch drywall.

I do, however, have to worry about my annoying baby cousin sneaking up on me.

Juliet breezes into the room like she owns it, not even bothering to look up as she flicks a hand over her dark red dress and starts speaking.

Not that she's interrupting anyone—once the boys get a look at her, both of them fall silent. Pierce's mouth hangs ajar, while Brad runs his eyes over Jules on a loop.

It has been this way since we were kids. Friends, colleagues, and neighbors all pant after my cousin, and she laughs in their faces. Thankfully, there's no need for that, now that she has Graham Everett's enormous engagement ring on her finger.

"*Primo*." Jules smiles, her expression sly as she glances at her phone screen and then presses it into her chest.

I wonder what she's hiding. Probably just dirty texts from her fiancé.

I really need to kick that guy's ass.

"I just came from Grayson's office, and he wants to see you," she carries on. "Walk with me?"

Her gold-brown eyes flash over to my crack team, who both still look like they've never seen a woman before. She pins me with an amused, slightly derisive look. "Unless you're busy?"

Clearly, they look about as competent as they actually are. I sigh, scrubbing at my face. "Yeah. Hold on."

I rattle off a few directives to the guys. Barnes is on Ella Duty. Which means I need Pierce to go through all of Ted Stryker's bank records. I dispatch Brad to do one final run-through of the security measures in place for Grayson's bachelor party, knowing I will check Ella's handful of destinations myself, since I'll be the one escorting her and her friends.

And Alice, who will be out with her.

Anxiety knots my gut every time I think about my shy, sweet girl going out with Ella. Paparazzi will be rabid for pictures of their party.

The whole plan feels wrong to me. Just like the engagement party that ended in disaster... I can't explain why, but I can't shake the feeling that the worst is yet to come.

Honestly, three weeks have passed since I made Alice my girlfriend... and she is just about the only thing going *right* in my life.

We spend most evenings together, debating philosophy, reading her smut books, making love all over my apartment. Sometimes, we don't feel the need to talk. With Alice tucked next to me, even silence is a joy.

The Wedding of the Century is only six weeks away, and Ella has handed the reins over to my sweet girl completely. She spends her days working nonstop, often groaning in frustration over the safety measures I've kept firmly in place. Although I know I'm going to have to lighten up soon—she and Ella have final meetings all over town, next week.

I still don't like it.

The pieces of this puzzle don't fit together yet, but each feels vitally important. Paparazzi finding Alice in the first place. Daniel bleeding out underneath me. Ted's bloated corpse. The bullet holes in his body—two in the heart, one in the head.

And then there's the one memory that bothers me more than the others: Alice's apartment door, hanging wide open. Everything inside untouched.

I've checked every bit of footage pulled from nearby street cameras a dozen times. I never see anyone go up her stairs or come down them. She has to be right about Tris leaving the door ajar, given her roommate's general thoughtlessness and the fact that no one else even approached their stairs.

The roommate in question gives me an over-the-top wink as Jules and I exit my office and pass by her glass cubicle. Juliet waves at her before leaning closer to me and muttering, "So. Anything you want to tell me?"

My teeth grind together again. "Such as?"

Juliet snorts at me. "You haven't been to Abuelita's in a month. You called Graham to ask for flower shop suggestions. All your goons are giggling about you watching endless surveillance footage of a certain woman. And Ella told me she helped you set up your apartment for a date. Are you hiding your new girlfriend?"

My cousin grins, sensing an easy victory. "Perfect. Family dinner next Saturday. Try to be on time, and maybe take the stick out of your ass beforehand."

Having gotten what she wanted, she abandons the premise of walking with me to Grayson's office, flouncing back toward the legal department. But not before shooting Tris Dunn a wink.

Honestly, the fact that they planned this whole thing doesn't even surprise me.

And it certainly isn't enough to distract me from the alert that pops up on my screen.

Holy fuck.

I stand frozen, watching the black-and-white video streaming from a surveillance camera. My entire plan for the afternoon disintegrates. Hours of work and checking up on a certain special project I'm working on in the background... It's all impossible to focus on, now.

Holy. Fuck.

I turn on my heel, heading for the exit.

And I don't look back.

fifty

I AM NOT an easy man to surprise.

Anticipating other people's moves is my essential skill, honed over a decade.

So the fact that I'm in utter shock by the time I stagger into my apartment is quite an accomplishment for my sweet girl.

I started ripping my clothes off in the elevator, equal parts pissed off and turned on. Did she do this to lure me here? Is she teasing me? Or was stripping naked in the living room and rolling around on my couch with her hand between her thighs meant to be a private moment? One I will *undoubtedly* be interrupting.

My tie and my jacket are already fisted in my left hand when I step over the threshold, giving no care to the slamming door or my heavy footsteps.

Let her hear me.

Naughty, sweet girl.

Over the last few weeks, I've had Alice just about every way I could have imagined. Showered her with all the praise and softness she deserves. Given in to the blossoming dynamic between us, fulfilling her desire for direction and approval.

She's never needed to be *punished* before.

But if she's done this on purpose—taunting me while I'm at work, sending me head-first into arousal so feral, I'm not even sure which company car I took to get here...

My handcuffs are a solid weight in my back pocket. An image springs to mind, but it's obliterated a second later when I walk into the living room. And see *her.*

Fucking hell.

She's lying on her belly, with her knees bent and her ankles crossed behind her. And—God—her body. Pale, creamy curves. Ripples of softness, all sensual grace. Laid out in the afternoon sun, bare and burnished. Like a fucking *banquet.*

Her Kindle glows from its place in front of her as her head snaps up.

I expect surprise. Maybe even guilt.

Instead, her blonde brow arches.

As if *she's* caught *me.*

Alice tilts her head, offering an innocent, coquettish look. "Marco," she says softly. "What brings you home so early?"

Her expression gradually sinks in. Understanding dawning.

She did this on purpose.

Because she's figured out I've been watching her.

The brilliance of this woman hits me all over again. My hard cock ticks fuller, pounding with its own pulse. I have to work to keep my lips from tipping up.

She isn't as circumspect. Her lush mouth pulls up in a well-deserved smirk.

"You know," she says, he voice still light and smooth. As if she isn't completely, beautifully exposed. "I heard something interesting today."

I step toward her, blood singing. Feeling like a wild predator with prey in its sights. "Is that so?"

She shifts, her glorious ass jiggling while her hips squirm slightly. "Something about my—Tony."

I'm not sure whether I want to growl about her nearly referring to that animal as "her" anything, or if I want to praise her for stopping herself. My jaw clenches. "Huh?"

An unexpected flash of vulnerability gilds her azure gaze. "How did you know?" she whispers. "That he was..."

Trash?

I take another careful step. "Because what he did to you had nothing to do with *you*, Alice. You were never weak or stupid; just kind and giving. He was the fucked-up one. Only a cruel dumbass would throw someone so valuable away. I know men like that— and I know they will always find a new low to sink to. Because bad men do bad things."

A new light sparks in her eyes. "And good men catch them."

She's talking about me. Calling me good, despite all the ruined pieces of myself she's seen up close and personal. Confessions and scars and mistakes.

Even now, knowing I haven't been able to keep myself from watching her all these weeks.

She thinks *I'm* a good man.

Now I'm wondering if she did this as a way to thank me for the strings I pulled to catch her ex in his latest scheme. While also calling me out for my stalking. And turning me on.

Because—*goddamn it*—she's *perfect*.

I reach into my pocket, pulling out the solid metal cuffs. I hang them from two fingers, curling them toward me.

"Get in my bed," I husk. "Now."

fifty-one

HE DOESN'T GIVE me time to follow his directions.

The second I'm on my unsteady feet, Marco scoops me off the floor, tossing me over his shoulder. My bare thighs press into the V of exposed skin under his half-buttoned shirt as he turns his face into my hip. Nuzzling there before delivering a sharp nip with his teeth.

I squeak, and he chuckles, the sound dark. His other hand cups my ass. The cool weight of his handcuffs presses between his palm and my naked side. My throat thickens along with my blood.

He's always so gentle with me. Softening his hard edges to make sure I feel safe.

But this version of Marco excites me just as much.

He storms into his bedroom, his motions rough as he tosses me onto his mattress and flips me toward his headboard.

"Hands up, Miss Moore."

I don't think he's called me that since the first night he showed up at my apartment. I recognize his stern tone, though. It's the same one he used at the hospital, when I confessed I thought he was pretending to be into me.

I've pissed him off.

And turned him on.

My stomach swoops as I balance on my knees and reach for his wrought-iron headboard. The click of his cuffs sends goosebumps sweeping over my spine. He positions himself behind me.

He must have removed his shirt because the warmth of his skin melds into mine as he hooks one open shackle around my left wrist and pauses to murmur in my ear, "Do you trust me?"

The rasped undercurrent in his voice puts a hoarse lump in my throat. After everything I've told him, I know he understands why that question pierces me so deeply.

When I give a breathless nod, he exhales, rubbing his nose over my temple. "Good girl. I—" He pauses, his silence as heavy as the solid weight around my wrist. "I trust you, too, Alice."

For a man like Marco, there is no higher compliment. Unexpected tears spring to my eyes, and I turn toward him, letting him see. He rumbles low in his chest, the sound pure masculine approval, tinged with tenderness.

"How did I get so fucking lucky, baby?" he mutters, shucking his pants. "Such a beautiful, brilliant, naughty, sweet girl."

The second he's totally naked, he takes his handcuffs and deftly snaps them into place. Tethering me.

He glides one of his brawny hands down my back, squeezing my ass with a quiet growl. When I glance over my shoulder, I find his dark eyes burning paths over my bared body.

He captures my gaze with his. Intensity freezes the air in my lungs. All the muscles below my waist tighten and gel, molten arousal seeping from my core.

"Who do I belong to, Alice?"

I know what he wants me to say, but *God. Look* at him. *How could he ever—*

His palm lands on my backside with a hard smack. The other envelops the slick head of his cock, stroking it roughly. "Tell me. Who does this dick belong to? Who made me come running home this afternoon without saying a word? Who would I get on my fucking knees for every hour if I could?"

I can barely speak, but the blazing entreaty in his eyes demands a reply.

"M-me?"

Another spank, this one less harsh, followed by a soothing caress. His voice softens, but he reaches for my nape, fisting my hair and pulling insistently. "Say it again, baby. Like you mean it. Who do I belong to?"

He tugs and drops his free fingers to my core, swiping through the wetness pooled there. I gasp, unable to resist blurting, "Me. You're *mine*."

He smiles against my shoulder as he stretches over me to leave a line of kisses there. "I am yours," he assures. "But I want you to show me."

I don't know what he means until he suddenly disappears. Dropping from his knees to his back. Positioning himself with his head between my legs.

I start to protest, but he grips my hips with startling desperation. Begging. "Sit on my face, sweet girl. Grind this pretty pussy all over me."

I can't help it; my core clenches viciously. A burst of cream slips from my slit. And Marco *sees* it, groaning, "Fuck me, *yes*."

If I had any working brain cells, I might hesitate. But I don't. The moment he latches on to my clit—with a raw, starved lack of finesse—I forget why I should be embarrassed.

My moan is so loud it echoes off the walls. His handcuffs chafe my wrists when I try to grab his thick hair.

He hums, tracing circles around the swollen bud pulsing for more. Muttering filthy praise against my soaked center as he spears two fingers inside me. He finds the rough patch he calls "our spot," drawing circles over it until I cry out sharply, more pleasure dripping from my pussy.

It's so *good*. I thrash and sob, riding his mouth the way he asked me to. Unable to feel shame or guilt—unable to feel anything except the building pressure pulling at my core. When he sucks my clit into his mouth, the tension pops. Warm, wet release squeezes all of my inner muscles, dousing his face.

He growls, the sound so feral, my nipples tighten to the point of pain. My hands pull at my binds again, but he reads my mind, repositioning us effortlessly, kneeling behind me.

This time, he doesn't tease. His thick cock surges right into me, impaling the tender muscles still trembling from my climax. He feels so perfect—hard heat, stretching and rubbing and tugging until it almost hurts. I cry his name, scrabbling to hold on to the headboard as he balances on his knees and reaches around to knead my breasts. Pinching the aching tips until I clamp around him all over again.

"Fuck, Alice. Yes. Squeeze me with this perfect pussy. Come for me and I'll fill you up." His snarled praise pushes me over the edge.

I moan, and he roars, losing all semblance of control. His rhythm turns frantic. Fucking me harder than ever. His teeth sink into my shoulder as a hot lash of cum warms me from the inside out.

Marco doesn't collapse on top of me. Instead, he catches me, hooking a bulging arm around my middle and bringing me into the cradle of his big body. "Hold on, love."

Love.

My heart spasms and flips. He reaches over to his nightstand, extracting a key. The handcuffs rattle when he unlocks them.

He rolls us with ease, tucking me into his side. Settling his steady strength around me as he says, "Move in with me."

fifty-two

MARCO PROMISES he won't wake up at five to work out on Monday morning if I promise to stay in bed with him.

Instead, his phone goes off at five-thirty.

With a volley of text messages he tries his best to ignore, pulling me into his warm, naked chest. Until the buzzing gets so out of control that I have to laugh at his attempts to pretend he doesn't hear it.

"Always fucking something," he groans, huffing onto his back to slap his palm around until it hits the iPhone on his nightstand.

While he deals with the notifications, I burrow into the crater of body heat he left in the mattress beside me, tucking my face against his pillow.

Move in with me.

It's been five days since he made his offer and left me speechless. The fact of the matter is, even now, firmly embedded in his life and his home, none of this feels real.

I'm beginning to think it won't be until the Strykers' wedding is over. *And then, if he's still around...*

Either way, I told him I need to get back to reality soon. It's been *weeks* since the engagement party fiasco and the alleged break-in at my apartment—and Ella and I have go to her final dress fitting today.

Marco exhales heavily, as if reading my thoughts and disapproving. Or perhaps facing some new burden.

He bends over me and drops a kiss to my brow, pausing for a second too long with his lips brushing my skin. Sighing again, deeper. "Go back to sleep, sweet girl."

And I try, but I can't quite shake the feeling that there's something he isn't telling me.

I MAY BE able to get Marco Amir to soften.

But I haven't quite mastered getting him to bend.

MARCO

Barnes will pick you and Ella up for her fitting today.

Remember: no subways.

I will know.

I'm still torn between pouting at my phone and giggling when I walk out the door. I settle for looking at his hallway camera, holding his messages up, and giving an exaggerated eyeroll.

Ten minutes later, the Strykers' terrifying British bodyguard arrives. As Ella sits next to me in the backseat of the Mercedes, chirping happily about cake flavors, I do everything I can to avoid the gruff man's silver gaze in the rearview mirror.

He's unsettling, somehow. Watching me more intently than he needs to.

I almost text Marco to tell him, but Ella is a delightful distraction. Her genuine joy sparkles all the way to the East Side boutique guarding her gown. I find myself grinning as she talks, feeling...

Proud.

Of myself.

I did this, I think in awe. *She needed help, and she couldn't trust anyone else. Now she gets to have her fairytale wedding.*

If anyone gets the importance of that, it's the woman with a shoebox full of tattered hopes and dreams.

Her fitting goes off without a hitch. The strapless form-fitting lace-and-silk confection she's chosen will knock Grayson out. Although I suspect his favorite part will be the colorful flowers adorning her veil. They're so Ella.

The shop owner seems nervous, which I understand. It's not every day you have a celebrity bride, and not one, but two hulking security guards. By the time we finish, Marco's protégé, Pierce, has joined Barnes by the door.

He must be as unsettled by the older gentleman as I am, because when Barnes grumbles about driving me "home" to Marco's place, the younger bodyguard winces on my behalf. Seeing my expression, he takes pity on me and offers, "I can take her. I'm already going in that direction to meet up with the boss."

Barnes doesn't seem to care much. He silently nods, then casts Ella an expectant look. She beams a winning smile at him before turning it on me.

"Thank you, Alice," she says, snapping me into a hug. "Everything is coming together *perfectly*. You're amazing."

Fresh pride inflates my chest as I squeeze her back. I resist the urge to argue with her or minimize her praise, Marco's stern look sailing through my memory. Instead, I whisper, "You're welcome."

Even picturing his approval does crazy things to me. I leave Ella with her scary security, following the much meeker man to his company car. It looks just like the others—all white sedans.

Pierce turns out to be every bit as awkward and nervous as I am. He nearly trips getting me into the backseat, muttering an apology as he closes the door just a little too hard to be considered professional.

I smile to myself as he settles in the driver's seat and fiddles with his seatbelt while he rambles. "So, Marco hasn't told me much about you. But he doesn't tell anyone anything, am I right?"

That wrings a little laugh out of me, although I really can't picture my strong, silent man bragging about me to any of his employees. I make a mental note to ask Tris if she's heard him talk about us at work.

Pierce starts the car and taps his fingers on the wheel as he pulls into the street. Unlike Barnes, he doesn't stare me down in the rearview. In fact, each time our eyes meet, his skitter away. "So, uh, anyway... thanks for being so cool about everything."

I don't understand what he means, but I nod along and make my best guess. "Well, this is an unusual situation. I know Ella and Grayson were in a tight spot."

Our car turns at the nearest intersection. I'm not sure which direction is best to get back to Marco's, but I'm sure I don't need to tell this guy. He drives people around for a living.

Pierce inclines his head to the side as if only partially agreeing with me. "Still," he argues. "It had to be hard on you."

Hard on me?

"I think Ella's probably the one who's suffered the most."

Grayson, too, really. I'm still angry on their behalf that so many people are clamoring to invade their privacy.

We head Uptown, the day's gray drizzle streaking our tinted windows with a muddy sort of mist. "That isn't what I meant," Pierce says, his tone oddly flat. "I was talking about what Marco did to investigate you."

A sudden rush of blood through my ears mutes the soft patter of raindrops. My heart trips against my breast. My lips go oddly numb.

Investigate me? I think back through our relationship, trying to recall a time when he'd mentioned any sort of *investigation.*

I remember every word he's ever said. But he's never said *that...*

Maybe it was naive of me not to assume he did a deeper dive than he let on. He *is* a former detective. He directs the *security* for an entire company. If he looked me up when we started dating, to be sure I wasn't hiding anything... It hurts that he didn't tell me, but I almost feel stupid for not thinking of it sooner.

"O-oh," I stutter, biting into the side of my thumb. "Did he, like, background check me or something?"

Pierce shifts his jumpy gaze back to the rearview. "No... I meant the undercover investigation," he repeats, as if that should trigger some sort of memory for me. "You know? How he was pretending to date you?"

My vision tunnels. A thick pulse beats in my brain. Slow and unsteady.

What is that? Drums? Some sort of drill? An earthquake?

It doesn't really matter. In this moment, I would welcome an act of God to wipe me out.

He was pretending to date you.

Pierce sighs heavily. "We all thought it was callous, if I'm being honest. But you know the boss; he was determined to make sure you weren't a threat, by any means necessary. Even if it meant... um..." He coughs. "You know."

The snippets of information float into my brain and expand,

hovering over my seized-up consciousness like expanding balloons.

It all makes terrible, perfect sense. How he approached me at the coffee shop when he "wasn't supposed to." The fact that he was watching for me the day I got attacked. The way he came over to my place unannounced, and then insisted I stayed at his.

The investigation.

Pretending to date you.

Too harsh.

By any means necessary.

You know...

Pretending *to date you. Pretending to date* you. *Pretending. Pre-tend-ing.*

He had been... pretending to date me. Pretending to like me. To want me.

For how long? And when did he stop faking it?

Did he stop faking it?

Why would he lie about that? Didn't I basically call him out for this exact suspicion weeks ago, before we ever slept together?

Because part of me knew all along. I never believed this could be real. For good reason.

An anvil sinks into my stomach, sending sickening waves of nausea through my center.

Pierce glances into the rearview mirror. His eyebrows jump, revealing shock that doesn't match his voice. "Oh," he says, reaching up to cover his mouth and his chin. "You didn't know?"

My mind works in a detached, halting sort of way. Drops of water hit my chest. Is it raining inside the car? Is the window cracked open? Why is the rain in my eyes?

Oh. I'm crying.

"No," I reply. "I knew."

Somewhere, deep down. I always knew.

I DON'T KNOW how long Pierce lets me sit in the backseat, crying into my hands.

At first, as he continued to drive me toward Marco's, he kept apologizing. Then, once he parked on the curb and I burst into shuddering sobs, he got quiet.

My entire chest aches, and my eyes feel raw when I finally hear a sound that makes me look up. Pierce is fiddling with his suit again, his movements fumbling.

His hands still for a beat before he feels my eyes on him. With one quick pitying look in my direction, he makes a *tsk*ing sound and shakes his blond head.

"Damn shame," he clucks, turning so his whole upper body faces me. I see it then, firmly gripped in his right hand—a *gun*.

I barely have time for a skitter of panic to race down my spine before he sighs. "Don't worry. This probably won't hurt as much as what he did to you."

And then he shoots me.

fifty-three

"WHY ARE YOU HERE?"

Grayson's pointed question would probably be insulting to anyone else. I return his glower, gesturing to our less-than-optimal surroundings.

"You said you needed to come down here and cancel your wedding registry," I return. "So, technically, this is your fault."

He huffs a quiet scoff, turning a salad bowl over in his hands. "I actually think it's my mother's fault for making the damn registry in the first place."

Given the Strykers' wealth, Ella refuses to receive wedding

gifts from anyone. Looking around here, I have to agree with her; they don't need any of this stuff.

But I do.

Grayson is on to me, it seems. He slants another sideways glance. "Still. I assumed you'd have Brad or Pierce drive me here. You hate shopping nearly as much as Ellie."

His special nickname for his fiancée no longer fills me with wistful envy. Now, I smile, the warmth in my chest a heartening reminder of why I'm here.

"I need new book shelves," I admit, sheepishly rubbing the back of my neck. "I figured two birds, one stone."

My boss smirks. "You finally decorating?"

Actually, I'm going to designate one of my spare bedrooms as the library Alice deserves. My lips curve up, but I keep most of my excitement to myself. "Something like that."

Grayson chuckles as I examine the options in this department store's furniture section. A sales person finally walks by, and he stalks after them, intent on his original purpose for our trip.

I use the spare moment to check my messages. A bolt of alarm strikes me when I don't see a reply from Alice.

My last text hovers there unanswered. I fire off another, asking if she and Ella have finished up at the dress store yet. Pierce is supposed to take her straight home afterward.

I suppose I could track his company car, although that feels extreme. I'm sure I'm just being overprotective. She's probably still busy with work. After all, there's no logical reason for Alice to avoid me.

Except for the fact that you asked her to move in with you and she hasn't given you an answer yet.

With a grimace, I send Pierce a text instead. He answers within seconds.

MARCO

Is the fitting over?

Do you have Alice?

PIERCE

Yes, sir.

Strange unease spreads through my gut. The same one I woke up with this morning. My instincts are on edge—and I know better than to ignore that feeling.

I grit my teeth, shoving down the anxiety to type out a warning.

MARCO

She goes straight home, got it?

Something feels off today. She needs to wait for me there.

PIERCE

You got it, boss.

I'll take good care of her.

The last message settles my stomach as much as anything could. I nod, slipping my phone back into my jacket pocket.

I'm being paranoid, I think, shaking my head. *Alice is going to be fine.*

I ALWAYS JOKED that I would die alone.

That was always an inescapable fact of my existence. Something I took as a given.

I *knew* it, but experiencing it is... different.

I got shot. I'm dying. And I am alone.

But the dying part doesn't hurt the way I expected it to.

I mean, it hurts. It does. The place where the bullet hit me feels like... well, like a *bullet hit me*. A hot, stinging, piercing pain, right in my chest.

My vision goes out, but I can feel things. Cold, mostly. The sort that slowly creeps over damp skin.

Oh. Blood. My bullet hole is bleeding and cooling.

My whole body seems colder, actually. I wonder why, trying to distract myself from the physical pain as much as the mind-melting misery of everything Pierce said before he shot me.

Part of me wants to believe he was lying.

After all, the guy did, you know, kill me. He clearly isn't a loyal employee. And I'm sure if he has no qualms about murder, a little dishonesty wouldn't deter him.

But I can't *think*. And my fake relationship is less of a concern than bleeding out.

Still, as everything fades into darkness, I imagine Marco's face.

That's a whole different sort of pain. I'll never get to kiss him again. Or wake up next to him. Or see the way he hangs on my every word, even when I struggle to get them out.

The way he pretends *to hang on my every word, maybe.*

If I weren't already dying, I think the hurt seeping into my soul might kill me.

Luckily, though, I am dying. That explains why I feel so cold —I am bleeding out.

Right in the middle of... wherever I am. Somewhere... hard? The surface under me is definitely hard. Apart from that, I can't wrap my mind around much aside from the soup of awful sensations swamping my body.

Yes. Thank God I am dying.

My heart can't break if it isn't beating.

fifty-five

I ONLY LAST four hours before I find myself outside Alice's apartment, knocking on the door.

I still haven't seen any sign of her, at my place or hers. Still, I have no idea where else she could be. Her things are still packed in a tidy pile in the corner of my closet, and her laptop tracker hasn't moved from my living room.

Ella said Pierce took her to my apartment. I even pulled up the tracking record from his company car—including the five minutes he spent parked on my curb before driving himself home.

So where the hell did *she* go?

And why is her phone turned off?

The software on her laptop is designed to ping all tethered devices in case of an emergency. I vowed to myself I wouldn't use it unless I had to... but when I tried to activate the cell's tracker and found it disabled, panic began to set in.

Did someone take her off the street? Some money-starved paparazzi or a crazed celebrity stalker, hellbent on using her for info on Grayson and Ella? Were they waiting for her inside my building?

Or did she simply... leave?

She has the freedom to do whatever she wants, but somehow, I can't picture her doing this. She'd know I would worry. She would *care*.

The red door jerks open. Tris stands on the threshold, her hazel gaze laughing. "Well, well, if it isn't the roommate stealer. Looking for our girl? Last I heard, she was on her way back to your—"

I brush past her and start walking. "She isn't at home. I haven't talked to her all afternoon."

I shove into Alice's dark bedroom. It's cramped, full of too many things for such a tiny space—but I only see the pieces that are missing. My pieces.

All the things she brought with her to my home. Her top bookshelf is missing most of her favorites. The nightstand doesn't have her phone charger or her day planner on it. There are no sketchbooks or wedding photos laid out. The corner of her bed skirt is stuck to her comforter—likely from where she took out her special shoe box when she had to pack in a hurry.

She isn't here.

And hasn't been.

Tris comes up behind me, crossing her arms as she rolls her eyes. "I told you, dude."

Panic spurs me forward. I move into Alice's space, my eyes scanning for any clues. Because I *know*, something isn't right here.

My stomach lurches, hoping against hope that I'm mistaken.

"Try calling her," I mutter. "Maybe she just blocked my number for some reason."

With a wary look, Tris pulls out her phone and dials Alice's. For half a second, I hold my breath. Instead, Tris sighs. "It's off."

I clench my teeth so hard, they make a cracking sound. "Come on. We have to move."

Fear widens Tris's eyes. It's the first time I've ever seen her look concerned about anything. "What are you saying, Amir? Spit it out."

I start dialing my phone. "I'm saying Alice is missing."

alice

IT IS pure luck that I don't open my eyes right away.

I wake up because of the noise. A scraping sound, distant and scratchy.

Oh my God.

I'm not dead.

Not yet, anyway. Consciousness filters in slowly as I do my best to remain utterly still. Marco once told me that his brain does sweeps of his surroundings before he even opens his eyes in the morning. Without moving, I cast my mental net out as best I can, cataloging anything and everything.

First, I am in pain. Horrible, gut-clenching, visceral pain that originates from the same place in my chest where the bullet pierced my skin.

It hurts, but it also feels... empty? As if the bullet isn't lodged there anymore.

Am I in a hospital? Did they do surgery and save me?

My heart wants to hope, but my senses tell me *no*. This is decidedly *not* a hospital.

For one, I am slumped on my side, lying on a surface that feels much too hard to be a cot or even a gurney.

The floor, probably. Not a stone one, because it isn't *that* cold, but it also isn't a cozy, carpeted room. Probably some sort of industrial laminate or tile.

The smell in the air hints at the first option. There are a few layers to it. I recognize the must of age, the peppery bite of dust, all underscored by a chemical fragrance I know but can't place. Gasoline? Alcohol?

No, something in the middle. But it definitely isn't the sterile, medicinal scent of antiseptic.

Oh God. Okay. I try not to panic, but it gets harder by the minute. Pierce shot me and then, somehow, took the bullet out? Did he do it without drugging me? Is that why it hurts so badly?

And... who is whimpering?

Is it *me*?

I don't know whether I should feel reassured or even more terrified when I do another check-in and discover that I am, in fact, the one making that sound.

My mind races as I smother the noise in my throat. Trying to determine if I'll have an opportunity to get out of here. Wherever here is.

The odds of escaping whatever situation I am in seem devastatingly low... maybe even impossible, given the searing pain that roils through me when I so much as flinch.

Okay, what would Marco do?

It hurts to think of him, but it's my best chance. He's only told me little bits and pieces about his job—clearly—but it will have to be enough to help me.

What would Marco do?

I need to open my eyes. That's the only way to really see what I am dealing with. I do my best to mentally brace myself... then I blink.

It's... dark. Nighttime?

No. But the room is vast, without any windows. So who knows what time it is?

The floor looks like some sort of covered metal, the top layer a kind of rubbery coating intended for heavy tread. Or maybe it's just to make it easier to clean up after he murders me. The walls are difficult to make out in the darkness, but I think they are comprised of enormous metal sheets.

The shifting behind me abruptly stops. In its place, a shaking voice whispers, "He's gone. You can stop pretending to sleep."

The sound is so unexpected, I have to turn toward it. When I do, a fresh bolt of pain rips through my chest. I bite down on a shriek, slamming my eyes shut.

"Shhh," the voice soothes. Someone shuffles toward me on their knees. Two small hands land on my shoulders and guide me onto my back. "Do not move so fast. I had to take the dart out with my hands and pack the wound. It was not the cleanest removal, but you needed to stop bleeding."

"A-a d-d-dart?" Bile rises up my throat while I squeeze my eyes shut, willing the piercing pain to subside.

"Yes. The coward shot you with a tranquilizer gun. One intended for shooting animals from a distance, by the looks of it. The needle on the dart was much too large for a human. He must have been standing close when he hit you because it left quite a hole."

I wait until I'm sure I won't vomit—from the pain or the idea of having a *hole* in my body—and then open my eyes. A slender, feminine face looms over mine, her fine features drawn tight.

There is a smear of blood on her cheek—hers or mine, or maybe both. Her eyes are panicked and dark brown.

Familiar.

"A-are y-you—" I search my brain for her name, knowing Marco has mentioned her many times. "E-Esme? Marco's mom?"

"Yes," she whispers, her gaze wide, but shrewd as it flits over mine. "You know my son? Who are you?"

Everything Pierce said swirls through my muddled mind. None of this makes *sense*.

"I—I'm no one," I whimper.

Esme frowns deeply. "You would not be here if you were no one." Her brows crease, understanding settling in the lines of her visage. "You must be *Alice*."

I don't have time to process how she knows my name. *If Marco never really cared about me, why would he tell her?*

Esme suddenly hears a noise outside, her focus flying to the corner of the warehouse. *That must be where the door is.* "Try to be quiet. I wasn't when he put me in here, and..." She holds up her limp arm, showing me where a bone nearly protrudes through her skin.

Holy shit. Oh my God. Oh my fuck.

I try to think, but a rising tide of panic works against me. "I—I d-don't understand. Why would h-he d-do this?"

Esme's dark eyes, so like her son's, narrow slightly, the same way Marco's would. "The blond one with the boy's face? You know him?"

I need to cough, but I'm scared it might make the pain worse. Instead, I rasp, "P-Pierce. He w-works for M-Marco."

I guess he does have a boyish face. Somehow, that only makes what he's done more unsettling. Esme looks shocked, too. "He *works* for my *son*?" she murmurs, soft but urgent. "You are sure?"

I try to nod but wince when shooting pain claws up my neck. "Yes. I'm s-sure."

Her expression is grim. As if my confirmation hammers the nail into our coffin. "W-what?" I whisper. "What is it?"

She drops to her backside and wraps her good arm around her knees, staring straight ahead. "His face. I would remember it anywhere."

A bolt of surprise joins the stabbing ache between my breasts. "*You* know him?"

How does she? If she knows his face, why doesn't Marco? He never forgets *anything*.

"That boy," his mother says, her voice as morose as her expression. "He's the one from the police station. The son of the man who shot my husband."

The thought pings around my brain for a full minute before it sinks in. "S-so that means…"

Esme's despair-filled eyes drift shut. "Marco killed Pierce's father."

And now, he's going to return the favor.

BY THE TIME I realize what the fuck is happening, the sun has set.

Tris is with me at the police station Uptown, where the chief immediately leaped into action when I called. He has units combing the city while I contact everyone I can think of who might have a clue as to where Alice might be.

Juliet calls four times before I finally answer, ready to roar a reaction and hang up. Her panting panic cuts me off. *"Primo?"* she cries. "Listen, you need to go to Queens. Your mom never came home from her night shift last night. Abuelita is freaking out. Esme's phone is off. We don't know where she *went*."

The room around me goes silent as my ears buzz. Pieces snap together.

Alice.

My mother.

If they're both missing, this has nothing to do with the Strykers.

It's *me*.

I'm the common thread.

I'm the one they're after.

The one my girl needed protection from.

"Fucking hell," I yell, unable to contain my fury. "This can't be fucking happening. Alice is gone, too. Nowhere."

Pierce is at home, but I've had him log in remotely and check every camera in the entire damn city. Twice.

Juliet is a powder keg. Anytime someone else's temper erupts, hers does, too. When I tell her I have my best guy on it, she shouts, "Well, you better call his pimply ass and tell him to start checking every motherfucking camera in *Queens* as well, *primo*, because your mother is *missing!*"

Oh God, what is *happening*? A swell of panic hits, so strong it locks me in place. I can only hear my own gasping and the sound of Juliet's heels as she runs.

"I'm getting in a cab," she huffs. "I'll find you when I get there."

It doesn't make sense that I can hear myself breathing, because I can't *feel* it. My brain resembles a snowstorm—a blank expanse of white, howling wind, and chaotic flurries.

A long-fingered hand gently grips my chin and brings me back to reality. Tris turns my face toward hers, hovering only a few inches below me.

"Hey. Big guy."

She sounds like a chain smoker; her usual husky voice grated down to nothing from all the crying she's done since we left her apartment. I blink at her slowly, trying to focus eyes that have gone blurry.

"I heard what you said. And I can see you're freaking out. But you can't do that right now. Because if someone took them both, that person is after *you*. And that means *you're* the only one here who can save them." Her nose twitches as her lips pinch around a ragged breath. "*Please*, Marco. Save my best friend. Because I need her, okay? And I'm pretty sure you do, too."

Her plea snaps something inside of me. I move, clipping across the main floor of the station to the holding area in the back. I push my way past clusters of officers, meeting Barnes as he comes in off the street.

"I went to Pierce's address," he reports. "He wasn't there. But this was."

The elder Brit shows me his phone screen. I blink at the smear of dried, dark blood he took a picture of. Proof that someone had been dragged from one vehicle to another."

Alice.

She got a ride from him. In—

"His company car?"

Barnes's jaw sets. He swipes his screen, revealing a photo of the Mercedes's familiar cream interior. Splattered with red.

My mind whirls. Misshapen shards finally fitting together.

Holy fuck.

I thrust his phone back at him. "We will find him," I intone, staring the other man down. "And when we do, he's *mine*."

If my demons want to dance, they're sure as hell not going to do it with my girl.

alice

BY THE TIME it truly gets dark, I've been in and out of consciousness for a while.

I can barely speak, but Esme explains that my body is likely in shock and trying to save me from the agony I feel every time I move. When I manage to keep my eyes open, we compare notes in hushed whispers, combing through what little we remember about how we got here.

She had been leaving work, coming off a night shift at her hospital in Queens. When she paused beside her car to search for her keys, a gloved hand covered her face with a chloroform-soaked rag. She stayed conscious just long enough to see Pierce's face and realized he planned to stuff her into her own car and drive off with her in the trunk.

She remembers thinking that he could drive her anywhere, move her to another vehicle, and dump hers. Or use her car to further his own agenda under the radar. As the widowed wife of a cop, she knew the possibilities were endless.

Unlike me, Esme knew right away why Pierce had taken her. She is Marco's only living parent... and Marco killed Pierce's only living parent. She assumed he wanted to settle the score.

It all made perfect sense to her... until I showed up.

In my brief moments of lucidity, I'm confused by Pierce's choice, too. After all, he admitted that I was nothing more to Marco than a mark. He claims his boss doesn't really care for me. Why would he use me to hurt him?

The warehouse is nearly pitch black by the time we hear the crunch of gravel under tires. Esme's head snaps up, her gray-black ponytail sliding to the side of her head as she cocks her head to listen.

Is it him? What if it isn't? Maybe someone would hear us and come help. We should scream.

I throw my head back, ignoring the protest my chest makes as I inhale deeply, and screech as loud as I can. Esme all but tackles me to the floor. "No, no, no, no," she chants. "*Mierda!*"

The door of the cavernous room swings open, revealing a dark figure carrying one electric lantern. The light twists his features from the vaguely familiar man I recognize into someone much more sinister.

He flashes an unhinged smile. "I see you didn't warn her what happens if either of you screams," he chuckles, stepping inside and slamming the heavy metal door shut.

Oh Lord, she did *warn me. She even showed me her broken arm.*

"She did not know," Esme lies. "I forgot to tell her. Please, she is already very injured."

"Hmm." He tilts his head, sending a strange shadow slithering up the nearest wall. "Who do I punish? You for forgetting to teach her the rules? Or her for breaking them? Maybe both."

His boots stomp directly toward us. I gasp, moving to rear back. Of course, pain explodes through my body all over again as I flop onto my front. Pierce takes advantage, charging forward and punting me in the side. I can't contain the shriek that flies out of me.

He keeps going, kicking mercilessly until I finally manage to bite down on my screams and fall into silent sobs. It takes every single ounce of my concentration to stay quiet. I squeeze my eyes shut and try to stop breathing, hoping I might just pass out again. I hear a soft grunt before Esme's body slumps beside mine.

"Now," Pierce says, "if you two are about done? I have some questions for you."

Esme doesn't move. I try my best to reach for her, but my entire torso screams, and I whimper. Pierce steps between us and drops into a crouch, his hand sealing around my jaw in an iron grip. He jerks my head to the side and waits for my eyes to focus on his face.

I see Esme's point about his young features; even twisted into a snarl, he doesn't look much older than a teenager. When he speaks, though, his words are those of a very bitter man.

"Such a pitiful excuse for a whore," he grumbles, eyeing me with distaste. "I couldn't fucking believe it when *you* popped up on my radar. He made investigating you sound like a death sentence. But then, when he finally ruled you out, he wouldn't quit seeing you. He even moved you into his fucking apartment." His enlarged pupils swing to my pelvis. "You have a golden pussy or something?"

His focus snaps back to my face as his thumb brushes roughly over my lips. "Or maybe it's this mouth. It is a pretty one, I'll give you that."

Some wild burst of fury darkens my vision. On impulse, I open my lips and take a snap at his fingers, hoping to bite one off.

If I'm going to die, I want to make sure I take a chunk out of my murderer. I figure Tris will be proud of that, at least.

Pierce barely gets his thumb away, hissing, "Fat bitch." He examines the damage, the place where blood trickles down to the sleeve of his black dress shirt. "I was leaning toward killing his mother first, but now I think maybe I'll take you out instead."

I spit blood at his feet, along with all the saliva that floods my mouth when my stomach clenches at his threat. My mind races, trying to figure out what to do with what he said.

"D-did y-you s-s-seriously take us b-both because y-you—" I pause, panting through pain to get out the rest of my insult, "—couldn't *decide* who to kill first?"

It isn't like me to taunt someone or voice my disdain. But, honestly, I seem to be at a point where things simply can't get any worse. I've lost the man I love. My career will unravel in my absence, along with the Strykers' wedding plans. And now, I am going to be killed by a psycho.

All because of a guy who possibly never wanted me in the first place.

"Shut your whore mouth," Pierce growls. "Do you think any of this has been *easy*? Do you think you could have done *better*? I infiltrated his team and dismantled it from the inside out. I tried to cost him his job by letting that crazy bastard Daniel into the party. It didn't work because Grayson is a pussy, but I still collected a nice little paycheck from that sicko Ted. Killed him and made it look like Barnes did it. Took the money and paid for this warehouse. Got into your stupid apartment to my own tracker in your laptop. *Then*, I managed to take you both without tipping him off. Even though that asshole Amir hasn't let you out of his sight in *weeks*."

I think back, my mind foggy and halting. So many things make sense, now—like that day we came back to my place and found it wide open, with no evidence anyone had been there aside from Marco's own team. Or how they had "missed" Daniel walking into Ella and Grayson's engagement party.

My abdomen heaves with the urge to vomit. Still, I refuse to cower. I will get all the answers I can before he does whatever he intends to do to me.

"H-he's smarter than you," I add, the jeer losing its edge because of my breathlessness. "H-he knew there was still a threat."

And he did *everything* he could to keep me safe.

Come to think of it, if he never truly wanted me, isn't the fact that he opened his home to me even more gallant?

Or have I just lost *a lot* of blood?

I hate the haze settling over my mind almost as much as I hate the tears that gather in my eyes. But I hate Pierce most of all.

He fully focuses on me—and, behind him, I see Esme slink up from her slump on the floor, using her knees and her one good arm.

If I keep him distracted... keep him talking... can she get the gun holstered at his hip?

I let my eyes drop to the weapon for one split second, hoping she sees me and gets the hint. When she inches closer, I hurry to keep talking. "I-if I m-meant nothing t-to him, why t-t-take me?"

It's the first question I can come up with, but it's also a good one. If I've just been a mark all along, how does Pierce believe killing me might possibly hurt Marco as much as harming his mother?

Pierce leans forward slightly, frowning. "Because he wouldn't *leave you the fuck alone.* I couldn't figure out why until one night when he had me posted on Ella, and he called her to ask for help setting up a surprise for you." He snorts. "I didn't see that one coming. I mean, you should have seen the last girl he tagged. *Goddamn.* And then... *you?*"

His words don't sting. They barely even hit me. Esme is almost close enough to stretch up...

Pierce goes on, "This week, I thought maybe he'd caught onto me and was trying to use you as a way to throw me off his precious mother. *That's* why I took her first. But then, I saw you two together this morning—when he hadn't even *realized* I had his bitch mom—and I knew I'd made a mistake."

His smile somehow looks unhinged and cool all at once. I'm not sure which I should be more afraid of—the detachment or the mania.

Pierce barks a laugh. "Fuck. I can't even imagine how good it will feel when he has to watch you *die*."

I want to ask him how he is going to do that. There's no way he thinks he'll be able to overpower Marco and actually bring him here, right? *Maybe he plans to record the whole thing.*

Esme is only two steps behind him now, struggling to rise to her feet when she only has one arm... and an ankle that also looks mangled.

I blurt, "S-so you've decided, then? It's going to be me first?"

I don't want him to say yes. The baser, panicked part of me is praying he'll decide I'm not worth killing. After all, if he plans to exact his revenge in the most logical way possible, killing Esme is perfect. The proverbial eye for an eye.

But then he will win.

He wants Marco to suffer. He wants his pain. To torment Marco the best way possible: not by hurting him, but by hurting someone he loves... and making sure he feels responsible for it, the way he feels responsible for what happened to his father.

I can't allow that.

Plus, if Pierce is busy hurting me, that gives Esme more time to get his gun and escape, right?

The decision is so simple. Of course Marco will choose to keep his mother alive over me. Of course I will die, so Marco doesn't suffer the loss of the only parent he has left.

Esme has a whole extended family who love her and depend on her. Like Marco's grandmother. I doubt my family will even miss me until my mom needs someone to pick apart. She'll probably get more clout from publicly mourning me than she ever got from claiming me while I was alive.

Tris is the only person who might wish I were still around.

And I can't sacrifice Esme's life just to keep my bestie from having to find someone else to watch The Real Housewives of New Jersey with.

Pierce cocks his head at me. "You saying it shouldn't be you?"

The look of petulant suspicion on his face reminds me, again, how old he probably is. Marco mentioned a boy and a girl waiting at the station the night he shot their father... even if Pierce was fifteen or sixteen at the time... he'd still barely be nineteen or twenty, now.

Behind him, Esme does everything she can to rise up and tackle him. Her entire body shakes violently when she pushes onto one hand and one foot, though. I watch out of my periphery as she tries to find balance but can't hold her weight. I realize the crunch I heard before was her lower leg... and now she can't stand.

She won't get the gun like this.

A calm sort of clarity settles over me. I know what I need to do.

I take every last nerve trembling in my body and force my voice up a few octaves, feigning panic. "Of course it shouldn't be me! I—I—He doesn't love *me*."

The words are melodramatic in just the right way. Edged with enough fear to make them sound... false.

It's the truth, carefully packaged as an all-too-obvious lie. I have a feeling it will work. Clearly, in Pierce's mind, Marco is the villain of this story. It makes sense for a bad guy to fall for an equally bad woman. One who would throw his widowed mother under a bus to save herself. I just have to play into the narrative he's already constructed for himself... and maybe I'll be able to save Marco's mom.

"Kill her first!" I shriek, weakly flinging my hand out. I catch Esme's eyes, wide with terror, through the gap between Pierce's calves. When she sees my brief glance, recognition lights her gaze... She freezes and slumps back to the floor seconds before Pierce whips his head around.

"*Obviously*," I cry, laying it on thick, "*she's* more important to him!"

The reverse psychology starts working. I can see Pierce doubting his own logic. His eyes narrow at me. "But he talks to you all day, every day. He *moved you into his apartment*. And he told me he even asked you to *stay* there after the wedding."

I can't think about why he asked me to do that. None of it makes any sense to me, now that I know the truth about why we started dating. If we ever *were* dating...

I pretend that Pierce's questions panic me. "Uh—um—he didn't really mean that! Obviously. He was just... um... trying to get me to..."

It isn't hard to pretend I have no clue as to the man's motives; I really don't. The only thing I know for sure, now, is that I have to save Esme.

And die trying.

"She's the one you want!" I insist, panting as the full weight of what I am doing crashes into me. "I—I'm not—" A whimper escapes me before I can help it. "I don't want to die."

The words ring true, because they are.

Those five words are the ones that seem to convince Pierce. A sharp, maniacal gleam glazes his eyes while he chucks another look over his shoulder at Esme—lying stoically on the floor—and then back at me.

"Oh," he chuckles. "This is *perfect*. Well, guess what? You're first."

He shrugs one shoulder, and a slim backpack falls to the ground. He bends over to pull out a camera.

Oh God.

"We'll have to make this quick. I have to be on a plane to Russia by dawn. The family my dad worked for hooked me up with a new identity. It's the least they could do, since they got him fucking killed. So by the time they scrub this warehouse, I'll be in Moscow, and your ashes will be dust in the wind."

I try to swallow, but I can't. The darkness has started to creep and smother. There's no air touching my lungs.

Pierce keeps his entire focus locked on me, his eyes climbing over my limbs the way a butcher might assess a whole cow before hacking into it.

"But first, I'm going to make a little home movie to send to your self-righteous piece-of-shit son, Esmeralda. Only one of you can be the star, though. The other has to hold the camera. Then I'll finish up and let my new friends torch both of your asses."

Oh God. Oh shit.

He leans over and pats my hair. "You'll scream real nice for me, won't you, blondie? You'll scream so sweet I won't need to be dramatic when I carve Mami up, too, right?"

fifty-nine

I CAN'T BELIEVE I had that fucker Pierce doing all of our surveillance.

One of the many tasks he purposely botched was the check on Ted's bank account. Barnes re-runs the scans while I brief the SWAT team on our suspect and our victims. When he comes back a moment later, he has two pieces of paper for me.

The first sheet shows a transaction, two months ago, from Ted's offshore account into Pierce's savings. The second is a recent real estate contract for... *a warehouse?*

When my mind snaps together what he is implying, I almost vomit. "Where?" I croak.

Barnes levels me with his too-knowing gaze. "I think you know where."

Fucking hell. I *do*.

I'm not sure why I'm not more surprised. If Barnes has known about my past all along, it would make sense. He was the one who hired me, once upon a time. He likely saw the word warehouse and instantly put the whole thing together.

Just like I am now.

The police chief behind me nods. "Let's move out."

For her safety, I insist Tris stays behind. I drive the Mercedes I arrived in, with Barnes beside me. While we navigate our way off Manhattan, to the warehouse district on the nearby shore of New Jersey, I try to stay focused and not think about my mistakes.

I still don't know how, but I know Pierce must be related to the man I killed, somehow.

Which means he wants revenge.

The two people I love most in the world are in danger. Because of me. And if anything happens to them... well, I'm not sure either know how much they mean to me.

"None of that." His clipped British accent has softened into a murmur. "The regret won't help you now, boy. Save it for later."

We surge on, breaking every speed limit until we skid to a stop at the yard. *Fuck,* it is huge. SWAT releases a truck-full of hounds, setting them loose among the shadowy metal buildings.

"He'll be in one of the units at ground level," I direct. "Look for more blood."

Everyone grabs a radio and fans out. Seconds pass by, then minutes. It has been almost ten when someone's voice finally comes through the speaker. "Amir? You in the northeast corner?"

"Yes," I reply, running faster, my eyes scanning the darkness.

"We have a vehicle," the voice reports. "A blue Camry."

My mother's car.

I break into a sprint, turning the corner to find the unassuming sedan parked behind a mountain of empty pallets without anything stacked on top. "Affirmative," I radio back. "This is us."

A line of SWAT officers creeps up quietly, following a couple of dogs who sniff Mami's car before going wild, each indicating they've found their mark. I run toward the warehouse without thought, already drawing my gun and locking the clip into place.

I hear it, then. The terrible sound of a woman trying not to scream. My sprint turns into a series of leaps as I launch myself closer.

I know the protocol. I'm supposed to wait for backup and try to sneak up on them as quietly as I can. If he hears us, there is a chance he will panic and kill whoever he is currently tormenting.

But my stomach flips inside out as another muffled shriek echoes inside. And the next thing I know, I'm shooting at the lock and ramming my shoulder into the all-too-familiar door.

It gives, bending inward when I batter it with my full weight. Pierce barely has time to turn his head and move his hand to his holster before I pull my trigger, sending two shots at his torso.

He crumples, dropping whatever implement he has in his hand and going down hard to his knees. When I realize he is still trying to take his Glock out, I train mine on his head and shoot him dead between the eyes.

Noise erupts around me, but I can't hear anything. Only the echo of those three shots, rebounding through my brain. My weapon falls from my hands. I drag my gaze up, up, up. To the woman chained in front of me.

My mom.

She is *chained* to the fucking wall. Thick metal links wrap tightly around her torso and her hips. She stands on one leg, leaning heavily against the panel behind her, where her left arm hangs limp in its own set of binds, holding a video camera duct-taped around her knuckles and wrist.

She has a strip of cloth tied around her head in a crude gag. While I stare at her, my chest heaving, she frantically nods and yells as loud as she can through the fabric. I realize that was the voice I heard outside—my mother, trying not to scream.

The thought spurs me into action. *"Jesus Christ."*

I rip the gag out of her mouth, and she immediately shouts, "Alice! Get Alice! *ALICE!* She wouldn't scream, Marco! He wanted her to scream so he could torture you with the video, and *she wouldn't scream*, so he—he—"

I follow the crazed bobs of her head to the opposite, darker corner... where the love of my life lies motionless in a pool of her own dried blood.

sixty

XANDER FINDS me sitting against a wall with my head in my hands.

Through the echoing emptiness inside of me, a dumb, blank voice points out that I am in the hospital where he works and I hadn't even thought to text him. That is probably stupid; he knows people. But I couldn't think long enough to even look up and check the hospital logo emblazoned on every wall.

Wordlessly, my former comrade slumps beside me, crossing his arms over his bent knees and reaching over to grip my bicep in a vise. It's a grounding technique we've used before, usually while riding in the back of tanks. This time, it doesn't work.

Still, he keeps his fist around my arm, squeezing.

"She's dead?"

"She *died*," I correct. "They were—they're trying to—"

I can't speak. Xander nods, staring across the hall while he speaks for me. "I talked to the terrifying British dude. He's an asshole, by the way. But once I told him how I knew you and the situation, he came around a bit. Told me it was that sniveling little bitch boy you hired all along?"

Barnes has already set to work, unraveling the false identity Pierce used to gain employment with us. Turns out, his real name was Pierce Prescott. And he had planned to torture and kill the two people I loved most because I'd taken his father from him.

Fresh shame burns my lungs. If I'd only had the fucking courage to face up to what I'd done that night... If I'd looked that scared teenage boy who'd just lost his dad in the face... then I would have recognized him the second he came in to interview.

"I tried to call his alleged wife." I don't recognize my own voice, bleak as it is.

Xander growls. "Why would you call that piece-of-shit's wife?"

It seemed like the right thing to do at the time. I kept picturing my mother the night Pierce's father shot mine; a new widow, lost and alone in the world. But when I asked the precinct to pull up Pierce's wife's information, they informed me that their system had no record of a Mrs. Pierce Prescott. Only a *Miss* Sarah Prescott—his seventeen-year-old sister, not his wife.

Xander listens while I explain, grimacing as he says, "I hate to give the guy credit, but lying to you makes sense. Anyone who observed you for any time at all would see that the easiest way to gain your trust or respect is to be a good family man. He probably passed off his sister as his wife to seem like a stand-up guy. Plus, it's easy. There were probably already pictures of them on social media and all that shit. Didn't you say she was pregnant?"

My nod feels mechanical. "He showed me pictures and everything."

"And a pregnant teenage sister would be even more motive for him to work with Ted. Once you explained the situation with the Strykers, I'm sure he approached those evil fuckers for a paycheck. Take care of his sister, get himself out of town. It was a good plan."

My voice rasps. "And here I thought he just helped Daniel assault Ella to make me look incompetent. Thank God there was a fucking reason for it."

Xander sighs. "I didn't mean it like that. I just meant... The kid was deranged, obviously, but he also had to be somewhat intelligent if he managed to fool you. He probably figured making some cash on top of ruining your career couldn't hurt."

I hear what he isn't saying—any way we slice what Pierce has done and why, it all comes back to me. *I* was the one he was after. *I* was the one who should have known better.

I'm the reason my sweet girl might be gone.

All of this is my fault. Every failing I have, every time I tried to make things better but only fucked up more... it all led to my mother on an operating table and Alice bleeding out on the dirty floor of that fucking warehouse.

If I lose either of them and somehow manage to live through it...

Well, I mostly hope I won't.

sixty-one

PRETTY SURE I died and went to heaven.

There are a few ways I know it is an ethereal plane of other-worldly goodness. The first is the distinct smell of my very favorite candle mixed with my very favorite tea and a very new book.

The second is the warmth. The type that only comes when someone holds you. The sensation of affection internally warming your body the same way the other person's presence heats your skin.

Even better—the warmth *moves*. It cups my cheek—or, you know, where I *used to* have a cheek—and strokes the place where I once had hair. It's nice, I think idly, that I still feel like I have a body, even though I'm some wandering collection of soul dust.

The last clue isn't the voice. Although the voice *is* very good—a perfect imitation of the one I love most in the whole world, quiet enough to feel intimate but loud enough to hear with perfect clarity.

No, the voice is *good*… but what really sends the whole thing into heavenly territory is the absolute *filth* it recites. Top-tier smut through and through. All wrapped in my preferred package of petticoats and dashing lords.

That's how I know I've actually died and somehow wound up in heaven. Because if heaven isn't the sexy love of your life—who never actually loved you on Earth, but who cares, now?—reading an amazing smut book while he cuddles you and brews your favorite tea… then what *is* it?

Sighing with all the contentment unfurling where my chest used to be, I float closer to the voice.

Which suddenly… stops reading?

"Alice?" My name is a hushed, hopeful breath. "Baby, can you hear me?"

The warmth moves again, shifting all around me. How is that possible, I wonder. How can it be under me and over me and against my sides? Is it more heavenly magic?

"Mmm," I reply, surprised to feel a vibration where I once had a throat.

A sharp intake of breath and more shifting. A buzzing noise that does not, in my opinion, belong in heaven. But then the voice comes back, and I forget to care.

"Alice? God, I hope you can hear me. And if you can… I love you, Alice. I love you so much. And I thought you were going to die not knowing that I—that you're *everything* to me."

Is it normal for my thoughts to be slower in heaven? I think it must be, because I can't grasp anything the voice told me. It touches my consciousness and then slips right over it.

I try to concentrate. This voice *sounds* like *Marco*. And it's telling me... he loves me? No, not possible. But it also said he *thought* I was *going to* die, which means... I didn't? If that is true, how is he here with me?

There's a sudden burst of shuffling and low, tense mutters I don't catch. The warmth all around me shifts too much, peeling away from my body. When cold tingles over my senses, I whimper, bereft.

Maybe this isn't heaven, after all. Maybe hell gives you everything your heart desires and then rips it away over and over again.

A woman's tenor interrupts my morbid musings. "Alice? Alice Moore? Can you hear me? If you hear me, try to answer, Alice."

She has an insistent way about her that makes me want to obey. I go looking for that vibrating sensation where my throat once was, but I can't find it.

"She's frowning," the copy of Marco's voice murmurs, urgent with hope. "Is that good? Is she in pain?"

The tenacious woman ignores him. A burst of red suddenly streaks in front of me. Then another. "Alice? Do you see the light? Open your eyes if you see the light moving."

Is that a flashlight? It looks more like a flare. But it's *there*. I see the color and feel the heat of it on my—

Eyelids. I really have eyelids.

Which means...

I put every bit of focus I possess into fluttering the lids open. Blinding yellow light instantly assaults me and I cringe, another odd sound reverberating up my vocal cords as I try to recoil.

That's a mistake.

Good Lord, everything *hurts*. My back, my front, my chest, my shoulders. A pained noise flies out of me as I squeeze my eyes closed, willing myself to go back to the semi-conscious state where I heard my favorite voice.

But then, it speaks to me again.

"No, Alice, no," he whispers, desperate. Large hands fold

around the sides of my head. "Please don't leave me again. I know it must hurt, but try to stay with me, sweet girl."

Sweet girl.

Somehow, those two words are my undoing. I blink, needing to see if he's really there or just a figment of my imagination.

His handsome face looms over mine, dark eyes tense and excited all at once. The set of his square jaw tells me he is barely holding himself together. His perfectly sculpted lips part, releasing a quiet breath of awe.

"Your eyes," he murmurs while his swim. "I thought I'd never see them again."

Oh God.

I am *alive.* I am *awake.* And that means...

Was all of that real? Was any of it?

THE PAIN PULSING through every part of me sharpens while my lungs push and pull, trying to gather air I can't collect. Some monitor beside my bed goes haywire. Marco's focus flies to it while two nurses rush forward, each gently maneuvering him away from me.

"You need to step out, Mr. Amir," one says. "Miss Moore will call you back if she wants to."

The no-nonsense doctor explains that I'm likely having a panic attack and asks if I'd like to be sedated. She tells me that they've already sedated me a few times, and it's taking longer for me to wake up after each dose. Because this is the first time I am lucid enough to give consent, they want my feedback before continuing to pump me full of whatever has kept me calm all week.

All week? I think, blinking back the last of my tears.

"N-no," I croak. "I—I want to b-be awake."

The barest layer of sympathy covers the doctor's face. She nods, assessing me carefully. "Alright. Try to stay calm, then, Miss Moore. You've had surgery. Raising your blood pressure right now will only put you at risk of complications. Do your best to relax, and I'll call your emergency contact."

I can't focus long enough to wonder who that might be, but a horrible thought suddenly occurs to me. I try to lurch forward before falling back. Face twisting with fresh pain, I pant, "W-what happened to Esme?"

The sympathy on the doctor's face doubles. "The woman you were found with? I'm sorry, but I don't know. I understand your boyfriend is her son, though. Would you like me to send him back in?"

I really don't know how I will stay calm if Marco comes back in, but I have to know if all my efforts to keep Pierce's hands off Esme succeeded. "Okay."

The doctor leaves, and Marco strides inside barely ten seconds later. He comes straight for me, only hesitating when he gets close enough to touch. I flinch away, and he takes the hint, dropping into the chair at my bedside without even grazing the bed sheets.

Floral bed sheets.

It finally occurs to me that my room doesn't look like a hospital room at all. It has the high ceilings and sterile white walls one would expect, but the rest seems... homey.

The bed isn't a lumpy cot—it's a full-sized double bed with sunny daisy sheets and an array of sky-blue pillows. Those match the painting proudly propped up on the counter beside a sterile sink—one of my own pieces, in shades of sunshine and tangerine. Both pair with the rug filling the space where the speckled laminate floor should be.

There are miniature versions of my favorite candles burning

on a small antique side table. A romance book is laid out beside them. And an electric kettle quietly steaming on the windowsill.

Marco watches my wide eyes sweep around the space and gives a small, apologetic smile. "I may have gone overboard. I wanted you to have your favorite things here when you woke up."

It's a lovely thought. One that would have made me swoon, before. Now, though, my heart aches just as fiercely as the rest of my body.

"Where's your mom?" I whisper. "Is she okay?"

Intense emotion fills Marco's perfect face. His hands fall to mine, scooping one up and burying his face against my fingers. "Yes," he husks. "She's okay. Because of *you*."

He swallows as he lifts his head, meeting my eyes with his haunted gaze. "She told me what you did. How you tried to save her. How you tricked him. How you refused to scream for his video so you wouldn't traumatize me. Alice, he tortured you for over an hour before you passed out. They've done so many surgeries to try to—to—"

At a loss, he grips the top sheet lying over me and peels it back, showing me the crisscross of stitches covering my upper thighs. I know there are more cuts on my abdomen. I remember each of them with horrifying clarity.

My vision blurs while new tears gather there. Marco makes a small, comforting sound, covering me back up and swooping for my hand again. His lips brush over my knuckles while he speaks.

"Don't worry about the scars. I tracked down the best plastic surgeon in New York for you. Most of them are on your body where no one can see, but he promises every scar will fade into invisibility within six months."

His eyes make a liar of him, jumping to a few spots on my face that, I figure, show the remnants of my scarring.

I wait for self-consciousness or anxiety to trickle in, but neither does. If I have scars, so be it. If I look even worse than I ever did before, that's fine.

I no longer care.

I'm alive. I survived and saved the woman who raised the man I love. I will never regret that.

I remember every taunt Pierce threw at me as he tried to slice away my will to live. They were all cruel, vicious jeers, designed to carve internal wounds matching the external ones he created. But none of them hit me, because I chose not to hear them.

It never occurred to me to just... choose not to listen. In all the years I've been teased or criticized, I never tuned it out. Now that I have, I can face anything.

I know who I am. I like how I look. And as long as I'm okay with both, who cares what anyone else has to say?

Marco bends over my hand, holding it in both of his while he takes audible breaths and rests his forehead against my wrist. "I'm sorry," he whispers. "For so many fucking things, but right now I'm especially sorry I'm doing a shit job of explaining everything. I should be comforting you right now, but I— It was a *week,* and you still hadn't woken up. I was starting to think you might... not."

My left arm may as well be made of lead. Stitches itch and pull as I slowly lift it to set my free hand on the back of his head. His thick, black hair is as long and disheveled as I've ever seen it, curling in coarse waves under my fingertips.

"I'm awake," I soothe. "I'm here."

He takes my touches as an invitation to move closer, carefully pressing his face against my hospital gown, right over my middle. Another knife to my heart, but I keep combing through his hair anyway.

"Tell me more about Esme," I request, needing the distraction. "Tell me everything that happened."

Marco exhales deeply, his muscular back deflating under the black Henley stretched over it. His eyes squeeze tighter as he recounts the way he figured out who took us and where we were. Once he gets to the end of the story, he pauses, hesitating.

"I didn't think," he finally admits. "I couldn't. I just walked in and shot him. Three times. He went down right there, and I stepped over him… He was standing in front of Mami, so I saw her first. She was frantic, trying to talk around the gag in her mouth. The second I took it out, she screamed at me, telling me to go to you. I turned around, and you were there, in the dark, bleeding out…"

His bronzed skin looks ashen as he raises his head and pins me in place with stormy brown eyes. "How did you get him to stop?"

"He thought I was dead," I confess. "He took a…" I have to stop to gulp. "… a particularly vicious stab to my side, and I thought, *It would be a miracle if that didn't kill me.* Then I realized I could use it to play dead. So I pretended, and he stopped."

I leave out the part about how, after he left me slumped on the floor, bleeding out, I wished he really had killed me because of all the pain. "D-did he hurt Esme more? She already had a broken arm and ankle…"

Marco shakes his head, a look of relief crossing his face. "No. I got there just as he was about to, but she's fine. She's already doing physical therapy and walking in a boot." A somber little smile kicks up the side of his lips. "They wouldn't let her in here while you were unconscious. I don't think I've ever seen her so mad."

"How did *you* get in?" I ask, holding back a laugh because I'm afraid of the pain.

His wry expression takes a turn toward utter chagrin. "I… may have implied that we were long-term partners. And I made a few" —he coughs, clearing his throat, which is his tell— "minor donations. To get this room and permission to decorate it a bit. Nothing, uh"— another throat rumble— "nothing crazy."

I look around again. The room really is perfect. Beautiful and thoughtful, just like everything he's ever done for me.

Only, he was doing those things to get information from me. Is he doing them now out of guilt?

Someone else will probably charge in here any minute, which means I only have a little time left with him… and I need an explanation.

"Are you—" I fight past my raspy throat and fuzzy brain, forcing coherency. "Can you tell me the rest? The truth about why you did all this?"

Marco's brows crease. He traces his thumb along my cheek. The tender gesture slices my heart. "What do you mean?"

The air between us grows thick, even before I sigh. "Pierce told me the truth. That you were using your charm to get me to do what you needed me to do. To keep Ella and Grayson safe."

Marco jerks upright. His eyes swirl, two dark pools of agony. "Alice," he half-growls.

Memories fly through my mind. The same ones that brought me comfort when I thought Pierce was going to end me; they all cut jagged chunks out of my soul, now.

"Was it all pretend, then?" I ask, a watery, humorless laugh bubbling out. An edge of mania creeps over my voice. "God, I *believed* you. I really, really did. It would have been one thing if it were just a bunch of pretty words or sweet nothings, but you— you went *all in*. Setting up those dates, the roses, the candles. Making me *stay* with you." I sniffle. "I even gave you an out! I told you, you *didn't have to pretend*. So why would you—"

Marco moves so fast, I almost hurt myself jerking back. He clasps his hands around my head, holding me in his thrall while vehement brown eyes snap with golden fury. His voice drops low. "None of it—not one single, godforsaken second—was *ever* pretend. The fact that he made you think that—let you nearly die believing I never cared about you—*fuck*. If I could bring him back from the dead to kill him all over again, I would."

I blink, forcing myself to slow my breathing. "B-but y-you—"

"Love you," Marco rumbles, his thumbs brushing tears from under my eyes. "I *love* you, Alice."

A rueful smile curls his lips. "Even when you were supposed to be a possible threat, I couldn't stay away. I wanted to talk to you. I wanted to *know* you. Before any of this—all the way back at that coffee shop. Do you remember?"

Of course I do. If I close my eyes, I can still picture him, appearing over me. Gazing into my eyes. Staring at me with some foreign intensity I didn't understand.

Thinking of it now sends tears streaking down my cheeks. "Yes."

Marco gently leans his forehead against mine. "I worried about you. I couldn't fucking *stop*. Coming to get you that day outside the damn subway. Showing up at your place. Following you to the bookstore. Jesus, Alice. You were some blend of obsession and salvation I didn't even *understand*."

More tears rush down my face while Marco continues, "You were so smart and kind and quietly sharp. *Beautiful*. Your apartment, your clothes, your skin, your hair. Fuck, even the way you made *tea*."

His body settles closer to mine with another sigh. "I was a goner that first night, but I told myself it was just a blip and talked myself into continuing—knowing damn well it wasn't a job. That it *never* was."

Dark eyes pierce me. "It was an excuse. A reason to be around you when I had no business letting myself into your life, dragging you into this danger.

"As long as I focused on my job, I could let myself do shit, like tracking your laptop and following you to Book Club that one morning." A wistful half-smile tugs at his mouth. "Christ, you were cute. And brilliant. You blew me away."

Heat sinks into his gaze. "By the time I showed up at your place to borrow a book, it was too late. You were under my skin. I was already halfway in love with you. And then you kissed me. And kicked me out. By the time I left, I knew I needed you."

Steady intensity builds between us. "I still do," he finally roughs out. "I always will. Because you're the one I've waited my entire life for. And *I love you*."

WATCHING Alice absorb those words fills me with relief.

Hell, at this point, watching her *blink* fills me with relief.

Over the last week, I've thought of little else aside from telling her that I love her. It was my greatest regret—I could have *lost* her and she didn't even know how I *felt*.

So I say it again. Deeper and clearer, this time. "I love you, Alice. And I want you to be mine. Not just today or tomorrow or for now. I want you forever. Always."

A tear rolls down her cheek. Her hands tremble in mine as her hoarse voice replies, "Marco... you don't have to say all of—"

I normally hate to cut her off, but not this time. My head shakes firmly. "No. Alice. *I fucking love you.* And I don't care how much time it takes for you to believe that. I will wait for you. Until the whole wedding is over—and even after that, if you need me to. As long as it takes for you to see that this isn't some whim."

More clear droplets fall from her crystal eyes. She sniffs. "I-it might take a long time."

Fuck, I don't *care.*

I'll fight her every damn day of forever, if she'll let me.

The realization puts a wide grin on my face. "Actually," I murmur, kissing the backs of her hands. Inhaling the fact that she's here and whole and *mine.* "I'm hoping it takes the rest of my life."

"ALLEY CAT," Tris whistles, leaning into my doorjamb. "Hot *damn*."

After adjusting the fit of the front of my dress, I toss a glower at my roommate. "Tris. We talked about this."

Her winning smile only grows. "Yes. Right. Absolutely. My bad, *Alice*."

It took two months of therapy before I finally worked up the courage to tell my best friend how much I hate her nickname for me. About the same amount of time it took for me to find the nerve to tell my mother that I would no longer be taking her calls.

Suffice it to say, the first conversation went a lot better than the second.

But the thing is... I still had them. Because, as my counselor loves to remind me, I can do hard things. And I deserve to be heard and understood just as much as anyone else.

My weekly sessions are one of many gifts from Marco that I halfheartedly refused, only to give in and accept, eventually.

In the initial weeks after I woke up, he surprised me almost daily. Boxes of exotic tea. Books. Flowers. Silky pajamas. And—my favorite—handwritten letters.

At first, I groused over everything, except for those. Somehow, I couldn't be exasperated by papers full of his messy, masculine scribbles.

They're so personal. Long and honest, and full of the innermost thoughts I only got to see behind his eyes, ordinarily.

Each time I huffed over a present, he merely chuckled and—occasionally—offered a spanking for my brattiness.

But he never stopped.

In fact, he outright *insisted* I take his offer of therapy. He wrote that it was keeping him up at night, worrying about the psychological effects of Pierce's actions, and asked me to please accept the sessions. I relented because I hated the thought of him torturing himself almost as much as I hated the trauma I had endured.

Dr. Laura also sees Ella and Grayson, though we never mention them. Slow and steady, she helped me unpack everything that happened since that fateful day when Marco and I connected in the coffee shop.

We've discussed how I never genuinely believed he would be interested in me, and how that only made it more devastating when I thought I'd found out that he really wasn't.

Now, though?

Well, some days—the good ones—I open my door to whatever trinket he's left for me, along with his daily letter, and I think, surely, he must love me.

Why else would he spend months diligently trying to prove as much? He's a free man. And a practical one. I doubt he would carry on for *months* under some misplaced sense of obligation or guilt or even gratitude.

After all, his mother has firmly taken care of the gratitude thing. She now shows up on my doorstep every Sunday morning with piles of Colombian delicacies, courtesy of herself and Abuelita. She bustles her way into our apartment, never once commenting on how small my kitchen is, and sets to work, preparing feasts for us to enjoy together.

I'm not actually sure how it happened. All I know is that she shows up, fussing over me as a proper mom might, and I allow it.

We never speak of Marco. Instead, she tells me old stories about her late husband, her childhood in Colombia, her colorful mother. Sometimes, she tries to teach me Spanish, remarking that I'm a much better natural student than *some* people—though I don't know if she's alluding to Marco or Graham Everett and his infamously terrible accent.

Every week, before she leaves, Esme snaps me into a fiercely maternal hug and coos over some part of me she thinks looks particularly pretty that day. Her Spanglish compliments leave me with a goofy smile on my face as I close the door behind her, already wondering what she'll turn up with next time.

Tris jokes that she gets spoiled by the Amirs just as much as I do, considering Esme leaves more food than I can eat by myself—and Marco always makes sure to include treats for my grubbing roomie whenever he sends something edible.

Her hazel eyes trail down over the soft pink sundress I've chosen for today's event. Her gaze sits on my boobs just a beat too long before she flashes a salacious grin. "Looks great!"

My shoes are partially hidden under my bed, still in their box. I snatch the lid off and grab them, sitting on the edge of my mattress, tying the ribbon-like straps of the heeled sandals over my ankles in a crisscross pattern.

I cast one last look in my mirror, smiling. The blush dress

really does bring out my blue eyes. And I love my curly hair even more now that it has grown longer.

The air in the room suddenly feels tight. Tris's smile fades from her face. "So... you ready?"

My stomach drops. My mind spins through the dozens of details I need to see to as soon as I get to the venue. It's a huge, modern loft—completely blank, the perfect canvas for all the extravagant fixtures we rented to fill it.

Tonight, we'll have Ella and Grayson's rehearsal dinner.

And tomorrow, my biggest wedding ever.

Plus, I owe Marco an answer. The man has been waiting for the last two months, reminding me daily of his offer to share his apartment with me.

I want to. More than anything. But despite all the work I've done for myself, I still can't shake the fear that he'll disappear as soon as this wedding is over. When the only thing holding him to me is...

Well. *Me.*

A dart of pain brings me back to earth. I look down and realized I've chewed my thumb to the quick again. My lips flit up when I imagine the way Marco will scowl at my abused fingers. I also notice a bit of yellow paint on my pinky nail that will make him smile.

"I don't know," I murmur to Tris.

Maybe we never feel totally ready. Maybe all of this is just a leap of faith.

Maybe it's time for me to jump.

Her eyes glow with understanding. Her voice sounds thicker than usual. "For what it's worth, babe, I'm proud of you." A sly smile splits her serious expression. "I mean, *I* obviously knew you could do this, but still. You were brave. And look what happened."

With that unexpectedly poignant thought, she saunters away. I let her words sink in for way too long before I notice the time.

Scurrying to gather up my things, I kick the now-empty

espadrille box under my bed. It hits something blocking its path, and I reach down absently, plucking out the other item.

Oh.

My embarrassing box of high school hopes, all wrapped in pink-heart paper. I stuffed it back into its hiding place the day Marco helped me move home from the hospital, not wanting him to see it or get curious about its contents.

It was probably monumentally stupid for me to bring it to his apartment in the first place. But back when we didn't understand the danger facing us, when he said to take everything essential with me... I just couldn't leave it behind.

Now, I wonder if I need to burn it before moving in with the man of my dreams or simply find a new hiding place.

Lord only knows what I put in this thing.

Cringing, I lift the lid to peek inside.

And it's all Marco.

The bouquet I loved so much on our first real date. A few magazine photos of intimate rooftop meals. One of a bedroom lit with candles and sprinkled with rose petals.

New horror dawns on me in a slow roll.

Oh my God. He found my box. And *looked in it.*

Did he read the articles? Or, God forbid, my mortifying *lists?* If he did, why the hell didn't he run away screaming?

He must think I am the most pathetic person who has ever lived. Did he do all those things out of pity? Oh my God, I will die. I can't see him ever again. I need to leave the country. Oh my Goddddd.

Across the room, my phone alarm chimes.

I want to have a nervous breakdown, but there isn't time. It will have to wait until after I do everything in my power to avoid Marco for the entire evening...

A goal that might be impossible when I open my front door and find one single white rose, laid across our welcome mat, along with his shortest note to date.

I'll see you soon, sweet girl.

honeymoons
keep out - top secret!

sixty-four

"*PRIMO*, are you sure you don't want a drink?"

I resist the urge to snarl at my cousin, forcing my face into a fierce scowl instead. "Yes. I'm sure."

Juliet rolls her eyes as she adjusts the thin gold chains holding up her dress. If you can even *call it* a dress. The damn thing is basically two scraps of blue gauze tied together with chains at her shoulders and sides. It goes with the ridiculous shiny heels strapped to her feet. And the color matches her light blue toenails.

It reminds me that I am decidedly out of my element in an all-white suit. Because, apparently, everyone needed to be on theme.

The thought should probably annoy me, but I only feel the urge to grin. *Alice.*

Graham Everett groans, shuffling notecards. The best man has been anxiously stomping around since I got to the venue for the rehearsal dinner. Having checked and re-checked all the security measures in place, I stopped here to make sure everyone in the wedding party knew their positions.

Turned out, Grayson and Ella had snuck off for a moment alone. Which left me with Graham Fucking Everett.

He paces in place, running a hand through his slicked-back hair. Looking ludicrous in a blue linen suit, the exact same shade as Juliet's dress. A gold waistcoat flashes from beneath his open jacket as he pivots on his heel and wears another path into the floor.

"I think your fiancé is the one who needs that drink," I mutter.

Juliet casts him a disapproving frown. "He's had one. Didn't help. I'm running out of ideas..."

Graham freezes, pointing a glare toward us, until he catches Juliet's eye. His expression goes slack, then twitches into a smirk.

"Amir, get out. We need twenty minutes."

"Jesus Christ," I grumble, standing and striding for the door.

"I only need ten," Juliet calls out, wringing a laugh from Graham as I slam the door to their suite behind me.

I have shit to do anyway.

Ella, the woman of the hour, appears with Grayson glued to her back. They take a break from beaming at each other to glance at me.

"Everything is secure," I report, nodding at my boss before grimacing. "Are you sure you're okay with this?"

Ella grins, floating forward. "We *insist.*"

They have *insisted* this entire time. In fact, I'm the reason they booked this venue for their rehearsal in the first place. After I told Ella my plan, she made it her mission to be my accomplice.

Her made-up eyes dart over my shirt. A small smile betrays her amusement at my new outfit.

"I look ridiculous."

She huffs. "Oh, come on. New chapter, new look. Is everything ready upstairs?"

"Yes. Is she here yet?"

A rush of nerves rolls through me. I wonder if Alice has recognized the building yet. It's a pretty basic brick structure... and it was dark the night we came.

Over Grayson's shoulder, my sweet girl has worked her magic on the huge entertaining space. The theme is an ode to the changing season—all white furnishings, colorful lounge furniture, spring blooms, and loose masses of greenery.

It's pretty, but none of it holds my interest. There's only one sight I want to see, and so far? I haven't even caught a glimpse of her.

Then again, I know she is excellent at fading into the background when she wants to. It will be easier for her to hide now that most of the guests are arriving, filling the luxurious space with a sea of bodies.

I scan the space, making sure I recognize each individual face. Grayson steps up behind Ella, casting me a look. "I thought we agreed you were off duty for the next two hours."

Now that our team is solid once again, I've tried to learn to let Barnes take the reins from time to time. He's more than qualified —and I need to get better about carving out intentional time for Alice. Especially if my plans for the evening go well.

Though before I can get to that, I have to find my girl.

Ella smiles wider, reading my mind.

"Go," she says, "I'll send Alice to you."

sixty-five

THE SUN HAS JUST STARTED to sink beyond the horizon when the elevator dings behind me.

On the roof, New York shows off its first warm spring evening of the year. Humid air whips overhead, slightly cooling the heat that's soaked into the floor during the course of the day.

Before I heard the lift, I was standing at the Lucite wall framing the rooftop, staring at the brilliant colors of the sunset and wondering who the hell Grayson paid to make sure they had such perfect weather for their party.

My insides lurch when the chime reaches my ears. I do one

last check to make sure everything is where it needs to be and stride toward the elevator. The doors glide open, revealing the single most welcome sight I've ever seen.

Alice.

God, she looks so beautiful. More beautiful than yesterday, somehow. Her light pink dress sets off the creamy rose of her skin. Her blue, blue eyes.

The riotous blonde curls I love to bury my fists in are growing long, looking looser and lighter from more time spent outside in the spring sunshine.

In addition to being gorgeous, she just looks *good*. Happier and more comfortable in her skin. Pride swells through me at the way she holds herself, the gentle, confident sway to her hips as she steps out of the cab and onto the roof.

She has her phone in her hands, typing furiously for a moment before she slides the screen into a hidden pocket along the skirt of her sundress and swings her face up, stopping short when she sees me.

"Oh!"

Her wide-eyed shock and the perfect little circle of her lips are just so Alice; joy erupts in my aching chest. My breathing goes ragged. All the words I prepared evaporate as our gazes mesh.

She blinks, clearly startled. I wait for her surprise to ebb, staring at the violet blue I adore. Eventually, her bewilderment fades. Our connection snaps into place.

Hi, I say silently.

Another sweet, owlish blink. *Hi.*

She floats forward a step. And I let my racing heart take that as a good sign. "W-what are you doing here?" she asks. "Ella told me—"

Her words die as realization dawns. I wince.

I do feel bad about the white lie. It was the only part of the plan that worried me. But Ella practically insisted we use her as bait when I told her I needed a way to get Alice up to the roof.

Instead of slinking back in embarrassment, my sweet girl

draws herself upright and folds her arms under her chest. I don't dare let myself glance at the way her breasts push up.

"Marco Amir," she snaps, voice shrill with indignation. "Did you *trick me* into coming up here?"

For the first time all day, I actually want to laugh. A chuckle rumbles out of me as I take a cautious step, closing some of the space between us, and shrug.

"I thought you might remember the view."

She can't see the whole roof from just outside the elevator. I was counting on that. But she still turns her head in either direction, looking around before sliding her eyes back to mine. Hers are a bit brighter with a sheen of tears glossing them.

"O-oh," she stammers. "Is this... this is our rooftop? But how did you..." More wetness gathers on her lashes as she puts it all together. "You asked them to choose this place?"

I take another step. Hoping to cover as much ground as I can before she tells me to stop. "Yes. I have something to show you." With one last breath, I offer my hand, palm up. "Will you come with me?"

Alice raises her arm and freezes, halfway to stretching it out. "I... I don't know." She sounds smaller when she adds, "I *want* to come with you. But Marco, listen, about this rooftop... Did you see a picture of something like this under my bed? Did you go through my box?"

alice

IF I THOUGHT Marco was the most handsome man to ever live when he wears black, seeing him in a white suit only confirms it.

His bronze skin looks incredible against the ivory fabric. Golden light glints off his black hair and the fine layer of stubble along his square jaw. Magic hour fills his deep, dark eyes, too, highlighting all their depths.

I want to run to him.

That's my first instinct. The second our eyes meet, everything inside me simply melts and sighs. Relief extends in my soul, softening parts of me that have only ever yielded to the man standing in front of me, silhouetted by the beginnings of sunset.

He has something to show me. On the very same rooftop where I realized I was head over heels in love with him months ago.

The notion reminds me of how he knew to plan that date on the roof to begin with. When I asked about the box under my bed, he winced.

I wait for the placations. Of course, Marco will tell me not to be embarrassed, even if he doesn't mean it…. Right?

Instead, he blows out a deep breath, keeping his hands extended while he sways toward me slightly.

"I was hoping to get to tell you myself." He sighs. "I had a proper apology planned, and I was going to give you this."

He bends to the side, picking up a wrapped parcel tucked against a post. He brings it to the space between our bodies, presenting me with…

A shoe box.

Wrapped neatly in periwinkle. Still romantic and pretty, but not quite as embarrassing as my pink-heart paper.

Our eyes lock—dark to light, both drenched in gold. *Here*, he seems to say. *I made it for you.*

I take it and pry the lid off, my fingers shaking. Inside, there are pictures I don't recognize. Townhouses, family-sized SUVs, vacation rentals.

"What is this?" I breathe, trembling.

But I know. Even before he smiles faintly and exhales a reply. "You had your box. This is mine."

A quiet sob sticks in my throat. "Marco."

He cups both hands around my face, his tense gaze burning into mine. "Or… it could be *ours*. I want us to build a life together. Everything in here, everything you want to add to it… It's yours. Because *you* are the one I waited for, Alice Moore. And I'll give you anything."

My heart reacts without my head's permission, unable to bear the deep-rooted tug of his soul to mine one second longer. My frozen hands finally move, setting the box beside our feet before reaching for him.

Sparks skitter under my skin, leaving goosebumps over my arms despite the warm nearly-summer wind buffeting our rooftop. Marco's arms snap me up, straight into his body.

Lord, I love how hard and huge he is, towering over me and my heels. Curving around every bit of the body that used to feel too large.

Not anymore, though. In his embrace, I feel delicate and precious. The perfect size to fill his arms without even coming close to the sheer *broadness* of him.

His hug starts out sweet, but soon his hands are clutching at my dress while his chest heaves against mine. "Fuck," he murmurs, pressing his cheek into my temple. "Alice."

Relief rolls over me, leaving pure euphoria in its wake. The feeling tingles down into my dangling toes as I smooth one palm down his back and reach the other up to touch his hair.

Marco always told me that there was a moment when he knew I was the one for him. His letters described it often, always with reverence. I have my own memories of it, but didn't fully relate to how he felt until this very second.

The deepest part of me settles into an unwavering sort of certainty.

I belong with this man.

He was *made* for me.

The answer to every hope and prayer I ever had. The one who has been waiting for his soulmate all his life, because he believed *I* was out there. He believed *I* would be worth it.

He still believes that, even after I've done everything I can to question him. Despite all the mistakes we have both made. He's here, fighting for me every bit as hard as he has from the beginning. Waiting until I'm ready to accept all the things he wants to offer me.

Because, to him, I am worth anything. *Everything.*

My whisper sounds watery. "I'm here," I tell him, meaning it in so many different ways. "I'm here, baby."

A quiver rocks through him along with another pant. Slowly, every bit reluctant, he sets me on my feet. His fingers release my sundress, gliding up to my shoulders, then down my arms to tangle his grasp with mine, squeezing gently.

"Come with me," he says.

The gruffness of his voice puts a tickle in my throat, more tears threatening. Still, I nod and follow as he walks backward, leading me from the recesses of the elevator to the center of the rooftop.

It's full. And completely transformed into four smaller alcoves, each under its own bower of flowers, all different colors and themes and...

Oh my God.

"What is this?"

The words sound as numb as my lips feel. Marco moves to stand behind me, his arm banding around my hips briefly to offer an encouraging squeeze.

"I figured if you were going to trade your old box for a new one, I should at least give you some of the things you had in there first."

When my mouth drops all the way open, his rueful smile turns teasing. He nods, urging me toward the first tent on the right. "Go see."

I feel like I'm floating as I wander to the makeshift gazebo-like structure, stepping into a canopy of lush red roses and crushed velvet. The quiet pulse of sensual house music fills the little space, along with dozens of gorgeous lingerie sets. It almost looks like... a high-end lingerie store? Or a modern take on an old-fashioned honeymoon trousseau. The kind I've secretly always dreamed I would have.

Or not-so-secretly, it turns out.

The more I look, the more familiar the pieces feel. They aren't exact matches for all the ones I kept pictures of in my box, but they are very close.

Marco waits at the threshold of the sumptuous space, his smile small and soft when I turn back to him. "You have good taste," he says simply, shrugging one big shoulder.

A giggle slips out before I can stop it. "I think *you* have good taste. Or just a very, very good memory...?"

Another sheepish shrug, but his grin grows for a second before his face suddenly becomes unbearably earnest. "I will always remember everything about you."

I nearly swoon into him. "Thank you," I breathe.

"You're welcome, sweet girl," he rumbles, wrapping his arms around me and grazing my ear with his lips. "Come on. There's more."

He isn't kidding. The next canopy is an ode to all my pictures of Paris. Pink silk, blush flowers, and a table full of the most delicate, beautiful pastries I've ever seen.

The third tent is concealed by dark burgundy curtains. When I step in, I can barely breathe for the swell of joy that threatens to pop my lungs.

A library. The entire space is one continuous round bookshelf, taller than me, stuffed with every classic and romance novel I can imagine. In disbelief, I pick up the nearest one, sure it must be a prop. But, no, it's one of my favorite Scarlett Scott novels, in perfect condition.

When I whip my face around to gape at Marco, he flashes my favorite grin. "You should see my Amazon book suggestions now," he teases with a mocking shake of his head. "Shameful."

I feel dizzy as I laugh, swaying into him. "Marco, you didn't have to—"

His lips swoop down, silencing mine with a chaste press that's far too brief. "Hush," he whispers, "I wanted to. Come on, one more."

I'm a sniffling mess by the time we get to the last little alcove on the roof, lying directly over the spot where we once had dinner. Marco holds me through every bout of overwhelming gratitude that swells into tears, his solid certainty every bit as calming as ever.

Finally, he leads me to the final space.

This room has no walls, its frame open to the beautiful view around us and wrapped in floral vines. Candles flicker all around the floor, creating a perfectly circular patch at the center.

Marco steps into the empty space. For a long moment, he just stares at me. Soft warmth fills his strong features, the look practically worshipful. He extends his hand again and waits for me to join him.

Dazed joy sparkles through me. I close my eyes and settle my cheek against his chest. "I can't believe you did all of this." My arms flex around his middle. I whisper, "I still can't believe you'd want anything to do with me after seeing what was in that box."

He leans back, finding my eyes and pinning me in place with his fervent gaze. "Never be embarrassed by what you have in there, sweet girl. Never."

My answer laugh is weak, wilted by chagrin. "But you saw... everything."

Sincerity burns in his depths. "That's the thing, Alice. When I found that box, and I saw what was in it, do you know what I realized?"

My brow folds into another grimace as I stare up at him. Do I even want to know?

"...w-what?"

His smile warms while his eyes snap with molten intensity. He steps back, reaching for his pocket. Pulling out a small ring box as he drops to one knee.

"I realized that all of your dreams were my dreams, too."

I CAN'T DECIDE whether my bride looks more beautiful in her dress or out of it.

The soft ivory concoction of lace and silk keeps me on the edge between lust so hot I worry it will singe my veins to ash, and love so profound I think it might actually stop my heart before the desire finishes me off.

Even when her hand lands in mine for the hundredth time, I can't help but skim my eyes down the flared bodice covered with tiny lace-and-pearl flowers, across the cool sweep of thin silk cascading over her hips.

If someone put a gun to my head, I wouldn't be able to tell you what style or design it is. But here, in the glow of a hundred candles, my bride looks like some dazzling combination of an angel and a siren, wrapped up in white.

For me.

My bride.

I will never tire of thinking the words or saying them out loud. Of all the things I've worked for in my life, the honor of waiting for Alice at the end of the aisle is by far my greatest accomplishment.

A warm vein of amusement and pride cuts through me every time I recall the way she put me through my paces. The months I spent rebuilding her trust, attending therapy on my own and with her, planning every date I could think of.

I built her library. Her art studio. I had hard conversations with Grayson about my role in the company and my commitments to the family I want to create. I got to use every long, exhausting, wonderful day to prove myself to Alice and let her love me back.

Nothing has ever been more worthwhile.

Now, Alice's delicate hands slide over the lapels of my tuxedo while her blue eyes beam up at me. With her wedding makeup and soft curls framing her gorgeous face, she's honestly never looked more beautiful. Or happier.

Her gaze tracks my expression. The lush curves of her lips quirk to the side. "Ready to go back to our room, Mr. Amir?"

I should have known she would see that I desperately want her to myself. With a rueful chuckle, I sweep her closer, pressing her hips to my thighs. "I'm that obvious, hmm?"

Her sweet little laugh bubbles between us. She leans back and sweeps her gaze over our reception. "I think I'm ready, too, actually."

She sounds surprised. I *definitely* am. Planning a wedding with a professional wedding planner is one thing—but planning one with a woman who has been dreaming of every detail for her entire life? The process was intense, and the results are spectacular.

I look around, hoarding every last facet of her brilliance. The soft, snowy drapes of fabric, thousands of candles, crystal chandeliers dripping with orchids so white they sparkle, a canopy of greenery swaying over everything.

It took a lot of work for Alice to admit that her dream wedding couldn't happen in New York City. She still hates to feel burdensome or demanding, even though I constantly assure her she's neither. Eventually, in one of our therapy sessions, she admitted to feeling unworthy of grand, special things.

That conversation unlocked a lot for us. She finally started to work through that nagging sense of unworthiness, and I turned my attention to proving it wrong through actions. Two days later, I booked a block of rooms at Maui's Four Seasons. A week after that, Alice discovered the venue of her dreams, and I placed a nonrefundable deposit before she could talk herself out of it.

But every moment of anxiety and every cent I've spent has been more than worth it. The hotel is already a beautiful setting, but once my sweet girl got her brilliant hands on it, the place became a masterpiece.

My bride finishes surveying our surroundings and shudders through a deep breath. Tears brighten her eyes when they flit back to mine. Her palm smooths over my jaw, gentling me before I can get concerned.

"You made all my dreams come true today," she whispers. "Thank you, Marco."

Ah, hell.

I already teared up when Alice appeared at the end of the aisle and started walking toward me. Then—and I'll never admit this —I fought back more emotion during Graham Fucking Everett's toast.

But I can't attempt to hide the way my vision mists when I see that look on her face.

My arms cinch around her body, lifting it into mine while I

hide my face against her neck. "For you? Anything," I murmur, repeating the promise I made that night on the rooftop, and again during our vows.

When I finally put her down, my focus shifts to figuring out how we can extricate ourselves from our own wedding. Before I get very far, Jules appears, smirking. Mischief gilds her gold eyes while they bounce between our faces. "You guys making a run for it?"

Her dress matches the champagne clutched in her hand. Alice spent weeks agonizing over the color, wanting one that looked good on *all* of her bridesmaids. I personally haven't noticed whether she succeeded or not.

Alice's cheeks pink as Jules's smile grows suggestive. A second later, Everett staggers over, drunkenly hooking his arm around his wife's waist and pulling her in for a sloppy kiss to the cheek.

"Mm, *bijou*," he groans. His bleary eyes slip over to us, grin widening. "Oh-ho, you guys gonna go off and do it?"

Two years have gone by and I still cannot decide if I need to kick his ass.

"Everett, this is our wedding," I remind him.

He shrugs loosely, rumpling the ridiculous gold-trimmed dinner jacket he insisted on wearing over his white groomsman shirt. And—dear God—is that a glittery bow tie? Where and how did he stash that away?

"We tried to tell you to bang it out before the ceremony," he taunts, still smirking. "But you two wanted to go *traditional*."

It's true. Aside from a few stolen moments in hotel hallways, Alice and I haven't been alone together in days. We decided to abstain from sex for the week leading up to the wedding, and I have big plans to make up for lost time on our honeymoon. I have big plans for the honeymoon, period.

"Ignore him." Juliet laughs, rolling her eyes. "We'll get you out of here."

I look at Alice for approval. She's the one who knows what

our big photo-ops are. A sly smile slides over her beautiful face, glowing up at me.

What do you think? she asks silently. *Time to sneak away?*

I gather her closer, flashing a grin. *Past time.*

Graham rubs his hands together, snickering. "So, we need a diversion, huh?" A wicked smirk clears the bleariness from his gaze. "I've been preparing for this moment all my life."

He slings my cousin toward the dance floor, spinning her into the center and lunging after her. All of our guests clap and cheer, fully immersed as Graham whirls a laughing Juliet into a dip that has her hair brushing the floor.

Alice's musical giggle has me hauling her into my arms, bridal style. "Come on, Mrs. Amir," I rumble, nuzzling her neck. "I believe you have a honeymoon suite waiting for you."

"And you," she replies.

But it isn't waiting for me—I was already in there earlier today, making sure everything would be perfect for my bride.

If she notices how I know the path to the room by heart, or how I have a key card waiting in my back pocket, Alice doesn't comment. She keeps her sparkling blue eyes on my face, smiling softly while I carry her all the way to the west-facing portion of the top floor.

I shove into the room with my shoulder, pleased with whichever turndown staff member has followed the instructions I left behind. They've dimmed the lights exactly as I requested, showcasing the flickering candles and snowy orchids floating in dozens of clear glass bowls scattered along the edges of the room.

"Oh my God!" Alice whispers as I gently set her on her feet before the foot of the massive, white-trimmed bed. "This is *beautiful.*"

My wife's awe makes her impossibly more lovely. A fresh surge of pride tightens my chest while I take her in, wanting to remember every single moment of our first night as husband and wife.

The wonder stays on her face, but a pinch of suspicion

appears between her eyebrows. "Marco..." She twists toward the bed, with its custom white silk sheets and the pink rose petals scattered over them. "What did you *do*?"

I shrug, trying to play it off while I wrap my arms around her middle and step up behind her. "Nothing, really. Just the flowers. And a few other things."

My sweet girl turns her dubious eyes to mine. "A *few other things*?" she cries quietly. "Are you saying that every honeymoon suite comes with my favorite bottle of wine?" She points a finger at the Tuscan red on the dresser. "And they all smell like my favorite candles? And have white silk bedding?"

I wince, not wanting to lie to her. I knew she'd be familiar with the suite's standard amenities, but I hadn't expected her to immediately pick up on *everything* I've added to match the photos from her shoebox the second we walked into the room.

Well, almost everything.

As if reading my mind, my wife reaches down to scoop up the train of her dress and marches toward the bathroom... where the suite's brand-new jetted tub burbles quietly, petals and bubbles spinning graceful circles on the surface of the water.

Alice blinks at the scene, including the matching satin robes with our married monogram—AAM—embroidered on the fronts. There is a black one for me and a white one for her, exactly like the photo that inspired the idea.

When she spins back to me, her arms are crossed, but a tiny smile plays at her gorgeous lips. "Marco Amir. This room did not have a jetted tub. I specifically asked when we booked it and checked again when I finalized things last month."

I can't help the grin pulling at my mouth. "I may have made a few improvements for my bride."

Alice slowly soaks in our surroundings again, trailing her gaze over the little things I've thought of to make the night more special for her. When her eyes finally land back on mine, her lower lip starts to tremble.

"Baby, no," I murmur, rushing to gather her into my arms.

"This is nothing more than what you deserve. I can't tell you how fucking happy I am that I could do this for you."

Her tears tickle my neck when she sniffs. "It's perfect. All of my dreams come true. Just like I said."

But I know that wasn't one hundred percent accurate. Yet.

"Not all of them," I husk, skimming my lips over her creamy shoulder. "I believe I saw mention of your husband making love to you on your wedding night on quite a few of those lists. Maybe even *all* of them."

My sweet girl blushes, her cheek heating against my palm while I turn her face up to mine. "A-are you sure?" she asks. "You're not too tired? You didn't have too much to drink?"

I don't tell her I've only had the mandatory sips required during toasts, to ensure she gets the wedding night she has always wanted. It isn't important how I made all of this happen—only that I did. And I will for the rest of my life. For her.

"You are all I can think of," I admit, skimming my lips over her temple. "All I want."

Alice melts into me, whimpering while I take her mouth with mine. I start out slow, but my patience gets away from me within seconds as the stress of the day falls from my shoulders.

It's done. We're married.

She's *mine*.

The soft, warm light gilds Alice's light hair and bright eyes while I slowly peel her dress off her, revealing perfect naked skin underneath. I smile when I see that she still doesn't have any panties on—a fact I discovered earlier when I went up her skirt to remove her garter.

The fact that we're alone now doesn't stop her from blushing just as fiercely as she did when I emerged and shot her a pointed smirk that said, *Naughty girl*.

She'd whispered that her dress had lining and cups sewn into it, to eliminate the need for undergarments. I'd whispered back that I could have used some warning to avoid getting a semi in the middle of my wedding reception.

Now, though, there is no reason to hide the way my blood pounds at the sight of her. Golden candlelight fills the dips and hollows of her form, turning her into a Renaissance painting of a shy, beautiful goddess.

What choice do I have but to go to my knees?

MARCO'S dark eyes burn with devotion as he carefully slips off his tuxedo jacket and the shoes from my feet.

He helps me step out of my dress and drapes it over a nearby armchair, taking care to keep it away from the bowls of candles on the floor. His jacket and shirt follow, leaving him in his trousers while he stares up at me from his place on his knees.

His solid hands bracket my hips, grounding me, while I run my hands down his neck and shoulders, reveling in his hard heat. Even though it's only been seven days, I've missed him so much.

Not just for his perfect body. I've missed the way he is looking at me right this second—as if I'm the answer to every question he's ever known and every prayer he's ever spoken.

His head falls forward, forehead pressing into my belly. I no longer feel the urge to push him away when he expresses his love for that particular piece of me—the part so many others conditioned me to scorn. Now, I let him glide his lips along the spot beneath my navel while his thumbs draw circles over my sides—

and all I feel are tingles of pleasure while he shows me just how much he adores every piece of me.

Marco moves lower, trailing open-mouth kisses from one hip bone to the other, gently biting at the thin skin covering each until I'm molten and squirming.

His voice is smoke and velvet as his lips curve into a grin against the freshly waxed skin where my panties should be. "Did you miss me, Mrs. Amir?"

I nod, tightening my grip on his thick, glossy hair. "Y-yes."

"Mm," he rumbles, kissing lower. "How much?"

Instead of waiting for me to answer, he skims his brawny hand down my backside and dips to the cleft between my thighs, a groan vibrating out of him when he feels how wet I am.

I can't help it, though. He looked *devastating* in his tuxedo. And the way he held me all night certainly didn't help keep my pantiless, champagne-drinking self from getting all worked up during every slow dance.

"My good girl," he praises. "So ready for me. So fucking sexy. So beautiful."

Like he simply cannot wait another second, he slants his mouth over my pussy and licks from my slit to the aching bud pulsing under his lips. We both cry out, my moan as shrill as his is deep. He instantly clutches at my body, steely fingers steadying me while his shoulders nudge my knees further apart.

I thought we'd tried every which way for him to taste me, but this feels different. Gravity is working with him, turning each clench of my inner muscles into a throbbing spasm. It only takes a couple of minutes for the tender squeezes to spur me into grinding myself against his working tongue. He hums his approval, sliding one hand up my thigh. *His left hand.*

He pulls back just long enough to meet my eyes while he flashes his solid gold wedding band at me. Before I take my next breath, he's sucked my clit into his mouth and plunged the finger wearing his wedding ring into my aching core.

I come the second I realize what he's done, locking down on

his ring finger and moaning loud enough for the sound to carry out of the open balcony windows, over the ocean tides crashing onto the shore below us.

For once, I don't care one bit. Especially when he immediately scoops me up and places me on the white silk sheets I just *know* he special-ordered.

He makes quick work of the rest of his clothes before sliding over me, resting between my parted thighs, and dropping his face to mine. I stroke down his back, urging him to push into me without waiting another second. He surges forward, gasping while my body seals around his straining cock.

Even though his whole body is taut with need, Marco turns his cheek into mine, nuzzling me like we have all the time in the world. A tremor moves through him.

"Is this everything you wanted?" he asks softly. "Everything you dreamed of?" I turn to catch his gaze, my heart aching at the tender love and *hope* deep in his warm brown eyes.

Tears rush over my cheeks while I cup his, pressing my mouth against him. "You're more than I could have possibly dreamed."

Marco deepens our kiss, locking us together and framing my head with his hands while he makes love to me. Until we both fall apart... and put each other back together again.

I SHOULD HAVE KNOWN BETTER than to hope that I might wake up before my husband and sneak into the bathroom undetected.

By the time I finish sweeping back my hairspray-fried curls and wiping the last bits of smudged wedding makeup off my face,

I emerge to find him sitting at the little breakfast table on our balcony, already wearing a pair of black linen lounge pants and pouring two cups of tea.

He grins when he sees me approach, holding his arm out to indicate that I have no business taking a chair of my own. I sit on his lap instead, turning to nestle into the bronze skin and dark hair covering his bare chest. He snuggles me close, expressing his love without a single word when he cradles my head in his palm and turns lax beneath me.

We stay that way, listening to the ocean, while the sun comes up. Eventually, he shifts and makes an odd request. "Sweet girl, would you mind grabbing the sugar on the other side of the table?"

I sit up, more from surprise than anything else—Marco *never* puts sugar in his tea. After shooting him an accusatory look, I stretch over, reach out my hand, and freeze.

My robe sleeve has pulled back, revealing an absolutely gorgeous white-gold bracelet. A simple braided design with enormous diamonds studding every nook. It's classy and gorgeous and so extravagant, my heart skips three beats before I finally manage to breathe.

"Your honeymoon gift," he murmurs. "I snuck it on while you were sleeping."

"H-honeymoon gift?" I repeat. "W-what—"

My husband shrugs, as if every woman gets a breathtaking piece of jewelry standard-issued with their wedding license. "Just a little something. I almost gave it to you yesterday, but then I decided to wait and do all the gifts at one time."

My mouth falls open. "All... *all* the gifts?"

A brusque nod. So very Marco. "Your wedding gift is here," he says matter-of-factly, reaching his long arm over me and tapping a collection of envelopes fanned out in a half-circle beneath the teapot. At first glance, I thought they were napkins.

But he hands me one of the slim, blue packets, setting his chin on my shoulder as my shaking fingers rip it open.

Two airline tickets fall out, along with a booking for the honeymoon bungalow at an over-the-water resort in Tahiti. There are other papers, too. Catamaran cruise tickets, receipts for couples' massages.

"You're... changing our honeymoon?"

I try not to sound disappointed. He's made our suite here so perfect, I don't ever want to leave.

Thankfully, Marco laughs. "No, sweet girl. This is our *next* honeymoon."

I am officially dumb again. "Our next—"

His broad smile melts what little is left of my brain. "You didn't think I was going to make you choose just one out of your box, did you?"

He spreads his fingers over the other envelopes, pulling them toward us. I check the date on the papers in my lap, seeing that they're bookings for next year, on our first anniversary.

"You didn't," I whisper, somewhere between horrified and swooning. "Marco, tell me you didn't."

"Book *all* your dream honeymoons? I had to. You had so many good ones in there, I couldn't narrow it down. Paris, Cabo, the Amalfi Coast."

He trails off after only pointing to three of the envelopes... which still leaves several. "But—but," I stammer, practically shouting. "There's no way we can do *all* of the trips I had in the box! There has to be, like—"

"Ten," he supplies, nodding again.

And, sure enough, when I count the envelopes...

Ten dream honeymoons and ten envelopes.

Marco watches me finish the math before gently gripping my jaw in his enormous hand and turning my face to his. "I made vows yesterday, and I meant them," he murmurs. "You're my soulmate. The one I wished for every day of my entire life. Your hopes and dreams are mine. Now and forever."

He catches my tears in his palm, running his nose along mine to comfort me. I lean closer, searching his face for any trace of strain or doubt. But all I find is my steady, solid husband.

"All of them?" I squeak, my eyes skirting back to the envelopes. Surely they *all* aren't *really* booked...

My mind says that, but I already know—in my heart—that they really are. Because that is exactly the man I married. Decisive, honest, and giving. Solid, safe, and devoted.

My soulmate.

His quick, mind-blowing smile flashes as he draws me into his embrace, settling us both with our matching mugs of tea and turning us to face the horizon.

"We're going for it all, sweet girl," he says. "Because that's what you deserve."

content warnings

CONTENT/TRIGGER WARNINGS ARE BELOW. PLEASE NOTE THAT THEY MAY CONTAIN SPOILERS.

CW/TW: general suspense, financial insecurity, fatphobia/body shaming, parental abuse (verbal) and neglect, negative self-talk, PTSD, violence, nightmares, weapons (guns, knives), grief/loss of a parent, threats/captivity, sex under false pretenses (past and off-page/not between main characters), torture, kidnapping, assault, bondage, impact play, praise kink.

acknowledgments

First and foremost, I always have to thank my best friend, Kelly. Without you, I most definitely would have given up on this book at least ten separate times. Thank you for helping me keep the faith and reminding me to be nice to Alice (and myself!). I couldn't do any of this (book stuff, mom stuff, life) without you!

Since releasing the first two books in my series, I've been so fortunate to find so many amazing book friends. I'm so grateful for all of the pep talks, practical tips, and help I've received from my fellow indie authors and the people who support us.

The most special thank-you to my editor, Katie! You helped me believe in this story and reminded me what I set out to do when I created Alice. You also made sure that all of the tea in this story was brewed properly, for which this pitiful American is eternally grateful.

Lastly, a special note to my husband. Matthew, I know this was a rough one. Thank you for being the foundation of our family while I was banging my head against my keyboard. And thank you for loving me the way Marco loves Alice—books and all.

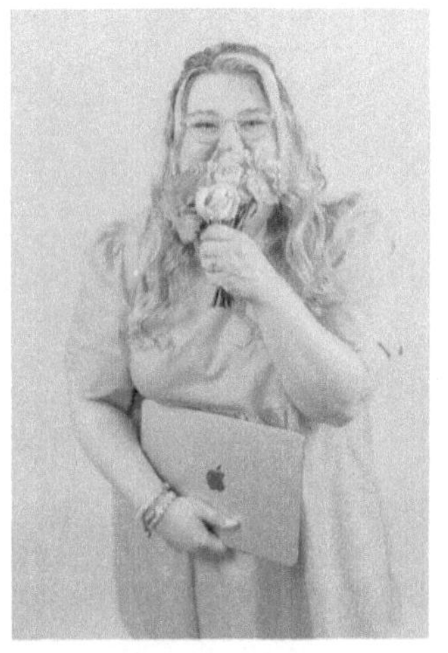

Ari Wright resides in a sun-soaked corner of the United States, where she spends her days raising littles, cooking, reading, consuming massive amounts of music, and doing entirely too much daydreaming. Ari began writing novels at the age of twelve. A passionate book-lover all her life, her mother once joked that she had to start writing her own stories because she had read everyone else's.

It has been her lifelong dream to share the worlds inhabiting her mind with others. Thank you for being a part of her dream come true!